CONFEDERATION

Gaea Ascendant 3

Eric S. Martell

Second Initiative Press

Confederation

Vox audita perit littera scripta manet.

This is a work of fiction. All the characters and events portrayed in this book are fictional, and any resemblance to real people or incidents is purely coincidental.

Contents

The Origin of the Confederacy of the Three Races

After aliens attack the Earth, the surviving humans exist in a post-apocalyptic world and are divided into groups that contest power.

One group has allied with two alien races. The disparate races have united in using technology captured from the original alien invaders.

Seemingly impossible tasks face this fledgling confederation: They must destroy the threat still posed by the original invaders while being involved in a conflict with barbaric remnants of the Federal government for control of the remaining population of the US. To complicate matters, they must simultaneously find a way to strengthen their working relationship, develop trade protocols and a mechanism for mutual defense in the face of potential incursions of unknown hostiles from outside their sphere of occupied planets.

This is the third story in the Gaea Ascendant Trilogy

DEDICATION

This book is dedicated to Hayden, Oscar, Elliot, Rowan, and Hazel – may you retain your curiosity always.

ACKNOWLEDGMENTS

Thanks to all of the authors who wrote the hundreds of science fiction books that I read while growing up. Your books may have taken time away from my school assignments, but if nothing else, you permitted me to exercise my imagination.

A Special Thanks

My grateful thanks to Krzysztof (Kris) Krygier for the original cover art. Creating a visual image of space battle using anti-matter projectors is a challenge that takes a special artist. Fortunately, Kris was ready for the task.

Chapter 1

"The Fourth Turning" by Strauss and Howe predicts many of the societal problems that have appeared in recent history. Perhaps most ominously, their theory indicates that one outcome of the current intellectual and spiritual environment could be "an omnicidal Armageddon, destroying everything, leaving nothing. If mankind ever extinguishes itself, this will probably happen when its dominant civilization triggers a Fourth Turning that ends horribly. For this Fourth Turning to put an end to all this would require an extremely unlikely blend of social disaster, human malevolence, technological perfection and bad luck."

Strauss and Howe didn't consider the possibility of a devastating alien attack as the trigger point.

The engines of the large shuttlecraft shut down with a whirring noise. The things were nearly silent in flight, but they always reminded me of a jet engine spooling down when they were turned off. I glanced around the cabin at our group. Our two Sunny pilots, Whistle and Frazzle, were at the controls. My beautiful, blonde wife, Liz, was seated beside me and my two old friends, Joe and Rudy, were in an adjacent row of seats. Despite the seats being a little too narrow for humans, they were more comfortable than any human-made military aircraft. The only one of us who had difficulty with the seating was the Sim-tiger leader, Kasm. His five-hundred pounds plus of six-limbed, muscular body just wouldn't fit in the seats. He'd settled between two vacant rows and braced himself against them, saying that he was fine. His position still looked uncomfortable to me.

A couple of minutes prior, we'd arrived over the grounds of the Stanley Hotel in Estes Park. We were flying the larger of our two captured shuttle-craft. It was now sitting on the remains of the old parking lot.

It had been obvious to Frazzle that the parking lot, cracked and disintegrating as the asphalt was, was the best place to land. It had been almost five years since the Pug-bears had destroyed our civilization with the EMP blasts they'd set off when I had destroyed their matter transporter network. The parking lot had not been maintained since, and the mountain climate had nearly destroyed it.

The shuttle was a heavy craft, and it sank into the surface as its weight came down when the engines were shut off. We climbed out to be greeted by a group of rather barbaric-looking men who walked over to stand guard over the craft. They looked us over carefully, and one man greeted Joe and Rudy by name. Those two had been loosely allied with the Warlord's men in the last great battle against the Pug-bears and Pugs and were well known. The men glanced at me but didn't comment.

The Sunnys and Kasm, on the other hand, elicited a buzz of low conversation. There were around forty of the Sim-tigers currently on Earth, and they were not unfamiliar to residents of the Denver Metro area, but there weren't enough of them around to make the sight of one commonplace. The two small, furry Sunnys were the only two currently on Earth. They were not incredible fighters like the six-limbed Kasm, but the men pointed at them, and I over-heard a comment about their technology that sounded positive and envious.

We walked in a loose group across the unkempt lawn towards the battle-damaged building. It was a clear day, and the springtime sun shone brightly through the thin air. I looked around with trepidation. The Warlord's men posed no threat, yet I was still getting the feeling of impending danger. In me, it manifested as a tingle on the back of my neck, and it was now acting up.

The wind was from the northwest and carried the chill of the snow-covered mountains. Jake, the Eastern Slope Warlord, and his party were already at the hotel and were waiting for us on the large veranda. We waved as we approached, and Jake raised his hand in a solemn salute in response.

As if his wave had been a signal, I heard the buzz of a high-velocity round as it flew by about knee-high. It struck the cracked surface right under Kasm, throwing pieces of asphalt that bounced off his green-furred stomach. He let out a snarl and leaped forward, turning as he did towards the nearest trees. I shoved Liz towards the hotel. It was now closer than the shuttle and offered the nearest shelter.

Rudy and Joe ran past me, and Rudy grabbed Liz's arm, dragging her along with him as she tried to turn to come back to follow me. I was close on Kasm's track, heading for the trees.

As I sprinted, I extended my mental perception, searching for the source of the shot. There was a second and, immediately after, a third shot. They were aimed at the rapidly moving Sim-tiger, but he was zig-zagging in his path, and they missed.

I mentally located the source. The aura I received was human and hostile. The shooter was in a building about four-hundred yards to the south. I linked with Liz and showed her the location. She was huddled in the shelter of a boulder by the front steps. When she received my thought, she yelled at Rudy and Joe to lay down suppressing fire on the location.

Jake was quick to follow suit, and the entire porch of the hotel erupted with a series of shots as the men blazed away with various calibers of weapons. I couldn't tell if they were hitting the building, but there was no more incoming fire.

I caught up with Kasm in the shelter of a stand of spruce trees. He glanced at me, and we connected mentally, that being his normal mode of communication.

"Dec! That was too close. The shooter is moving now. I can sense him. He's heading to the east behind that row of buildings," he sent.

"Okay. You cut him off, and I'll follow up around the west end. We'll catch him between us. Be careful! You were the target, and I don't know why. Let's try to capture him in talking condition," I responded.

He dashed down the line of trees, sprinted across a vacant space, and dropped into a depression that would provide some cover. I took a chance and ran out towards the west, heading diagonally towards the building to the right of the shooter's original location.

Our target was moving, and I followed him mentally. He wasn't thinking about shooting at the moment, just getting to some other point that might provide cover or the opportunity for a fourth shot. When I sensed that thought, I turned and headed directly for the west end of the original building. It was about three hundred yards from my position, and it took me longer than I thought it would. I guess that getting older has its drawbacks. I was gasping for breath as I rounded the southwest corner of the building.

I belatedly remembered that I was running into a potential ambush and jumped back behind the building's side. I dropped to the ground and peeked around the corner, but there was a loading dock directly in front of me, and I couldn't see around the abandoned box truck backed up to it. I jumped up and sneaked around to the front of the truck. Nothing was showing along the strip of buildings.

I stepped back and dropped into a meditative state. It didn't take long before I could sense Kasm's presence. He acknowledged me with a mental flick, almost as if he said, "Don't bother me. I'm working." He was moving in my direction, taking cover where he could, behind junk and rusting cars that hadn't moved since the EMP blast had killed them.

I widened my mental search and located the shooter. There was a kind of curious mental doubling about him. I couldn't figure out what it was, but I now knew that he was aware we were after him and had set a booby trap on the door into the part of the building where he was lurking. He was hiding near the front windows with their view over the Stanley property, and I could tell that he was still looking for a target. Sensing nothing else, I jumped up and ran as fast as my burning lungs would let me move towards the door. Kasm saw me in the open, and taking that as a sign that it was safe, he charged towards the same door. I linked with him again as I ran.

"Stop! There's a bomb on the door," I sent. I received a close mental analog of a frustrated snarl in return.

He arrived at the door before me and flattened against the wall. There was a window on the side of the door I was approaching. I ducked under it and paused to examine the door. There was no sign of a trap, but I was sure it was there.

I'd run past an abandoned length of electrical cable partway down the building, so I went back and brought it up. Kasm stayed in place in case the guy should change his mind and come out again.

It was pretty simple to tie the wire onto the levered handle, back up to its full extent, and yank the door open. There was a momentary pause and then an explosion that I recognized as a military frag grenade. Some pieces flew out past us, but we were about a hundred feet away behind a defunct pickup truck. Kasm dashed back to the wall beside the door while I lay down so that I could see under the truck. It was then that I realized that my forty-five had come out of its holster somewhere during the run, and all I had was one of the aliens' splinter guns.

This was an unwelcome development since I wanted the shooter alive. He'd almost instantly die if I hit him with one of the poisonous glass splinters. There was no such thing as wounding with the weapon.

I explained my problem to Kasm, and he grimly responded, "That's what you humans get for relying on weapons. Just leave it to me. I won't hurt him too much; maybe a bite or two."

"Try not to bite him so that he can't speak. I want to find out what he was trying to accomplish by shooting at you. We need to know why he is here and who sent him," I answered.

He thought back, "You're taking the fun out of this. Be quiet. He's coming now!"

I saw the man's feet in the shadows of the doorway. The tires of the truck I was crouched behind were flat, and I couldn't see much through the space between its bottom and the ground. I could sense the man's puzzlement. He'd expected a body, but there was nothing in sight. I didn't want him to look around the corner and see Kasm, so I let out a low groan, pretending that the blast had wounded me.

That worked like a charm. The shooter stepped out of the door just in time to find out what it felt like to be hit by a leaping and enraged Sim-tiger. By the time I got there, Kasm had one forepaw on the man's chest and held the guy's arms with his secondary forelimbs. His manipulating arms were at least as strong as those of a strong human, and he was restraining the shooter's attempts to reach a pistol holstered on his belt.

I removed that and grabbed the rifle he'd dropped when Kasm hit him. Kneeling, I frisked him with one hand. He had two knives and another pistol in an ankle holster. I stepped back, saying, "Okay, buddy. I'm going to have my friend let you up. You can't outrun him, and you can't out-fight him, so don't get any ideas. We're going to march back over to the Stanley Hotel, and you're going to tell us everything we want to know."

Kasm stepped back, and the man cautiously climbed to his feet, eyeing the large alien with fear in his gaze. I got the man's attention when I asked, "Why did you shoot at my friend?"

He just shook his head in denial. At first, I thought he meant he didn't do the shooting, but then I inserted myself into his mental aura. He feared the Sim-tiger and had been instructed to kill it. The thoughts were fragmentary, but it was clear that someone else had sent him.

"Who sent you, and why do they want my friend dead?" I was getting a little impatient, even though we had only gotten started.

"No one sent me!" he snarled.

I knew that wasn't true, so I asked again, "You were sent by someone. Who was it?"

This time I got a momentary picture of our prisoner in uniform, facing a superior officer. He had little natural mental shielding, and I could read his thoughts easily. The only problem was he didn't have much mental dialogue.

"Okay. So you are in the military, and you're on a spying mission," I said softly.

His eyes grew wide in alarm, "They told me that some of you freaks could read minds! You're not readin' mine!" He grabbed something from his belt and jammed it into his mouth.

I jumped forward and grabbed his arm, but the poison pill had already taken effect. He was frothing at the mouth and gasping for breath. Instead of wasting time trying to help him, I shoved an intense mental probe into his frantic mind. The sense of mental doubling intensified, and I followed it to its source. The man had some kind of implant in his brain! It seemed to be acting as a store of information, but it was also linked to some areas of his brain related to pain sensations. I backed away from the thing. It had a dirty, nasty feel or something akin to that. It's hard to describe mental sensations verbally, but that was what I felt. I regrouped and tried again.

Brushing off the desperate, struggling thoughts, I quickly sifted through as much of his normal memories as I could access before his mind stilled in death. It was like being in a large room as the lights gradually went out in sequence. I exited before the darkness reached me. I didn't know what riding along with a mind on its descent into death would be like, and I didn't want to find out.

I blinked a couple of times as I returned to my normal state and then bent to inspect the body. There was a scar behind his right ear. Whatever it was I'd sensed, it had been surgically implanted. I wondered who had that technology, especially now. The scar looked relatively new. This was something that I found very alarming, but without any additional facts, there was nothing that I could do except to shelve the issue for later.

I turned to Kasm and spoke aloud, "He was a member of the government of what used to be my nation. He came from the east to spy on us. I got the impression that they're planning on attacking the front-range area. They've expanded their hold across the eastern half of this continent and are now approaching Jake's territory. They know something about your people, and I believe they want to purge the planet of all alien creatures. It seemed almost like a religious thought in his mind. He viewed it as his sacred duty to rid the planet of invaders."

Kasm shrugged his secondary shoulders slightly and headed towards the end of the buildings. I glanced at the body and followed. It seemed callous, but that was the way things were in the here and now. There had been too much death in the past few years to waste time with a corpse.

As we walked, we conversed mentally. Kasm could speak some English, but it was difficult for him. On the other hand, his people were telepaths as was I, since my mind had been irrevocably altered by my encounter with the powerful leader of the invading Pug-bears years ago.

I'd killed the leader, but his mental attack had ripped my mind open in a way that led to me developing the latent psychic abilities that all humans have. Through constant practice and many hardships, I'd grown powerful in my own right.

"Kasm, the man was a member of a group that was a department in our old government. This continent was mostly ruled by a central governing body that eventually grew so powerful that it dominated all of the people."

I paused as he interrupted my thought stream. "That would never happen with my people! No single group could control everyone. We'd leave their area."

I responded, "That couldn't happen here. It did in the past, but for many years our population has been so large that there was nowhere on the planet that a dissenting group could go. Besides, the central government was too powerful. It somehow grew to control everything; all the resources; all of the people."

He looked at me and drew his lips back, exposing his large fangs in distaste. I continued, "They controlled travel and long-distance communication and food. They used resources as bribes to keep themselves in power. I'm afraid that my people were so focused on their own needs and desires that they were easily led and then captured in self-induced misery. They set up organizational structures that seemed unchangeable to those mired within them. I'm not proud of it, but the fact is that our species was not progressing quickly, either socially or scientifically. The invasion of the Pug-bears and Pugs might turn out to be the event that allows us to progress, despite killing nine out of ten humans. If I can figure out a way for us to work with your people and the Sunnys, together we might create a better way forward for all of us."

He stopped showing his teeth and replied, "That may well be. I confess that I was ashamed of my people also. We've lived for many generations, content to be simple hunters on our planet. We'd reached an equilibrium in our population. No groups fought with other groups, and each tribal group had its own territory. Natural and accidental deaths balanced out our birthrate. We were happy in our existence until the Pugs attacked. That was a shock! We didn't know how to cope with their advanced technology at first. It was fortunate that they were so easy to ambush when they came into the jungle."

He changed his topic suddenly, "I've been thinking about the same thing, Dec. I'd like to see if your people and mine can live together peacefully. There's no question about the Sunnys." He snorted, making a derisive sound. "They can't even consider fighting without having a near breakdown."

I sent back, "Yes, but they are plenty devious. They have methods of defending themselves, even if they are far more pacifistic than either of our peoples."

My concentration was broken by discovering my old Sig-Sauer lying near some dried weeds. I remembered stumbling as my foot caught in them and realized that stumble must have bounced it out of its holster. I picked up the pistol and returned it to its usual place. The safety strap was intact and snapped shut. I had thought that I might have bumped it against something, unsnapping it without noticing, but maybe it had just worked loose.

Kasm had paused while I recovered my weapon but turned almost immediately and continued. I hastened to catch up with him.

I continued our discussion as I followed, "That sniper was a member of a government group that used to be responsible for internal security. I read in his memories that they are now an occupying force in the lands to the east. They call themselves 'The Motherland Army' and are ruled by a single individual they call 'The President'. That person desires to project his power and dominate all of the lands and people available. In that way, they're much like the Pug-bears."

We walked for a while without communicating, then he suddenly added, "And, Pugs. That one wasn't a Pug-bear. He was just a sneaky, ambushing, and stinky Pug." He simultaneously sent a comedic image of one of the aliens trying to hide behind a tree with its rear end sticking out.

I laughed out loud at his humor. We were approaching the porch of the Stanley, and Liz came running out to embrace me, followed by Rudy and Joe.

As he passed Liz, Kasm brushed his shoulder affectionately against her and trailed his manipulating arm across her behind in a way I would have resented if he'd been human. He liked her, and that was just his standard greeting. Inter-species etiquette was somewhat of a moving target. He had done it to me before, although it had shocked me the first time he'd patted my ass.

Chapter 2

We walked up the long flight of stairs, and I shook hands with Jake. He looked at me, still holding my hand, and asked, "Did you get him?"

"Of course. Kasm captured him, but he took cyanide before I could get too much out of him. He was a member of the leftover federal government, a member of what he called 'The Motherland Army,'" I answered.

Jake's eyes shadowed, "I've heard a word of those guys. They're setting up all across the eastern half of the country. They dominate everything east of the Mississippi now and are moving through Missouri and eastern Kansas. I'm going to have to fight them, I think." He shook his head and continued, "Let's discuss it later. I've set up a party for us. Let's eat and recover ourselves. We've got a lot of topics to discuss later."

That was true. We had tentatively agreed to set up a working arrangement to exist as close neighbors without conflict. The second issue was what we would do about a possible third attack by the Pug-bears. Now we were presented with the undeniable presence of a hostile group of humans with eyes on our territory. I nodded and moved to shake hands with his Lieutenant, a large and hairy mountain of a man.

Jake took his time, greeting everyone as if we were all equal, although, if the truth be told, he controlled far more territory and men than were in our little community over the mountains at Grand Lake.

I guessed that we more than made up for our lack of manpower with our alliance with the Sunnys and Kasm's people, not to mention the captured FTL spaceships that we controlled. My armed FTL carried three anti-matter weapons that could easily devastate any part of the Earth. It was apparent that Jake knew and respected that power and, I suspected, was trying hard to figure out a way to gain control of it.

We'd only seen the one EMP burst over Kansas, but the Pugs had set off several others over the face of the globe. The electromagnetic pulses generated had successfully destroyed almost all of mankind's electronics and the electrical grid. One moment, things were much as normal, and the next, there were no working automobiles, trucks, or airplanes, and our communication networks had failed.

It had been a hard five years after that. Many of the original invaders were dead or were killed shortly after the bursts, but millions of people had starved or died of medical problems in the first month. The death toll gradually declined and leveled out, but we'd estimated that nine out of every ten humans had died before we figured out how to survive. The average human now lived a life on the level of a seventeenth-century man. Nearly everything that we'd taken for granted existed no longer.

There were still some Pug-bears surviving on Earth. The alien monsters mainly were in remote areas where they didn't encounter many humans, but they were usually killed whenever they did. Defeating an intelligent Pug-bear would typically be difficult for a human; the feral, non-intelligent ones were hard enough to kill. Fortunately, they had almost uniformly suffered from some unknown pathogen-induced loss of intelligence, making them easier to destroy. No one had taken the time to figure out what was sickening them, though.

Jake, a retired marine, had somehow taken over the Denver area and now ruled the entire front range from Pueblo to Fort Collins. He had no interest in coming over the mountains since there were not enough resources to make the effort worthwhile in the Grand Lake area. That made us neighbors, although the initial relationship was uneasy. We'd worried that he might attack us until the second Pug-bear invasion was underway.

Three of his people and I had gone through the new matter transporter that the Pugs had sent to Earth and had freed some of the Sunnys and captured an FTL spaceship. We'd used the ship to help liberate one Sunny planet from the Pug-bears, and then we'd flown to Kasm's planet in search of allies. It had been difficult, but the decision was a good one. The Sim-tigers were fierce fighters, easily capable of defeating a Pug-bear, and together we'd formed a rough alliance that allowed us to defeat the second Earth invasion in the early winter of last year.

We'd spent the rest of the winter consolidating our forces and relationships. Now, I'd determined that we absolutely had to carry the attack to the Pug-bears. It was apparent that they wouldn't leave us alone unless we rendered them incapable of further aggression.

They were a primitive race and had no real civilization. Their ability to telepathically attack and capture prey paired with the symbiont-induced intelligence of some of them had allowed them to capture a Sunny exploration group and their spaceship. The acquired ability to travel in space had hit the Pug-bears like a bolt of lightning. They read the Sunnys' minds and quickly realized that an untold number of planets were available for them to attack. Since their genetically-programmed ambition was to dominate as much territory as possible for each individual, they quickly captured the Sunnys' six planets and then the planet occupied by the Pugs.

Using the iron-age Pugs as troopers and menials, the Pug-bears forced the Sunnys to build more spaceships that they used to attack and dominate many other planets. They'd destroyed five alien civilizations that I'd heard of, only being stopped by Kasm's people and now, humans. I suspected that they'd come back in more force and continue to try to capture the Earth unless we took direct action against them.

Since my group didn't have enough people, I wanted to come to a working agreement with Jake that would allow us to use his men. It could be beneficial to both sides. My concept was to build a confederation of independent states, including the Sunny civilization and the Sim-tigers. The Sunnys had technology that was far advanced over that of humans, and I believed that with the proper organization, we could benefit from it.

They would benefit by our providing protection for them. They were congenitally unable to engage in violence, even to protect themselves.

On the other hand, Kasm's people were highly intelligent telepaths who lived as roving hunters on their own planet. They had no technology but were so flexible in outlook that they could quickly adopt it. Of the two friendly aliens, the Sunnys and the Sim-tigers, the Sim-tigers were the closest in worldview to humans. We had a lot in common, considering that we were vastly different in physiology.

Kasm initially looked familiar. He was shaped like a large, stocky tiger with no tail, six limbs, and green stripes. His middle limbs were manipulative appendages with hands that allowed him to use some of our technology. However, his people had never seen the need for weapons since they were heavily armed naturally, with razor-sharp claws and fangs.

He and I had discussed our differences, and I'd concluded that at least part of human advancement directly resulted from our lack of natural weapons. Probably the first tool used by primitive man was a stick or rock pressed into service as an improvised weapon. One thing led to another, and we progressed; weapons technology often leading the way. For example, the transistor, which led to integrated circuits and the digital age, was an outgrowth of the nuclear missile program. Vacuum tubes could not stand up to the launch stresses placed on them by early rockets.

Jake led us through the hotel and out onto the back patio where the Eastern Slope people had built an enormous fire and were barbecuing two hogs and what looked like the rear quarters of a mule deer. I looked at Jake, and he smiled, saying, "We'll talk as we eat. I'm not one for formality, and this cool air makes me hungry."

"Okay," I answered, "sounds good to me. Do you have any of that deer leftover that hasn't been cooked? Kasm doesn't believe in applying fire to his food."

That was a significant understatement. The Sim-tigers only ate raw meat, and Kasm had initially been horrified that humans preferred to burn their food before consumption. His people had discovered that they loved mule deer and elk. That meant they could spread out over the mountains and hunt, an activity that fit well with their traditional lifestyle.

We lined up by the fire and loaded up on food. The cooks had reserved the rest of the deer for any Sim-tigers that would show up, so that was no problem. Once we'd helped ourselves, we sat at some of the tables that had been cleaned up and arranged across the patio.

The last time I'd seen those tables was before the EMP bursts. A large group of Pugs had been using them as shields during the pitched battle against my group. It hadn't helped them. I'd used an anti-matter rifle to dissolve a lot of them, and Rudy's people had killed the rest.

Jake was paying particular attention to my wife, Liz. They had not previously met, and he was making every effort to be charming. We sat down at a table, and she moved her chair close to me, letting him know with a smile that his effort was not unappreciated but showing that he didn't have a chance.

We began to discuss the situation as we ate. Two hours later, we were still talking. The main issue finally came down to whether or not Jake would get his own spaceship. We agreed on the confederation idea, and having Jake's men help us as fighters was not an issue, but he was holding out for one of our two FTLs. I didn't want to give them up, seeing the need for the transportation and fighting ability of the two, even though one was as yet unarmed.

Jake had been very impressed with the spaceships' capability after he'd seen the results of the single, low-orbit pass while firing the anti-matter cannon on burst mode. It had wiped out the majority of Pugs and Pug-bears, along with a vast swath of real estate, neatly dividing the city of Boulder into two parts.

He was worried about the Motherland

Army horde that was heading our way. Apparently, there were thousands of men in their army, and they were burning villages and killing anyone who showed any signs of resistance. On hearing some of the tales, any residual loyalty to the prior order that I still held faded quickly away.

We were doing all we could, maintaining our way of life and gradually working back towards a civilization of sorts. There was no way an invasion by a bunch of rapacious semi-barbarians would contribute to our survival.

I agreed to provide orbital support for any military action he would be forced to take against the remnants of the old government, should they attack. That led to him agreeing that I'd keep our spaceships as long as he had dibs on the next one we captured. I didn't speak my mind, but inside, I wondered if a spaceship might not lead him to think of becoming some sort of glorified space Viking or pirate. His reputation was good among his men, but he had conquered a lot of territory and showed no qualms about conquering more.

The meeting went on into the night hours as we worked out details of creating what was to be the Earth's first space force.

Chapter 3

It had been a long two months. I was hard-pressed to cope with the tasks involved in setting up an expeditionary force to attack the Pug-bears, but now we were on our way, moving out of Earth orbit and heading slowly towards Uranus. We were still training our crews and were in no hurry, so we kept the acceleration very low. It would take us three weeks to approach Uranus at the rate we were going.

We'd recruited men who had military experience before the EMP. We had enough to provide each of our two ships with a couple of squads of what I'd tentatively named Space Marines. Each ship also had a small crew that was supposed to handle flight duties. I kept the title of expeditionary force leader for myself and appointed Rudy to captain the second, larger ship. Joe was his Exec, and Whistle filled the position of pilot, ship-driver, and also maintenance engineer, should there be any mechanical or electronic problems. That last was doubtful since the Sunnys built their ships with multiple redundant systems. There was a Lieutenant under Joe and Rudy to command the Marines and a couple of general crewmen and a cook.

The cooking wasn't too tricky. The Sunnys had created a complete set of food synthesizers, some of which were set to create human-specific food. Granted, it didn't taste good, but Frazzle was working on tuning the machine's output. I'd noticed that my meals were gradually getting more palatable.

Rounding out the crew of each ship was a small group of Sim-tigers. At Kasm's insistence, we'd asked for volunteers from his people and gotten ten out of the original fifty-six that were left after defeating the Pug-bear forces on Earth. Most of the Sim-tigers had spread out over the front range, where they gave every appearance of enjoying life as the apex-predator. Some were loners, but many had affiliated themselves with human families or individuals. The two races got along well, and something about the mutual relationship seemed to fill an empty space in the Sim-tigers' worldview. They certainly were appreciated by the humans. Having a Sim-tiger living near or even with you made you a lot less desirable target for any outlaw that happened by.

Even so, there were ten who felt strongly about carrying the battle to the Pug-bears. We divided them into two groups of five, one on each ship. They were nominally Marines and integrated with the humans, but their proper role was shock troops. A squad of five, armed with their now preferred weapon, the Katana, could easily overwhelm double their number of Pug-bears and any number of Pugs, providing the Pugs were unarmed. Pugs with anti-matter weapons were a different matter entirely, one that required human assistance.

Liz stayed on the smaller ship with me. I'd refused to leave her and our two children behind. I'd done it previously and nearly lost them, and I wasn't going to leave them behind to be involved in the next wave of fighting.

The final member of our crew was our battle-scarred tomcat, Jefferson. He had been with us for nearly five years and had an unerring instinct for locating Pugs. He hated the aliens intensely and had shown that he was perfectly willing to risk death by attacking them directly, although there wasn't much he could do against one of the tough-hided creatures. Liz and I had thought about leaving him at our homestead but were unable to trust that he'd be okay. Besides, he had such an outgoing personality that everyone on the ship liked him.

Liz was plenty busy. She doubled as my Exec, at which she was competent, and as the mother to an active five-year-old boy and our four-month-old daughter. Frazzle and Mrs. Frazzle, commonly known as "Red," seemed to enjoy the presence of my children. Red quite often served as a nanny for the two. Despite her petite size, she could control Michael, and she quickly learned how to deal with a human infant.

The Sunnys were egg-layers but carried their hatched babies in their arms until they were more mature. Red had her own ideas about diapers. Having a full coat of multi-colored, reddish fur that she was inordinately proud of, she was reluctant to risk getting human waste on it, so she was cautious with diaper changing. It was actually kind of cute to watch her carefully wiping

Rowan's nether parts. I don't think any human baby had ever had such a clean posterior.

This was something that I'd never considered. Having an alien nanny, I mean. It's one thing to think about being friends with a being from another planet, but it's totally different to think about them caring for your child.

Our ship had a smaller contingent of Marines than Rudy's larger one. We had less space. I had recruited a cook and a couple of ex-submariners for other personnel, thinking they would help me organize the crew. It seemed to work. Even though I had no idea about the challenges we'd face, things were moving smoothly.

We'd set up classes so that the Sunnys could teach our people about safety issues and what to expect from the ships during daily operation. The Marines were a little restive at first, but then the Lieutenant in charge, Mr. Holmes, came to me and asked for permission to use the ship's largest area, the loading bay, for exercises and drills.

It so happened that Frazzle was nearby, and he came up with a good suggestion. "Dec, do your fights people (the Marines) need strength?"

I stopped my response to Holmes and turned to him. "Yes. That would be helpful. I'd like them to be ready for all possibilities when we start operations against the Pug-bears."

I'd taken to circumlocution when it came to talking about possible violence. The Sunnys were so averse to fighting that even speaking about it caused them to flinch.

"I can set de gravity ups in the hold," he said. "Would dat make them stronger?"

"As long as you don't set it too high. We don't want any injuries due to too much stress on them," I replied.

Mr. Holmes' mouth was hanging open in astonishment. I don't think that he'd even considered the rather remarkable fact that the ship had a gravity field.

"Sir! That would be great. Could we make it, so weight is increased by twenty-five percent?"

He was already planning exercises, and I had a brief pang of sympathy for the Marines. Then I felt even worse when I realized that I'd have to participate. I was one of the fighting forces, and I didn't want the men to think I was going easy on myself or any crew. With a brief thought of "What am I getting myself into?" I agreed.

It was ridiculously simple. Frazzle turned back to the control boards and made a couple of adjustments, then turned back to us and said, "Watch outs when you go into de hold. Gravity is now up, and your foots will be heavier when they cross the entry to the transporter. You be careful and don't fall down."

Holmes, Kasm, and I strode over to the inter-ship transporter and re-materialized in the hold side. The door opened, and, just as Frazzle had warned, I almost stumbled. My leading foot and leg suddenly weighed more as I swung them through the door. I recovered myself and carefully walked into the hold. I suddenly weighed about another fifty pounds, and it was like carrying a heavy backpack.

Holmes was experimentally doing squats, and then he went down on his knees and moved into a prone position. He went through twenty-five quick push-ups and then climbed back to his feet with a grin, "Those are much harder than normal. I usually don't feel this much burn until I reach a hundred. This will be great for working the boredom out of the men!"

I nodded and sighed, then got down myself. Twenty-five push-ups later, I was breathing heavily. I climbed back to my feet ruefully and glanced at Holmes. He immediately said, "That was very good, Sir!"

Kasm, who had shown no response to the additional gravity, except for a brief sigh as he took on the load, snorted and sent, "Dec, you'd better be in here with me every morning. I don't want you to run out of energy just when things start getting interesting."

I don't know how he managed, but he could add a slightly disparaging overtone to his mental communication. I quickly responded aloud, "No worries about me."

Then in response to Holmes' inquiring glance, I added, "Holmes, you don't have to try and flatter me. I know I'm not in as good a shape as I'd like to be. I know it took me twice as long as you to complete those. I'm going to work out with your men daily, and so are the other ship staff. We all need to be in fighting trim when we engage the Pug-bears and Pugs."

"Yes, Sir. You don't have to be so hard on yourself, though. You're a lot older than me," he replied.

"I don't call ten years older," I sighed. But it was true. Even though I lived a rough and ready life, Kasm was correct. My fitness wasn't what it had been.

Going back into the transporter was funny in a sort of silly way. Just as my foot had dropped when I stepped out, it flew up higher when I stepped in, making me look like I was attempting a clumsy goose step over the threshold. I grinned at Holmes as he tried it, "I guess we'll get used to the change with practice." He nodded. Kasm snorted sardonically.

Work-outs proceeded daily, and everyone, including Liz, who insisted on participating, benefited. After the third day, I got the idea of teaching the men to maneuver in zero gravity, and after that, we moved from heavy workouts to flying about. I reasoned that the change was good for the Marines. There was no telling where they'd be called upon to fight.

The most challenging problem I encountered with the zero-g workouts was the habitual orientation of the guys. Everyone initially wanted to orient as if the floor was the floor. It stopped after I lectured them with my feet hooked under a beam on the ceiling of the hanger.

"When you're fighting in space, the soldier who insists on viewing things as if they were on the ground is at a grave disadvantage," I

started. "There is no right or wrong orientation in zero gravity. The primary orientation you need is towards your objective. If we're assaulting an enemy ship, the ship is the target. Call it 'Down,' and then things become easier. The target is always down. Let's make that a habit."

There was some discussion, but after that, the men loosened up, and it wasn't long before they were sailing around the room in all sorts of positions relative to each other. It made the concept of attacking easier when you didn't have to stop and try to figure out whether you were upside down or your cohorts were.

The exercise got more interesting when the Sim-tigers decided to participate. We worked on drills and coordinated attacks that used the strengths of both groups. Humans armed with unpowered, anti-matter weapons and Sim-tigers with padded sticks in place of swords. Several days of such training led me to conclude that our force would be more than able to out-match a reasonable number of the enemy.

After the Marines worked out, Liz and I would take Michael and our daughter, Rowan, into the zero-g environment. I wanted them to become familiar with the sensation. It might be vitally important should the ship ever be damaged so that the artificial gravity went off.

Regardless of the importance, both children had a blast. I had to train them not to bash their heads on the walls, but after they became used to the idea of rotating and landing carefully, both became adept at moving around the large space. Rowan could not yet walk, yet she quickly learned to push herself gently off the hold's wall. She would drift slowly across the space with an excited grin on her face and somehow stick out a foot or arm just in time to fend off the wall as she approached.

After watching her, Liz and I agreed that the children would probably become far better at zero-g movement than we'd ever be.

That night, Liz woke me. The kids were asleep, as were most of the crew. We'd set up two main periods, but the later-day crew was only one human who sat watch and either Frazzle or Red who stood by, should the ship need attention.

Chapter 4

It was alt-day shift, and most of the crew were resting in their cabins. Liz grabbed my hand, shushing me with her finger held across her lips. We slipped out of the door to our room, and she shut it carefully.

"The kids will be fine for thirty minutes or so," she whispered.

"What's this about, Liz?" I was curious. I thought I knew what she had in mind, we were so closely linked mentally, but I wanted to hear her say it.

"I've been wondering about something, and I want to find out," she answered.

We went through the transporter to the hold. It was still in the zero-g mode, that being a little more economical on the grav-system. When the door opened, we floated out, both giggling like kids. Clothes sailed off in various directions as we came together in mid-air.

It was a workout. We had to hold tight to each other, and there was no gravity-assisted coming-together. Even so, it was exhilarating. We were able to take positions that would have been far too difficult with gravity. In the interest of decency, I'm going to leave our actions to your imagination.

Thirty minutes later, we floated back into the transporter, stepping down into normal gravity. Liz embraced me with warmth as I activated the thing, still radiating passion. "Dec, that was the most amazing thing! We have to do that again," she said.

"I agree, but it might be a little difficult if the men find out what we've been doing. There aren't any other women on board, and I'm pretty sure they'd be very envious," I said.

"Yeah. Why is that, anyway? Why no women?" she asked with a frown.

"I guess I thought I was outfitting just a fighting force. I should have been a little more thoughtful. Women can handle weapons too. And, zero-g fighting would more than equalize any strength differences, unless it came to grappling."

"We should pick up some women crew members at the first opportunity," she responded. "Make sure they're willing to fight. I don't want them to sign up thinking they're just here to keep the men happy."

"Okay. We'll come back to Earth and add some crew eventually. We've got to get the Pug-bears out of our system first, though."

I was considering the grappling concept. "Liz, you're trained in judo. What do you think would work in zero-grav? You can't do throws the way you would on the ground."

She paused to consider, "No, obviously not, but I think that joint locks and things like armbars or chokes would work fine. We ought to get the Marines working on those sorts of things. They've just been practicing with unloaded guns so far."

"Yeah," I responded. "We should see about using knives, too. I think that would be handy."

As a result, we began to work out techniques in human-style hand-to-hand. The process fascinated Kasm and his people. They even went so far as to join us.

I cautioned them about claws and teeth before they started. Kasm told me not to worry. His people were completely aware of the natural advantages they held over us puny humans. I wasn't so sure about their ability in zero-g. Strength is acceptable, but leverage is critical. As Archimedes said, "Give me a lever long enough, and I can move the world," or something like that.

We entered the hold, and the Sim-tigers watched as we did our usual workout. One experimentally jumped a couple of times to see how the heavier gravity affected him. He was so strong in the legs that it didn't seem to matter. He easily jumped high enough to touch the ceiling with his manipulating arms. The others joined in, leaping around for a few minutes. Then they laid down at the side of the room and watched us sweat our way through the rest of our grappling workout.

When we finished, Frazzle gradually lowered the gravity, and we relaxed into zero-g. The Sim-tigers didn't seem bothered by this. After a minute or so, Kasm gently floated over to where I was.

"Dec, show me how some of those hand-grabbing things work," he rumbled in his growling voice.

"I'm not sure how they will work with you," I answered. I tentatively caught one of his manipulating hands. He pulled me close and wrapped his front legs around me in response. I started to pull back but felt his claws against my back.

"This is not to your advantage," he said. "I can dig my claws in and pull my arms apart. You'd be seriously injured."

"Yes, and you can bite too," I agreed. He was holding me loosely, and I hooked a leg across his hips, spinning myself as I shoved up under his chin. The maneuver allowed me to slip downward and simultaneously twisted him around to face away from me. His manipulating arms were jointed roughly like a human's, and I held onto his wrist as I floated free. I had been thinking about the concept of an armbar, and it seemed natural to slip one leg on each side of his arm and across his chest and then pull. It was precisely the type of thing a human wrestler would try on another human. It worked. I was able to extend his arm, but then he used his rear paws to shove my legs towards his head, twisting me out of my position.

"That was interesting," he admitted. "You might have been able to hurt my arm. It's not as strong as my legs. I still could have bitten your leg, though."

I grinned and shrugged, "Well, I don't think any human would voluntarily get in a wrestling match with you. Let's try this."

I spun around and shoved off the ceiling while holding to his arm. My momentum dragged him around, and I let loose as he started to turn towards me. The result was he went sailing away, and I flew towards the wall. He fetched up against the opposite wall and leaped towards me, but I shoved at the floor with my hand and gently moved beyond his reach as he went past. I got a sense of amusement from him as he mentally sent, "We could dance around like this for a long time without touching each other."

I answered, "Striking with a blunt object like my fist or foot wouldn't work very well. I'd fly off the other way, and the blow would be weaker than if I was standing on the ground. Your strikes would be more damaging simply because of your claws. Perhaps we'd be better off using knives or your sword."

"That's what I was thinking," he growled aloud. Then he sent, "I can see how I'd have a little more trouble with the sword. I'd spin away from the blow in reaction, but I think my target would be cut, nevertheless."

I sent, "That's right. Every action would have an equal and opposite reaction. Your added mass would make you more dangerous than a human, though. The thing is, a zero-gravity fight would probably be in a hard vacuum. We don't have a vacuum suit for you, but if we can create one, your sword would allow you to penetrate an enemy's suit, and the vacuum would kill them if nothing else."

"I want vacuum suits for my people," he responded.

"I'll ask Frazzle if we have the facilities to make them for you," I said aloud.

We used the rest of the time for human-on-human practice. Kasm spent the time communicating with the other four Sim-tigers. They were analyzing what we were doing and figuring out if they could use some of the same techniques. The problem was that none of the Marines wanted to practice with them. They definitely were intimidating.

Things were going along about as well on Rudy's ship. Whistle was a competent pilot and kept the larger ship within a few hundred yards of ours. Rudy reported that his Marines and tigers were working out in heavy g and zero-g, just as ours. He wasn't participating as yet. He was still undergoing treatment on his injured arm.

He'd taken a bullet in an ambush over a year ago, and his left elbow was locked, rendering him unable to straighten his arm. The Sunnys had a medical device that was gradually stimulating a gentle healing. He now had recovered almost his entire range of movement, but Whistle refused to allow him to endanger the arm.

"Rudy, you got to keep de arm from being hurt," he cautioned. "De regenerator works, but arm not strong enough to do much yet. Let it heal for a long time, and then I tell you when it ready to work hard."

Rudy followed his advice and stayed out of the wrestling, only doing some of the exercises in heavy-g to keep in shape.

We gradually approached Uranus. The in-system Em-drive was so powerful that we could have gotten there much faster, but I felt that we needed the time to get used to our new environment and get organized into at least a semblance of a fighting force.

However, the day came when we were close enough to see Oberon with our naked eyes.

Chapter 5

We slowed our approach to a relative crawl, and I called a meeting in the bridge to discuss how to proceed. We'd been scanning the moon carefully, and there were no changes that I could see. The surface had transparent domes scattered about among the many craters in the few level locations.

I'd taken the time to learn a little about Oberon before setting out and found it very interesting. It was a curious moon, but most likely, it wasn't going to be a nice place to visit.

I'd learned that Oberon's mass places it ninth out of the entire solar system. Herschel discovered it in 1787, and it was named after the king of the fairies in Shakespeare's A Midsummer Night's Dream.

The aspects of Oberon that make it curious is that its orbit is the most distant of Uranus' five major moons at 584,000 kilometers, and it is almost right over Uranus' equator. The moon moves quickly, making one revolution around Uranus every thirteen and a half days. By coincidence, Oberon's rotation is the same length, making it similar to our moon with the same face always pointing towards the gas giant. There is heavy bombardment by the solar wind since Oberon is in such a distant orbit that Uranus' planetary magnetic field does not protect it.

The most unexpected fact that I found was that Uranus has a polar tilt of almost ninety degrees, orbiting the Sun lying on its side. This means that Oberon spends one half of the planet's year with its poles in complete darkness and another half with them in full sunlight. Since Uranus' takes about eighty-four Earth years to revolve around the Sun, this makes for long days and nights on parts of the moon. The surface is rugged with lots of craters and steep mountains; all told, not what a human would call the garden-spot of the universe.

Because of the roughness of the place, the aliens had scattered their domes widely. There were craters inside craters, and each of them seemed to have mountainous piles of ejecta surrounding them along with steep central mountains. After studying the moon through high magnification, I concluded that it would be nearly impossible to determine how many domes there were. Giving up in disgust, I relied on my standard fall-back tactic. I asked Frazzle, "How many domes do the Pug-bears have on that place?"

He considered with his hand rubbing his stomach. I'd noticed that he tended to do that while meditating. I was relatively confident that his brain was in his skull, so it must have just been a habit.

Finally, he answered, "I don't know, Dec, de Great Ones, er... Pug-bears might have moved more of their kind onto the moon in the time we were going to Kasm's planet. We know that one new FTL arrived. I don't know how manys of dem were on that vessel. Nor, how many Sunnys or Pugs either."

"Can we contact the Sunnys with radio?" That had worked in the past, and I wondered if there was a chance of it working now.

He answered with a negative sounding chirp, "Not working well. I been listening for radio calls, but nothing is happening. Dere no space traffic and no mining, so all is quiet."

I considered in turn, "Let's try calling on the frequency that your people usually use for their own radio traffic. Just say something innocuous. Maybe pretend you're lost or something, just in case the Pugs might be listening."

The Pugs sometimes monitored radio traffic, but they were of a more primitive mindset and didn't habitually do so. As for their masters, the Pug-bears, they could care less about radio communications between what they considered the lesser peoples. They weren't physically equipped to create or use technology anyway. Their claws were designed for hunting and fighting, but not for fine manipulations, so they depended on the Pugs and Sunnys when it came to such tasks.

Frazzle turned to the communications console, dialed in a frequency, and made a short whistle that was his version of an interrogatory sound. Nothing happened for several minutes, but then a cautious set of whistles and clicks came back. He responded and shortly was in an animated dialog with the Oberon Sunny contingent.

He paused after a bit to explain to me. "Dec, deys all Sunnys in just a few domes. There not many Pug-bears; only three, but a whole bunches of Pugs. De Pugs and Pug-bears have their own habitats and don't stay with my people."

I started to say that was a good set-up for us, but he held up a webbed, furry paw and lifted one of his stubby fingers, so I paused.

He quickly said, "De problem is that the Pug-bears have a bunch of Sunny servants. There always some of us with dem, so separating the Sunnys to where the transporter link is can't be done. Maybe we have to go down and rescue Sunnys in person."

It made me grin a little. His reluctance to engage in violence or even consider it made him phrase things oddly. What he meant, in plain terms, was we'd have to attack and clear the domes on foot, and that was a hazardous business. Both the Pugs and the Pug-bears were difficult to kill and deadly fighters.

I didn't want to risk my men clearing out a group of enraged Pug-bears if there was any possible alternative. Fortunately, Kasm came wandering into the bridge area, and I mentally posed a question to him.

"Kasm, we're going to have a problem getting the Pug-bears away from the Sunnys and the Sunnys to the Oberon transporter. Any suggestions?" I sent.

He answered quickly, "How many Pug-bears?"

"Only three, but they keep a lot of Sunny servants with them at all times," I answered.

The cat-like alien paused briefly and then said, "Here's something that might work. When they invaded our planet, we found that some of them made nests and laid eggs. We learned that the hatchlings' distress calls would cause any nearby adult to come to their aid quickly. It made a great way for us to set up ambushes and traps for the stupid things."

He was exaggerating a little, something that he often did, tending to be a little over-confident in his outlook. The Pug-bears weren't stupid, or at least the symbiont-infected ones weren't. They were quite cunning but still acted in an animal-like and ferocious manner. Those that did not have their brain augmented by the symbiont only functioned on their natural animal level and were only as cunning as perhaps an earthly bear. Even so, I could imagine that either kind would come charging in response to a distress call.

"So, what you're suggesting is that we set up some sort of ambush for them?" I asked. I still couldn't see what he was getting at. The presence of the Pugs would complicate matters. They would fight hard if they discovered us.

"No, silly!" he sent. "All we have to do is to broadcast a hatchling distress call from a distant dome, and the three Pug-bears will do everything in their power to get there quickly. They'll leave the Sunnys behind, but they might take a force of Pugs with them. Then all we have to do is to destroy the dome."

To be honest, I was preparing to argue with him about being called 'silly,' but his idea made so much sense that I forgot about it. I realized for about the hundredth time that I continually under-estimated him. It was easy for my human eyes to simply see a large, green-striped tiger and we aren't used to thinking of tigers as quite so devious.

"That could work. We'd have to figure out how to get a recording of a hatchling, though," I thought out loud.

"Let's ask Frazzle to find out from his local people," he replied. "It might be that the Pug-bears have laid some eggs somewhere, and maybe we could steal one."

Frazzle called and almost immediately found out that the Pug-bears had a separate dome for breeding. They had been on Oberon long enough to lay several nests worth of eggs.

One of the Sunnys was assigned to turn the eggs periodically. Apparently, that helped the embryo develop, but the Pug-bears weren't noticeably concerned with domestic chores and gladly assigned the task to a hapless Sunny. He was in constant fear that the eggs would hatch and the hatchlings would attack him. He was also afraid they wouldn't hatch, and he'd be blamed.

The first batch of them was just now showing signs of readying for hatching. The eggs became more brittle immediately before the event so that the young spider-like hatchlings could easily break out.

When I asked the location of the hatching dome, Frazzle showed me by pointing at the video monitor. It was near the central Pug-bear residence dome and connected by a long, meandering, inflatable tube.

The Pug-bears avoided the matter transporters for the most part. The symbionts that gave them their intelligence were hypersensitive to the transporter process and would die if the Pug-bears undertook more than an extremely short jump. This meant that the Pug-bear would arrive at its destination in its feral state. It could eventually regain intelligence by consuming parasite eggs until one of them attached to its brain, but that often took a long time. This situation was not optimal for the Pug-bears, but it was all they had. Transportation between domes via matter transporter was limited to Sunnys and Pugs. The Pugs had no problem with the transporters, and neither did humans, Sim-tigers, or Sunnys.

There were no transporter heads in the egg dome, making it difficult to formulate plans to raid the place. It promised to be a chancy venture. We'd have to slip into the Pug-bears' habitat and then travel down the tube with the attendant possibility that they'd discover us.

I briefly considered wearing a vacuum suit and just shooting my way through the outside of the dome, but that would undoubtedly evacuate the entire complex and kill the Sunnys I wanted to rescue, so that wasn't an option.

From our insider information source, the Pug-bears' habitat dome had a transporter head used by the Pugs and Sunnys when their masters summoned them. The transporter was near the entrance to the tunnel that led to the nesting area, and it seemed like it might be possible to slip through undetected. Then I happened to realize that there was an almost equal possibility that the Pug-bears would sense any unshielded mental emanations and attack before we could go through. That meant that only the Sim-tigers and I would be able to go. The Sim-tigers naturally shielded their minds, and I was confident that my mental shield would keep the Pug-bears from sensing me. The rest of the humans did not have the ability or were too weak in their shielding, as in my wife's case, to be able to sneak through undetected.

It was at this point that Liz came through, "Dec, you've been looking at this thing all wrong. Why do you want to capture a hatchling? To record its distress cries to lure the Pug-bears into an ambush. Well, the creatures are all in one dome now. Just go in and kill them and try to save as many Sunnys as you can. Forget the egg dome."

I felt like slapping my forehead and saying, "Doh!" She was right, of course. I sent a thought message to Kasm, "How long will it take before you and your friends are ready to attack the Pug-bears' dome?"

The answer was immediate, "We're ready now! We'll be at the transporter waiting for you."

They were as good as their word. The Marines and Joe and I arrived together and were greeted with Kasm's guttural voice asking, "What took you so long?"

The Sim-tigers were all armed with their choice of words, some with an extra weapon strapped around their mid-section. The humans were carrying anti-matter weapons.

I had no doubt about my ability to use the weapon sensibly, but the Marines, having been recruited before we shipped out, didn't inspire my confidence. Considering the fighting abilities of the leathery-skinned Pugs, I had decided that it would be best to bring two Marines along with Joe and me. We'd be armed with anti-matter pistols backed by the two men who'd have anti-matter rifles. That would allow maximum maneuverability paired with stealth.

I decided that I'd better have a brief talk with the two Marines. "Listen up! The rifles you're carrying are incredibly destructive. They will easily shoot a hole in anything at which you point them. That includes the dome structure we're going to raid. If one of you is careless enough to dissolve a hole in that dome, it will evacuate, and we will die. There isn't enough atmosphere on this moon to count and what there is, isn't breathable by any stretch of the imagination. All shots must be single shots; no pulse bursts! And, all shots must be backstopped by either buildings or other aliens or the dome's floor. If you shoot downward, you'll be less likely to kill us all. Understood?"

Joe just looked grimly amused as the two chorused back a muted, "Yes, Sir!"

Sighing, I judged that was the best I could do. I looked at Kasm, and he made a face that I had come to recognize as indicative of him finding something humorous.

He sent, "Don't worry, Dec! We'll most likely have them down and dead before your people come through. There will be no need to shoot."

I only hoped that he was correct. I looked at the Marines again as Kasm and the small group of Sim-tigers entered the ship's transporter and disappeared. We followed, and I pushed the button, and things got blurry for a moment as they always did, then we came out into the alien's dome.

There were two dead Pugs directly in front of us, and nothing else was visible. I could hear some fighting coming from the far side of the dome. The place was like the first dome I'd ever seen. A garden or plot of uncultivated vegetation was in the center, with cubicles spaced evenly around the perimeter. The vegetation was between us and the fighting. I could hear some Sim-tiger snarls mixed with the weird, moaning noise the Pug-bears made.

I waved the two men towards the left and led Joe around the right side of the central garden, taking care to stay well back from the alien vegetation. Before we could get started, a huge Pug-bear broke through the plants coming right towards us. It was missing a couple of legs on one side, and there were some deep slashes in its carapace on the other, but it was coming fast, and it was obviously enraged.

I shrugged off the impact of its mental attack and then realized that neither the Marines nor Joe could do the same. Out of the corner of my eye, I could see the three of them standing, paralyzed with their weapons drooping. The Pug-bear had come out somewhat behind my position just as one of the riflemen passed close by the central plants. I should have warned them, but I hadn't foreseen the layout.

Before I could complete my turn and aim, the swollen, spider-like alien had slashed the marine with one of its venom-tipped claws and was reaching for the next. I brought my pistol up and then had to step to the side because Joe was standing, stunned, between the Pug-bear and me. It struck at the next marine but only succeeded in knocking his weapon out of his grasp. Before it could try again, my anti-matter pulse had burned off two more of its legs and dissolved a basketball-sized hole in its side. It wavered, staggered, and then fell over, still reaching for its last target. The remaining marine was standing just a little out of its reach.

The thing wasn't dead, and I suddenly sensed a difference in its mental sending. Instead of commanding that its prey stand still, it switched instantly to summoning them. The targeted man shuddered and then turned, starting to step towards his death as did Joe. The alien lifted its remaining forelimb to strike, but a green-striped fury charged by and struck with its sword, lopping the threatening foreleg off near the carapace.

Then, the Sim-tiger turned and chopped with all its considerable strength, cleaving the Pug-bear's skull in half. A stunning mental shriek emanated from the thing's symbiont as it died. Then all was still.

I stepped over and pushed the semi-paralyzed and stunned man away from the venom-dripping claws. There was no sense in risking an accident. As I moved him away, Kasm came up beside me and sent, "I don't think your people should fight these evil things. Most humans can't resist their mental commands the way you can."

"You may be right. I'd forgotten just how powerful an intelligent Pug-bear can be," I sent with a mental feeling of regret. My lack of preparation had resulted in the death of one of my men, and I didn't feel worthy of command at the moment. I'd made a stupid mistake.

Kasm brought me back to the immediate situation. "How many of these things were there supposed to be?"

"Only three, according to our informant," I responded.

"There are three dead ones on the other side of the plants. This one is the fourth, and I think some others ran down the tunnel to the hatching dome." He was still worked up over the fight and finished his mental sending with a ferocious and loud snarl, making the remaining marine jump.

I turned to the man and ordered him to set up a guard over the transporter portal. It wouldn't do to have enemies arriving behind us when we were in the tunnel. Then I said, "Joe, please check each of the cubicles. Carefully! There could be a Pug-bear in any of them. I'll have one of the Sim-tigers go with you, just in case."

The marine stepped towards the portal, and Joe headed for the nearest cubicle along with one of Kasm's people. As for me, I turned and followed the rest of the Sim-tigers into the tunnel.

Chapter 6

Frazzle's informant had told us that only one Pug-bear at a time visited the egg-dome. The creatures were more fractious and likely to fight over nests when they were in an egg-laying mood.

Kasm had seen at least two escape down the tunnel before I'd arrived through the transporter, which meant there might be even more. The information we had received was wrong, and I was left wondering what we'd be facing when we got through the tunnel.

It was a long walk. The tunnel was some type of transparent, plastic-like material, but ice crystals on the inside made it difficult to see out. There was nothing outside to see anyway. I could more or less make out the outline of the nearby giant planet and some low, jagged mountains, but little else.

The tunnel meandered aimlessly across the terrain, bypassing craters and moving diagonally up and down slopes. The air was breathable but quite dry, something I'd expected, knowing the Pug-bears' preference for dry nesting grounds. I was near the end of the line of Sim-tigers. They were in no hurry since they realized there was nowhere their enemies could go to escape.

Kasm mentally suggested that I drop back and guard the tunnel entrance. "We're going to burst out and attack all of the enemies we find. Dec, you stay near the tunnel and make sure none get past while we're busy."

I mentally assented to his request and slowed down. The Sim-tigers gradually moved out of sight ahead of me. The tunnel was quiet, except for the sound of my steps and my breathing.

There was a sudden sharp right turn, and the dome appeared. It was difficult to see much. The dome, like the tunnel, was covered with tiny ice crystals and what looked like dust on its outer surface. The combination made it quite dim inside. This was a drawback to me, but the low light level didn't hamper the Sim-tigers much. Their eyes were more cat-like than not, and they saw better in the dusk than humans.

They charged out of the entrance, and the battle was instantly on. There were far more Pug-bears in the dome than I'd anticipated. The place held more than twice the number of my small force. The Sim-tigers, though outnumbered, attacked with their usual fury and were holding their own when the Pug-bears' numbers were suddenly reinforced by a large number of sub-adults, some so young that they were in the nasty, spider-like form that disgusted me.

The Sim-tigers chopped with their swords and raked with their claws while the Pug-bears slashed with their single-clawed legs and snapped at the tigers' legs with their dripping mandibles. The spiders climbed over the backs of a couple of the tigers, sending the tigers into a whirling spin as they tried to rake the things off of them. The spider venom was different enough from the adults' poison that it caused a reaction from the tigers. They were mostly immune to the adult venom, but the spider-venom was more concentrated, and the two beset tigers suddenly slowed in their movements and became shaky and disoriented. Some of the adult Pug-bears moved to take advantage of the disability.

I'd remained by the tunnel entrance and had been ignored until this point. I raised the anti-matter rifle I'd taken from where the dead marine had dropped it and systematically began to shoot at the adult Pug-bears. I took four down with four shots before they became aware that I was there. The rest instantly tried to overwhelm me mentally, and their attack was vicious. My sight blurred for an instant, but then my psychic defense rose to the challenge. My vision cleared just in time for me to sweep a burst of pulses across a rapidly advancing line of spiders and older juveniles, any of which would have instantly killed me.

I checked the ground nearby and zapped a couple of stray spiders, then went back to concentrating on the remaining adults. Two were trying to circle behind Kasm as he faced two more. I shot both of them but then had to dissolve some more of the younger ones. The situation was a mess, and I wasn't sure that we'd come out whole.

The battle suddenly resolved into one-on-one conflicts, which the Sim-tigers quickly won. One remaining Pug-bear sprinted away but was overhauled and cut down. There were still several spider forms and sub-adults wandering around, but they didn't seem to have any direction with the loss of the adults. I carefully shot as many of them as I could see, and the unoccupied Sim-tigers killed the rest.

The fight was over, and Kasm came back to me, stopping briefly to inspect his two wounded compatriots. They were still shaky and under the venom's effect, but it was starting to fade.

"Kasm, let's destroy the eggs in the nests before any others hatch," I said aloud.

He turned to the nearest nest and started crushing the large number of eggs there. The rest of the Sim-tigers followed suit while I used the rifle to wipe out distant nests. There were probably over a thousand eggs contained in almost a hundred nests. The blasted creatures were undoubtedly prolific.

We'd just finished the destruction when Joe came bursting out of the tunnel.

"Pugs!" he shouted.

We'd been flanked, and there were a large number of Pugs following him through the tube. They'd come through the transporter and killed the second marine before he could react. The remaining Sim-tiger had attacked them and taken out a couple but then had been hit with an anti-matter shot.

The next few minutes were frustrating for both my group and, doubtless, the Pugs also. Neither party dared shoot down the tunnel. It was a thin-walled plastic tube with too many turns. There was no way to fire an anti-matter weapon down it without hitting the side and evacuating both domes.

I was at a loss as to how to proceed. I didn't dare send Kasm and his friends down the tube. They would doubtless kill a bunch of Pugs, but there was almost a hundred percent chance that at least one of the Pugs would shoot at them and evacuate the domes.

We stayed out of the direct line of fire from the tube mouth while I tried to think of how to approach the problem. It turned out to be self-resolving. The Pugs, seeing no one there to meet them and only knowing that Joe had run down the tube ahead of them, approached the nesting dome in a large group. They paused several yards back in the tube for a moment, and I heard their sibilant speech.

There was a curious effect as I heard them talking in their own language and still gleaned the meaning mentally. Without realizing it, I'd reached out to their minds, nasty as they were, and tuned in. They were preparing to charge out and try to overwhelm Joe. They figured he'd be hiding in one of the cubicles; apparently, they didn't have a very high opinion of humans.

I waved the Sim-tigers out of sight, and they faded back into cover on the other side of the central jungle or garden, whatever it was. Joe stood in the open, looking at me for a cue. Chancing that the Pugs weren't quite ready, I ran across the mouth of the tunnel to Joe's location. There were a series of hisses, and several poison splinters flew across the space and struck the central plants. None had come close to me, fortunately. I was glad. I'd seen many humans die quickly and horribly from the toxin.

One of the jungle plants must have been sensitive to the poison in the splinters. It began to sway, and then its tendrils curled up almost as quickly as an animal could move. It made some shuddering movements and then perceptibly began to wilt.

The Pugs, having missed me, were now confident that there was only one human there. I don't think they differentiated me from Joe. They let out a loud series of hisses and came charging out into the central part of the dome, looking for easy targets.

By then, Joe and I had taken cover around the edge of the nearest cubicle, and no one was in sight. I summoned Kasm mentally.

"Kasm, they are all out in the open, and none of them have anti-matter weapons. They only have splinter guns."

That was quite to his liking. The Sim-tigers were immune to the Pug-bears' venom, and the glass splinter toxin didn't seem to affect them at all. The Pugs were just getting organized when the tigers charged around the plants with loud roars.

Two Pugs fell immediately to the sharp swords, and the rest bolted variously towards the tunnel and the nearest cubicle. The two that came towards the cubicle ran right into my single anti-matter pistol shot. I'd carefully aimed downward so that the dome floor would dissipate the bolt, should I miss, but I didn't. Their lower halves disappeared with the weapon's characteristic crackling noise. The Pugs dropped. The nearer one was dead, but the other had been struck lower down in the legs. It made an effort to recover and shoot splinters at us. I quickly shot again, and this time, the bolt dissolved the creature's head.

Only one survived to make the tunnel opening, but it was pursued by two Sim-tigers and didn't make it very far down the tunnel before being pulled down. By then, the rest of us were in the tunnel mouth and heading back to the transporter head. I wanted to get out of there before more Pugs showed up and trapped us again.

When we reached the main dome, a small group of Sunnys stood indecisively near the tunnel entrance. They started to run when the Sim-tigers charged out, but Kasm dashed in front of them and headed them off. The rest of the tigers surrounded the nearly hysterical small, furry aliens, preventing them from trying to escape. Joe and I came out of the tunnel a little after the tigers. We weren't nearly as fast.

The Sunnys had been preparing to die, not knowing what the Sim-tigers were, but at the sight of us, they perked up a little. It was apparent that they recognized humans.

Not having time to fool with amenities, I simply forced contact with their minds and ordered them into the transporter with Joe. Then I contacted Frazzle, ensuring that he had the ship's

transporter linked to the outbound function of this one. Joe looked my way, and I nodded and pointed my finger at him. He waved and pressed the button, and they were off to the ship. I waited a minute and then hit the call button. The rest crowded in when the door popped open. It was pretty tight, but we all managed to squeeze in. Kasm was last, and there was no space for him, but he solved that by simply jumping onto the tightly packed backs of his fellows. This put his face right next to mine, and we looked companionably into each other's eyes.

I pressed the go button, and the transporter did its thing. It still made me feel a little woozy, despite the large number of transitions I'd made through them. The Sim-tigers weren't bothered by the effect as far as I could tell.

The door opened just as Kasm opened his mouth and licked my ear. I recoiled, shocked, only to sense that he was mentally laughing. Sometimes his sense of humor was a little ridiculous. He growled in his low voice, "You don't taste too bad. Better, at least, than those spider things."

I responded in kind, "I don't mind you licking me, but better not let Liz see you. She might be jealous."

He was quick on the come-back, "No. She knows I like her more than you."

I snorted as he turned and jumped out into the cargo bay.

We were shortly back in the bridge area. I started to explain to Liz and Frazzle how the raid had gone, but then I realized that we had not captured any of the hatchlings or recorded their distress cries. My face fell.

Liz asked, "What's the matter?"

"We failed to get the distress call that we need. I lost two men, and we failed," I responded.

"No. You rescued twelve Sunnys and killed a bunch of the enemy and, look!" She pointed at one of the other Sim-tigers. He was clutching a battered spider. Three of its legs were missing, and it looked about half dead.

He held it up for me to inspect. As if on cue, it made a thin squalling moan. I grabbed the digital recorder from my belt and thumbed it on. I judged that we had what we needed and nodded at the tiger a minute later. He simply squeezed tighter, and the spider's carapace crunched. It went limp, and he dropped it in the waste disposal.

"How many Pug-bears are left?" asked Liz.

I thought about it a moment, "Well, there were only supposed to be three, according to Frazzle's informant, but we found more. I think it's safe to assume that the information was wrong, and we'd better proceed as if there are many more."

"I don't think it matters," Liz said. "Our luring tactic should work on one or many. Now, let's see about bunching any remaining Pug-bears."

Frazzle had been searching through the transporter network on the surface. Several of the domes had transporters, although the Pug-bears only used tunnels. It was pretty easy to see that only a few of the domes were connected with tunnels, and we figured that those would be the only likely ones for Pug-bears.

I turned the recorder on and listened carefully to the sounds. Simultaneously, I reached out on the Pug-bears' mental frequency and broadcast the distress call along with the sense of it coming from the most isolated dome.

I hadn't tried to sense the aliens before. Somehow, it didn't always occur to me to use my mind that way, but now I could feel that there were many of them from the strength of their response. They were moving quickly through the connecting tunnels and heading towards the remote dome. I kept the distress broadcast going for a moment longer, then stopped.

"Frazzle, can you get in contact with the remaining Sunnys?" I asked.

"Already done dat, Dec," he answered. "Deys ready to run to the transporters and come up to the ship."

"Have them start then. How many are there?" I asked.

"We have room, barely," he answered. "Dere nearly a hundred of them."

I was surprised. This would make the ship very crowded. "How about Pugs?"

"Deys mostly in their own habitats over that way," he pointed. The Pugs needed a different air mixture to be comfortable and tended to stay segregated from the Sunnys and Pug-bears unless under orders.

"Let's give them something to worry about," I said and nodded at Liz. She was sitting at the weapons station and immediately fired an anti-matter burst at the central Pug dome. The center of the structure disappeared, and the walls collapsed, followed by a burst of condensation that shot up from the evacuating, linked domes. I figured that would take care of the Pugs. Now we just had to wait for the Sunnys to come through.

That took about thirty minutes. Whistle called up from the cargo hold and chirped at Frazzle over the intercom. The Oberon Sunnys were all on-board and safe.

That was Liz's signal to shoot the Pug-bears' domes, and she did, destroying most of their surface installation.

She was finishing her destruction when Frazzle let out an excited whistle, "Dec, Dec! Deres another FTL coming! It just dropped out of FTL status and is heading this way."

"How long before it gets close enough to detect us?" I asked.

"Maybe not too long," he answered. "Deys moving pretty fast."

Chapter 7

I stepped over to Frazzle's control station and looked at the video display, but the incoming ship was not visible. It had dropped out of FTL about sixty light minutes out towards the edge of the solar system at a position above the ecliptic. Instruments now showed that it was proceeding directly towards Uranus from an angle of about thirty degrees above the planet's orbit.

Our two ships would be easily visible as the intruder approached. However, I didn't want to send any radio signals that would warn them that we were there, so coordinating with Rudy on the second ship required a mental effort. I'd touched Rudy's mind years ago when I gave him a little training in mental communication, but he hadn't enjoyed the process and, out of respect for that, I hadn't linked with him since. Now, I was a little unsure whether or not he'd even notice that I was trying to contact him.

Liz and I were in a continuous low-level linkage that didn't take much to escalate into clear communication. I glanced at her and then at the disk of Uranus showing in the upper left part of the bridge window. She read my intention and nodded, then spoke, "Yes, I agree. We should move to put the planet between them and us. We can hover just out-of-sight and direct detection until they shut down and start trying to determine what happened here."

Frazzle looked inquisitively at her and then back at me. He nodded when she'd finished talking and added, "I start moving us slowly with the in-system drive on low. We can get dere fast so that they don't sense us."

I gathered from this that he'd be able to keep our emissions low enough to allow us to remain unseen. With that assurance, I immediately linked to Rudy. He was in the bridge of the larger ship, and I could sense his tension. He physically jumped when he realized that I was linking with him, and his thoughts raced for a moment and then came through to me, a little disorganized, but clearly: "Dec, enemy coming. What to do? Detect us, maybe?"

He then tried to shut his thoughts off to give me time to respond. It wasn't necessary; mental communications don't work precisely the way conversation does. Messages can go both ways simultaneously.

I sent, "Set the Em-drive at twenty percent of power and move towards the other side of Uranus. Let's move into a low orbit. We can stay out of sight until they've shut down their ship, then we'll see if we can transport over and capture it."

I sensed his assent. The larger ship started moving, following beside us and a little behind.

"Kasm?"

"Yes, Dec?"

"We've got company coming. A ship just dropped out of light speed, and it'll be in position for us to try to board in about two hours. I expect that the incoming ship has a normal crew of both Pugs and Pug-bears with a few Sunnys. See about getting your people ready to transport onboard."

"Okay! Looking forward to another chance at them!" he sent with a mental snarl.

The marine Lieutenant was watching our preparation from the rear of the bridge, and I motioned him to step up to the command console with me.

"Mr. Holmes, we've got company, and I hope to capture their ship. I'm not sure how this will play out, but I want you to get half of your men ready to transport onboard in about two hours. We'll wait until they shut down before we attack."

"Yes, Sir!" he replied, turning to go.

"Just a minute. Let's get the other half suited up for vacuum. We might have to board their ship without using the transporter system," I added as an afterthought.

"I'll have B-squad in suits, armed and ready in the cargo hold near the outside lock in about ninety minutes."

"That will be adequate. Let them leave their helmets off and get them something to eat. It'll be about mealtime before we're ready, and they'll probably fight better with some extra energy." I didn't want them to be distracted with hunger.

"Okay. That makes sense. With your permission, I'll have A-squad stop by the cafeteria and eat prior to assembling near the transporter head."

"Good! Now, let's see about getting ourselves a third spaceship," I replied. He saluted, turned, and headed out to assemble his men.

I looked at Liz ruefully. I still wasn't used to his constant saluting. She just smiled and shook her head. I received a sense that she thought I'd better get used to that treatment.

We moved back into the gas giant's shadow. Oberon was transiting the middle of the day-side of Uranus, and we hovered just inside the shadow, in the edge of night so-to-speak. All external lights were shut off, and we dimmed the bridge lighting so that nothing was visible externally. As far as a distant observer could see, both of our two ships might have been a couple of rocks, maybe a little too symmetrical, but nothing that looked like a threat, I hoped. Our engines were shut down, and our energy emission profile was as small as we could get it.

When the new FTL coasted up into a low orbit around Oberon, Frazzle carefully made a quick attempt to link to her transporter. Here we met a stumbling block. This was an older ship, and it didn't carry a transporter unit. All travel to and from it would have to be made by shuttle-craft or docking tubes.

I was digesting this information when two shuttles left the newcomer and headed for the damaged dome system on the moon. They communicated back and forth via radio using the Pug language if a series of hisses and sibilants could be called a language.

We watched as the shuttles landed near the now-destroyed central dome. Their radio chatter ceased, and I realized that the crews were preparing to go outside and investigate the disaster. Their false assurance that they were the only space-traveling group in the area was true-to-form. Neither the Pugs nor the Pug-bears seemed to grasp the idea that they might not be alone. Basic security measures eluded them as a result.

I called Mr. Holmes on the intercom, and he got all of his men suited up and in the large shuttle. We still hadn't solved the problem of spacesuits for the Sim-tigers, so they were left pacing back and forth in the cargo bay, all ready for a fight, with no way to get to it.

The Pugs entered the wreckage, and Frazzle said he could detect radio traffic coming from the remains of the domes. I took that as a signal to dispatch the Marines. The large shuttle disconnected and gradually accelerated on an intercept course for the new FTL. It increased speed until it was well on its way, then coasted until it was time to brake to position in orbit, gradually overtaking the FTL.

The shuttle matched up with the FTL, and I received two clicks on the assigned radio channel from Holmes. That meant he was ready to attack.

I nodded at Frazzle, and he spoke a series of clicks and whistles into the radio. The other FTL had to be piloted by Sunnys; Pugs usually didn't bother with flight training – there were too many opportunities to do more exciting things, such as fighting over breeding rights or eating, for them to bother. Besides, that's what Sunnys were for – flying and using technology, along with serving as an occasional snack.

Frazzle cranked up the magnification on our video, and we could see tiny specks that were our Marines drifting from the shuttle over to the FTL. They landed and moved towards the airlock. Once they started transiting through, Rudy and I brought our ships out of the shadow and accelerated towards Oberon.

Holmes' voice suddenly came through on the radio, "We're encountering stiff resistance. Requesting back-up, stat! The ship is full of Pugs, and they're all armed and spoiling for a fight. Get here as quickly as you can!"

"On our way. Try to hold out for fifteen and keep your spacesuits on," I sent back.

Someone in the new FTL had been monitoring the radio waves because our sensors suddenly pinged as an active search signal bounced off of our hull. The enemies' ship started to move, and we could see a transparent wave disturbance in space emanating from their Em-drive.

"Frazzle! They're going to accelerate away from us!" I said. "Try to catch up with them."

"It hard to match if dey accelerating," he relapsed into his pigeon English.

"Okay," I grunted. Liz had risen from the weapons station a few minutes before and was looking over Frazzle's shoulder. I jumped over and dropped into the seat. I powered up the system and locked the bow anti-matter gun onto the enemy.

"Get us as close as you can, Frazz!" I ordered.

We were catching up quickly, having had a head start at building acceleration. The Em-drives didn't exactly accelerate rapidly. The net effect built up quickly enough over time to allow easy in-system travel.

We approached, gradually slowing in our relative motions as the other ship sped up. When we were at our closest point, I took manual control of the gun and fine-tuned it to the ship's tail, between the FTL vanes. The Em-drive was located there in an external housing.

I double-checked my aim and then triggered off a single burst, praying as I did that my aim was exact, and the burst wouldn't be so powerful that it took off the entire end of the other ship.

My results were mixed. The Em-drive housing disappeared, as did part of the hull. A puff of condensing atmosphere shot out of the gap and sprayed tiny drops of ice out into the void. I hoped that the Marines had followed orders and had kept their spacesuits sealed.

I needn't have worried. Holmes radioed in immediately after that, "Atmosphere is gone in the main part of the ship. Resistance has ceased. There are decompressed Pug bodies all over the place. I think they're all dead."

A couple of minutes later, he checked in again, "The bridge is shut and locked. There must be a crew in there."

I transmitted back, "Hold there, Holmes. We'll be up to you shortly and will lock on with our gravity generator. Then we'll see about patching the leak."

Frazzle turned to me at about that time and said, "Dec, dere

some Sunnys in the bridge. They locked airlock to try and keep away from fighting, so they alive. But none of Pugs or Masters – errr – Pug-bears in bridge with them."

Things were working out nicely. The Pugs and Pug-bears were dead, and the Sunnys were safe. We had a new spaceship, even if the Em-drive was gone and there was a hole in the hull. From past experience, I knew those things could be fixed in a matter of days.

Our shuttle had been left behind but now came creeping up to our position and docked with its grapples. The only loose end was the two shuttles full of Pugs that had landed. I called Rudy.

"Hey, buddy! How about going back to the moon to see what you can do about those two shuttles?" I radioed.

"No problem, Dec. We're on our way." The larger FTL dropped back and then accelerated towards Oberon orbit.

Chapter 8

We'd assembled the rescued Sunnys in the hold. It was the largest space on the ship, and we needed it because there were so many of them. The place echoed with their whistling speech bouncing off the hard ceiling and walls. They milled around conversing but steering clear of the two Marines posted by the access transporter portal. Frazzle came through the transporter with Kasm, Liz, and me.

When the occupants noticed our presence, the volume level doubled, sounding like a convention of songbirds that had suddenly noticed a cat entering the room. We made our way across to the end of the hold. There was a slightly raised area there for cargo storage, and we jumped up onto the platform, then turned to our audience.

Frazzle raised his webbed hand, and the gathering stopped talking immediately. Liz looked at me and cocked an eyebrow as I caught her thought: "More polite and attentive than humans would be."

Frazzle spoke for some time, making a combination of whistles and clicks that would have made no sense to me except that I was mentally monitoring his meaning. He explained to his audience that we had rescued many Sunnys and allied with their race and the Sim-tigers. We intended to free all of them from the domination of the Pug-bears, and we needed their help. He paused momentarily to indicate each of us, pointing with his webbed fingers as he mentioned our names by way of introduction.

Then there was a lengthy dialogue with an older-looking Sunny who was roughly in the middle of the front line. I understood from the discussion that he was their elder and was nominally in charge of their group. They were discussing the repair of the shot-up FTL.

Frazzle finally turned to us and said, "Dec, dey have lots of techs in this group. If we link to de damaged ship so they can access it, they can repair in maybe two or three days."

I was greatly relieved. I really wanted that ship. We needed all of the space travel capacity we could get, and I had been kicking myself mentally for not having the foresight to close with it and latch on with our point-gravity source.

The anti-gravity system in our ship could be focused outside the hull and could place a considerable pull on external objects. That was how we'd previously dragged an ice-ball comet to one of the Sunny planets to water bomb the Pug-bears' breeding grounds. I figured that we could maybe have grabbed the new FTL and slowed it enough so that it couldn't have escaped.

Instead, the only thing I'd come up with was blasting the Em-drive area of the ship. The thing was, the anti-matter cannons weren't exactly surgical in their precision. Things hit by an anti-matter burst tended to disappear, and you couldn't accurately predict in advance how much of them would vanish.

I realized that the effect was one-to-one. A normal matter particle would cancel one anti-matter particle, but when you projected anti-matter bursts, you couldn't tell in advance how many normal particles would be struck. I mean, if you shot at a solid structure, it would evaporate to a certain extent, but if the target were partially vacant or had low mass areas in it, like a spaceship, then much more of the structure would disappear.

In this case, we'd successfully knocked out the Em-drive and a lot of the rear hull. I didn't think we'd damaged the FTL vanes. Those were the part of the ship that transferred the FTL generator's effect into the quantum plenum so that the ship could be boosted along by the naturally occurring torsion waves – or so I believed in my admittedly limited understanding of the system.

I responded to Frazzle mentally, boosting my gain and doing my best to broadcast to the entire group of Sunnys. They were not telepathically endowed like the Sim-tigers and Pug-bears, but they could understand thoughts that were carefully placed into their minds.

"I'm pleased that you have agreed to help us salvage the damaged ship. We desperately need more spaceships in our quest to stop the Masters (their term for the Pug-bears). We will attempt to provide as much support as possible for the effort. My men (here I pointed at the Marines) can assist. They are not experienced with your technology, but they are more than able to help position items for attachment to the ship.

The elder turned to me and formally raised both of his arms. "We agree to help your quest. We accept the relationship that you have set up with these other Sunnys, and we petition you to adopt us into that relationship," he whistled.

I gleaned his meaning mentally and simply raised my palm to stop Frazzle as he turned to translate.

I responded, "We are pleased to acknowledge your presence as valued members of our confederation. I hope to free your people, to quarantine the Pug-bears and Pugs so they can never be a problem again, and to build a mutually beneficial relationship with both the Sunnys and the people of the Tukola system, that we call Sim-tigers."

Kasm stepped forward and looked them over, then nodded his head in a very human-like motion. He wasn't able to broadcast his thoughts to them, only to his own people and to select telepathic humans. The elder Sunny lowered his arms, and the ceremony was complete if such it could be called. The Sunnys immediately began to chatter as they organized to file out.

Frazzle turned to me and said, "Dec, I go back to de bridge and fly us up to the other ship. Then we can link up and start repairs."

"Okay. That's great! Do we have an extra Em-drive?"

"Not in dis ship, but the other one, Rudy's, has an extra drive in storage. It's not unknown for drives to break, so we sometimes carry extras. Putting it on the ship may be a problem. We have to fix the support structure so it will handle the stress of acceleration," he said, then paused and held up a single webbed finger. "Dat might not be too hard to do. We have plenty of extra hull metal in our workshop here."

We returned to the bridge where we'd left Red, Frazzle's mate in charge. She indicated the short-range communication system, saying, "Call Rudy. He got problem."

Rudy had approached Oberon rather circumspectly, but the two shuttles full of Pugs had been alarmed by the sudden cessation of communication from their ship and had both launched. They flew towards his ship, probably thinking it was one of theirs. When he couldn't speak the sibilant Pug language, they'd accelerated directly at him and given every sign of attempting to destroy the big FTL by ramming it.

The Pugs' small ships were more maneuverable than the interstellar vessel, and he had fired on them. The shots were accurate, and both of the shuttles were reduced to fragments of metal along with some decompressed and frozen Pug corpses.

It was a bit of a setback as I'd hoped to capture those shuttles also. We needed more of them.

As we approached the damaged FTL, I suddenly realized that it held a third shuttle-craft latched to the grapples on the far side of the ship. I hadn't noticed it in the excitement. When I pointed it out to him, it made Rudy feel a little better.

We matched up with the damaged ship. It drifted in an orbit that would eventually decay and drag it down into Uranus' gravity field. It would be a race to get the drive system working in time to prevent that from happening.

We closed on the ship and extruded our docking tube. It mated with the access port and locked, providing a pathway for the attacking Marines to return directly to our ship. Lieutenant Holmes and a couple of his men stayed on board, although they had no way of controlling the derelict.

Holmes had thoughtfully directed his men to bring back as many Sunny spacesuits as they could carry. They came floating through the vacuum in the tube, pushing a giant tangle of the things. Since the damaged ship had lost its atmosphere, there was no sense in pressurizing the docking tube. They had to cycle through the airlock into our ship slowly.

The Sunnys were waiting and quickly donned the suits and made their way back to the ship. From that point onward, I left the repair job in their hands. Rudy brought his ship close, and we used a shuttle to haul his spare in-system drive over to the salvaged hull. The Marines helped the Sunnys push the bulky package around and position it above the welding crew, who were already busily engaged in rebuilding the dissolved attachment points.

By the end of the watch, Liz and I were tired and ready to take time to play with our neglected children for a little while before eating and bed.

Jefferson came with us into the cafeteria and made a general nuisance of himself, poking his nose into everyone's food when they weren't looking. He didn't want to eat much. He just touched the items with his nose in that smug and irritating way that cats have when they want to demonstrate that they own something. I had to go and get more meat twice as a result.

By the subsequent wake period, the repairs had progressed enough so that the damaged ship was air-tight again and the atmosphere had been restored. The Sunnys had re-mixed the air to be similar to Earth normal. The Pugs liked a combination of gasses that humans couldn't easily breathe. The Sunnys could breathe both mixtures, although they preferred our atmosphere over that of the Pugs.

Our Marines were working alongside the Sunny crew in shifts and were now in the process of fitting the Em-drive to its new mounting brackets. Once it was attached, the control system had to be hooked up and tested.

We were ready to head back to Earth by the end of the third day. We weren't in a rush to return. There was one other task I wanted to be completed first.

I had the Sunny crew working on a gun mount for the bow of the new FTL. We'd unmounted one of our two waist guns, and I wanted it on the new ship. Having an unarmed ship just wasn't in my plans.

Chapter 9

I had two items on my agenda. First, I wanted to gather a fighting crew for the new FTL and possibly some women crew members for all three ships. The second thing I needed to do was locate a scientist, preferably a medical doctor capable of research or a biologist, who could help me figure out why the Pug-bears' brain-enhancing symbionts were not growing correctly on Earth. The last I'd heard, no one had encountered an intelligent Pug-bear for over two years.

By the end of the second day of our return to Earth, the Sunnys, aided by some of the Marines, had the gun mount prepared on the bow-deflection plate of the newly captured ship. At the same time, another crew had been busy detaching the gun from one of our waist mounts.

I hated to weaken my ship's offensive capability in that way, but I felt about as confident as you could get that we weren't going to have another space battle anytime soon. I'd won my first space conflict handily, but then I'd been fighting shuttle-craft that were more lightly armed. Our two remaining anti-matter cannons were far more potent than the shuttle-craft plasma projectors and the smaller anti-matter guns. Another advantage was the connection of the weapons to our ship's power rather than relying on battery power; they'd shoot until the ship failed.

Despite having discussed the weapons at some length with Frazzle, I was still ignorant of their true capabilities and limitations. Like all the Sunnys, he was reluctant to discuss or think about anything relating to violence, and apparently, weapon technology fell under that category.

All of this was in the back of my mind while I was playing with Michael and Rowan. She was getting to the point where she could sit upright without falling over, and we were engaged in a kind of tickle game with a stuffed bear. As I poked it into her tummy, both she and Michael laughed.

The inoffensive bear was grabbed and immediately conveyed to her mouth. She wasn't yet teething, but she drooled all over its ear. Michael thought that was funny also.

The bear reminded me of our enemies. For about the hundredth time, I regretted calling our main enemies Pug-bears in the panic-stricken moment when I realized that we were about to be rushed by a large number of them that we'd encountered in a Nebraska Air Force hanger.

The Sunnys called them "Masters," but that didn't sit well with me. I wasn't going to give them that degree of respect. I reluctantly concluded, once again, that I'd continue with the Pug-bear designation.

I sighed and stood up. I'd have to go and try to coerce Frazzle into talking about the anti-matter technology. If there were any chance the guns would fail or do something unexpected, I figured that I'd be better off knowing about it in advance.

Liz had been watching our play-time with a pleased expression that turned to concern when she saw my change of attitude.

"What is it? I know you too well, Dec. You've got some problem on your mind, and you're trying to figure out how to handle it."

I smiled and shook my head. There was no way I could put anything over on her. She was too perceptive.

"Take over with the kids, Dear. I'm going to talk to Frazzle about anti-matter. I've got some questions for him," I responded.

She moved over to the children just in time to cushion Rowan's head as she toppled over backward. "Go easy on him, Dec. You know how he gets upset about weapons."

"I will. I'm going to try and keep it on a technical basis, so maybe he won't freeze up on me," I said, going out the door of our cabin.

A few moments later, I came through into the bridge. Frazzle wasn't there, but it turned out that he'd gone into the cafeteria with Red to get something to snack on.

I went through the transporter to the cafeteria. When the door opened, the two of them jumped as if they were guilty. They'd been snuggling and making out or whatever Sunnys called it. I was stricken with a bit of guilt myself. I hadn't intended to break up their personal time since they had little of it due to their duties.

Frazzle spent almost all of his time at the ship controls. He was also what I'd taken to calling our chief science officer since he was the most theoretically oriented of all of our Sunnys. Many of the newly rescued Sunnys were technically adept, but Frazzle seemed to have their respect, and they almost always deferred to him on ship maintenance.

As I've mentioned, his wife, Red, spent a lot of time babysitting for us. Since Liz and I were nearly always planning or meeting with the Marines or Kasm's people, that meant that she and Frazzle didn't have the extended togetherness that I'd learned was normal for newly married Sunny couples.

I turned to go back, resolving to wait until they came back into the bridge, but Frazzle called out to me, "Dec! Wait. It okay. We want to talk to you."

I caught an undercurrent of concern from both of them simultaneously, and it halted me instantly.

"What is it, Frazzle? I didn't mean to interrupt you two. You don't get enough time alone anyway," I said.

Red let out a series of whistling sounds that I'd learned was their laughter, then recovered herself and said, "We get enough time. Dats what we wanted to tell you."

Frazzle looked at the floor, and I could swear that he was embarrassed. "Dec. We having a baby."

I was both relieved and concerned. "Will Red be okay on the ship, or do we need to get back to Earth or somewhere?" All I could think of was that maybe she'd need some special environment or something.

He answered in the negative. "No, it be no problem. Sunnys lays eggs, and dey don't hatch for many days. The babies are strong, too, so no problem for us. We just worried that your babies need care and now ours too."

"I'm very happy for both of you. Don't worry about my children. Michael's old enough to require less care, only watching to ensure he doesn't get in trouble and Liz and I can take care of Rowan. So, anyway, it shouldn't be a problem. We've been very grateful to Red for watching our children. It was very helpful, but she doesn't need to worry about it." I paused, "When will you have your baby...uh, egg... whatever?"

That was awkward, I thought. Fortunately, both the Sunnys and the Sim-tigers were socially robust and nearly impossible to insult.

Red laughed again and responded, "We have de egg in a few days now. The baby have to be kept warm for many days in egg before it ready to come out."

Frazzle added, "We got incubator fixed in cabin, so egg will be warm."

This was news, but it wasn't the reason I'd come, and my mind turned back to the anti-matter gun. Frazzle saw my change of expression and asked, "Whats you want to talk about, Dec?"

"I don't want to upset either of you, but I need some information about anti-matter," I answered, trying to ease into the conversation.

Frazzle let his shoulders droop, and I knew he was upset, but Red suddenly gave him a hard shove. "Get over dat!" she said. "You and me both know dat there be plenty of need for the shooters. Tell Dec what he need to know."

Frazzle sort of shook himself and then asked, "What's you want to know. I can talk about the technology, an I tries not to think about the use."

I considered how best to ask. "What I want to know is a simple explanation of how they work and what could go wrong with them unexpectedly. I don't want to be surprised at a critical moment."

He seemed to be thinking it over, so I added, "I'd also like to know about their limitations and true capabilities. I feel like I've been lucky so far, and I need to know more."

He drew a breath and began to explain, "Making de anti-matter particles normally takes much energy, but we cheats. The weapon creates a field that gathers positively charged virtual particles from the sub-field of space –"

Here I interrupted, "What's that mean?"

He continued, "You call it de quantum plenum. It's full of particles of all sorts coming and going, so there plenty of anti-particles to grab with the weapon field. The power of the weapon, the little power packs for the hand weapons, and the ship power for the big gun first are used to grab these particles. All sizes of guns work the same. Just the smaller ones can't grab as much particles."

He paused for breath, and I interrupted again, "What happens to the particles once this field captures them?"

He smiled, a closed-lip tightening of his cheek muscles, and looked aside at Red. She nodded her head.

"Dat a good question, and it's the next thing that the power pack does. It powers a circular field that uses the strong magnet force. The positive particles pulled from the virtual plenum become real here and are trapped in the circle field. When the shoot button is pushed, the field opens, and the particles, whoosh –" waving his hand wildly, "fly out. The direction tube (by which I thought he meant the barrel) has magnetic field that keeps the particles in the tube and away from the sides. That field also makes the particles to go faster. It uses electric force to make them accelerate to close to light speed. An you know what happens when anti-particles hit regular matter. Fswhoosh!" He threw both paws up in a gesture intended to represent the resulting annihilation.

"Okay. That sort of explains how the things work," I said, thinking about what he'd just told me. "What can go wrong with the system? Does it wear out or break?"

"De direction tube and the place where the circle field is can sometimes get erode by leaking particles. Dis happen most when the power pack is low and the magnetic field not strong enough. So, we put limiter on the weapon. It won't work if not enough power. The handheld ones have flashing red light when power packs get too low. But this not a problem for the big shooter attached to ship-power. It not run out of shots, and power is enough to keep erosion very low."

He scratched his nose and then continued slowly, "De only problem you

have with the big ones is that regular atoms in air or space dust get dissolved and thin anti-matter pulse down. If too much dust or try to shoot through too much air, the pulse gets used up and no damage to the target happen. Same happens to small guns if try to shoot too far."

"Frazzle, I've always thought that anti-matter reacting with ordinary matter would create an explosion. Why doesn't that happen?"

"The shooters project a long burst of particles. Not much hit at once, though very fast. Difference like dripping water on dirt compared to dumping whole bucket at once on dirt pile. Best I can 'splain," he shrugged in a very human-like gesture.

Our, or maybe I should say, my grasp of physics wasn't up to much more than this anyway, so I went on to my next question, "How far and how fast do the big ship cannons shoot?"

"De direction tube on the big ones use lot of energy with each pulse. By time the pulse reach the end of tube, it going nearly light speed. That gives very fast shot. Distance determined by matter in between like I 'splain. Only thing is shooting at long, long-distance, pulse take a while to get there, so target can move," he answered, waving his finger in the air with an attitude of admonition.

"Okay, so keep the targets fairly close. The atmosphere must not be too much of a problem for the big gun. It had no problem burning a wide path through the middle of the Pug-bears position from space."

"Dat's correct. It more a problem for handheld weapons. They not nearly as powerful. But when we shooted Boulder to get the Pugs, I boosted power in the gun, so circle magnetic field built up much more particles than normal. Can't do that much, and it take some time. Try too often, and erode becomes a problem," he answered.

I judged that I'd gotten about as much information as I could understand. "Thank you! I'm going to talk to Rudy. You two continue where you left off."

They laughed as I turned to the transporter. I was still smiling myself when I came back into the bridge.

Chapter 10

It took a couple of weeks to return to Earth orbit. We used the time to drill our Marines in Pug-bear fighting. They hadn't been ready for the all-out combat style of the aliens, and I didn't want to lose any more men.

Rudy, Joe, Liz, and I, along with Lieutenant Holmes, held lengthy discussions about space battle techniques. The new information about the anti-matter cannons proved very helpful since it forced us to plan out combat techniques more carefully. I realized that I'd been fortunate the first time I'd fought the Pug shuttle-craft. The entire engagement had taken place at close enough range and high enough speed that the shuttles couldn't dodge. They lacked the interior anti-gravity field of the spaceships, and the occupants were subject to inertia. Tough as the Pugs were, they couldn't survive the g-stress of a violent maneuver to dodge an incoming shot, even if they could see it.

Another thing was, you could see plasma bursts coming. Their speed was slow enough that I thought they could be dodged if seen far enough away. However, the anti-matter pulses were invisible unless there was dust or some matter in between the gun and its target. Anyway, the anti-matter traveled at nearly light speed, so it would be as challenging to duck away from it as dodging a laser beam. Nearly impossible, in fact.

When we got close enough, we inserted our ship into Earth orbit and adjusted our path until we passed over the front range of the Rockies about every hour. The first order of business was to take the shuttle down to visit Jake. We needed supplies and more personnel.

I knew that he'd want the newly captured spaceship for himself, but I didn't want to give it up as yet. I decided to promise him two spaceships, provided I could capture two more. Meanwhile, since we had four shuttle-craft, I thought I'd bribe him with the smaller shuttle, leaving just the large one for my ship.

As we descended into the Denver area, we could see columns of smoke rising at various locations on the high plains out to the east of the town. The sites were too distant to tell what was burning. All we could see was the dark smoke.

We were meeting with Jake at his headquarters in Mile High Stadium. We'd brought the larger shuttle down and landed on the fifty-yard line. Now we were sitting in one of the private boxes looking out over the field.

As usual, Jake had been the perfect host and was doing his best to be charming, not only to Liz but also to the rest of my group. I'd brought Rudy, Kasm, Frazzle, and several of the newly rescued Sunnys. That left Joe, Holmes, and Whistle in charge of our fledgling fleet.

The enemy seemed to focus on the outer reaches of the solar system, and we agreed that it would be unlikely for an enemy FTL to show up in near-earth orbit. Nevertheless, the three ships were actively scanning the solar system. If a ship dropped out of FTL status anywhere on this side of the Oort cloud, we'd have plenty of time to reach orbit and prepare. I didn't expect any incursions from the Pug-bears, so I wasn't worried.

"Well, Dec, I understand that your raid on Oberon was successful," Jake started. "I hope that my men were an asset and acquitted themselves well." He paused and then added, "I trust that you haven't forgotten my requirement for helping you, either."

"No," I answered, "I haven't forgotten. Let me brief you on the situation as it now stands."

"That would be good. I want to be more involved. If only I could solve my immediate problems here, I might have time. Frankly, flying in space would be a big relief compared to my current difficulties," he said.

That was a little curious. "What kind of problems are you having?" I asked.

"No. Give me the status first. We'll talk about my issues afterward," he ordered.

"Okay. We took the two ships to Oberon and rescued the Sunnys held there. The resident Pugs and Pug-bears were all killed. Another spaceship showed up while we were there, and we captured it. The problem was that we had to shoot the drive out to prevent it from fleeing. We've got the thing mostly repaired now, but it will need some time at a real repair facility before it's space-worthy and combat-ready. We've done only enough so that my technical crew (I meant Frazzle) thinks that it will be able to make it to the closest repair dock at one of the Sunny planets."

Jake considered, "Won't there be a problem with the enemy there? How will you get the ship repaired?"

"We attacked that planet and disrupted the Pug-bears' rule pretty seriously," I smiled in remembrance. "We dropped a huge ball of ice on their nesting grounds and flooded them out."

Jake pushed his chair back on its rear legs. "Will they have recovered enough to keep you from getting repaired?"

"Well, we'll have to take all three ships," I started. He opened his mouth to interrupt, but I continued quickly. "We'll need the two undamaged ships to clear the system in case\ any of the enemy that has shown up. If there are, we'll try to capture their ship also. It'll be much easier with two ships. I know I promised you a ship, and I'm going to get one for you." I looked directly into his eyes for emphasis, "In fact, how about I deliver the next two I capture to you. Meanwhile, I can provide you with one of our spare shuttlecraft and a Sunny pilot along with some maintenance personnel. Would that help?"

Jake was a shrewd negotiator, and I was prepared for a lengthy session. He thought for a moment and then asked, somewhat unexpectedly, "Can the shuttle be armed with one of those disintegrator ray things?"

I glanced at Frazzle and lifted an eyebrow in inquiry. He picked up on my unspoken question and answered mentally. "We can put one or two of de plasma shooters on it. We don't have any more of the big anti-matter shooters."

I turned back to Jake and asked, "What do you need that kind of weapon for?"

"Well, this leads into the 'afterward' phase of our discussion nicely. The remains of the US government, acting under the name of the Motherland Army, is threatening us. That sniper you caught was one of their men, just as you told me. We've caught a couple of others trying to infiltrate our lines while you've been gone. They have also been raiding a lot of the smaller towns to the east, and we're getting some refugees as a result. I sent out some scouts to try and find out what's going on. The results were mixed. We learned that there are a lot of them, and they're gradually heading this way. I pulled back my scouts when they caught a couple of my men and strung them up!"

He was angry. "I'm going to have to retaliate, and I'm not sure that I have enough force. I've got a fair-sized group of men, but they aren't anything like a trained army."

"I know your guys are good fighters, though," I inserted. "They made mincemeat out of the Pugs that came south out of Boulder. How big is this Motherland group, anyway?"

"That's just the problem. I don't know what kind of force they have. My scouts reported that there were a lot of them, but they're widely separated right now. They seem to be in a large number of small groups. The refugees we've interviewed have reported that they've been raiding farms and towns all along the Kansas-Colorado border. There may be more of them than there are of us," he concluded.

I smiled encouragingly. "That's where the shuttle will come in very handy. You can use it for reconnaissance and, if we arm it, you can really mess up their operations, provided you can catch them in a sizable force."

"That would be nice, but wouldn't a spaceship be a better weapon?" he asked, somewhat plaintively.

"It would for a set conflict; similar to when we used it against the Pug-bears. It would hardly be worth using against small groups." I was deliberately omitting to mention KEWs. As far as I was aware, he hadn't thought of that as a viable weapon, and I wanted to convince him that the shuttle was better for smaller operations.

"Look, Jake, we'll be as fast as we can. If you can stop this gang or army or whatever it is with the shuttle and your men, then no problem. If they attack in force, you'll have to hold out until we get back. I think that will be in roughly a month. We can set them back then." I may have over-promised on the month time frame. I hoped not.

"I don't see them grouping to invade us very quickly. It has mostly been minor raids so far. They certainly wouldn't have the fuel and operational vehicles to mount a motorized campaign against us," he said, thinking aloud.

This was pure speculation. However, it was a good guess. The EMPs had taken out almost all of the world's vehicles. Some older cars with old-fashioned distributors were still working, but we knew of no remaining fuel. I supposed that some military vehicles were EMP hardened and could have survived, as could a sizable supply of fuel, provided it was under close control of someone who could defend it.

The government had disintegrated, and this new group may have been composed of some of the survivors. Still, in my opinion, they had no more authority or right to invade us than any other group of outlaws. However, I realized that when it came to government, force was always the deciding factor that determined the right to dictate terms.

Something else hit my mind about then. I remembered that I needed to see if Jake knew of any biological scientist or doctor who would be able to help figure out what factor was interfering with the Pug-bears' symbiont's growth. If something in the Earth's environment was attacking or suppressing the things, I wanted to know about it.

When asked, Jake first drew a blank but then beckoned one of his men over and asked, "Fred, what was that professor's name? You know, the one from Colorado State? The guy with the weird hair."

Fred thought for a moment and then answered, "Boss, I don't remember his name, but he's living downtown in a place off East 23rd near the natural history museum. I think he's doing something with the museum specimens or ... well, something like that." He shrugged apologetically.

Jake turned to me and said, "Don't worry about it. I'll have him picked up, and we'll talk to him tomorrow if he can be located. People have a way of disappearing these days."

I smiled at the comment. It was worse than that. Not only did people move unexpectedly, but the mortality rate was also far higher than before. People died unexpectedly also. Infections and disease were the leading causes, but accidents happened, and fights were also the cause of many deaths. Jake did a lot towards maintaining order, but I didn't think he was even aware of much of the disorder in his territory. It was too large, and his organization was too provisional as yet to suppress conflict uniformly.

We finished our meeting. I promised to deliver the shuttle I was going to give him after I'd had a weapon mounted on it. I figured that a plasma gun would be adequate. That should do everything he wanted and then some. The shuttle could be used to strafe troops and even motorized convoys if there were any such things. It wouldn't burn through heavy armor, but a direct hit would destroy an ordinary truck or car.

I shook his hand, and we returned to our shuttle for the short jump up to our ship.

Chapter 11

When we arrived back on the ship, I had Holmes find out how many had wives or girlfriends from his men. I had determined to give them the chance to come along. Not only did I not want morale problems due to the fact that Liz was the only woman on board, but it had occurred to me that something might happen to us. If, for example, we were marooned somewhere, it would be much more conducive to our survival if we had the basis for a small colony. A group of men, alone, would probably end up killing each other or themselves if there were no hope of rescue.

As a result, we took the large shuttle down the next day along with the smaller one. The Sunnys had spent some late hours rigging the smaller shuttle with a plasma shooter, and it was ready to be delivered to Jake. I had asked some pilots to go along with it to train the humans to fly the thing. There had been some intense discussion among the Sunnys about the idea. Eventually, a couple had volunteered for the job, despite the group's nervous consensus that there might be too much violence involved.

I was relieved. Apparently, the Sunnys were able to overcome somewhat their adverse feelings about violence with a belief in duty or perhaps the realization that their entire race would benefit from their participation. The two that volunteered were two of the newly rescued ones. They were an elderly mated pair, past the egg-laying age. I'd taken some time to meet with them, and they were both ready to serve as instructors, non-shooting pilots, and, for my purposes, observers who would keep an eye on Jake's doings.

The large shuttle was full of men. Nearly everyone had decided to go down to try and convince women to come with us, even those who had no relationships at present. They were excitedly talking. The roar of conversation filled the passenger compartment as I took my seat and prepared for the flight. I smiled to myself at their excitement. Frazzle, who was piloting, noticed and made his closed-lip smile back at me, but I could tell he was a little puzzled.

In explanation, I jerked my head backward at the noisy passengers and then sent him a mental message. They were so loud that I doubted that I could make myself heard. "They are hoping to find mates, or they're excited about meeting their mates," I mentally sent. The puzzlement in his eyes disappeared, and he smiled again with more confidence.

We separated from the ship and were shortly leaving orbit, descending to the Denver area. The smaller shuttle was a little behind us and a few miles off to one side. The two volunteers were flying it down with a single passenger, Lieutenant Holmes. He had confided to me that he was just as excited about the chance to meet his girlfriend as the men. He'd been trying hard to hide it from them. I judged that he thought riding in the smaller craft by himself would make it easier. He wouldn't have to officially notice their boisterous behavior as a bonus.

Once we'd landed and the crew had departed on their hopeful romantic quests, I met with Jake's second-in-command.

Judith was an older woman than I'd expected. She appeared to be in her early fifties, and her appearance was one of a no-nonsense school teacher. Due to her age, she rarely left the Warlord's headquarters, preferring to monitor reports and coordinate activities. She was rather brusque and very business-like. She somewhat surprised me. I'd expected some kind of Viking-like fighter as Jake's second, but apparently, she had the admin experience that he needed.

She was a new addition to his staff. I thought that perhaps she'd taken Erin's place, now that Erin and Frank were married and living in Grand Lake with our friend Stormbreaker and his wife.

"Glad to meet you, Dec. I understand that you've got a shuttle for us. I hope that you've got someone who will fly it for us also. The thing isn't so easy to fly that anyone can do it with no training, is it?"

"Good to meet you, too, Judith. No, the shuttles are more than a little complicated. They are made for alien pilots, either Sunnys or Pugs. The Pugs are more our size, so shuttles designed especially for them are a little easier for a human to fit into the pilot's seat. The Sunny-sized seats are really too small for humans, as are the control keys."

In fact, Sunnys have webbed-fingers with rather pointed nails. You couldn't call them claws by any stretch of the imagination, but they were pointed enough that the Sunnys used them like a human would use a stylus. Some control switches were inset into the keyboard so that they couldn't be pressed by accident. A man would have to insert the tip of a stylus to activate one. These mainly were the important ones, like the reactor controls and engine power. The comm controls were regular buttons. The net result was that it would be challenging for a human, even an experienced pilot, to fly one of the shuttles. The day before, I had been speaking to Frazzle about making changes to the control set-up to accommodate humans better. He'd indicated that it could be done fairly easily.

"We make shuttles for de Pugs to fly, no problem. We can change the Pug seats for human seats and modify the controls and displays for human eyes. It maybe takes a few days if we have access to a full repair facility," he said.

"It'll have to wait until we return to one of your planets, then. In the meantime, the older couple can fly the small shuttle for the Warlord," I replied.

"Dey can do that, but they might have problems with shooting," he cautioned.

"That's why we set the fire-control panel up for the third seat," I reminded him. "A human will ride along and serve as weapons officer. We don't expect Sunnys to operate the weapons."

This conversation replayed in my mind as I led Judith over to the small shuttle-craft. It was sitting close to the goalposts in the football stadium, and we walked across the end zone to the small ship. I stepped up onto the edge and opened the cockpit. The transparent cover slid back, and I reached down and assisted her as she climbed up to where she could inspect the interior.

"My goodness! It's very tight in there," she said.

"Just big enough to get three people in," I answered.

"You call those furry aliens people?" she asked, in some puzzlement.

"Look, Judith, humans are used to being the only sapient beings on the planet, and we're used to thinking of ourselves as the only ones who count. Both the Sunnys and the Sim-tigers are just as smart or perhaps smarter than humans, and they both have a sense of personal identity that is just about the same as ours. They think of themselves as people and accord us the same status. In short, I'd say they are people in the same sense that we call ourselves people. You'd better get used to treating them that way." I realized that I sounded admonitory, but her attitude had taken me by surprise, and in fact, I found it somewhat offensive.

"I guess you're right," she apologized. "It's just that they seem so strange. I hadn't thought about it much. I'll make an effort to ensure that everyone treats them with respect."

She was obviously embarrassed and trying to make amends.

"Don't worry about it. Once you get used to them, the physical differences won't seem so odd. Of course, we humans have held even smaller differences against members of our own species, so maybe it's a built-in sort of thing," I replied.

I hadn't thought about it in this way before. Humans can have funny ideas. If we can hold a ridiculously minor difference in skin tone against each other, we might also develop some form of prejudice against members of other intelligent species.

I sort of snickered to myself as I realized that I certainly disliked the Pugs. However, that was due to their aggressive nature and the fact that I'd seen them kill many humans without showing the slightest bit of empathy and not due to any in-built prejudice I secretly harbored.

The Sunnys were so cute that I didn't think they'd suffer from people disliking them. If anything, the humans that knew them tended to want to treat them as attractive pets. Their high intelligence and cheerful nature allowed them to blend in well with groups of humans, and they didn't seem to be offended if a human wanted to stroke their fur. They were just as likely to stroke our bare skin with a similar attitude of fascination.

The Sim-tigers wouldn't arouse that same emotion. They were a little too fierce-looking, but I knew from experience that humans and Sim-tigers could get along as friends.

"Look, Judith. This is an unprecedented situation for humans. We're going to have to adapt to this quickly. These people are our friends, and I think that is what really counts. Not shape or color or fur, but willingness to be friendly and a certain similarity of world-view. The enemy, the Pug-bears, and the Pugs don't think the same way. They see us more as inferior species that are only useful as slaves or food. From what I understand of their mentality, they don't see things in terms that map directly into human consciousness. You can be friends with a Sunny, but you'll never be able to be friends with a Pug."

She thoughtfully commented, "You know, if we'd had enemy aliens all along, we probably wouldn't have felt the need to discriminate against members of our own species. Being attacked by the Pug-bears makes the differences between human races seem non-existent. Having to pull together to avoid extinction has focused a lot of people on what is actually important."

That was an insightful remark, and I briefly thought that it could mean humanity was on the verge of reaching a new level of maturity. I sighed and nodded my head in agreement with the idea.

We closed up the shuttle and went back into one of the offices under the stadium to conclude our discussion. Judith led the way. As we walked down the hall, she spoke over her shoulder, "I've got someone for you to

meet in my office. He's...well, I think he's qualified to do the research you want. He's a biology professor or something like that. He was teaching at the university in Boulder and escaped to our lines when the Pugs attacked."

We entered the office. The Professor was sitting with his back to the door and stood when he heard us come in. He was about my height but older, perhaps sixty or so. His wiry, reddish hair was fading slowly to gray.

We shook hands, and he introduced himself, "I'm Ian Martin, Professor of molecular biology. I've been engaged in a wide range of brain research on primates and lower mammals also."

"Professor, or can I call you Ian?" I started.

"Ian will do. I'm afraid that my professorship evaporated when the university was destroyed by the –" he paused, "I guess you call it, anti-matter weapon."

"Yes. That's what we used to wipe the main Pug force out. I'm sorry about the university, but most of them were in an area between the Pearl Street Mall and the university, and the anti-matter beam was wide enough that it got most of the university along with the Mall," I answered.

"No matter. I understand that you've got some kind of problem with the big aliens that you want me to figure out. I'm afraid that the Warlord has been very non-specific," he looked past me at Judith with a kind of accusing glance.

She chimed in, "Professor, in our defense, we don't know what Declan has in mind. None of us know any more than the aliens are deadly, and their venom kills humans easily. Not to mention that they have a regrettable degree of mental control over almost all humans. I don't know anything else about them."

"Don't worry about it," I answered, looking at her. Then I turned to the Professor, "Ian, the thing is, I know quite a lot about them. I was attacked by their expedition leader on Titan almost six years ago, and it somehow opened my mind to a whole spectrum of what you'd call psychic abilities. In the attack, the alien somehow downloaded the entire contents of its memory into my mind. I can't usually recall things at will, but when I ask the right question, the answer usually pops up."

He didn't look like he believed me. At the risk of seeming like a stage magician, I reached into his mind and pulled out some information. "You were born in Kansas. Emporia, I believe. You've been married twice and have two natural children, and have adopted some others. You lost your second wife a few years ago, and –" An image popped into his mind. I shied away from it as a little too intimate but then went ahead and told him, "You've been involved with one of your graduate students for the past two years." Her name popped into his head, and I added, "She seems to be a good researcher, and her name is Sherry."

He turned a little pale for a moment, then responded, "You could have researched my past somehow, but I'm not sure how you found out about Sherry. We've been very careful not to be ... I mean not to be, uh, obvious, if you get my meaning."

"Yes, I understand, and I'm not making any judgment about it. As far as I'm concerned, your personal life is yours. I just need you to do some research for me."

I began to explain to him how the Pug-bears achieved their intelligence. "The aliens are the top predator on their home planet. They have a natural mental ability to stun or paralyze their prey. This is something that also affects humans. I've seen unintelligent Pug-bears hold several humans in thrall so that the humans could not move or fight. There is a way to fight the control, but that's not the point now. The aliens sometimes pick up a parasite or symbiont that lodges in their braincase. The symbiont grows and merges with the alien's brain and confers a high level of intelligence in so doing. They become thinking creatures, not what we'd call rational, but able to think. When they reach this level of mentation, their primary urge is to expand their territory as much as possible. They want to dominate all forms of life and all planets. Until they came to Earth and we set them back, they had successfully attacked and dominated quite a number of planets. They're very dangerous and have no limit to their ambition."

"But what do you want me to research?" he interrupted.

"The thing is, we've killed quite a number of them here on Earth, and something seems to be suppressing the symbiont's growth. The older ones we've killed with symbionts should have a much larger skull. It grows as their brain becomes enlarged. Most of them don't show the growth that goes along with the higher intelligence, and their symbionts are somehow stunted. I think that there must be some environmental or biological factor here on Earth that is causing this and, if such a thing exists, I want to know what it is. Most especially, I want to know if we can isolate and weaponize the factor."

"That might be very difficult. Most people think weaponizing a biological agent is easy, just spray some germs around and, well, you know what I mean, but it's not easy. It can be complicated," he said.

"Yeah. I know, but I'm faced with a difficult problem. There are five planets full of Sunnys enslaved by the Pug-bears. There is no way we have enough ships or men to free the Sunnys on even one planet. I've got to find something that will kill or disable Pug-bears without harming Sunnys, and I need it fast."

Our discussion went on for some time. I explained how the Pug-bears were usually widely separated and mixed in with the Sunny population, so they were not good targets for KEWs. I told him about our comet bomb, and he agreed that its effectiveness was a special case. The Pug-bears' breeding grounds were a good target because of the planet's geology. Not every planet would have a high mountain valley that ran entirely around the globe's circumference. Dropping a massive ice-ball of a comet on most planets wouldn't have the desired effect of wiping out the Pug-bears' breeding area without washing the Sunny civilization away also.

We ended with Ian's agreement to work on the problem and Judith's promise to set him up with all the equipment and facilities he needed. There were still a few Pug-bears on Earth, and, in fact, Jake had issued a reward for live ones. As a result, the Denver Zoo was being used to hold several of the things. The keepers had gradually developed a sort of immunity to their mental control. It seemed to lose effectiveness after a man had been exposed to it repeatedly.

I didn't exactly feel confident that Ian would come up with a solution, but I was left with some hope that his research would bear fruit.

Chapter 12

The ship's hold was full of people all talking at once. It was about as noisy as an equal number of Sunnys. The din was echoing off the overhead, and I had to shout to get everyone's attention.

"Hey! Listen up! Quiet!"

They settled down and turned towards me. Since every man had brought along a wife or a girlfriend, our group was almost doubled. Most of the couples were going to bunk together, although a small number of women were actually unattached at the moment. I momentarily wondered if that would cause problems later in our voyage.

"Marines, fall out to the rear. Ladies, please gather a little closer to me, so I don't have to shout so loudly," I bellowed.

Once the shuffling had finished, I addressed the women.

"Ladies, I know that you've never been in space, but there is a lot to learn. The ship is quite safe, but if there were an emergency, you either know what to do and do it quickly, or you die. We've got to get you up to speed with ship operations, and I also want to find out how you can assist in running the ship. I don't want any of you to think all you came along for is to lie around and make your man happy periodically. We're all going to have to work." There was a stir, and I raised my hands in a calming motion.

"With so many people, duties will be very light. The cook will need some help, and everyone is expected to keep their quarters and the ship in general in order. Finally, we'll be giving classes on hand-to-hand combat, weapons use, spacesuit use, and giving you a chance to find out about flying both the shuttle-craft and the spaceship, if you're interested. Ms. Dunham will be your primary supervisor. If you have any complaints or questions, see her first."

I glanced at Liz. She was trying to look as pleasant as possible, but I could tell from her mental radiation that she would make me pay for springing that on her. I grinned at her and then continued, "You'll find that, aside from the scheduled classes, ship life is leisurely. There will be plenty to eat and plenty of time to sleep. I don't think you'll find it too difficult."

I paused and held up an admonitory finger, "On the other hand, idleness can lead to discord. That is something I won't have on this ship. From the point of discipline, I want you to understand that you are now crew members and expected to obey orders from any of the more experienced crew. That's all I've got to say. You're free to go find your cabins and begin learning about the ship."

There was a rustle, and some subdued conversation as the couples rejoined each other. I'd turned towards the exit but then had another thought. I turned back and said, "Men, I shouldn't have to say this, but start teaching them about the ship immediately. Also, any disputes or relationship problems –" I looked around to make sure they were watching me. "Bring them to me immediately. Breach of discipline will be punished appropriately."

I didn't know what I would do if there were problems. We could assign extra duty or even lock miscreants up in a storeroom. I hoped that would be the extent of what I'd have to consider.

Liz and I stopped by our cabin to check on the kids before heading to the bridge. They were fine, and Red was doing a good job keeping them occupied, so we headed back to the bridge, talking as we went.

"Dec, you're not handling this very well," Liz started. She had that look in her eye that let me know I was going to have to listen to her. From experience, I knew that she'd probably make several good points that I hadn't considered.

"Look, Liz. You know me. I'm not very good at setting up organizations. How do you create a space navy or whatever you want to call it from scratch and with a bunch of civilians, too?" I asked.

She smiled one of her charming smiles, "Yes. I know that you're much better at breaking enemy organizations than building friendly ones. Let Holmes handle the discipline. You know, set up a chain of command."

She paused and, before I could speak, added, "You should also put the Sunnys and Sim-tigers in the organizational table. We can't continue in our previous informal ways. We've got to have a better organization."

She was right, as usual. I agreed to work out how the women would fit into our system.

Once on the bridge, we got the three ships moving in close formation and headed for the outer system. When we were moving fast enough, we'd transition to FTL status. We were on our way to the Sunnys' planet on which we'd dropped the ice ball. I wanted to use the repair facility to work on the damaged ship. I also hoped to add to our offensive capability. I'd gotten the idea that we needed at least one main gun facing directly aft in a position where it could cover shots targeting the Em-drive and FTL vanes. I'd taken out the Pugs' ship with a shot at the undefended engine section, and I didn't want to be similarly vulnerable if any Pugs got the bright idea to emulate my actions.

Much to my pleasure, the organizational problems worked out during the weeks of the voyage. Holmes handled all of the problems himself without coming to me. He'd promoted one of the Marines on each ship to the rank of lieutenant, and they either took care of problems or kicked them up to Holmes.

Since he was in charge of our third ship, I'd promoted both him and Rudy to Captain's rank. Rudy had asked Joe to be his Executive Officer, and I thought that was a good idea. While I was assigning ranks, I told Liz that she'd have to be the Captain of our ship, a position she took somewhat grudgingly. She also laughed at me when I told her that I would be the Admiral of our small fleet.

I addressed her sternly, "Captain, I won't stand for disrespect. I'm in charge of this fleet and this expedition, and I'm going to have to take action if there's any additional insubordination."

She laughed again and asked, "What are you going to do about it?"

Since it was alter-shift, the kids were asleep, and we were in our cabin. I proceeded to show her just what I was going to do. After a few minutes, she sighed and said, "I going to be disrespectful often. I think I need as much of that kind of punishment as I can get."

The next day, she appointed Kasm as her XO. He took the job with a bit of puzzlement, confiding in me that he wasn't sure what he was supposed to do.

"It's like being a hunt leader," I answered. "You take general directions from Liz and figure out how to best implement them."

That seemed to clear things up, and our organization began to shape itself into a working unit. The new crew members, the women, were going through training and learning as if their lives depended on it. It seemed like they took the voyage seriously. There were few fights, although there had been some reshuffling of relationships. There had been a few instances of women arguing about certain assigned tasks, but that was because they didn't understand their importance.

By the time we arrived in the Sunnys' system, our three ships had reasonably functioning crews. It was a good thing because we no sooner got there than we had a fight on our hands.

Chapter 13

Faster than light travel allows you to glimpse only a distorted view of the Universe. You can see blurry stars streaming by on either side. They move slowly at first and then shoot by as the ship approaches their position. The view dead ahead is distorted by the virtual matter in the quantum plenum. FTL travel relies on the ship's engine somehow converting the vessel and contents into a wave-packet that is passed along at a small fraction of the speed of the underlying torsion waves. Since torsion waves move approximately a billion times faster than light, even a little boost by them moves the ship's wave-packet significantly faster than light. In practice, we found that our maximum velocity was roughly a light-year every two days.

Approaching the Sunnys' star, we could see our destination dead ahead, but the details of the system were blurred and could not be made out. Something about the virtual particles streaming past distorted photons' paths rendered us incapable of seeing smaller obstructions in our way. The deflection shield and bow armor plate were for those things we couldn't see.

Typically, we'd exit FTL status out far enough from the destination star to give plenty of time at sub-light speed to approach carefully. A solar system is a pretty big place; for example, light takes about five and a half hours to reach Pluto from the Sun. Progressing into a system while slowing to system speeds requires a complex calculation, but let's just say you approach at a fifth of light speed on the average. It would take over a day to travel that distance, so you can see that there's usually enough time to do things sensibly.

Only this time, there wasn't. As soon as we dropped out of FTL, Frazzle let out a squeak of alarm, and the main boards lit up in yellow. He jabbed at some buttons, quickly focusing the display on another FTL ship directly ahead of us and only about two minutes-light ahead at that.

Speaking over his shoulder as he adjusted our braking speed, Frazzle said, "Dat a Pug ship. Must have dropped out just a little time ago. It's a long way out in the system."

"How soon can we close on it?" I asked.

"We closing fast, fast. I don't know, maybe three – four minutes we go by them," he answered.

"I don't want to go by. I want to match velocities with them and try to grab them with our gravity field generator," I replied.

"We can't do," he answered. "We going too fast and too close. Can't slow down fast enough. We go by."

Just at that moment, another warning light came on. He checked some things and said, "Dey's seen us. They're going faster. Turn on Em-drive. Look like they are running. See!" He pointed at the display. "They're turning away from the star. They're leaving the system."

I didn't want them to spread an alarm. With any luck, we could get the needed repairs done in maybe a week, give or take a day for contingencies. They could possibly be back with reinforcements within that time. I didn't think the enemy had any armed FTL vessels, but a whole ship-load of Pugs trying to re-take the space station might be more than we could handle while laid up for repairs.

We'd been making progress training the women, and one of them was crewing the weapons station. I turned to her, "Meghan, lock the bow gun on that ship, but don't fire until I tell you."

"Target acquired, Sir," she replied after a moment's manipulation.

"Frazzle, what are they doing now?" I asked.

"Dey still speeding up, Dec."

"Any chance we can match speed with them?" I wanted to ensure that we didn't have a chance before I shot at them.

"No, dey turning and speeding faster. By the time we get close, they may be going fast enough to go FTL."

In contrast to his name, Frazzle was very calm in most situations. He pointed at an indicator and said, "See, dis show they reach FTL speed in seventy seconds."

I turned to Meghan. She was watching me closely, so I just nodded.

She understood my command and triggered off an anti-matter pulse. I turned immediately to the screen and was just in time to witness a flash on the ship. Its Em-drive engine was gone, and its reactor had overloaded. There was no place for the driving energy to go, and there suddenly was a brilliant secondary flash as the ship vaporized.

I was disappointed because we needed every ship we could capture. I tried to console myself with the thought that this one, at least, wouldn't be bringing a wasp nest of reinforcements down on our heads. I turned to Frazzle, "Okay. Let's proceed to match orbits with the space station and see about getting the repairs we need."

The situation on the space station was about what it had been when we had left it to head to Kasm's planet. The Sunnys were trying to provide material and moral assistance to their compatriots on the planet's surface.

On our previous visit, we'd dropped a huge, water-ice comet on the equatorial belt of the planet to flood the Pug-bears' breeding grounds. The planet had offered a perfect set-up for this tactic. The north and south hemispheres were mostly ocean, and there was a broad belt of land entirely around the equator. The planetary crust had moved towards the equator on both sides, pushing up large mountain ranges on either side of a high and normally dry plateau. The desert climate of the plateau had been ideal for the invading Pug-bears' nesting activities.

In my first encounter with the Pug-bears' eggs in Carlsbad Caverns, I'd learned that they rarely hatched in moist environments. They needed to be kept dry. When we'd dropped the comet on an equatorial trajectory, it had broken up as it descended, creating a veritable Noah's flood of rain that mostly landed on the high plateau. The resulting deluge had destroyed all of the Pug-bears' nests with the added benefit of drowning a large number of the Pug-bears.

The excess water that had landed on the outer slopes of the mountains mainly had drained into the sea. The Sunny cities were all arranged along the ocean's edge, an almost resort-like setting for the water-loving, otter-like creatures. Due to the proximity to the sea, the cities had good drainage. There were periodic storms that mandated that water control be a priority. The Sunnys hadn't suffered from the extra rain. Their suffering had come at the hands (actually claws) of the crazed Pug-bears.

The surviving Pug-bears were wildly angry over the destruction of their future on the planet and made every attempt to raid the cities. Since the Sunnys were almost pathologically pacifistic, they had difficulty defending themselves.

With the aid of the Sunnys on the space station and the six that I'd transported there from Titan, they managed to create automatic booby-traps. Those caused so much damage to the attacking Pug-bears that the remaining few had retreated into the mountains, only occasionally coming down for a raid. The blasted creatures were predators, and the Sunnys were about the only animals on the planet suitable for food. As a result, the cities had taken on the aspect of forts. The Sunnys had built large, impassible walls blocking all access to the interior.

After some discussion on the comm unit, Frazzle informed me that the general consensus was that the Pug-bears were gradually starving. He estimated that the planet would be free of them within a few more weeks.

"Dec, de Pug-bears on the planet are dying!" Frazzle was excited at the news, but then his aversion to violence took over, and he momentarily looked mournful.

"That's great news, Frazzle! Don't feel bad about the Pug-bears. They don't belong there, and we have to get rid of them," I said. I was pleased with the result. That meant that I only had to figure out how to clear the Pug-bears off the other five Sunny planets.

I tried not to think of that aspect of the problem. So far, I didn't have a clue as to how to accomplish the task. The comet bomb was a "one-off" situation, and I couldn't expect it to work so well on the remaining planets.

A week later, we'd finished repairing the damaged third spaceship. Several large anti-matter weapons were being manufactured to the Pug's specifications in an asteroid facility. The Sunnys were okay with making the things. I guessed they just tried not to think about their ultimate purpose.

We'd sent the big shuttle out to pick up nine of the weapons and had now mounted four on each of our three spaceships. We replaced the waist gun that I'd moved to Rudy's ship and added another mounted where it had a clear field of fire to the rear of our ship. The FTL vanes interfered to a certain extent, which caused some problems, but we mounted the weapon near the Em-drive pod on a gimble mount with built-in limiters that kept the weapon from pointing at the vanes. It could shoot between the vanes and offered a reasonably good field of fire.

There were the blind areas where the vanes interposed, but I felt a lot more secure now that our tail had been covered. Mounting weapons on the other ships required installing better fire control consoles. Rudy's had just been a simple joy-stick rig. We hadn't had the time to create another weapons computer similar to the one on my ship.

The station Sunnys had outdone themselves in this task, and I ended up waiting for an additional half-day while they completely replaced the weapons console on my ship with a significantly advanced system. It was a significant upgrade that enabled us to track twelve targets simultaneously and switch from one target to the next automatically after a shot had been fired.

Once the work was done, we headed out again. Our destination this time was the Pug-bears' home planet. We had to make sure they were isolated to stop any attempted invasions before they started.

Chapter 14

Our three-ship squadron dropped out of FTL near the Pug-bears' and Pugs' homes. They came from a loose double system where the two small suns orbited each other in a kind of long-distance, elliptical dance. Their size and spectra were identical, so I thought they'd probably been formed at the same time and place. At this point, they were separated by almost two light-years, a distance that led me to believe they were gradually moving farther apart. If so, the pair would eventually separate, and each would go its own way.

Neither star provided much light to its planetary system. They were dim, and both systems were full of fine dust particles that attenuated the primary's light. This explained why the Pugs seemed to prefer darker environments. The Pug-bears' planet orbited fairly close to its sun. The Pugs' was farther out. I'd noticed that the Pug-bears didn't have the same degree of aversion to light that the Pugs showed, and that was probably the reason.

The entire stellar system was barren, with only a single planet and a paucity of smaller objects. The dust probably accounted for most of the matter in the system. Why it hadn't condensed into planets was a question I couldn't answer.

As sisters, the stars had much the same chemical composition, a fact that probably accounted for some of the alienness of the two races. I had initially learned these facts during the latter part of our voyage to the planet of the Pug-bears' only failure – Kasm's planet – unless you could consider the Earth a failure, but the outcome there was still in doubt.

We dropped out of FTL in the outskirts of the Pug-bears' system. The Pugs' star was on the far side of the Pug-bear system, and that fact made me feel a little more secure. If the Pugs were in possession of some FTL ships, it would provide a little more time for them to reach our position should they be minded to investigate or assist their masters.

From the instant we arrived in normal space mode, our passive sensors determined that the single planet that orbited the star was currently attended by four FTL ships parked in close proximity to the sole space station. The light we saw was about six hours old, though, so the ships might have moved. The only other objects that we could locate were some small moonlets that orbited the planet at a far distance. The space station was well inside their orbit, and there might have been a few comets, but we didn't look for those.

Frazzle was carefully observing his instruments, as was Liz, and I watched from the observation seating. He eventually pushed back and said, "Dey have four ships, and maybe one being repaired now. What's we going to do?"

I answered rather more casually than perhaps I should have, "Do? We're going to capture all four of them."

He turned to look directly at me, his eyes wide, and asked, "How?"

"See if you can pick up any Sunny comm chatter. Getting in contact with the Sunny part of the crew has worked well in the past. They'll probably let us board, and then we can clear out the enemy crews."

It had worked before. I saw no reason that it wouldn't work this time also, except for the necessity of coordinating boarding attacks on four vessels simultaneously.

"I already tried Ansible comm for Sunnys," he replied. "Dere's no sign of any of my people on the comm. I don't know if they are in those ships or maybe all dead – killed by Pug-bears, maybe."

The Pug-bears did have that regrettable habit. They were so sure of themselves that they didn't hesitate to kill and eat members of their ship crews, either for amusement or because they just thought they needed a snack. It seemed short-sighted to me. They couldn't fly an FTL themselves. On the other hand, perhaps the ships were crewed by Pugs.

"Frazzle, do you know if any of the Pugs can pilot an FTL ship?" I asked. I knew they could fly the shuttle-craft. The shuttle seats were designed for their narrow rear ends, making them somewhat uncomfortable for humans.

"Dey didn't fly the big ships before –" He hesitated, thinking about it. "Maybe dey do now. I don't know, but I remember some talk of making the ships friendly for Pugs so they could be flying. If the Pugs are the only ones on the ships, they won't let us board through transporters. Maybe we have to use spacesuits and go through the cargo holds?"

I didn't like that speculation, but it might be our only approach. We'd have to coordinate our attack and move very quickly. I didn't want our people outside our ships if the Pugs decided to fire up their engines and flee. We'd have to stop to pick up everyone and wouldn't be able to give chase.

The other thing that bothered me was that our arrival wave was irrevocably heading towards them at the speed of light. It would take a little over six hours from where we'd dropped in to reach their position, so we had to plan quickly.

The barren system didn't offer any cover for sneaking up on them either. We'd approached in the shadow of Uranus before, and that had allowed us to get closer than we might otherwise have done. I turned to Liz and asked, "What do you think?"

My wife once again proved that she wasn't just a pretty face. There was a very sharp mind behind those good looks.

She answered, "Let's load all of the Marines and Sim-tigers into the available shuttles. The three shuttles will carry nearly everyone, and we've conveniently got three shuttle mounts on Rudy's big FTL. If he moves in as if he were one of their ships – have Whistle do all of the talking – he might be able to get close enough for the shuttles to dump the suited men where they can attack the ships."

I liked the idea and added, "We can hang back to intercept if any of them get their wind up and try to get away. If Rudy approaches from the right quarter, it will take him close by two of the three unattached ships. Some of the men can move from his hull when they're close. The big shuttle can take the Sim-tigers onto the space station. We don't have suits for them, so they're limited to either transporters or docking tubes. If the shuttle can mate up with a port on the station, the Sim-tigers can clean it out and take the attached ship while they're at it."

She grinned in anticipation, "That might work. I think we'd better be on our way in as soon as the attack starts. We might have to pick up a lot of men if they somehow miss their jumps. I don't want any of them to go on a one-way trip."

The regular comm system wasn't limited to radio transmissions. It could also use directional laser carriers. We linked up with low-powered lasers and shortly had the plan hashed out with Rudy and Holmes.

Our Marines moved into the shuttle, as did the Sim-tigers. I started to go, but Liz grabbed my arm and said, "Where do you think you're going, Buster?"

"I've got to go with the men," I replied.

"Oh, no, you don't. Your place is here. They can do their job just fine without you participating in every boarding action. We need you onboard where you can direct any ship action. If they start to escape, you'll have to decide how to handle the situation. I'm not going to do it myself. Remember, you're the only one of us who has any space-combat experience," she said.

Honestly, I hadn't given it any thought. I'd always been the go-to guy who did all the fighting. It didn't feel right for me to stay back while my men went into battle, but she was right. Having survived a battle with five armed Pug shuttle-craft, I was the only one who had more than a theoretical grasp of how to fight with our FTL. I took a deep breath and then settled back in my seat, "Okay, you're right, as usual. Let's get this show on the road."

Rudy's big ship was braking hard as it approached the space station. He'd accelerated quickly to nearly light speed to give the Pugs as little warning as possible. Rudy turned his ship and ran his Em-drive full out as he tried to slow down.

Our initial arrival wave would expand as it traveled, and we'd arrived far enough out that I hoped the Pugs wouldn't detect it, or if they did, perhaps they wouldn't realize that three ships had dropped in together. Rudy's larger ship might confuse them. It was big enough to cause a more significant signal. With any luck, they'd think it was large enough to account for our entire entry wave. That seemed to be the case since it was now almost at the point where our entry wave would have reached the enemy's location. So far, they hadn't responded.

I found it irritating to have to wait through the communications lag period. I'd noticed that the Pugs wouldn't use the FTL communication system for any in-system purpose. They reserved it exclusively for interstellar distances. Accordingly, we limited ourselves to radio comm as we attacked.

At the rate Rudy was approaching, the Pugs would have maybe another couple of minutes before their query signal would reach him. That was assuming they saw our entry wave and responded with a query.

That assumption wasn't actually based on their expected behavior. The Pugs were so used to being the only ones with spaceships that they didn't keep regular watches. The Sunnys would have done that, but if there were none of them on the ships, it was just possible that the Pugs were fooling around or fighting among themselves. Their race was a non-technologically oriented, iron-age society. They didn't live very long, and their primary interest lay in competing for resources and breeding rights. This kept them busy and focused on each other rather than other possible threats. I hoped that we'd get lucky in this regard.

The minutes passed, and then our FTL communicator clicked twice. Rudy had activated his system and sent out two pulses which meant that he'd received a query from the station or the ships. They knew he was coming. I hoped that Whistle was on the comm, sending them a convincing story. He could speak enough Pug to communicate with them on a fundamental level.

In another thirty minutes, Rudy's ship would be in attack range for the shuttles. We'd given him a thirty-minute lead and then followed at the same acceleration. I wanted to be there shortly after the attack started.

Our two ships were braking rapidly, and our ETA was about right. I judged that the Marines would be inside the enemy ships when we arrived at a reasonable shooting distance. Our anti-matter guns had an infinite range in vacuum, but the beams would rapidly attenuate in this dusty solar system.

From that point, things happened quickly. I think my mind goes into combat mode and is highly focused on each aspect of action, but time doesn't seem to amount to much whenever I'm in a battle.

As we approached, we could see that the shuttles had separated, and the larger one was approaching the space station. There was no way we could see the individual men against the background of the planet. They were to keep radio silence until they'd breached the hatch of the most distant FTL ship. That group would then let us know they were inside. That signal would free the other two groups to broadcast their status.

We had slowed down to planetary speeds. Our ship's internal gravity system compensated nicely for the deceleration and allowed us to carry out maneuvers that would have killed humans on a more primitive ship.

Suddenly, the radio crackled, and the party began, "We're in target three. Encountering no resistance in the hold or corridors."

Team two chimed in, "We must have all of them. We've got heavy fighting going on. They're shooting at us with some kind of projectile weapons. I've got two men down and needing evac."

I waited to hear from team one, but they were quiet. That didn't seem right to me. Their target had been the smallest FTL, and as a result, we'd only assigned a light strike force. I hoped they hadn't encountered anything they couldn't handle.

Before I could call them, the shuttle that had headed for the space station reported that the Sim-tigers were through the hatch. They hadn't had any difficulty mating up and docking. The tigers did have a radio, but their first instinct was to fight, and I doubted that I'd hear from them before they'd cleaned the place out.

Team one was still quiet. Team two was gradually making progress, and team three was about to reach the bridge of their targeted ship. They called in shortly after that and reported that all resistance had ceased. They'd killed all of the Pugs on board and hadn't found any Sunnys or Pug-bears. That was one down and three to go.

Right after their report, target one's Em-drive fired up, and it began to accelerate at maximum rate, heading out of the system. I tried calling the lieutenant in charge but got no answer from anyone.

We didn't want that ship getting away and going for help, and as a contingency, I'd been ready with the weapons console. The system was tracking all three of the free-floating ships. I focused on the accelerating ship and carefully aimed at the drive package. The ship was heading directly away from us, and it was a simple shot.

The gun did its work, and the drive simply disappeared along with one of the FTL vanes. A gout of atmosphere shot from the breached hull, and the ship's lights went out. It was coasting away from us but no longer accelerating.

Team two reported that they were in possession of their ship. They'd killed a large number of Pugs in the process, but that didn't hurt my feelings. I radioed back to transport their wounded to the shuttle bay and stand by for pickup. Rudy's ship had the most complete medical system, and the wounded would need to go there for treatment.

We now held two ships, but the third was disabled. I dithered for a moment, wondering if I should chase the disabled ship to find out what happened to the attack squad or head to the space station to help the Sim-tigers.

My dilemma was solved when Kasm contacted me. "We've taken the station. There were a lot of Pug-bears here, but we killed most of them. There are still a few barricaded in one arm of the station with some Pugs, but we've got everything under control. The FTL that we thought was being repaired is apparently being salvaged. It's gutted and just a hull. We couldn't go in. It's hard vacuum there. We've also rescued a few Sunnys," he sent in his clear mental voice.

That left the disabled ship. We pulled alongside after a brief chase, and Frazzle grabbed the thing with our gravity field. A small boarding party jumped across the gap and entered.

They quickly reported back that there was no life on the ship. Then they changed that story when they found one of the Marines still alive and locked in a storage closet.

Several Pug-bears had ambushed the boarding party. The creatures had taken mental control over the men and had frozen them in place. The last man to board had somehow managed to avoid mental capture and had locked himself in a cabin before being sensed.

The Pug-bears had realized he was in there, and he'd suffered their fearsome, mental attack and had been unable to move until we'd shot a hole in the ship. The vacuum had killed the Pug-bears, but they'd ripped the other nine members of the boarding party to shreds first.

I felt terrible. This was a loss that we could ill afford. I hadn't considered what would happen to men who couldn't shield themselves against the Pug-bears' mental attack. The loss focused my mind on the desirability of creating spacesuits for the Sim-tigers.

The Sim-tigers were immune to this kind of control and were more than a match for the Pug-bears. One-on-one with no weapons, the Sim-tigers could win almost all of the time. With their swords, it was no contest between the two creatures. The Pug-bears always lost.

If a human could shoot, they'd usually win, provided they'd hit the Pug-bear in a vulnerable area, but if they fell under the alien's mental thrall, they always lost. I was the only human that I knew of who could fight the enemy's mental control and win.

I resolved to include at least two Sim-tigers on every boarding raid from now on. If the strike force encountered a Pug-bear, the Sim-tigers could take care of it. The humans could handle the Pugs. That way, the paring of our two species provided an immense advantage.

We'd cleaned up the mess, transported the wounded to the medical facility, and evacuated the space station. The Sim-tigers had eliminated all of the resistance there shortly after their last communication, and we were happy to discover that the station held enough spare parts to allow us to patch up the damaged ship.

We'd ended up with twelve casualties and gained control of three FTL ships and three more small shuttles. One FTL was seriously damaged, and I wasn't sure it would be repairable. We looked it over briefly, and I regretfully decided to scrap it. There was too much damage and no parts. Not wanting to leave the hulk floating around for someone else to salvage, we used the gravity point-source to boost it into a sunward orbit.

As far as I knew, there had been no signals from the station or ships requesting help, but I still wanted to get out of the system quickly. There was just one task to accomplish before we left.

I wanted to isolate the Pug-bears on their planet. They may have had some shuttles on the surface, but we'd seen nothing of them. Even so, I didn't want to leave the space station in place. It gave them access to FTL travel, which was the central part of the problem.

If they'd stay on their planet, I was willing to let them live. I just didn't want them free to raid other planets. They were too dangerous.

I realized it was a nasty thing to do, but I decided to lock onto the station along with the gutted FTL. Our gravity point source could slow it down enough so that its orbit would decay. I didn't care about the environmental damage or the Pug-bears enough to worry about what would happen when the huge mass fell to the surface.

The station massed enough that it took both my ship and Rudy's to slow it down. We strained against it for over an hour before it began to descend. Then we released the thing, retreated to a more distant orbit, and watched.

When the station struck the atmosphere, it created a spectacular light show as it broke up and fell. It was so large that the majority of it didn't burn up. Instead, it fell in three huge fragments that probably gave the local Pug-bears a considerable headache when they struck.

Fires were visible on the surface as we accelerated out of the system on our way to the planet of the Pugs.

Chapter 15

As I mentioned, it was only a couple of light-years to the Pugs' star, so it wasn't long before we dropped out of FTL in the extreme outskirts of their solar system.

Their system was almost as dusty and barren as that of the Pug-bears; only one planet, but there was a wide belt of asteroids sunward of the planet. The asteroid belt was oriented at an acute angle to the planet's orbit and gave the Pug's planet something interesting in terms of its annual climate.

The asteroid belt was quite dirty and dense. From our observation point far out in the system, it blocked a significant amount of sunlight. It looked like the Pugs' planet passed through its shadow twice a year. Since their planet had a rather extreme tilt, whenever the shadow passage coincided with their winter season, the winter would be frigid, indeed.

With that kind of planetary setup, it was no wonder the creatures didn't care for very bright light. I also thought that the harsh environment would select for the toughest, most survival-oriented individuals, and that seemed to square with my experience. They all seemed tough.

On the other hand, I didn't care how bad their living conditions were. I wanted them isolated. Maybe if we could separate them from the evil influence of the Pug-bears, they might eventually turn into creatures we could deal with on a civilized basis, but at the moment, all I wanted to do was to keep them from ever reaching space again.

Our sensors could detect a single, smallish space station in orbit with no ships nearby. We might be missing a ship or two if they were somewhere else in the system, perhaps approaching at a slow rate from the other side of the star. That was always a possibility, but we couldn't abort our attack on just a possibility.

As we approached, we detected some shuttle traffic in the system. It appeared that the Pugs were mining in the asteroid belt. There was an intermittent stream of traffic between the belt and the space station and from the station down to the planet's surface. We'd have to disrupt that enterprise, probably by destroying all of their shuttle-craft and the station. I didn't think their grasp of technology was high enough to rebuild without the Sunnys' help.

Frazzle tried the comm trick, but there was absolutely zero Sunny chatter. There had only been a few Sunnys on the station in the Pug-bears' system, and we guessed the situation was the same here.

The station was unarmed. The lack of viable inter-stellar competition led to an overwhelming lack of security steps, something that I realized we should learn from. Earth needed to expand into space as quickly as possible, and we needed to keep a sharp watch for approaching ships; plus, we needed our space presence to be heavily armed.

My mind wandered back to the way it was before the alien invasion. In its quest to maintain political power, our government promised its citizens all sorts of free benefits. The benefits were paid for by a sort of Ponzi scheme that involved creating unbacked, fiat money out of thin air. Since the money essentially was free, there was no reason to tax the life out of working people and businesses, save to keep them off-balance and under control.

The biggest crime, in my opinion, was that we failed to spend more than a pittance on the type of technological development that would result in our moving into space. When the first alien invasion reached its climax with the EMP bursts that took our civilization apart, we'd only just begun to allow private investment into space travel. Before that time, the government maintained a monopoly on space. I felt that we had been almost terminally stupid, but perhaps, with our newfound friends, we'd have a chance to do things right for a change.

The lack of any large ships meant that we didn't try to hide our approach. We traveled directly towards the station as quickly as possible. When we were about a million miles out, the Pugs belatedly became aware of our approach and called on the radio.

Frazzle answered, speaking the hissing Pug language. I figured he had a Sunny accent because it seemed like he had to repeat himself several times, but I really couldn't tell if he was saying the same thing.

He finally turned to me and said, "De Pugs think we are Pug-bears coming to check on them. They say the last Sunnys died, and they need more to works on shuttles."

He paused and looked sad, then continued, "De stupid Pugs don't maintain anything and a bunch of shuttles are broke. They want them fixed for gold mining. They been finding some gold in the asteroids and want more."

I interrupted, "I think they are going to be disappointed. We're not going to fix the shuttles. We're going to destroy them."

I got Rudy and Holmes on the radio to coordinate, and we all three fired a long pulse with our bow-cannons at the station. One moment it was floating there with a few shuttles drifting in space, sparkling a little in the light of the dim sun. The next moment, there was a flash, and the entire installation ceased to exist, leaving nothing at all. It might seem inhumane, but I'd seen too many humans killed by Pugs to care.

I delegated Holmes to hunt down all of the shuttles he could find and either capture them or destroy them; his choice. Meanwhile, Rudy and I brought our ships closer to the planet and began a detailed scan.

After several orbits, we determined that there was only one spaceport on the benighted place. There were several shuttles on the small landing field, but they didn't survive our next orbital pass. The waist guns destroyed the spaceport with the same efficiency that had wiped out a belt across the enemy's position in downtown Boulder several months ago.

Leaving the surviving Pugs to their own devices, we joined Holmes in his search of the asteroid belt. He'd captured four shuttles and destroyed three others by the time we got there.

A further search didn't turn up anything other than a small mining colony on a large chunk of rock. They didn't have a shuttle, and I figured they probably didn't have much in the way of supplies. I'd previously decided not to deal with Pug captives. They didn't respond to kindness and were just too troublesome to fool around with. We could have wiped out the colony, but I decided to leave them to their own devices. This, too, might seem cruel, but they wouldn't have hesitated to kill as many humans as they could get their bony hands on.

We reformed our small squadron and loaded up the new shuttles on the docking hard-points. Regretfully, we didn't have enough storage for all four and had to destroy one. We sent it in a trajectory that would end in the sun. Then we turned towards Earth.

I still hadn't figured out a way to help the Sunnys rid themselves of the Pug-bears on their planets, but I had an idea that maybe Ian's research would lead to a solution.

Chapter 16

A couple of weeks later, we were back in our home system. The Pug/Pug-bear system wasn't far away, and humanity had been lucky it had taken them so long to find us. It had been simple chance that they'd initially started their conquest of space in a direction that led them away from Earth and towards the Sunnys. They were so primitive and random in their behavior that they could easily have headed towards us.

The Sunny planets were strung out like a series of islands in a rough chain that ended about thirty light-years away. That final link on the chain was where the initial Earth invasion had originated. That was a long-distance for them to travel at the sub-light speeds that were the only possibility when they started on their quest to conquer the Universe.

If the aliens had started from their system and headed directly to Earth, they would have arrived well over a century ago, and the result of the invasion would have been vastly different. Earth might no longer have humans as the dominant species.

The Pug-bears would have taken a more direct approach to their invasion. They'd destroyed several primitive civilizations in the past, so eighteenth or nineteenth-century Earth would have posed no problem to them. They would have strafed the major cities with an armed shuttle and ruthlessly suppressed any resistance. We'd all be either slaves or dead as a result.

I considered that I'd been fortunate to have discovered the transporter network. They'd been carefully setting up the infrastructure to disrupt our ability to govern ourselves with the intention of making it nearly impossible for us to respond to the planned attack with any coherence. Somehow, I'd managed to create enough havoc within their system that the attack plan failed. Of course, one could consider that their use of multiple EMPs had successfully destroyed our civilization, but they'd been kicked off Earth and mostly out of the solar system at the same time.

Their attacking force and primary base had been destroyed, and now we'd taken the fight to them, something that they were totally unprepared to meet. They were no longer as much of a threat.

They might have other FTL ships, and there were undoubtedly Pug-bears on the remaining Sunny planets, but that just reinforced my intention to help the Sunnys rid themselves of the occupation. It was urgent for us to get rid of all of the Pug-bears on their planets. Given enough time, they'd force the Sunnys to build more spaceships, and they would probably rebuild the space station in their home system. I felt a considerable amount of pressure to forestall that possibility.

This time, we had returned to Earth with five FTL ships. The one that we'd had to shoot in the Pug-bear's system had not been repairable. The anti-matter pulse had destroyed the entire rear end of the ship, including the FTL drive and the reactor. We carried some repair parts and had some extra Em-drives, but the reactor and FTL system required a fully functioning repair facility. I'd reluctantly dropped the damaged spaceship into the system's dim sun on the theory that it was better to destroy it than risk the possibility that it might be repaired and used against us later.

On the way in from the farther reaches of our solar system, we took the precaution of checking the various moons where the aliens had previously established bases. There were no ships in attendance at any of the destroyed bases, a fact that I viewed with mixed relief and regret. I was relieved that they hadn't shown up with reinforcements but regretful that we didn't have the chance to capture any additional ships.

At this point, I wasn't very worried about any force they would bring against us. Their FTLs were not armed as a matter of course, and my armed ships would make hash out of an unarmed vessel.

We didn't have any spare weapons for the two newly captured ships, so they'd have to stay out of any potential conflict. They were being flown by a small crew of Sunnys with some Marines on each to assist. I'd insisted on the

Marines being included on each ship. The Sunnys were generally interested in cooperating with us, but I didn't want to risk the possibility that they might decide to break for one of their home planets rather than continue to Earth with our tiny fleet. As it was, things went smoothly, and we arranged all five ships close to each other in the low Earth-orbit we'd selected.

We brought the large shuttle down to Denver the second day after arriving. Some of the women wanted to be left on Earth. Space travel hadn't turned out to be what they'd expected. I hadn't been too surprised. It had been evident to Liz from the start that some of the women were not going to adjust well. We collected them from the other ships along with a couple of the Marines who had also proven to be trouble-makers.

I intended to replace the two and recruit some additional crew members to replace those killed. We didn't need as many recruits as I'd thought we might since some of the women who were staying had worked their way into the marine force. They weren't as strong as most of the men, but they could shoot just as accurately and were acquitting themselves well enough in hand-to-hand.

It had been around two months since we'd left. What with the repairs and attacks and so on, the voyage had taken us longer than I'd thought it would. As we flew down to the Denver area, it was apparent that the so-called Motherland Army was moving into position to attack. There were many plumes of smoke out to the east of the front range where they'd set homesteads and entire small towns on fire. I didn't know why they were so destructive, but that had always been the usual order of business for invading armies throughout human history – break things, loot, and kill people. It was disappointing to see. You'd think that with the alien attack, people would be more focused on preserving human life instead of turning on each other.

Jake met us on the stadium landing field. He'd usually let us come to his office, and I recognized his choice of meeting place betrayed his anxiety. We greeted each other and walked into the tunnel to his office.

He started without paying any attention to amenities, "I'm glad you're back. Those barbarians out there to the east have been causing us no end of troubles. I want you to delegate more shuttles to help us stand them off."

"We've been pretty successful on our errand. Among other things, we've now got several new shuttles. I'll start getting weapons mounted on them so we can provide air-cover for you," I responded.

He sighed and said, "I'm sorry to dump my problems on you, Dec. I've been really worried. We don't have as many men as those invaders, and there has been a large stream of refugees coming from the burned-out towns and farms. That's taking a lot of our resources and time. I need help."

"No problem," I answered. "We've got the resources, and we'll have the shuttles armed in a couple of days. I think most of them will have plasma guns, though. We don't have any more anti-matter cannon available. The ones we've got mounted on the big ships are too large for the shuttles to carry, but the plasma-bolt guns will work well."

"What kind of effect will those have on land targets?" he asked.

That startled me. I'd left a shuttle armed with a plasma-bolt weapon in his control.

"What happened to the shuttle and pilots I left with you?" I asked.

He looked embarrassed as he answered, "The two Sunnys you left to fly the thing refused to fly it. They didn't want to be involved with killing, I guess. They locked it up, and we haven't been able to do a thing with it."

"Where are they now?" I asked.

He shrugged, "I didn't want to imprison them. They're too – I don't know – innocent, I guess. I let them go, and they are living somewhere near some lake up in the mountains. The shuttle is undamaged and ready to go if you can get me pilots who have fewer scruples."

That explained the problem. Thinking about it, I realized that he had experience with anti-matter weapons, but although he'd seen the plasma bolts that the Pugs had shot at his forces, he hadn't realized what they were.

"I'm sorry about the two Sunnys. I thought they'd be more reliable, but they hate violence, and that must have been the deciding factor. To answer your question, the plasma-bolt guns are the weapons that shoot that large ball of fire. You've seen what they can do," I answered.

He grinned, "Oh! Those things. Yeah, we hated those things. They burned through about anything in front of them, and the results were usually that the target would explode from the impact. Will the things have enough range when shot from the air?"

I said, "Yes, I'm pretty sure they can reach out far enough to give the enemy a real headache. We can mount them pretty easily, although the mount will be solid with no aiming capability. The shuttle pilot will have to be pointing the entire shuttle at the target. The guns can shoot a burst every four or five seconds. They'll be similar to the one you haven't been able to use."

I didn't know how far the plasma bolt would travel in the atmosphere. In the vacuum of space, the thing seemed like it would keep going until it finally hit something, but I thought it would dissipate more quickly in the air. I left that unsaid. I figured that they'd be adequate for their intended purpose.

We moved on to other topics.

Jake said, "I sent for your pet scientist. He should be here any time now. I think he's got some good news for you. I hope so, anyway. He's been a pain in the ass for me, asking for us to catch Pug-bears about every other day. You know the damned things have become very scarce, what with everyone hunting them. We haven't been able to find any for about a week now."

"Really? That's pretty good news. We don't need any of them on this planet, they're too dangerous, and they breed too quickly," I said.

"Yeah, but Ian's been going through them just as quickly. I think he dissects one a day, at least. Be sure to take him with you when you go out the next time. I'm tired of his demands," He shook his head in mock despair.

There was a little commotion at the door, and Ian came in. He looked disheveled and even more like a mad scientist than usual. I stood and shook his hand briefly.

He greeted us and then helped himself to a glass of moonshine from a bottle Jake had on a sideboard. He sat down in a vacant chair, took a large gulp, and then, ignoring Jake, he looked at me with a smile, "I've got your solution, Dec."

He paused for another sip and then sat, waiting for me to respond. I don't like playing games of that nature, and my response was a little acerbic.

"I hope you're not wasting my time, Ian. We've got to have an answer that will allow us to clean the damned creatures off of five planets," I held up my finger and added, "without killing or hurting the large population of Sunnys on each planet or damaging the local ecosystem very much."

He looked a little unhappy at that. "Well, I can't promise that the local ecosystems won't be impacted. I don't know anything about them, after all."

He brightened, "But I'm willing to come along if I can have the chance to study them."

I glanced at Jake to see that he had a big grin on his face at hearing that. For a fact, Ian wasn't an easy person to deal with.

I said, "Look, Doc, you can come along and study all you want, but our main agenda is to get rid of the Pug-bears. That's all."

He considered. "I'll come anyway. It's too good a chance to miss. Imagine seeing alien life-forms on their native planets. Yes, I definitely want to come."

"Okay, you're invited, but what do you have as a solution?" I couldn't wait any longer. My curiosity was killing me.

He grinned again, "I cut open the brain-cases of a bunch of the creatures. The younger ones had healthier-looking symbionts."

He started discussing the amazing way the symbiont blended with the Pug-bear's brain, and it looked like he'd continue on that topic, but I stopped him rather rudely.

"Look, Ian, that's interesting, but not to the point. What is causing the symbionts to fail to develop?" I asked harshly.

"Oh, yes. Well, it was apparent that they were being choked by something. The circulation systems in the young ones were clear, but the longer they'd been growing, the more clogged the circulation system became. In fact, the larger Pug-bears eventually lost their entire symbiont. It died from starvation, and in some, the whole symbiont was totally replaced by the competing organism. It's most remarkable," he concluded, taking another sip.

"Again, that's nice, but what is the attacking organism, and can we use it somehow?" I was getting impatient.

He continued, "It can be a problem for humans since it's a commonplace organism on Earth. It's yeast. Saccharomyces Cerevisiae to be precise."

I looked puzzled, and he continued, "Er... Brewer's yeast to give it its common name. It usually doesn't bother people, although some are allergic to it. Candida Albicans is the organism that causes most of the pathology in humans."

Several questions occurred to me all at once, "Where can we get this stuff? Is there enough to cover a planet? And, how can we distribute it? Oh, and will it hurt the local ecology?"

He grinned at the first three questions and then shook his head negatively as I asked the fourth.

"It so happens that there is a large supply of Brewer's yeast here locally. The Coors brewing plant has a lot of it, as do the micro-breweries and health food stores scattered over the metro area. Now, most of them aren't operational any longer, but I've taken the liberty of having the Warlord's men scavenge as much of it as they could find. We have a few hundred pounds of it in our possession right now."

I started to speak, but he interrupted me, "And before you ask, I believe that will be enough to seed several planets. You can spray a liquid slurry of it over an extensive area. It will propagate rapidly if you mix it with water and nutrients, so you shouldn't run out, no matter how much you use. The only thing I can't vouch for is its impact on the planet's ecology. It may not survive long if there are stronger organisms that compete for its niche or eat it, or it may take over. I just can't say."

I considered, "Well, we've been drinking some beer, or rather the Marines have. They smuggled several cases on board."

I looked at Jake. He was still grinning. I continued, "What I mean is that the Sunnys found out about the beer and have taken a liking to the drink. The alcohol doesn't affect them the way it does us. They don't get inebriated, but they do like the taste, and none of them have shown any reaction to the yeast that they must have been exposed to, so maybe it won't hurt them if we spread it around."

Not to be distracted, Ian rather pompously began to lecture us on the various kinds of yeast and how common the strains are on Earth. Jake interrupted him with a question, "Look, Doc, that's fine, but will spraying the stuff on these planets get rid of the Pug-bears?"

Ian paused as he considered his answer and then said, "Well, it won't get rid of the Pug-bears per se, but it will reduce or even prevent them from acquiring intelligent status. The exposed individuals will lose their symbionts and be reduced to animal level mentation. In my opinion, that should suffice. The local inhabitants, uh, Sunnys, I believe you call them, will be able to either hunt or capture the creatures since they won't be smart enough to avoid traps."

I could see that this would be a problem for the Sunnys. "The Sunnys are non-violent, so hunting is out of the question, unless –" an idea occurred to me. "Maybe we can get Sim-tigers to do the hunting. The Sunnys will be able to set traps, though, so, between the two, we should be able to gradually rid the planets of the pests. I think this will work."

We made arrangements to load the ships with the available yeast and some tanks to mix and grow the stuff. I figured I'd have to rig spray units on the shuttles, and Jake said he'd have his men look for that equipment.

In return, I agreed to start mounting weapons on shuttles immediately.

Chapter 17

The Mother-effers were coming again. Hazel had been doing her best to avoid the soldiers for the last week. She'd been hiding in a dry, concrete culvert that went under the narrow, asphalt road a mile from the remains of her parent's farm. Hazel had been in shock for the first three days, but now her emotions were beginning to crystallize. Physical discomfort and hunger seemed to increase the effect, and now she was experiencing nothing but cold, hard anger.

Last Saturday had been bright and sunny. She'd been gathering eggs when her dad had come running around the barn shouting for her to hide. Soldiers were coming. There had been smoke from burning farms in the distance for the last twenty-four hours, and she and her parents had realized that something terrible was coming. Now it had arrived.

Last night, over supper, they'd argued. She had wanted to run, but her parents were adamant that they had to stay with the farm.

"Hattie, the animals need us. They won't be able to survive alone," her father reasoned, calling her by her nickname. "Besides, if it is His will that they come here and find us, then nothing we can do will change that."

She wished that her parents weren't so religious. Since society stopped years ago, their faith had only grown deeper and firmer. Now, they wouldn't leave, and she knew they'd take no steps to defend themselves. "Turn the other cheek," her father always said.

Her mother added, "The cows have to be milked twice a day; otherwise, they may get udder rot. We owe it to them to stay. They've supported us well in the past, and we need them, too."

They'd made it clear, though, that if armed men found them, she was to hide. Her father and mother looked at each other with worry in their eyes, and then her mother had said, "Hazel, you're too pretty to take any chances with invaders. They would probably kidnap you, and you might be seriously hurt."

Hazel knew what they were talking about. "You mean they'd rape me, don't you. You needn't think I'm totally ignorant. I'm nearly an adult," she fumed.

Her parents looked shocked. That had pretty much been the end of the discussion. Her mother went into the sitting room to read her bible by candlelight, and her dad went out to the barn to repair something or other. Things were always breaking.

Two weeks ago, a refugee family had come by the farm. They were headed for the mountains, the distant mountains. They hadn't seen any soldiers, but they'd heard tales of atrocities, and that was enough to drive them towards safety.

Hazel had only dreamed about the mountains. She'd never seen more than a faint purple line against the western sky. Before the EMP blast, back when she was still a child, her parents had told her that they'd take a vacation to the front range, but it never happened. They never made enough money on their small farm since it was barely a subsistence-level enterprise. They always had enough to eat, but there was precious little left over for clothes, let alone luxuries like vacations or even birthday or Christmas presents.

She'd gone to school in the small town that was eighteen miles to the south, and that was just about the limit of her exposure to the outside world. That and reading. There hadn't been any school since the EMP burst, and she'd read and re-read every book in the house.

She had turned sixteen three months ago. In her heart, she had harbored dreams of a life that had more in it than gathering eggs.

At her dad's shout, she'd put the egg basket up against the side of the chicken coop and dashed off into the cornfield to the west of the house. There was a drainage ditch on the far side of the field, and she made her way to it. Once there, she scrambled down into the dry ditch and waited, hoping her parents would show up.

There was a rustling in the corn. Hazel peered over the edge of the ditch in trepidation, wondering if the soldiers had followed her or if it was her parents. Shortly a black and tan muzzle came through the corn. It was Katie, their aged border collie.

She snapped her fingers, and the dog came over to the ditch, wagging her tail. It took some pulling and lifting on her part, but she got Katie down over the edge. The old dog was so stiff that she couldn't jump or scramble down easily.

It was hot, and there was only a slight breeze. They sat in the ditch listening to the insects buzzing in the corn, waiting.

Suddenly there were two shots, then three, and then after a pause, a fourth echoed over the cornfield. Katie whimpered.

Hazel could hear men shouting off in the distance towards the farmhouse. She waited for a few minutes, wondering what to do. Her mind was abruptly made up for her when she saw a column of black smoke rising from across the field. Then she heard the squealing of their pig, Blackie. She'd named him in jest since he was a white-colored animal.

His squealing rose in terror and then abruptly faded in a gurgling sound. She'd seen hogs butchered before, and this sounded like he'd just had his throat cut. She thought about creeping through the corn to see what was happening, but a sudden cold fear came over her, and she turned resolutely and followed the ditch down towards the culvert, taking care not to leave any footprints where the dust had blown up into thick, soft patches.

She took the dog into the culvert, and they huddled behind a bunch of dried weeds that blocked the narrow tube. She'd had to push her way past the weeds, forcing the dog ahead of her and checking carefully for snakes as they entered. Once inside, another blockage of debris and weeds provided shelter from the other end.

She carefully crawled back to the entrance and backed in, brushing out the signs of their entry with a piece of tumbleweed. Then she and Katie lay on the dry sand and kept quiet. After an hour or so, a group of men came down the road and walked over the culvert. She could hear them talking as they walked.

One said in a loud voice, "Pretty poor pickins at that last place, not even nothin' much worth stealing, stupid sumbitches."

He was answered by another who spoke more quietly, "Yeah, but we got some good bacon, and that woman wasn't too bad either. Too bad for her that she had to fight so much."

Loud-mouth came back with, "Did ya see that stupid farmer. Imagine him trying to fight us with a pitchfork."

Another added, "He looked pretty surprised with that hole through his head."

Hazel sniffled and tried to suppress a sob by biting her lip. Nevertheless, one of the men said, "Say, there was some smaller-sized dresses in the second bedroom. There might'a been a girl lived there. D'ya think we'd better look under the road here?"

She quivered in terror and held her hand on Katie's muzzle to suppress a possible snarl or bark. There was a scrambling sound as the men came off the roadway and bent down to peer into the culvert.

"Na, there's nothing in here but a bunch of weeds and crap," Loud-mouth shouted. "It's so plugged that ya can't see through. No tracks going in, either."

Hazel was glad that she'd taken the time to blur the signs of her passage, erasing their tracks. She quivered in an agony of fear that one of them would try to crawl in and discover her hide-out.

"Hey, Tim, get yer ass down here and look in this here hole," shouted Loud-mouth.

There was another scrambling sound, and someone said, "It's pretty plugged."

Loud-mouth said, "Why don't ya slide in there and see what's what?" He seemed to have only one volume setting for his voice. Hattie couldn't see him, but she imagined that he was fat and filthy.

Tim answered with a tone of disgust, "Whyn't you? It's too damned tight for a man to go in that hole. An 'sides, there might be a rattler or two in there. I ain't a goin' a do it."

Loud-mouth cursed, and Tim called him a 'Damned fool.' There was the sound of a little scuffle, and Loud-mouth grunted as if he'd been struck in the stomach, then said, "I'll get you for that someday, you sumbitch."

Tim replied, "Maybe, but I ain't waiting down here for it. I'm going to catch up with the rest of the guys."

There were some more scrambling noises as they crawled back up onto the road, and then all was quiet.

She remained still until dark when thirst drove her and the dog out and back to the farm.

It hadn't been a good day, and it became far worse when they reached the farmstead.

Chapter 18

She now thought of herself as Hattie. In her mind, she was Hazel no longer. That was another person who'd lived in another time. Hattie was a stronger name, someone who didn't feel grief, someone who survived, and most especially, someone who lived for revenge.

She wore a pair of her father's overalls. The legs had been cut off at ankle length, and the suspenders were cinched up to the max. A couple of tee shirts covered by a baggy sweatshirt camouflaged the fact that she had breasts. She'd chopped her ponytail off, and now her hair hung in a ragged mop that could have been a boy's.

A belt around her waist carried her Dad's hunting knife, a butcher knife in an improvised sheath, the small hatchet, and the twenty-two Ruger pistol. It was a nine-shot, semi-automatic covered with rust, but it was deadly accurate and always hit where she pointed it, as several rabbits had found out to their disadvantage.

She was very careful when she approached the culvert, stopping and inspecting the ground for signs of an invader and ensuring that she left no track of her own.

She was alone now. Katie had quietly died the second night they were in the culvert. Perhaps it was just old age, or perhaps the dog felt as much grief at the loss of her family as Hattie did. Either way, it didn't make any difference. When Hattie woke up, Katie was stiff, and her body was cold.

She'd dragged the last member of her family into the cornfield to bury. Then thinking better of it, she'd carried the dog into the farmyard and left her body to decompose behind the barn. There were dog dishes and food on the remains of the porch, and the dog's absence might make an enemy suspicious. Better to just let nature take its course.

By now, the crows and other birds had been at the bodies. Hattie wanted to bury her parents, but the same consideration held. The act of burying implied survivors, and survivors meant there was someone to hunt. She didn't want to send that message.

She'd been lucky to find the pistol hidden in the tin box under the floorboards. Her Dad hadn't believed in guns, but for some reason, he had hidden the small pistol and three boxes of long-rifle ammo along with the deed to the farm. The box had also contained her parent's marriage certificate, two hundred dollars in paper money, some older silver coins, and three gold coins.

The paper money wouldn't buy much. She knew from hearing her parents talk that the only thing most people would take were silver coins. Nevertheless, she carefully hid the box under a rock at the edge of the field. She'd keep the marriage certificate in remembrance.

The deed to the farm had no meaning in this world. Things belonged to those who were strong enough to take and hold them. That was an obvious truth to her. Her parents hadn't been strong enough.

She'd hidden through two additional incursions of the Motherland Army. The last time they'd been in the farmyard, there had been a lot of cursing about the fact that the place was already stripped. One of the ragged men had gone on about how big a mistake it had been for him to join the Motherland Army and ended by calling it the 'Mother-effin' waste.'

Hattie thought that was far more appropriate. Motherland somehow had the connotation of a desirable thing. The army she'd seen was in no way desirable or admirable. She was dead set on staying out of their hands, and their appearance reinforced that desire. She had no delusions about what would happen to her if she were captured.

She was lurking just inside the edge of the cornfield watching the mostly burned-out house. She'd seen a small group of men heading down the road towards the homestead, and she'd finally decided that she was ready for revenge.

Today's group of self-styled soldiers was coming down the road. There were just three of them, walking cautiously along, keeping a close look-out for trouble. They rounded the barn and immediately took to cursing, just like the last group.

"Damn it! Some greedy SOB has already taken this place down. There ain't nothin' here worth the walk," said the apparent leader.

His nearest companion added, "Looks like two dead homesteaders here. Woman over there probably put up a fight, or they'd a taken her with them."

The leader responded, "Maybe, less she wasn't pretty enough. I'd as soon shoot an ugly one as have to listen to 'er complaints."

The third turned with a laugh and said, "You'd shoot her alright, but what gun would ya use?"

They all laughed at that.

Hattie didn't laugh. She was aiming the little Ruger at the leader.

The pistol snapped viciously, and the leader grunted and then said slowly, "What?"

He opened his mouth again, and a stream of blood ran out over his beard. He slowly put his hand on his chest and then toppled over.

Both of the others were trying to look in every direction at once, their rifles at their shoulders. The single-shot had echoed off the barn, and the men were looking suspiciously at the barn door, the chicken coop, and the hay-mow window, which was hanging open.

Hattie aimed carefully and shot again. The third man screamed, dropped his rifle, then clapped his hand to the side of his neck. A bright red gout of blood sprayed through his fingers. He sat down in the dust. The drops of blood were splattered across the area to his right, making a somewhat artistic display, bright red against the light-brown dust.

The last man was shooting at the barn. He still hadn't figured out where Hattie was hiding. She waited for him. His rifle fired several three-shot bursts, and then the bolt locked open. He started fumbling at his belt, trying to open the magazine pouch there. Just as he got it open, Hattie shot him in the stomach. The little slug splatted home, and he grabbed his gut with a curse.

She shot again, and he dropped the rifle when the bullet hit his upper arm. He cursed and started towards the back of the house, heading around the cistern and staggering away from her. She stepped out of the corn and yelled, "Hey, Mister. You came to the wrong place."

He turned slowly to look at her. His face betrayed amazement, "A stinkin' kid! I been shot by a stinkin' kid."

She just nodded and answered, "Yep. That's the way it is." She paused, but he didn't say anything, so she added, "And, I'm going to finish the job."

He started to hobble faster. She lifted the little Ruger and carefully shot two rounds into the center of his back. One of them must have hit his heart. He slowly folded at the waist and toppled forward, landing face-first in the bloody dust.

She sighed, shook her shoulders to clear the tension as she popped the magazine out of the bottom of the pistol's grip. Seconds later, she had reloaded it with six more cartridges. Her mind was blank, no emotions at the moment, just attending to business.

She collected the three rifles and the soldiers' knives. One of them, the leader, also had a nine-millimeter Glock. She took it along with two full magazines he had in a pocket. Next, she checked the others' pockets. One had some jewelry that she kept for possible barter, and the other had a nice pocket knife.

The rifles were military carbines of a standard sort. She didn't know much about weapons, but these looked like the ones she'd seen somewhere. She couldn't remember if she'd seen them in a magazine or on TV. It had been so long since the TV went out, and she'd been a child then. She didn't want to think about it.

After fiddling with the various buttons and knobs on one of the weapons, she figured out how to release the magazine and operate the bolt. The safety was a little rotating lever on the left side of the bottom by the magazine well. It had several positions, allowing for, she surmised, single shots, automatic fire, and a safety position.

She took a moment to climb into the barn and looked out the haymow window. The road was easily visible from this height, and no one was coming or going in any direction. She decided to experiment with the rifle. Sliding the safety lever to the first position, she shouldered the weapon and aimed at the first raider's body. The rifle banged, much louder than she'd expected, but the recoil was largely absorbed by a spring in the stock. The corpse jerked with the impact. Shooting the thing wasn't so bad. She pulled a rag out of her pocket and tore off a couple of small pieces to stick in her ears.

The next shot wasn't nearly as unpleasant. She'd aimed at the second body, and the round showed that it was far more powerful than the little Ruger. The corpse's head practically exploded. She laughed out loud in surprise, then shot the third man also. With her laugh, her emotions started working again.

She'd expected to feel horrified about killing people. She was amazed. She felt good. Empowered and, maybe a little bit, satisfied.

She carried all of the weapons to the culvert and hid the jewelry in the tin box under the rock, taking the silver and gold coins out and putting them into a small pouch she carried. Back at the culvert, she loaded up all of the magazines in a bag with a shoulder strap that she'd taken off one of the men, got her canteen and other supplies that she thought she'd need, and then deliberated for a moment over the Glock. She ended up leaving it in favor of the Ruger. She could hit with the twenty-two, and it wasn't loud enough to give her away if she had to hunt. She didn't know about the Glock, but it was undoubtedly a lot louder. She holstered the little twenty-two pistol and climbed up on the road carrying the best one of the three rifles.

Hattie looked both directions and then set out towards the south. The nearest intersection was there, and she was going to head towards the mountains.

Chapter 19

We had been busy trying to arm the shuttles during the following week. The work took place in orbit, and I didn't keep much track of what was going on down on the planet.

Arming the shuttles was always a bit of a problem. Their power supplies weren't compatible with the plasma weapons, and that created problems. The guns required a high voltage to charge them. The Sunnys had created power packs to make them portable, but each power pack was only good for a few shots. That might have worked for the Pugs in the past; they'd used armed shuttles to strafe planets, but I didn't think returning to base after having fired five or six shots was efficient.

The problem kept the Sunny engineering crew busy installing transformers and some other stuff that I didn't understand. By the time they were done, the shuttle-mounted guns could fire until the shuttle power was down to thirty percent of max. Then a relay cut out, and the gun could no longer shoot until the system had recovered somewhat. This was necessary to ensure that the shuttle's engine didn't suddenly shut down. Crashing on top of people you'd just been shooting at would be an embarrassing and potentially fatal thing to do.

We'd finally finished with the shuttles and then loaded the yeast, along with some industrial-quality spray equipment that had been discovered in a warehouse. So far, the Sunnys had adapted the sprayers to one of the mid-sized shuttles.

We had three sizes of shuttles. There were four small ones, like the one I'd given Jake, along with the really-large shuttle that we carried on our ship.

The rest were a step above the small craft, carrying a strike force of ten or possibly twelve unarmed passengers.

The work crew had installed a holding tank on one of these latter and welded a rack of spray heads across the bottom of the mid-section. Fortunately, the shuttle engine provided plenty of power for the dual pumps to spread the yeast evenly over an extensive area using successive passes back and forth.

I'd had the tank loaded with water, and one of the Sunnys flew the craft in the vicinity of our FTL's orbital path with the pumps running. The results were spectacular. The water droplets instantly formed a very fine cloud of ice crystals that refracted the sun's rays in a magnificent rainbow.

It didn't last very long since the tiny crystals quickly sublimated into an even finer gas and became invisible. Some of the Sunnys were watching through the bridge windows, and the display created a real stir among them. They whistled and stomped their feet appreciatively as the rainbow took shape. The test was an unequivocal success as far as I was concerned. I wanted to try the rig on the unsuspecting Pug-bears in the worst way.

The Motherland Army had continued its incursions, moving closer and closer to the Front Range area while we were busy. I wanted to take off to rescue the Sunnys, but Jake practically begged me to bring all of our shuttles down to discourage the invaders.

We held a brief meeting on Rudy's ship and agreed that we should help him before we went gallivanting off across the galaxy. I thought we could fly sorties for a couple of days and drive the Motherland people back. This would give Jake time to work on his defenses. It wasn't like he was unarmed either. His men had raided some old military installations and had some heavy field pieces along with a large number of BGM-71 TOWs. These were anti-tank weapons with optical guidance. They'd been stored in a secure facility that had been protected against EMP effects due to a built-in Faraday cage, a fine mesh of grounded copper wire. The electronics still worked, although the battery power was a little chancy.

Taken together with the artillery, the smaller weapons seemed like they would stop anything short of a major push. At the moment, neither Jake nor I thought the Motherlanders were up to such an attack.

He told me, "Dec if you'll try to strafe those guys so that their raiders fall back a couple of hundred miles, I think I can spare you long enough for you to finish off the aliens. I don't like this fighting on two fronts at once thing, though. One would think that fighting off alien space invaders would be something that would take precedence for all humans, but I've got to deal with these barbarians."

I agreed, "You're right. Getting rid of the Pug-bear threat is important for human survival. These left-over government gang members or whatever you want to call them are a severe pain in the rear. It's shortsightedness like that that almost makes me think that humans don't deserve to survive."

The next day, we started flying patrols out over the plains to the east. The raiders were usually in small groups and, since they liked to burn things, they were relatively easy to find. They contributed to their demise by shooting at us, revealing their positions. The shuttles were pretty much impervious to rifle bullets; they had to be tough since there was always the possibility of being hit by a micro-meteor. That type of impact would be at a far higher velocity than a rifle could generate.

We quickly developed the tactic of using one high-flying shuttle as a spotter. Once a group was located, the spotter would call in a low-altitude strike by a second shuttle loitering along a few miles behind. This worked very well. The plasma guns could fire maybe five times in the time it took us to make a run. The results of the shots were telling. We destroyed almost every group that we saw.

We had almost as much luck the second day, but the word must have gotten around by the third day. The raiders were apparently moving back to the east, just as Jake desired and a little harder to spot.

Whistle and I were flying one of the small shuttles. It had room for three, but there were just the two of us. His job was to fly, and I fired the gun when necessary. He'd gotten over part of his anti-violence attitude and was developing into a decent combat pilot.

We'd been flying for several hours, and it was late afternoon. Our spotter had run short of fuel and returned to base. We should have gone with him, but just as the Sunny pilot called to signal that we should return, we flew over a farmstead, and I looked down.

What I saw took all thoughts of leaving entirely out of my mind. The place was overrun with maybe a hundred of the Motherland gang. They had dragged the farmer and his family out into the center of the yard and had them down on their knees in a row with men pointing pistols at the back of their heads. It looked like a mass execution.

The thing that made it worse was the family was a large one with several children, and the kids were also lined up to be shot. We circled around, and then I saw something that absolutely set me off. The family was being forced to watch while two of the daughters were raped in front of them.

"Whistle, circle around again, and prepare for a firing run."

"Okay, Dec. I don't like what we see down there. We got to stop it," he answered. He was definitely becoming more human-like.

We came in on a firing pass, and I started the weapon. The first three shots were right into a large mass of the invaders, and the second two took out several more on the other side of the farmyard.

They started shooting at us as we came over the hill, and several of the shots bounced off our hull. The firing slowed as our shots took effect, and then we were too far away for them to hit us.

"Let's make another pass and see if the family can be rescued," I said.

We came back the other way, hopeful that we could do something, but the commander down there was vindictive. The prisoners were all lying on their faces, unmoving. The soldiers had shot them as we went past.

Whistle came back around without being told, and we shot up the place thoroughly. As we headed over the south hill, something exploded against our underside, and the shuttle bucked violently.

They'd had some kind of shoulder-launched missile, maybe a Stinger or something. The shot had taken dire effect. Our engine sputtered and then died. Whistle did his best with the control surfaces, and we skidded into a large, flat pasture, ripping the barbed wire fence down as we came in next to a large pond.

"Get out now!" I ordered. "They'll be here in a few minutes, and they won't be happy."

We jumped out of the shuttle, and I locked the hatch cover closed. I doubted that they could do more damage to the ship than they'd already done, and I wanted to keep them out of it since it might be salvageable.

We ran over to the pond. There were no trees anywhere in sight and nothing other than the pond dam to hide behind. I knew that wouldn't work for long. It was obvious where we'd gone, so I started looking for the best cover I could find.

The enemy showed up before I got settled. They came at a run, and I started shooting with my splinter gun. It was the only weapon I carried, not expecting to be shot down. It was small and didn't interfere with comfort when sitting in one of the narrow shuttle seats.

I was holding them off pretty well, although they were pretty safe from the splinters if they stayed back a hundred yards or so. The little weapon didn't carry very far. The splinters were just too light.

We were at a stalemate for a while until the sunset. I was still shooting at what I could see of them in the twilight when I realized that Whistle wasn't beside me. I looked around for him and saw a man towering up to my right. I rolled and shot the guy, but another one had sneaked along the base of the dam, and he hit me from behind with something. My eyes flashed, and things went black.

Chapter 20

I became aware of the pain in my wrists first. Something was cutting into them. I moved my head to try and see and inadvertently groaned. It felt like the back of my skull was caved in. My head was throbbing, and my arms were somehow twisted behind my back.

Someone came up and kicked me hard in the gut about that time.

"Bout time you came to, you sumbitch. You killed most of my men. I'm goin' ta take you back to field HQ, and we're goin' ta jam an implant in yer head. Then we'll see what ya know. Nobody can hold out against one of them. I figure a fancy pilot like you will know a lot about the Denver group. Ya just might earn me a promotion," he slurred.

I realized that he was about half drunk. Maybe the farmer had kept a supply of liquor. He kicked me again and staggered off towards what I now realized was a fire. My head was hurting so bad that I'd thought it was just a flashing in my eyes at first.

My next thought was to wonder where Whistle was. I tried to roll so that I could look around, but I couldn't see him. It was dark, but the firelight allowed me to see that only four men were in the group. I fervently hoped that I'd killed the rest of the blood-thirsty barbarians. Anyone who would kill innocents like that deserved to be gone from this world.

I tried to move my hands, and it seemed like they must have used zip-ties on them. They were so numb that I couldn't feel my fingers. If I did manage to escape, I might still lose my hands if they were too far gone.

The men at the fire opened another bottle of something and passed it around. They were getting louder as they drank more. As the bottle's level dropped, one of them got up to relieve himself. He came over to my location, unzipped his pants, and then pissed all over my back. His urine was hot on my skin but rapidly cooled in the chill air.

I lay still, and he stepped closer. I could see one of the men by the fire toppled over, too drunk to sit upright any longer. The one by me kicked my ribs tentatively. Suddenly it was all too much. I swung my legs around and swept his feet from under him. He dropped, hitting with a grunt as the air was knocked out of him. I rolled over and got my legs around his neck. I think he had a knife, but he was too drunk to use it. We rolled around a little until I got the proper leverage and broke his neck.

I looked over to see if the others had heard anything, but there was only one sitting upright now with his head on his chest. Two of them had passed out.

I struggled to my feet and started to move back into the darkness. After ten steps, someone moved right in front of me. I sighed. Maybe they'd been smart enough to set a watch, and I was caught, but then a low voice whispered, "Turn around, and I'll cut you loose."

It wasn't one of them. I turned around. There was some fumbling with my hands, and then my arms swung free. I immediately tried to work my hands. To my relief, they were still mobile. Compartmentalization hadn't set in, and I thought I'd probably be alright. I rubbed my wrists along my arms. I couldn't use my hands well enough as yet.

My rescuer stepped up beside me. He was small, a youth, I thought. Maybe one of the farmer's children.

"There's only three of them left. I didn't think you could kill anyone the way you did, Mister. You wait here. I'm going to finish this now," he said in a low voice.

"Be careful. They're a lot bigger than you," I cautioned.

He snorted, "I've killed a lot better ones than them. They're drunk and don't know what's up. Killing them will be almost too easy, but I saw what they did to those girls in the farmyard. They're dead now."

He stepped forward a few paces and raised his hand. There was a sharp snap and a little flash from the muzzle of the gun he held. It must have been a small caliber from the sound of it, but the seated soldier groaned and fell forward with his face in the fire. He didn't move, so the shot must have been immediately fatal.

The youth walked closer to the fire, carefully shot each of the other two in the head, and then stooped down to check their bodies. I walked up slowly. The kid, for so I judged him, was holding a small pistol in his hand while he searched the bodies for valuables. He paused over the second man.

I walked up and saw that the man's head had suffered some kind of explosion from within. The little gun wouldn't have done that. Puzzled, I knelt and examined the body. Fluid and blood were coming out of its ears, and both eyes had been pushed out of their sockets and were now hanging loosely on the corpse's cheeks. I turned the head and found a large hole behind the right ear. I suddenly remembered the implant that I'd detected in the sniper who had been trying to kill Kasm when we first met with Jake in Estes Park. Perhaps this was the same sort of thing. The twenty-two bullet had bounced around inside the guy's skull and struck the implant, triggering a self-destruct charge. It was a nasty device.

While I looked the body over, the youth had stepped to the third man and knelt. He fumbled around with the guy's equipment. After a moment, he unfastened a belt that held a holstered pistol and brought it over to me.

"Here, you might need this. You can shoot a pistol, can't you? You're not just someone who can shoot fireballs from an airplane, right?" he asked.

The implication that I was helpless irritated me, and I answered, "Yeah, I can handle a pistol, but we'd better get their rifles and get out of here before any others show up. You're taking too long looting them."

"Don't criticize me, Mister. I cut you free, and don't you forget it," he hissed.

I regretted my harshness and answered, "I know, and I'm grateful. It's just that we need to be going."

He stepped past me, and I reached out to stop him. My hand pushed against his chest and – He was a girl! I was momentarily shocked, and I gasped in surprise.

She swung her little gun up to point at my face and snarled, "So, you know! Don't get any ideas about me. I can take care of myself. Just because I rescued you doesn't mean that – that –"

She paused as if overcome by the implied thought.

I hastily interjected, "You're safe with me. I'm married with two children, and all I want to do is to get back to my wife."

She relaxed perceptibly. "That's okay, then. I've been moving towards the mountains. How far do you think they are from here?"

I was puzzled, "You don't know?"

"No, why do you think I asked. A person wouldn't ask if she knew," she said in an irritated tone.

I resolved to start over. "Look, my name is Declan, and you might be?" It was an idiotic line, but it had always worked for me before.

"You can call me 'Hattie,'" she said in an easier tone of voice.

"Hattie, where is my ship, and did you see any small, furry creature anywhere?" I was very worried about Whistle.

She snorted, "Your ship is about a mile over that way, and I haven't seen any dogs or cats or anything else but you and these dead guys." She paused and then added, "I did see a rabbit yesterday, but I shot it for dinner."

"That's not what I meant. The pilot of my flyer was a Sunny. They sort of look like big otters, but their heads are disproportionately large. They're intelligent aliens from another planet; and our friends," I added as an afterthought.

She seemed surprised but then said, "I heard there were space aliens here now, but I never expected to see one."

"Well, lead me to where my ship is, and we'll see if he's around there," I instructed.

A few minutes later, we were approaching the pond from below the dam. We climbed over the dam and looked. The shuttle should have been visible since it wasn't that dark. The full moon had started to rise, and its light was enough that I could see the shuttle was gone.

I exclaimed, "It's not here. The Motherland people couldn't have moved it, so – maybe, uh, maybe Whistle fixed whatever was wrong and took it back to base. At least that's what I hope."

We walked around to where we'd landed. The ground was torn up, but there was no sign that the shuttle had been dragged away. It had to have taken off.

I thought quickly. We needed to find some safe place to hole up before the next day broke. I didn't want to be captured again if any of the Motherland people were around. Assuming we could hide out during the day, maybe we could make our way back to Jake's territory.

I explained to her, and she snorted in response. "Look, Declan, that's just what I've been doing. There's a road back that way about half a mile, and we can follow that for a few hours until we get too tired. Maybe we can find a safe place to hide then. I've been doing pretty good, just going out into the pastures and finding a coyote den or a hole to lay up in. I'm going to keep on doing that. I suggest you come with me, but if you don't like that idea, you can just go on your own without me."

She was sure of herself. I liked that. The girl certainly had spunk. I said, "You can call me 'Dec.' It's shorter, and most people call me that. What's your real name?"

She hesitated then said firmly, "Hattie."

I asked, "Is that all? Just 'Hattie'?"

She nodded, "Just 'Hattie.'

We'd been walking towards the road she'd mentioned, and we had reached it. I stepped on the bottom fence wire and lifted the next one, making a gap for her to duck through. She did and then performed the same service for me.

Bending down made my head throb like fury and I kind of groaned.

She asked, "Are you alright? You must have been beat up pretty bad."

"I think I'll be okay. It's just that somebody hit me on the back of the head, and it hurts pretty bad," I answered.

"Bend down here so I can feel it," she ordered.

I did, and she gently probed my scalp. Finally, she said, "Well, it has clotted blood all over, and your hair is matted, but I can't feel any holes or anything, so I think your skull is okay."

I quickly straightened up and said, "That's a relief. I was kind of scared to feel it myself."

We walked quietly for several hours. She didn't talk much, only enough to let me know that my questions weren't welcome.

Along about dawn, we found a deep gully in a field. There was a clump of cottonwood trees on the gully bank by a small pool of water, and one of them had a large hole under its roots. There was enough room for both of us, and it looked as if it would be pretty good cover, so we holed up there.

Chapter 21

We were awakened by the sound of a shuttle passing overhead. Hattie jumped up, startled. Our shuttles were the only air traffic, and people had become unused to seeing vehicles in the sky. The only thing that flew today were birds or perhaps a kite or two.

I doubted that there were many kites. Life was too hard to waste time on frivolous recreation.

We crawled out of the hole and drank at the pool in the gully. My stomach was growling, causing Hattie to say, "You're going to have to wait for breakfast. Maybe we'll see a rabbit or two later."

My head still ached with a fierce, throbbing drum-beat, and my stomach was definitely empty. It wasn't nice of me, but I took that as an excuse to snap at her, "I hope the little fur-balls show up soon and you don't miss with that little pea-shooter!"

She gave back as good as she got, "Well, maybe I shouldn't have cut you loose, after all. You weren't doing too well back there on your own."

I looked around. The sun was shining, and a light breeze was stirring the weeds along the side of the gully. The scene was calming. I took a deep breath, rotated my shoulders to loosen them, and said, "Okay. I'm sorry. My head is pounding. Let's start again, shall we?"

Her smile was like another sunrise. Under all of the dirt and matted hair, I hadn't recognized how pretty a girl she was. And, as I looked closer, how young she was. She couldn't have been more than fifteen or sixteen.

I smiled back, "That's better. I'm sorry I'm grumpy. Something to eat will probably help my head, so we'd better get going. No rabbits in sight here."

"When you're as old as you are, it's okay to be grumpy in the morning," she said earnestly.

I didn't know quite how to answer that. I guess someone in their thirties does look old to a teenager, especially someone who'd been more or less concussed, tied up, urinated on, and generally mistreated after their shuttle crashed. After a minute, I decided to let it go. She was already heading towards the road we'd been following last night, so I followed along quietly because talking made my temples and the back of my head throb.

We reached the fence and then climbed up onto the asphalt. It was a poor excuse for a road. The lack of maintenance showed in the deep cracks and weeds growing up through the surface in random shoots and clumps. The good thing about the road's condition was that there were patches of dust in places where the wind had deposited them in the lee of weed clumps. These were softer, and any incautious travelers would leave their imprint there. There were numerous bird tracks, small and large. Some might have been grouse, maybe. There were also small mammal tracks left by rabbits, pack rats, coyotes, or maybe feral dogs, and once we saw the prints of a bobcat.

I noticed that Hattie kept well clear of the dust, and I mentally gave her a high mark for that. She was cautious about leaving a trail. That was something that was now natural for me. A few years ago, I was mostly an urban dweller, at least when I wasn't being a soldier. In the years since our technology died, I'd become a pretty fair mountain man, and being aware of my tracks was second nature. I feared, though, that it would also be second nature for any of the Motherland Army men.

We didn't see any sign that another human had traveled on the road until the sun was well up. We came up a hill and, at the crest, Hattie dove off into the ditch. I was a little behind her and cautiously stepped forward until I could just see over the top into the next valley.

There was the remains of a fire on a flat place in the middle of the road at the lowest part between our hill and the next. There was no smoke, and there hadn't been any odor, but the wind was quartering across and probably wouldn't have carried any scent to us.

I inspected the area carefully. It seemed safe. We had to keep going, so I decided to chance it. I murmured to Hattie out of the side of my mouth as I walked by her position, "Stay here and keep an eye out. I'm going down."

She hissed in response and slowly parted the weeds so that she could see better.

I walked slowly down the road, trying to use my mental senses to determine if there was an ambush after all. It was no use. I couldn't sense anything, but my head was still pounding, and that made it extremely difficult to slip into the relaxed mode that my mental sensing required.

When I reached the site of the fire, I stopped and looked around. The wind blew through the long grass of the hillside, creating surprisingly regular waves. A bird was calling from a small bush. It seemed cheerful and not at all alarmed. I kicked the ashes, and they were cold. Then I looked around again. Nothing.

There were a few bones near the side of the road. I squatted by them and picked up one. It was a goat, and it had obviously been cooked. It had been some time ago. There was no meat left on the bone. The small animals, mice, birds, and rats had cleaned off every scrap of flesh.

Standing, I waved for Hattie, and she stood up in the ditch, looking around. Then she ambled down to where I waited.

"Somebody was here, huh?" she asked.

"Yeah, maybe a week ago or so. The fire is cold, and the bones, there, have been picked by the mice," I replied.

She snorted and walked past, saying, "Well, standing around isn't going to get us to the mountains. Let's get going."

She wasn't making this easy on me. I followed along, hoping for something to eat and daydreaming about finding Whistle. Then it hit me. I must have a concussion. My mind just wasn't as fast as it usually was. I should have been trying to contact him mentally!

Hattie was a little ahead of me as we moved westward. I tried my best to ignore the pounding in my head, softening my steps to minimize the pain, which seemed to beat in time with my strides. I slung the rifle over my shoulder and let my hands hang limply as I walked, trying to slide into a state where I could push my psychic senses out far enough to sense Whistle or Frazzle or Liz! I was really foggy! I'd forgotten about her. She was far more sensitive than either of the two Sunnys.

I gradually drifted into a deep state of meditation as I walked. It's necessary for me to alter my brain frequency, slowing it down to a theta level, about four cycles per second. Human brains usually slow to that point just before drifting off to sleep. It's when we usually have a series of dream-like thoughts that gradually fade out as we doze off. Things were progressing well. I seemed to be able to continue walking as I meditated. My eyes were still open, but I was focused on other-where.

...Snap...

I jerked awake at the sound, and my eyes popped open fully. I'd dropped back and was about fifty yards behind Hattie. She was standing on the edge of the road, holding her little pistol. There was a small trickle of smoke exiting the barrel. She lowered the weapon and tucked it into its holster as I watched.

She turned to me and called in a low voice, "Hurry up. I got us a rabbit!"

That got my attention. She jumped the ditch and fence, and by the time I got up to her position, she was probing in some grass and weeds. Rising, she turned to me with a grin, holding a nice, fat, and thoroughly dead rabbit by the hind leg.

A few yards beyond her location was a small clump of woody brush. We gathered dead sticks and built a small fire in a barren area well away from the dry grass. It was the work of a moment to pull the skin off the bunny and gut it. Then we cooked strips of the lean meat on sticks held over the almost smokeless fire.

The meat tasted amazing. I'd forgotten what food was like, or so it seemed. By the time the fire died out, we'd cooked and eaten the entire rabbit. It hadn't been as big as it first looked, but I felt comfortably full, and my head was better. As I ate, the headache started to fade, and now, although I still had to move carefully, I almost felt human again.

"Hattie, I need to take a few minutes to try and contact my friends," I started.

"How? You don't have a radio, and I don't see any telephones around here either." She wasn't being sarcastic. She was just impatient and wanted to get moving again.

"It's a long story, but to make it short, I'm able sometimes to use my mind to contact people over long distances," I said, hoping that she'd take that as a complete explanation.

"Oh, you mean like telepathy?" she asked.

I kept underestimating her. She was filthy and her hair matted, but underneath was a beautiful and intelligent young girl.

"Yes. That's exactly what I mean. If you'll give me some quiet time, I'll see if I can reach them," I said.

"Okay," she replied.

I was surprised. No arguments; she just sat there with her mouth shut, watching me expectantly. I briefly wondered if she thought I'd go into some kind of fit or something. Her intense staring didn't help. I tried to drop into the meditative state, but her constant gaze made me self-conscious.

"Look, I can't get into the right state with you staring at me. It's embarrassing or something like that. Just keep watch and make sure we are secure or whatever," I pleaded.

She huffed a bit but then moved over to a small hillock that afforded a slightly better view over the surrounding terrain. I sat there by the remains of the fire, sensing the breeze as it gusted fitfully around me. The noon sun shone down brightly, and there were some bird calls in the distance. The grass waved and ...

I was drifting down into that twilight area that I wanted. My mind separated from my body and slid out to a great distance or an infinitely tiny distance, and there was no meaning to normal spatial measurements. I became aware of – Liz!

"Dec! Dec! Where are you? What happened? I've been so worried! Where are you? I love you." Her mental stream almost overflowed my mind.

"Calm down. I'm Okay. I love you, too. I'm walking back towards Denver, and I'm maybe twenty miles west of

where our shuttle went down. What happened to the shuttle anyway? It wasn't there when I got back," I sent.

She sent back, "Whistle got it rebooted, but you'd been captured. He slid into the pond and watched from out in the water. He said someone hit you on the head, and you went down. He didn't know if you were alright. They dragged you off, and he was afraid to follow, so he went to the shuttle, got it going, and came back for help. They went out to try and find you early this morning."

That was the shuttle that had waked us! They were probably poking around off to the east, trying to find me there.

"Are they still looking?" I mentally asked.

The response was clear, "Yes, they're still out there. Rudy and Joe and some of the Marines. Whistle is piloting."

"Can you radio them to follow the road that is about a half-mile south of the crash site? I estimate we've come about twenty miles," I sent.

"What do you mean, 'we'?" she asked.

"The Motherland guys grabbed me, but a girl rescued me," I sent back. "Her family seems to be gone, and she's a refugee. I'm going to bring her back. She's got a lot going for her, and she needs to be somewhere safe."

"Is she pretty?" Liz asked.

My wife! "She's so dirty that you can't really tell, but I think so. She's also pretty smart. I think that she's had an awful time." I sent.

"Dec! You make sure that girl gets back here safely! Frazzle has the shuttle on the radio. Get somewhere they can see you. They should be there in a few minutes."

She betrayed her worry by scolding. I hadn't realized that she could add a scolding overtone to her mental sending, but she had.

We hiked back to the road, climbed to the top of one of its low hills, and stood there waiting. I was looking to the east for the shuttle. I had just seen a distant flash as the sun glinted off of the craft's hull when Hattie grabbed my arm.

"Look!" she pointed westward along the road. There was a group of men coming. They were about half a mile away and had just come over a hillock into sight. We could faintly hear them shout as they sighted us.

They left no question about their identity and intentions. A rifle bullet struck the asphalt off to our left and whined away as it ricocheted off the hard surface.

We dashed eastward over the top of the hill. When we could just barely see them over the rise, I unslung my rifle and fired several high shots in their direction. The weapon was poorly sighted, and I wasn't sure where it was hitting, so I was surprised when one of them went down. They scattered, diving into the roadside ditches and leaving the fallen man to wriggle his way over to the edge of the road. It must have been too much for him since he stopped trying as soon as he got to the edge of the asphalt and laid still.

They kept shooting at us, but the bullets mostly bounced off the asphalt and flew overhead, whirring as they tumbled through the air. Hattie was crouched low, her eyes wide.

She looked at me and asked, "How do we get out of this?"

She wasn't panicked. She was obviously trying to figure out how to deal with a novel situation. I realized that she had never been in an actual firefight, despite the cold-blooded way she'd taken down the drunken soldiers.

I started to speak, but there was a loud whining noise, and the shuttle came to a hovering stop about a hundred yards over our heads. I mentally tuned in to the crew and contacted Rudy.

Our mental communication was sketchy. He could use his mind to send, but he was nowhere near as facile as Liz.

"Stay down, Dec. We're going to use the plasma weapon on those guys, and then we'll drop down and pick you up." His communication came through in bits and pieces, but that was its intent.

There was a flurry of rifle shots that either missed or bounced bullets off of the tough shuttle armor, followed by a screeching crack as the plasma cannon fired. There was a sense of quickly passing heat even one hundred yards below as the weapon discharged.

The surviving men in the ditches jumped up and took off running as if the devil himself were on their heels. The bolt had struck a little short of their position and started all of the grass and weeds on fire on one side of the road. I figured the men on the other side of the road knew they were the next targets because they all ran away in a tight group. That was a big mistake.

There was another crack, and this time the bolt struck right in the middle of the running group. It exploded with a flash, leaving no one standing.

Now, it may seem cruel to shoot retreating targets, but Rudy was nothing if not expedient. He had always gone for the throat in battle, and this was no exception. As he'd told me once, "The only good enemy is a dead one."

The craft settled with its characteristic jet-turbine whine and landed on the hilltop directly in front of us.

Chapter 22

During the two days that I'd been MIA, the strategic situation had firmed up for both sides. The Motherland forces had consolidated into a huge group and were now arranged in a miles-long line beginning north and east of Longmont and extending south in a giant crescent to a little northeast of Parker. That formation covered nearly the entire Denver Metro area.

As we flew past, a mile above the battle line, I could make out clumps and groups of men, horses, and steam-drawn artillery. They'd apparently converted some of the steam tractors manufactured in Kansas City for agriculture to war-like purposes, kind of the opposite of beating swords into plowshares. I thought it was a stupid waste.

The Motherland battle line wasn't solid. There were large gaps in many places; nevertheless, I was left wondering if Hattie and I could have found our way through without being captured. It was fortunate that we'd been picked up by the shuttle.

Our aerial viewpoint allowed me to observe that the Warlord's Army was considerably smaller. They were facing the other line in a convex arc with groups of reinforcements stationed at strategic points behind the lines.

There were long picket lines of horses near these groups. They'd be able to mount up and come at a gallop to any potential break-through points. That would allow Jake to maximize the strength of his line, even though he didn't have nearly the manpower that the Motherland commander had assembled.

I wondered how that group had evolved. As far as I knew, the Federal Government hadn't survived the EMP blast and the subsequent attack by the marooned Pugs and Pug-bears. Most of the population had died in the months after the blast. For them to have reconstituted themselves into such a massive force in the last five years was a significant feat that was even more impressive considering the difficulty of life in the here-and-now.

They'd also traveled a very long distance, at least some of them, to get halfway across the continent. My general conclusion was that they were tough and would be very hard for Jake to withstand.

The thing that predisposed me against the Motherland group was that they'd acted like any of an almost infinite number of barbarian groups in the past. They'd pillaged the land as they came. I doubted that there were very many untouched towns or farms behind them. From what I'd seen, they took what they wanted and left nothing and no one standing as they passed.

I had no problem comparing them unfavorably to what Denver had become under Jake's rule. Sure, there was violence in Denver. People got killed, but the thing was, they all had an equal opportunity to defend themselves. Jake didn't restrict arms, and the few courts he'd set up were as likely to set a killer free as hanging him, provided his motivation was relatively reasonable, and the deceased had been afforded a fighting chance.

I'd also observed that the people of the Denver area were noticeably more polite than city dwellers had been before the Pug-bear invasion. I guess that it is true that an armed society makes for a polite society. When everyone is armed and able to fight to the death, there's no sense in needlessly offending someone. Good manners are the best survival strategy, and the Denver people went out of their way to display them.

The other interesting thing was that men were polite to women and treated them with much more consideration than before. The women accepted it, too. Before society had been knocked to its knees, many women would have a screaming, feminist fit if some man had deigned to open a door for them. Now that life was so much more difficult, and survival wasn't taken for granted, the women-folk were generally happy about chivalrous actions.

It was true that a woman's chance of surviving giving birth was considerably less than it had been before. The lack of medical supplies was responsible for that. However, there was a far lower chance of a woman being raped or abused. Most of the time, the perpetrator didn't survive long enough to repeat the act.

It may have something to do with the fact that people who live leisurely, secure lives generally seem to amuse themselves by engaging in nasty political and social activities. I'd heard it said about academia that the politics in university departments are incredibly vicious, precisely because there is so little riding on the outcome. From my observations, it seemed to be true.

There was also a noticeable shortage of lawyers. Most of those who had survived now were gainfully employed in other ways. Suing someone for any insult was simply a thing of the past.

People seemed to be more serious and more concerned with each other. Of course, there were fewer people, but most were reluctant to engage in fighting. The consequences were too likely to involve physical death and destruction. Social conflicts were generally judged too trivial to risk insulting someone else.

I was tired, and my head still hurt, but I wanted to check on what was going on. We landed at the stadium and were shortly meeting with Jake. He had been out in the field, directing the Denver defenses, but he'd just now brought his shuttle back to meet with the mule-skinners who were to haul supplies to his lines. The mule-drivers used large, flat-bedded drays for their everyday work. They were taking the opportunity to lobby for assurance that Jake would reduce the standard tariff charged on loads of supplies brought into the Denver area once the battle was won.

He was shouting at a group of their leaders in the middle of the end zone when we unloaded.

"Look, you thick-headed lummoxes – you're as stubborn as your mules! I agreed to lower our city tariff for six months, but if you don't get out there and do your job, there isn't going to be any Denver for you to haul to!" he bellowed.

I'd never seen him so angry. His face was red, and his movements were rapid and jerky.

The leader of the draymen yelled back, just as loudly, "Takes one to know one! We want the tariff gone for a year afore we'll risk our animals out there. 'Sides, if those Motherlanders take you over, we'll just haul for them. Chances are they won't charge any tariff."

I could see this was going nowhere. The draymen were naive if they thought the Motherland forces would be better than Jake. I stepped in, "Look here, you men." I reinforced my words with a mental command, and they turned to me as I continued, "That army out there intends to conquer Denver, and the chances are very high they'll kill everyone here, steal everything that isn't tied down and burn the place to the ground. That's just what they've done to every place they've over-run so far."

This was probably an exaggeration. I didn't know what the status of their territory was back in the east. I was just going with what I'd observed in my limited experience. However, I thought my fear was very well-grounded.

They grumbled among themselves but then agreed to get to work. After they filed through the exit, Jake turned to me, still red in the face, and said, "That was none of your business, Dec. I'm capable of handling my own –" He caught himself with a jerk, took a deep breath and noticeably tried to get control of his emotions.

After a minute, he said calmly, "I'm sorry. They really pissed me off. Thanks for the help. How did you get them to agree so rapidly?"

I grinned and shook my head, indicating that I hadn't taken offense. "I added a little telepathic command along with my words. It just kind of slipped through their defenses and made them think about what it would be like around here with the Motherland group in control. They were being sensible, in their opinion, holding out for better terms, but they could see that your terms were better than being burned out," I said.

Jake looked at me thoughtfully and asked, "Have you ever used this kind of psychic power on me?"

That was a different matter. I replied, "Truthfully, I've thought about it, but you're so reasonable and have your people's best interests in mind that I've never had to do it."

"Make me a promise right now," he commanded. "Promise me you'll warn me if you feel the need to use mind control on me. I don't expect you to promise you won't use it; I wouldn't believe you if you did, but at least give me a chance to rethink for myself."

I nodded, "I will do that. I respect you too much to try to influence you that way, anyway. But I see your point about a promise not to do it."

He grinned and changed the topic, "I need help badly. There are too many of them, and there's no way my forces will hold for long. What can you do?"

I'd been thinking about that very topic. The main thing that had occurred to me was to back the Motherland people up by using one of the ships to make a firing pass with its bow cannon.

I said, "It will take some careful coordination. Will you give the order for your men to fall back en-masse? They'll have to drop back at least a couple of miles, so it will take, say, thirty minutes. Once they drop back, the Motherland group will start forward, and at that point, we'll burn a strip between the two fronts with an anti-matter cannon. That should calm them down a bit."

"Yeah, that should work. Demonstrating that we can wipe them off the globe might make them think twice about attacking," he added.

"The only thing is, you can't let them intermix with your people. I can't make a pass unless there is a clear target. If the battle is joined and forces are mixed together, the best thing we can do is to provide spot support with the shuttles," I said.

We set up a plan to have the Denver forces pull back at a radio signal from my FTL to Jake's shuttle. He'd be in the shuttle, watching from a few miles behind the lines. The major problem was disseminating the orders to his widespread front.

I hustled my friends and Hattie back into the shuttle, and Whistle had us moving quickly. We'd be in orbit and matching up with my ship within the hour.

Chapter 23

F our hours later, we'd moved the ship into an orbit that passed directly along the north-south axis of the Motherland Army's battle line every seventy minutes. I was satisfied that we were in position, so I called Jake and told him to have his men get out of the way.

We were just coming over the top of Canada, heading southward, when Jake radioed that all of his commanders had received the order to fall back. They were to wait until two hours after noon and then move rapidly back to the west. I calculated that would place us somewhere over central Asia when they started moving. It would take us about thirty minutes after that to be in position to fire. That timing was just about what we'd decided upon in our meeting.

Jake's message had ordered the fall-back but not explained why. We didn't want the enemy to know what was coming if they happened to get lucky and capture a messenger.

Immediately before the retreat, all of the Denver defensive artillery was to fire for ten minutes. The hope was that the enemy would believe the artillery barrage was intended to mask the retreat. If the Motherland commander was as aggressive as I believed him to be, he'd order an advance as soon as the shells stopped falling. That would potentially put many of his men in the path of our anti-matter strafing pass.

I wanted to drive the Motherland Army back, although I didn't think one pass would eradicate it. Practically speaking, any reduction in their force would be desirable.

Our ship moved inexorably around the globe from the night side to the daytime of the western hemisphere.

Over Canada, the monitor system displayed the enemy lines under extreme magnification. We could see that they were moving forward at a rapid pace. I was in an agony of worry. We were too far out as yet to start shooting since too much atmosphere would weaken the anti-matter pulses. I mentally urged the ship to hurry. I didn't dare let the Motherland troops mix into the defenders' lines. There would be nothing I could do then. Shooting under that circumstance would kill as many of our side as of them.

We'd over-charged all four of our cannons by thirty percent. I intended to shoot each in sequence. The ship was oriented so that the bow gun, one of the waist guns, and the tail gun would fire in close sequence. Then we'd rotate axially and fire the other waist gun as we moved away from the Denver area. Frazzle had told me that over-charging the weapons wasn't a recommended strategy. Still, they would handle a limited number of extra-high power shots before they began to suffer erosion of the capture chamber and barrel.

Time seemed to crawl, but finally, we were directly above the northern end of the enemy line. We began to fire a steady stream of anti-matter pulses at them.

The last time we'd used this technique, I'd been on the ground, so I'd seen the effect from that perspective. It had been impressive. There had been a giant ripping sound as if a mile-wide strip of velcro was being separated. The anti-matter bolt had erased everything on the surface and created a five-foot-deep trench a mile or so wide.

It was nearly as impressive from orbit. You could see the ground change from green to a barren, brown strip. The monitors were focused on the area directly in front of the beam, and we could see that a significant fraction of the Motherland Army was in the direct path. I thought that they might lose half of their force. Even so, that would still not give Jake an advantage. He could only field about a third of their number.

We'd completed the pass and were rapidly moving toward the equator when Jake radioed that the enemy was in disarray and was retreating. He was flying along their rear, shooting his shuttle's plasma weapon at them as they fled. He sounded exultant and was full of praise for the strategy as we moved out of radio range.

When we came back into range about an hour later, he was still pleased, even though he'd found out that over a thousand of his men had failed to fall back far enough and were now gone. He blamed it on incompetent group commanders.

The next orbit showed that the Motherland commander had rallied his troops, and they were now firing their artillery at Jake's lines. We were able to locate some of their batteries and erase them with short anti-matter pulses, but there were too many to get them all during the brief window we had.

We shot a few more during our next pass. It was getting late in the afternoon, and the shadows from the front range peaks were extending outwards toward the battle line. It would soon be dark, and we didn't want to shoot then. It was a little too difficult to tell who was friend and who was foe in the dark.

Jake called us and said that the Motherland commander had a working field radio and had called. He'd demanded Jake's surrender and gotten laughed at for his pains. Shortly after that, we picked up a call from the enemy commander addressed to all 'spaceships.'

He was offering to withdraw under cover of night, provided we would cease shooting at his forces. I looked at Liz, and she agreed. I called him back and told him to get his men moving back toward the east. By morning, I wanted them to be at least ten miles eastward of their current position. They agreed.

Morning came, and we could see that the Motherland forces were gradually withdrawing. Some of them hadn't made the ten-mile limit yet, but I didn't fire on them. They were close to that point.

During the day, Jake and the Motherland commander worked out a sort of uneasy truce. They agreed to back up a hundred miles as long as we didn't shoot at them from orbit.

I thought they'd use the respite to regroup and reinforce themselves while carrying out some form of spying or infiltration. I hadn't gotten the impression that they were ready to back off as yet; however, Jake had agreed to the truce, so we complied.

I left the FTL ship in the same orbital plane, but Frazzle moved it up to the extreme edge of the near-earth zone. There were possible conflicts with satellites and junk that were orbiting at a little lower altitude. We thought it best to move out of the way of possible collisions. The ship's bow armor and shield could handle minor strikes at orbital velocities, but there was no sense in risking damage.

Liz had taken Hattie under her care, and the girl was starting to recover from her harrowing experiences. She had been cleaned up thoroughly, and Liz had cut her hair, getting rid of the tangles and matted clumps. Now, she looked like a startlingly-pretty, high-school-age, brown-haired girl with blue eyes and a wary, suspicious attitude.

I couldn't blame her for her suspicion. She'd seen her parents killed and had killed several raiders herself. She'd walked for well over a hundred miles in occupied, enemy territory, avoiding capture, and she'd rescued me. Now she was in a spaceship along with two kinds of alien creatures that she'd never heard of, and she was finding it challenging to adapt.

I came into our cabin from the bridge and found Hattie and Liz playing with Rowan. The baby was laughing, and Hattie had a relaxed smile for the first time since I'd met her. She'd grinned at me a few times, but those had been tense grimaces more than genuine smiles.

Rowan rolled over, and Hattie tickled her, eliciting more laughter. I walked around the little group and noticed that Jefferson, always the opportunist, was curled in Hattie's lap. I extended my mental perception to the cat and realized that he had a distinct attitude of helping. He recognized Hattie's distress and was doing his best to help her out of it. He was a lot more sensitive than his numerous scars would indicate.

"Liz, I'm going to have to go back down to meet with Jake. We've got to make plans to free the remaining Sunny planets," I said.

Hattie looked up and asked, "The Sunnys – are they all harmless and friendly?"

I'd noticed that she had held back from contact with them, but I'd thought that she was just shy. From her question, it appeared that she had some doubts about their relationship with humans.

Liz answered her, "Yes, dear. They are very friendly, and they've got a mental block that won't allow them to think about violence. In a sense, we are their protectors. Besides that, I trust them. Frazzle's wife, Red, usually babysits Rowan. You'd have met her before now, but she's taken some time off. She's pregnant, and it's about time for her to lay her own egg."

Hattie's eyes grew very wide. "She's going to lay an egg?" she asked incredulously.

I said, "That's right. The Sunnys are egg layers. They lay one egg, and the baby hatches in a few months. Then they raise it in much the same fashion we raise our babies. The Sim-tigers –"

She interrupted, "I'm scared of them. They look so fierce."

I started to continue, but now Liz interrupted me. She'd recognized that I was starting to lecture, something of which she disapproved.

She said, "The Sim-tigers give birth to live cubs. They look fierce because they are. They're excellent fighters. Dec has gotten them to ally with humans, so they are our friends also. I'll introduce you to them more closely, and you'll find that they are caring and gentle with us."

Hattie started to speak, but then Liz added, "They do have a wicked sense of humor, though. They can be a little insensitive. You just have to remember that human rules don't come naturally to them."

Hattie asked, "What do you mean?"

"Oh, for instance, I know their leader, "Kasm' likes me. He's Dec's close friend, and I think he'd die trying to protect me, but he always fondles my behind as a greeting."

She hastened to add, "It's not a sexual thing. It's more like how we pat dogs or stroke cats in greeting. It startled me at first, but I've gotten used to it. Don't be surprised if one of them pats your rear."

Hattie laughed at the imagined action, "That's crazy. How do you greet them?"

I answered, "There's no problem with putting your hand on their shoulders or back. They don't care to be patted on the head, though. They'll allow it, but I think touching the head is an intimate thing for them. It's probably seen as a sexual sort of act. Maybe like a kiss is for us."

She sighed, "There's a lot I don't know. Are you going to send me back to Earth?" Then with a slight tremor in her voice, she added, "Or, can I stay here – with you?"

Liz looked at me, and I smiled. Liz reached out and pulled Hattie into a light embrace, saying, "You can stay here with us as long as you want. We'll make sure you learn everything you need."

I added, "Hattie, you saved my life. I'm not going to forget that. You've got a home as a part of our family as long as you want."

The girl looked even younger in my wife's embrace. She looked over Liz's shoulder at me with her eyes wide, and when I nodded affirmatively, she buried her face in Liz's neck and started to sob.

"I – I – my parents were poor, and the soldiers killed them – I – didn't know what was going to happen to me. I've been trying to be as hard and tough as I can, but it – it still hurts inside," she said through her tears.

"I know, I know, but you're safe here. Dec and I won't let anything happen to you. You can stay on the ship and maybe even learn to fly it. I'll ask Frazzle to teach you," Liz said.

"That would be nice," Hattie responded, wiping her eyes. "Flying in space. Are there any bad guys in space?"

"Unfortunately, there are, but we're working on getting rid of them too," I said. "Now I've got to go down and make sure Jake can survive while we go and rescue the Sunnys."

Liz stood and embraced me. We kissed while Hattie looked away in embarrassment. I patted her shoulder as I started to leave, and she surprised me by whirling and hugging me also. I responded gently, looking at Liz over Hattie's head. My wife smiled in a motherly sort of way and said, "Go take care of your business. We'll be fine here."

Chapter 24

Whistle and I took the smaller shuttle down to Earth. For a change, Jake wasn't at his stadium headquarters. We found him at a large encampment of his soldiers out near the eastern border of Colorado. It was located near a small town named 'Joes.'

The place was a little over a hundred miles from the Denver metro area, situated along highway 36, about twenty or thirty miles from the Kansas-Colorado border. I read the name from an old atlas we'd been using for navigation. The shuttles didn't have anything like our old GPS systems. If they had, it probably wouldn't have worked. Even if the GPS satellites were still operational, the Sunnys had no more concept of how humans mapped their planet than Jefferson.

When I told Whistle the town's name, he looked at me, puzzled, and asked, "Dis place belong to Joe?"

"No. It's just a name. Maybe it belonged to someone named Joe who lived here a long time ago. I don't know," I answered.

He seemed bemused for a bit and then commented, "Dat's nice. Place keep memory of human alive. Sunnys never think of this. All our places are named their own names, not related to Sunnys."

I smiled, "We come from different cultures. It would be strange if we did things the same way."

He was busy adjusting the shuttle for landing for a moment but then said, "Peoples all be different. You, me, Sim-tigers, even Pugs have their own way of doing things. Maybe no one way is right. Maybe every people got their own reasons for what they do. Who is going to say?"

That was a good observation. I added, "The only ones that have no set way are the Pug-bears. They just act like animals and do whatever they want."

"Yes, Dec. You know they are animals, only some of dem have the big brains and are smart. If we can get rid of the thing that causes their brains to grow, maybe they won't be problem any longer. We just have to keep them out of space. You crashed their space station. I thought that was bad. Now I understand that sometimes breaking things and being violent prevents more trouble later." He returned to his landing preparation.

I was speechless for a moment. It seemed that he was somehow overcoming the Sunny bias against violence. Previously, he hadn't been able to see that sometimes force applied at the right time and place can prevent having to apply more force later.

We had been traveling over a mile up. I'd thought it best to keep some air beneath us in case someone decided to take a shot at our shuttle. The things were heavily armored, but having had the engine knocked out before made me nervous and disinclined to take any chances.

The area surrounding Joes had been an agricultural center. From a high altitude, there were what looked like large polka-dots scattered around all over the place. The polka-dots were all that remained of what once were irrigated fields. The irrigation systems were hooked to artesian wells and had rotated around the wellhead, spraying water on the crops. Each of the dots was perhaps two thousand feet in diameter. The wells had either dried up, or more likely, the equipment had worn out and not been repaired. For comparison, you could probably have dropped two towns the size of Joes on one of the spots and had room left over.

We landed next to Jake's shuttle in a field behind the post office. A group of men came over to the shuttle to greet us and then escort us to Jake's location. He was sitting in the old community building about two hundred or so yards down the street from where we'd landed. There was a rag-tag group of officers gathered around him in a planning session.

As we came in, I heard the crackle of a short-wave radio system. Jake turned from his map at the sound and saw me.

"Just in time, Dec!" he said. "We're trying to get hold of the Motherland's main leader. I believe he calls himself the President." He smiled sardonically.

The radio crackled again, and then the operator got it tuned in so we could talk. It took some time to convince the Motherland people to get their leader on the line.

Finally, a man's voice came through clearly, "This is President Bashir. Who am I talking at?"

Jake introduced himself, using better grammar than the alleged President. The conversation shortly degenerated into a series of demands on the part of the President. I don't know if he really understood the idea of negotiation. It didn't seem like he did; his demands were all one way – his.

"I want you to retreat back to your city. We own all of the lands up to your city borders. You must pay us an annual tribute of either gold or slaves. If you don't, we'll attack your city, and the next time, we'll take it and kill everyone who opposes us," he said.

After that, his demands became even more outrageous. His following words were, "I require you to turn over all flying machines to me, including the rocket or spaceship that shoots at my men. The commander of the spaceship must be turned over to me alive. He must suffer torture for what he did to my forces. In addition, you must turn over all of his crew. They are all sentenced to death."

Jake looked at me as if to say, "See what we're dealing with?"

I didn't say anything. Instead, I stepped over to the set and held out my hand for the microphone. The operator handed it to me.

I paused, composing myself. The guy's demands had gotten on my nerves, and I was just about ready to tell him something that was very undiplomatic.

I shook my head to clear it and then said, "Your force is not powerful enough to take the front-range territory. Even if you could take it, you couldn't keep it. The tribute is out of the question, and so is the spaceship. We will also keep our shuttles. You may find that their armament is almost as potent as that of our spaceships."

I looked at Jake. He was grinning, and then he made a pushing motion, indicating that I should tell them to retreat farther.

I had held the mike button down, so the channel was still mine. I added, "We've told you to retreat one hundred miles from our territory. We've decided that isn't enough. Our territory now extends to the Mississippi River. Stay on the eastern side or risk attack."

Jake exclaimed in surprise, "Oh! Are you sure that we can enforce that boundary? We don't have enough men to do it."

"I know, but he's pissing me off. We can always back down a bit, but maybe it would be a good idea to have a no man's land as a buffer between us," I responded.

The President called back. He was sputtering in rage and somewhat incoherent. He finally said, "This means war! We will gather a force that is so great that it will be like a shadow over the land. You will have no chance, and we will give no mercy. Any survivors will be implanted with controllers, and they will be our slaves forever."

That was interesting. I looked meaningfully at Jake. We had discussed the implant that I'd found in the sniper. This was an indication that they had more and were probably using them on anyone whose loyalty was suspect. I wondered where they got the nasty things. Manufacturing mainly was still impossible, especially high-tech things, like the implants.

I went back on the radio and said, "In the interest of cooperation, we'll allow you to have the land up to the eastern border of Kansas. We can keep Kansas clear as a buffer between our territories. Any incursion into that territory will be met with extreme force. You haven't seen even the beginning of what we can do. I assure you that you won't like the results of angering us."

The radio was silent. I thought that the President was considering the expense of waging a long-distance war that his forces might lose. He came back on and said, "That will be acceptable for now, but you cannot withstand our might forever. We will give you three months in peace, and then we'll speak about this again."

There was a distinct click as the Motherland radio went off the air. I turned to Jake with a wry grin and said, "Sorry that I kind of took over."

He grinned back and said, "You did okay. I would have cussed him out." He glanced around and then added, "I'm a pretty good poker player when I set my mind to it. I'm positive he was bluffing. He needs time to regroup and gather more men."

I said, "I think you're right. He'll probably need more than three months to rebuild his forces."

I was still feeling guilty for taking the lead. He had been gracious about it, but Jake was Jake. He had to maintain his prestige. I added, "Listen, maybe I made some threats that you wouldn't have, but I want you to know that we're committed to helping you. I'll leave a force here through the whole thing, reinforcing your position. Oh, one thing, I wasn't exaggerating. We can do some things that they won't care for at all."

Jake asked, "What do you mean? I thought the anti-matter weapons were about the ultimate thing you have."

"They are, but we can also resort to a low-tech weapon that is potentially so powerful, it can destroy their entire territory," I answered.

He looked puzzled, and I continued, "We can easily drop KEWs on their positions, and a big one will have the power of many atomic bombs."

"Dec, slow down," Jake shook his head. "What's a KEW, and why haven't you told me about this thing before?"

"It's an acronym for 'Kinetic Energy Weapon' – a fancy term for throwing rocks," I started to explain more, but he interrupted.

"Quit kidding around! Throwing rocks, what –"

I continued, "We can easily capture some asteroids and cut off various sized chunks. When we drop one from orbit, it will gain an amazing amount of energy during its fall. We could even drop an entire asteroid on one of their cities. We do have to be careful, though; a big enough rock would kill all life on Earth."

His mouth dropped open, "Now I know you're exaggerating."

I replied, "No, I'm not. Our spaceships are powerful enough to drag a huge rock here from the asteroid belt. Do you know what killed the dinosaurs?"

"What?

Oh, dinosaurs – didn't a meteor – Oh! Now I see what you mean. You can do that? How accurate would it be?" he asked, jumping ahead to a critical part of the idea.

"Honestly, we haven't tested, but Frazzle tells me that we can drop a small rock within a hundred yards of any target on Earth. It will come in at thousands of miles per hour, and the impact will be of nuclear size," I answered.

"I like that idea," he shouted gleefully, pumping his fist in the air. "Let's call them back and insult that idiot some more!"

"Best to let sleeping dogs lie for now," said one of his commanders.

Jake gave him a stern look but conceded the point and nodded in agreement. He turned back to me and said, "I'm going to have to beg you for that spaceship. I need something more powerful than a shuttle to gather asteroids."

I grinned and said, "I've got a ship for you, but you have to promise to listen to the Sunny pilot. I don't want to return from my next voyage to find that the Earth is a dead world."

"I promise," he said solemnly. "When can I get my spaceship? Oh, and where are you going now?"

"The spaceship is in orbit," I answered, thinking of the older, smallest ship. It would be quite powerful enough for his purposes. "It's armed with anti-matter cannons also. You can probably defeat them with it alone."

"Great!" he answered.

I added, "I've got to go rescue the other five Sunny planets. They're still under the Pug-bears' control. We've got to save them."

"Won't you ever get rid of those blasted things?" he asked.

"I think that Ian's idea to dump brewer's yeast on them will work. We have to put it to the test, and if it works, they'll be out of the picture," I answered.

We finished by taking shots from a dusty bottle of scotch whiskey that someone had found in the remains of Jo's Liquor store across the street from the Post Office. The place had been looted, but this one bottle had somehow survived. It was far better than I remembered.

Chapter 25

Whistle and I left to head back to the FTL ship. After we took off, I got the idea to pass over the eastern half of the country. We climbed to ten miles and flew towards Washington DC slowly, moving at about a thousand miles per hour.

The shuttle's monitor displayed surface features under high magnification, and we put it to good use. I carefully inspected the area we flew over.

The Motherland Army had retreated from the site of our recent confrontation. It looked as if they were taking the threat of our spaceships seriously. We also saw some small groups of refugees moving along the smaller, western Kansas roads and heading towards the mountains.

Most of the farms and many small towns were burned out. For the most part, I couldn't tell if the undamaged ones were occupied or if they'd been raided. There were large stretches of burned fields. The invaders had burned wheat and corn fields indiscriminately, which was a stupid thing to do. The upcoming winter would likely starve almost everyone unfortunate to be caught in the destroyed territory, and the soldiers would be as likely to suffer as the remaining residents.

We saw several columns of soldiers marching in ragged order along the old roads. Like the refugees, they were heading generally west, leading me to wonder if they were intended to be reinforcements for the attack on the mountains.

As we reached the Kansas-Missouri line, it was evident that the Motherland Army had set up check-points along all roads. They weren't letting any refugees through. The lucky ones were simply turned back. The unlucky ones lay in rows and piles in the ditches near the barricades. I supposed that they'd had something worth stealing, or perhaps the check-point guards had just been in a bad mood.

We varied our course slightly from a straight line to fly over Kansas City, St. Louis, and Cincinnati on the way towards DC. The cities mainly looked abandoned except for some groups of soldiers moving in the streets. Perhaps the residents had left or were too afraid to go out of their homes.

I tried to monitor what was going on below mentally, but I couldn't seem to reach any specific individuals. The only thing I received was a general sense of distrust, hostility, and hopelessness.

I finally decided that we'd have to land somewhere to hear what was happening directly from someone on the ground.

We landed outside a little town in West Virginia named Buckhannon. It was the site of a small college, and I'd actually been there before, briefly, and had a good memory of the place as being relatively prosperous and friendly. The aura was now one of disrepair and danger.

We hid the shuttle in a clearing in the trees on the side of a steep mountain, and I walked out to the road, leaving Whistle in the vehicle. There were a couple of houses nearby, and I walked up towards the first one with my hands held out so that the residents could see that I was unarmed.

A white-haired man came out on the porch to greet me. He carried a double-barreled shotgun, but he kept the muzzle pointed at the ground, carefully not covering me. I felt that he wanted to be friendly but was too used to being suspicious to relax completely. Besides, he could see that I was carrying a weapon. My splinter gun was easily visible on my belt.

He greeted me with some reserve, and I responded, "I'm just traveling through, and I wanted to know what I should look out for."

He lifted the gun a trifle at that and then thoughtfully answered, "Your story doesn't make any sense, son. No one's allowed to travel these days. You can't be from around here, or you'd know what to look out for, so where are you from? You can tell me. I'm not a collaborator."

The word 'collaborator' came out of his mouth with a degree of vituperation that let me know he didn't think highly of such people. I decided to level with him. It seemed easier, somehow. Besides, I'd been mentally probing, and I received a sense of trustworthiness from him.

"You're right. I'm not from around here. I'm from the Denver area," I answered.

He gasped and then said, "I knew it. You must have been from a long way away, not to know that the Motherland Army controls everything here."

He indicated the front steps with a gesture and said, "Sit down and let me rest and we'll talk."

I sat, and he gave me as complete a briefing as you could want. He had been an Air Force officer during the Vietnam war. He and his wife had been trapped here at their vacation home when the EMP burst had stopped most automobile travel. They normally lived in Florida, but they owned the little cabin here, and here is where they had stayed.

"The situation was bad for nearly a year. A lot of people died, but I was able to keep us going by trading and by hauling things for people. I've got an antique car that still runs, and I've been able to get food by transporting people and goods around the area when the soldiers aren't around," he said.

"What about the soldiers?" I asked, "Are they a problem?"

His answer was discouraging, "The whole country is locked-down right now. They tell us we're under martial law, and they enforce a strict curfew. They've shot a lot of people for being out after dark. It's unreasonable, but they just execute anyone they catch without asking who they are or why they're out. No emergencies are allowed."

I replied, "It sounds like they are a problem then."

"That's not the half of it," he said. "They levy on our food supplies. If you can't pay the food requirement to them, they take everything you have. That's been real hard for a lot of people. People with kids or elderly people, like me. We have to be careful. If they come and take all of our supplies, we'll starve. A lot of people have starved."

He added, "Lucky we've got some apple trees, and I can use my tractor to plow a garden. It still runs, too, but getting diesel fuel is getting really hard."

The mention of a garden must have made him think of food because he looked at me and asked, "You aren't hungry, are you?"

I shook my head, "No. I ate breakfast a short time ago, and I'm not hungry now."

He sighed in some relief and then laughed, "I thought I'd probably have to feed you and we don't have much left right now. Most of the people in the area barely have enough to eat to keep from starving."

That meant that he wasn't alone. I reached out mentally and felt that someone was looking at me from a hiding place. It was his wife, and she was watching suspiciously, in case I turned out to be hostile after all. I didn't mention that I sensed her but went on with my questioning, "What about meat? Do you have any livestock, or do you hunt?"

He replied, "The Motherland taxmen have taken all of the livestock and shipped them to Washington for the big-wigs that live there. We aren't even supposed to hunt. No one is supposed to have any weapons. If you get caught walking around with a firearm, they execute you, no questions asked. I have to be careful with my shotgun not to let any of them see it."

He looked around and then added, "But a couple of the local guys have bows, and they're pretty good. We get venison once in a while. The deer come into my orchard and pick up the fallen apples, and who's to say if one less deer goes out than came in."

I grinned, "That would be the deer's problem and no one else's."

"Yeah, but you don't want to get caught with venison. We only take a little, spread it out among a lot of families, and we all eat it quickly. No sense leaving it to spoil or get us in trouble," he said.

His attitude turned from friendly to one of concern, "You're from the Denver area, you say?"

"Yes. From Denver," I answered.

"Is there anything you can do to help us? This Motherland group is just a bunch of savages. They rape any women they want, and their idea of justice is a travesty. In addition, they've taken off all of our young men to fight somewhere. I don't know where they're sending them."

I suspected that many of them had been sent out west to the Denver area, and I didn't want to tell him that we'd killed a bunch of them.

"There's not much I can do right now," I said. "Now that I understand what you're facing, I'll see what can be done."

I didn't want to promise any action. I might not be able to help, but if my idea of a confederation worked out, we'd have to have some minimum standards for treating the population well as a prerequisite for admittance to the group. Maybe that would be a way to get the Motherland leader and others like him to behave. I hadn't thought about it to this point, but I could see that it would be necessary to enforce some basic human rights somehow.

His mind had gone on to another question, and he glanced at me out of the corner of his eye as he asked, "If you're from Denver, how did you get here without being caught. They're just about everywhere, and it'd be difficult to get through."

I hesitated, then answered, "I flew."

He smiled widely, "That's the best way, but I didn't hear any aircraft. I used to be a pilot, you know. I thought that you might be some kind of spy or something." He paused and then quickly added, "Not that I'd consider turning you in or anything. They caught a man they said was a Canadian spy a few months ago. They've instituted the old medieval practice of drawing and quartering criminals. They make everyone in the area come and watch, too. It's a very unpleasant thing to see."

I ignored that sad news and answered the first part of his question.

"My ship is very quiet. You wouldn't hear it unless you were very close when the engine was running," I said. "I'm going to have to go now. We've still got a long way to travel, and I'm running late. Thank you for all of the information."

He leaned back and said, "Not at all. You come back and visit any time you want, young man. I've enjoyed talking to you. It gives me some hope that things might eventually get better."

We shook hands, and I walked back out to the road. Once I reached the place where I'd come out of the woods, I looked in both directions and then jumped the ditch and moved into the trees. Whistle was sitting in the cockpit where I'd left him.

We took off and headed on to pass over Washington. I wasn't worried about detection. There probably wasn't any radar still operating. They might see us visually, but electronic detection was unlikely.

The Washington area was heavily fortified. I could see lots of soldiers manning barricades along the approaches to the beltway. There were also wagons carrying produce streaming into the city along some of the main roads. The people inside the beltway seemed to be relatively prosperous. They weren't afraid to be out on the streets, either. There were a lot of pedestrians and horse traffic, along with quite a large number of carriages. I could see the occasional motorized vehicle, and once there was a large convoy of military trucks rolling along a boulevard. I assumed that these vehicles had been somehow shielded against the EMP blast.

Overall, the place looked like a well-to-do but heavily defended fort. We circled the city a couple of times, looking. I could see that the White House was occupied, and there were lots of people coming and going into the old government buildings. I guess even a barbarian-level government needs administration.

There was a long row of gibbets on the green in front of the old United States Capitol building. Most of them had corpses hanging from the projecting arms. It was a grim reminder of how the place was ruled, and despite the hustle and bustle of the scene below, I was left with a feeling of depression and a temptation to take a couple of shots at the place. I restrained my urge with some effort.

That's what our once proud country had devolved to, a totalitarian kingdom with public executions. I wondered if it was due to some kind of previously hidden structural flaw or if our government had just been an easily-replaced sham. Thinking back on pre-EMP times, I remembered that the constitution had been losing more and more of its meaning as the government gradually stripped rights from the people. Perhaps this barbarian empire was the inevitable result after a representative democracy disintegrated.

Whistle pointed the shuttle towards space and gave the engines full power. We shot upwards and out of the atmosphere like a bolt of lightning and were soon on an intercept path with the orbiting FTL.

Chapter 26

Whistle was more than competent at handling the complications of docking, so I closed my eyes and thought as we finished the flight.

The Pug-bears' attack nearly brought our civilization to a complete halt. The EMP destruction seemed to have caused the end of modernity. It seemed to me that the current situation could easily slip downwards into a version of the dark ages. The Motherland empire was leading the way with its focus on brutal military rule. Everyday life under their control was a pale and terrible shadow of what it had been before the EMP. We were headed for a complete collapse of science, culture, politics, and society.

The Motherland ruler had made life in his territory miserable, brutish, and often unnaturally short. If his army didn't kill you, you were likely to starve to death or succumb to disease. I suspected that most of the antibiotics and drugs in the world were now gone, and there wouldn't be any new supplies forthcoming, especially if what I'd seen of this group was representative of the rest of the world.

When it came down to it, the only hope for humankind was my fledgling amalgam of species. If humans, Sunnys, and Sim-tigers could somehow figure out how to live together, we might have a chance. Each of the three races had unique strengths that complemented those of the other two. The question was how to set up the arrangement.

No, on second thought, the first problem I had to solve was freeing the Sunnys from the remnants of the Pug-bears. The second was, in many ways, even more difficult. Somehow I had to come up with a way to organize and govern the remaining humans.

Allowing them to coalesce into various aggressive kingdoms or groups was just asking for a Mad Max scenario. We'd end up killing ourselves. So, I had to develop something or some set of principles.

The only thing I could think of was some form of a human confederation. If I could get human groups to agree on some basic set of human rights and treat their citizens fairly, then I didn't care if one area had a monarchy and another a dictatorship or a theocracy or even a totalitarian form of rule.

The trick was to protect the individual's rights in all circumstances and allow the individual freedom to emigrate to another territory with a more congenial form of government if desired. This would amount to a free market of ideas, and emigration would be a way of voting with your feet. Eventually, the poorly governed areas would wither away, provided I could keep them from warring against their more prosperous neighbors.

Keeping them from warring – that meant that I'd have to have some over-arching organization that had the power to enforce human rights and settle disputes. It would have to be both powerful and impartial, never stooping to interfere in the daily rule of any territory.

I briefly thought of the old United Nations organization, but that had been a massive failure. The UN was a sort of democratic hybrid that allowed constituents to vote on actions, and the group politics and corruption had led to it becoming ineffectual. The organization I was thinking of would have to be separate from the territories. The territories could only request aid and definitely not vote on the allocation of resources.

The main problem was how to keep the thing impartial. Then an idea occurred to me. I already had the most powerful force remaining on Earth in my little squadron of spaceships. If I formed a space force or navy and could keep it impartial, I was partly there. The force would have three responsibilities. First, it would enforce the basic rules that all human territories or states had to follow. Second, it would serve as an Earth Space Protection force, providing a means of countering alien invasions and dealing with piracy, which was a problem that I could foresee developing in the near future. Thirdly, it would serve as a point of contact with the main confederation that I envisioned between the three species.

The shuttle interrupted my musing with a clang as the grapples took hold. The docking tube was a minute or so away from connecting, and I stirred, preparing to enter the ship. At that moment, another good (I hoped) idea hit me. Why not ensure the impartiality of the space navy by appointing a member of one of the other species as commander. If the Earth Space Protection Force was commanded by a Sunny and the Sunny force by a Sim-tiger and the Sim-tiger force by a human, we might keep the forces from becoming an overwhelmingly powerful entity and meddling in the planetary governments.

That had always been the problem in the past. How could one find a man who was so immune to the exercise of total power that it wouldn't corrupt him in some way? It would take a saint or, more appropriately, a more-than-human being such as an angel. To the best of my knowledge, humans weren't capable of exercising such power impartially.

I couldn't really see how it would work, but the line of thought was promising. I shelved it for later as I moved through the lock into the FTL. I thought I'd run it past Liz for her opinion and then take it to Rudy, Joe, and Holmes. I'd talk to Kasm and Frazzle about the concept if they thought it had value. Perhaps with all of us thinking about it, we could work out the details

My wife was waiting as I came through the lock. When I saw her on the other side of the portal, it reminded me of the first time we'd met in the Pugs' transporter system. She'd been a captive, destined for execution, and I'd shot her captor.

I reflected on how funny life is. I could never have predicted the path we'd taken in the years since. She smiled and embraced me. Then we kissed, making me forget about my problems for a moment.

Chapter 27

We prepared to leave Earth space. I was taking my fleet of four ships back to the Sunny planets. We were going to dump yeast on the Pug-bears and see what happened.

It sounded like a plot for a comedy; defeating aliens by hitting them with one of the ingredients for beer. I could already see the bad jokes coming: "Did you hear the one about the Pug-bear who couldn't hold his brew? He lost his mind!"

Ian assured me that it would work, and I chose to believe him. As far as I was concerned, anything that would make it easier to rid the Sunny planets of thousands of the ill-intentioned creatures was worth a try.

If we went from Sunny planet to Sunny planet, the voyage would take almost three months just for travel alone. I didn't want to take that long, so we distributed the yeast and tanks to all four of our FTL ships. By now, all of the shuttles were outfitted with spraying apparatus.

I briefly thought about sending one ship to each Sunny planet but discarded that notion. There were still some FTL ships under Pug-bear control, and I didn't feel entirely comfortable that my ships were ready for a potential battle with another ship even though the Pug-bears hadn't armed any of their spaceships to this point.

The Pugs did have some armed shuttles, but those were used exclusively against planetary populations. The one time they came after our ship, I'd destroyed all of them. Even so, I'd been lucky. We had lost one of our FTL vanes, and only the fact that we were near a Sunny repair facility kept us from being restricted to in-system speeds and unable to return to Earth.

The Pug-bears' empire covered a lot of space, and we'd only begun to interfere with it. They controlled other planets besides those of the Sunnys. However, Frazzle informed me that these planets were generally not heavily populated by Pug-bears. The creatures each seemed to want to dominate a planet of their own.

The only planets in their control that could construct spaceships were those of the Sunnys. None of the other colonies save the planet of the Pugs even maintained their own ship.

The good thing about the Pug-bears was that they tended to stay there once they became established on the ground. Without help from the Pugs and Sunnys, they wouldn't be able to reach space again. I wasn't inclined to leave them alone for the long term, but I thought that exterminating them could wait if they were planet-bound.

If we captured the remaining FTL ships, the Pug-bears would be isolated, and we could safely leave their colonies to either survive on their own or become extinct. They'd never be able to create their own technology and would be biologically doomed by their physical structure to remain planet-bound.

I finally decided that we'd take the entire squadron to the first couple of planets and see how the liberation mission went. That would give me the chance to make sure that each commander was ready. If all went well at these two planets, I would dispatch Holmes and Rudy, who'd been promoted to his own ship, to handle the next two Sunny Planets. Joe and I would take the final one. It was far enough away from Earth that I thought Rudy and Holmes would be done with their two by the time Joe and I got there, dumped our yeast, and returned. We'd link up at the first Sunny planet and check on the progress of the yeast-dumping plan.

I would then take all of our ships to Earth. Once there, we'd check in with Jake. I wanted to make sure that he was holding his own against the Motherland forces.

When we got back, I had determined to disrupt their control over the territory they claimed. My conversation with the old veteran in West

Virginia had convinced me that something had to be done. There were too many people suffering needlessly due to their president's lust for power.

Perhaps they could be the basis of my planned human confederation, Jake's territory, and the North Park territory where Liz and I nominally lived.

If my daydreams began to materialize, humans would quickly begin to spread out over our single solar system and possibly others as well. For that to work smoothly, we'd have to have the various political and ethnic entities on Earth organized and getting along without conflict.

I'd had a chance to go over my ideas with Liz, and she more or less approved. She had pointed out that human society, as it had existed before the invasion, was a hodge-podge of over two hundred formal political entities and a bunch of informal ones too. Some were based on ethnicity, some on language, and some were conglomerations of various hostile factions forced together by outside influence.

She didn't think that they'd willingly agree to give up their customs and adhere to my proposed schedule of human rights. I was more of the opinion that the promise of the Sunnys' technology would lure them into agreeing to observe some basic amenities. If they didn't abide by these amenities, we would simply isolate them. They could then sink or swim on their own.

We had discussed the human tendency to cling to ethnic groups. In light of the new alien races that we now knew about, being biased against another human simply because they were different in terms of their national origin, religion, skin color, general configuration, or any of a number of equally ludicrous distinctions was the height of idiocy. Perhaps the fear of strangers bred into our genes from millions of years of what is essentially internecine conflict had once had a functional reason for existence. Now, it seemed like a left-over behavior pattern that would cause a fatal lack of cooperation, potentially resulting in the extinction of the human species.

I'd spent some time listing what I thought were necessary human rights. My list was getting very long and cumbersome when Liz took a look at it. Once again, she cut directly to the chase.

"Dec, you can't possibly list every right in every situation. You've got to come to grips with some principle that will cover all situations and then let the individuals involved decide if their rights are being denied. You'll have to set up some kind of universal tribunal that will handle appeals pertaining to rights. This can only work if you have a basic principle to apply," she said patiently.

As a result, I decided that the basic principles of libertarian philosophy were probably a good place to start. I did not want to rehash old ideas in their original form. Libertarianism was associated in many peoples' minds with the distortions imposed by propaganda for the old status quo. The truth is government, especially unfettered government, will do anything to obtain and hold power. I knew that libertarianism had received enough bad press to seem both trite and naive in the past when it was nothing of the sort.

After a considerable amount of thought during the early part of our voyage, I came up with a long set of ideas that I felt could be reduced to simple principles.

After writing and rewriting them several times, I again discussed my work with Liz. This time she stated that I needed to reduce the ideas to a simple list of principles that everyone could quickly memorize and understand. I agreed, but the task was a daunting one. I made a stab at it but eventually decided to wait, hoping that I'd have a moment of inspiration that would create the desired result.

I had another excuse for my lack of action since we had arrived at our first destination. The first Sunny system was awaiting liberation.

Chapter 28

We dropped out of FTL a long distance out in the first Sunny system. This was a far different type of solar system than we'd previously visited. It was jam-packed with objects. There were more planets than our own Sol boasted and correspondingly more rocks and debris, making in-system travel more complex at high speeds. If we struck a rock too large for our shield, well, that would leave the Pug-bears in control, and I couldn't fit that outcome into my world-view.

We observed carefully and used the ship's computer to analyze the system data. There were fourteen gas giants, ranging from the size of Neptune to larger than Jupiter, and three smaller earth-sized planets. The three smaller planets all orbited close to the star in roughly the same place as Venus, Earth, and Mars in our own system.

Two of the more remote gas giants orbited the sun on extremely divergent paths. Their orbital planes were both at about seventy degrees to the plane of the majority of the planets. It was likely that they'd been wandering objects that the star had captured. In fact, their paths were still unstable, and there was some indication that they would eventually cause problems for some of the other planets.

I could imagine two of the enormous masses colliding. Who knows what could happen? It might even result in the formation of a second star, and while I didn't think that it was a very likely pathway for the creation of a binary stellar system, it still seemed like it might be a possibility.

There was also a lot of debris floating in a wide range of orbits. The birth of this system must have been very messy. It had two wide asteroid belts separated by a gas giant. The early days of the system must have involved many meteor strikes.

The primary center of alien activity was the planet that was right in the heart of the Cinderella zone. That one was analogous to Earth, complete to a single, small moon that orbited it.

We detected signals coming from five mining centers in the asteroid belts, and our sensors showed two cloud scoops circling two separate gas giants. The Sunnys were making good use of the system's resources.

After some initial checking, Frazzle got a mining base on the radio and chattered for a few minutes. Then he turned to me to report.

"Dec, dis place is one I haven't been before. All of the Pug-bears on the planet. None in space, but there's three big, in-system ships full of Pugs that collect fuel and ore from the Sunny miners. Sunnys in system space is free, but work 'cause their families are on planet. It not a real bad place, except for the Pug-bears killing us when they feel like it," he said. He was excited, and his eyes sparkled. "Can we get Pug-bears out with the yeast? It be great if it makes them stupid again."

The Pugs' ships were armed freighters whose role was to collect tribute from the Sunny installations, then deliver it to a manufacturing base on the small moon that orbited the habitable planet. From there, goods and fuel were transported down to the surface for use by the residents and their rulers.

At the moment, the three freighters were on the far side of the system. They were approximately twenty light-hours away and wouldn't become aware of our entry for almost a day unless someone used an Ansible to alert them. I thought that we had enough time to start our spraying program before they'd realize we were there. Accordingly, we accelerated and headed in to try our luck with the Pug-bears.

On the way, I decided to send the full complement of shuttles from each ship with full loads of fuel and yeast. There was a lot of orbital traffic, and some of it was quite low. With any luck, my ships could blend in and make undetected sub-orbital passes over the single continent while they dropped their load.

The single planetary landmass was about equal to Africa and South America combined. The rest of the surface was covered with a shallow sea. We could see several hurricanes moving across the water as we neared the planet.

Due to the storms, most of the Sunny population lived farther inland, despite their predilection for ocean-side dwelling. The center of the large continent held a huge lake chain that made our Great Lakes look tiny. The shores of these lakes were covered with cities.

Frazzle contacted orbital control and was relieved to find that the staff was all Sunnys. The Pugs were apparently only used as tax collectors here.

It was easy to persuade the Sunny traffic controller to assist in our mission, and he collaborated with Frazzle to set up fake identities and flight plans for our shuttles. The crews took off on their mission, and we moved our squadron out past the moon, leaving Joe's ship behind to provide emergency support for the shuttle crews while we headed out to go Pug hunting.

Even though the planet only had a single continent, it would take the shuttles about ten hours to cover the area with yeast. We wanted to spread it as evenly as possible. We could have sprayed it more quickly, but Ian thought that wide dissemination would be a more successful approach. He had gone on the large shuttle to oversee the operation.

We left the shuttle crews busily spreading their tiny seeds of Pug-bear destruction and headed for the other side of the system on a course that passed close to the star and would get us to the Pug ships as quickly as possible.

They were loading fuel at one of the gas giants, far out in the outskirts of the system. The cloud scoop installed there pulled in raw hydro-carbons in vast amounts, and the chemicals were compressed and stored in huge tanks that orbited the gas giant in a distant orbit. The operation was so efficient that the Sunnys had to shut the scoop down for several days in between each visit by the Pugs.

It was a case where additional tankers were needed, but apparently, the Pug-bears weren't concerned about efficiency. There was enough fuel for their purposes, and if the system had to cease producing intermittently, it was up to the Sunnys to handle the extra labor of shut-down and start-up. A similar human installation would have had a continuous stream of tankers moving back and forth.

We approached the location where the tankers were loading the hydro-carbons. Two of the ships were attached to huge tanks with a series of giant hoses, while the third was floating off at a slight distance, either waiting its turn or waiting for the others to fill up so they could all depart at the same time.

Rudy shot the Em-drive pack off the free ship as soon as we got in range. I didn't want to destroy the vessels. The Sunnys needed the fuel for their society to continue functioning without hardship. Neither did I want the Pugs free to sneak around and shoot at us or our shuttles.

The other two ships began the slow process of disconnecting from the filling station. I could see space-suited Sunnys moving around near the hose connections.

Frazzle radioed them and told them to cease work. The ships were now in our possession. The Sunnys followed his orders and stopped the disconnecting operation, moving back to their small utility ships.

One of the Pug ships, the one that was nearly disconnected, started its engine and broke free of the final hose connection. The hose vented a long stream of hydrogen for several minutes, whipping around as the gas shot out and smashing into two of the Sunny utility ships, destroying them. It was a truly incredible sight. The thing was like a gigantic fire hose gone berserk. It would have continued for a long time, but the automatic shut-off on the surface of the large tank finally activated and stopped the flow.

We shot the Em-drive off that tanker also, but our anti-matter burst was too powerful, and we somehow holed the tanker's storage tanks. It sailed off, out of control, directly towards the gas giant, propelled by the venting hydrogen. Unless the Pugs could rig some kind of emergency engine, the ship was going to sink into the atmosphere within the next half hour.

The third ship's pilot seemed to be a little more sensible. He came on the comm system and apparently surrendered. As soon as we acknowledged their action, the crew boarded the tanker's small shuttle and made a run for the home planet, Em-drive firing at maximum.

I'd previously resolved not to take Pug captives, but I was saved the necessity of shooting at them. Holmes fired a burst, and their escaping ship vaporized.

I was congratulating myself on our success when a large plasma bolt flew by the bow of Holmes' ship. The first tanker was not wholly disabled. It had used its attitude jets to turn towards us and was now shooting.

All three of my ships accelerated instantly, moving us out of the path of the next bolt. We could see it coming a long way off, and I was relieved when we got out of the way.

In return, I used our waist cannon to fire an anti-matter pulse at their bow gun. It struck and erased the gun along with most of the tanker's bridge. A large gust of atmosphere shot out of the hole, the moisture in the air forming a cloud of ice crystals as it vented.

Frazzle, and I looked at each other. This hadn't gone nearly as well as I'd hoped. The second tanker was now too near the atmosphere of the gas giant to rescue, and the first was severely damaged. The only one we'd captured was the third, and that only was because it had been linked firmly to the chemical tank.

Frazzle spoke to the station Sunnys and told them they needed to continue the gas mining operation. They were going to try and repair the shot-up tanker and rig some kind of temporary controls for it. If they could, they'd fly both of them back to unload at the moon installation.

We couldn't afford to spend the time to help. Anyway, I figured the Sunnys could best operate their own systems. All we'd come to do was reduce the Pug-bears' influence on them.

Back at the planet again, we picked up our shuttles. They'd had no problems, and the single continent was now inoculated with brewer's yeast. We'd have to wait for a month or so to know if the scheme had worked. Meanwhile, we had more planets to treat.

The entire squadron turned and headed out-system under Em-drive, accelerating to near light speed in preparation for the transition to FTL.

Chapter 29

We were headed for the second Sunny planet to dump yeast on the Pug-bears. Despite the heavy in-system traffic, the exercise had gone well on the first planet. Our shuttles had managed to spread their payloads evenly across the sole continent.

Ian was nearly beside himself with excitement. He'd seen just enough of the first planet's ecology with the monitor's macro function to convince him that he couldn't wait for a chance to study the indigenous life forms. He was quite angry about me insisting that we continue on to the next planet.

"Damn it, Dec! How are we going to know if the yeast works unless we land and investigate? Jaunting off to another solar system is just a waste of time if the stuff doesn't do its job. Also, it might have some kind of bad effect on the planetary ecology. How am I going to know if we're doing the right thing?" he argued, nearly in tears from frustration.

I answered, "It will be enough if the yeast suppresses the Pug-bears' symbionts. The local ecosystems will have to take their chances –"

He interrupted my following sentence. "No! We could be doing irreparable damage –"

One interruption deserves another, so I continued, in a louder voice, drowning him out, "The local ecosystems are already being damaged irrevocably by the Pug-bears. The adults kill large animals indiscriminately, and the spider-form plays hell with small creatures. Allowing them to breed unchecked will do more damage than any amount of yeast."

I wasn't sure about that. The yeast could overwhelm the planet's life. I had nightmares of returning and finding that I'd converted the entire place to a planet-sized petri-dish full of fungus gone amok.

He shook his head in denial and responded with precisely that fear, "The yeast might do more damage than the aliens."

"Look, Ian, the Sunnys are aliens on these planets. They arrived on them years before the Pug-bears invaded. They are also technologically savvy. They can deal with whatever problems the yeast causes. They can't deal with the Pug-bears, so getting rid of them is our number one priority. You, yourself, swore to me that the yeast would suppress their symbionts, so we have to follow through with our plan. Every day that goes by sees more Sunny deaths caused by the Pug-bears. The Sunnys are not affected by the yeast, so I don't think the ecosystems will be affected either. The stuff doesn't attack the Pug-bears' physiology; it just chokes the symbionts out," I replied.

He thought about it for a moment, "Well, there is that, I guess. I'm fairly confident that most of our micro-organisms wouldn't be able to attack an alien life-form. They evolved to take advantage of Earth's ecological niches. But what happens if a local niche isn't available?"

"The only local niche I want the yeast to invade is the Pug-bears' brain-cases," I responded. "I don't care if it starves otherwise as long as it gets rid of their intelligence. If it does that, the Sunnys will have a fighting chance."

He latched onto my last statement as a weakness in my argument. "I thought you said they couldn't fight? How will they get rid of the Pug-bears, intelligent or not?"

"Frazzle provided them with plans for several kinds of traps. The Sunnys can build those, and the unintelligent Pug-bears will gradually fall prey to them. If necessary, we can help out later, but we've got to get the process started on all five planets to give them a chance. We've got to solve the problem posed by the Pug-bears, and the sooner, the better," I replied.

Liz had been listening to our discussion quietly, but now she chimed in, "That's true! There are still several FTL ships unaccounted for, and we don't want a ship full of Pug-bears showing up in our system planning on invading us again. They breed too quickly. We can't afford to give them another chance."

I added, "That's right. We've got to get them off all planets but their own and make sure they never get another chance to reach space."

I looked at him to see if he understood our urgency, then continued, "Besides, you'll have plenty of chances to study alien ecology. You can ride down on the next yeast-bombing run, and that will at least allow you to see two planets. Then later, when we come back to finish the job, you'll have a chance to visit the surfaces of all of the Sunny planets."

I was thinking of the surface of Kasm's planet and wondering if he'd want to study that as well. The odd beasts would provide subjects for years of study. It would be an irresistible attraction for any biologist despite the considerable danger the animal life posed.

During the next phase of our voyage, we allowed the yeast to divide and grow in our storage tanks. By the time we arrived near the next planetary system, the tiny fungi had replicated themselves so that we had more than we'd had when we left Earth.

Several days later, we arrived in the second Sunny system. Like the last system, this one was like nothing I'd visited in the past. The star was a young one, and the system, like the last, was full of dirt, dust, and rocks of all sizes but only had one single, massive planet. The planet was a gas giant that I judged was near twice the size of Jupiter.

It wasn't quite a second star, but it was close. There was a lot of radiation coming from it, and it almost certainly had some degree of fusion going on down below the miles and miles of dense gas that served as its atmosphere.

The Sunnys had colonized the largest of its moons. The moon was big enough to be viewed as a planet in its own right and had its own atmosphere. It was slightly larger than Earth in diameter, but its mass was less since it was composed of lighter materials.

There were numerous other moons, ranging from objects the size of Titan down to small rocks that orbited in a complicated dance around the giant planet. Their orbits intersected, which must have resulted in collisions in the recent past. The big moon's surface revealed several large scars and numerous craters, indicating that it was still subject to bombardment. I briefly wondered how the Sunnys expected to avoid being hit by the falling rocks and why they'd picked this location to colonize.

As our ships approached the star, I saw their answer to the meteors. It was an engineering feat that made me gasp. Twenty orbital stations traveled around the moon in crossing orbital paths but at slightly different altitudes. The Sunnys had set up an immense orbital deflection field.

They'd used the same system that protected their spaceships, meaning that the field was a derivative of their artificial gravity. This system provided gravity within the ships and could be used to repel external objects to protect the ships from being struck by high-velocity dust or micro-meteors. I now saw that it was even more flexible than I'd realized. It could be used across the entire surface of a planet, providing an effective shield against the young stellar system's debris.

Each of the orbiting stations contributed to the shield. Frazzle explained to me that it wasn't a single shield. Each station created its own shield, extending it as far as possible. The large number of the orbiting fields provided a moving web of deflection that pushed most of the junk away from courses that would directly impact the surface. Large objects that would have overwhelmed the station fields were dealt with individually, but they were, fortunately, few in number.

The lowest orbital station was the one that hosted calling ships. It was safely below the interlacing fields and was unlikely to be struck by objects. It currently hosted four large FTL ships. The Pug-bears and Pugs were here in force.

On seeing this, Frazzle commented that there were only two more unaccounted for FTL ships to the best of his knowledge. We'd destroyed some and captured others. The Pug-bears' Sunny-provided FTL-capable fleet had never been extensive. They had previously used colony ships to invade the planets under their control. The FTL ships were a new development.

This was an excellent opportunity for us. If we could capture or destroy these four ships, it would go a long way towards clearing the Pug-bears out of space. If we could get these ships and if we chanced on the other enemy FTLs at another planet, I could begin to see an end to this chasing around, trying to destroy the Pug-bears' empire.

We approached the moon over the next few hours, giving Frazzle time to use the comm system and contact the Sunny traffic control. Once again, this worked well. These Sunnys, like all of the others, were more than willing to keep the knowledge of our presence from their masters.

Our approach was far from smooth. The dirty system interposed navigational hazards that we had to avoid. Every so often, we had to change our course slightly to avoid a cluster of asteroids, and there was an almost constant flare around the bows of our ships caused by small rocks and dust striking the deflection shields. Once or twice, a distant clang was paired with a slight shock to the ship as larger stones made it through and struck the bow shield itself. I was apprehensive that one of those strikes would knock our bow cannon out.

That cannon was mounted on the exact tip of the bow shield, so it was a good target for rocks. Its power supply relied on an armored cable that led across the shield's surface to where it attached to the ship's power at the rear of the shield. This cable was an additional weak point. The cannon itself was heavy and durable enough to withstand minor strikes, but the cable could be easily severed if even a smaller rock happened to strike it. The gun would still fire on battery power if that happened, but the number of shots was strictly limited.

I reflected on the desirability of capturing the ships versus simply shooting them. Shooting them would probably be easier, but I wanted them to add to my growing fleet. I could

see the need to provide transportation to the Sim-tigers and the Sunnys, at least until the Sunnys had the opportunity to create more ships of their own.

We began to prepare for what would surely be a battle.

Chapter 30

The orbital station we were approaching looked strange to me. It was configured like a large disc, oriented to look like an immense Frisbee sailing around the planet. It had internal gravity and didn't rotate, so angular momentum wasn't a factor. We hadn't seen this type of station before.

The normal, rotating, starfish-shaped station used its arms for different purposes; some for Pug-bear residences, one for the Sunnys, some for storage or maintenance, and usually one for the Pugs. The Pugs' arm always had its own gas mixture due to their special breathing requirements. I'd drawn a few breaths of their air before, and, as far as I was concerned, it was foul, but they couldn't survive in our air for long without their skin-tight pressure suits. When attacking one starfish station, I'd shot a hole in the Pugs' residence arm, evacuating it and ridding us of most of the Pugs in one simple act.

This disc-shaped station didn't offer any obvious targets, and, as a result, it might be a harder nut to crack. We would have to invade and fight our way through the interior. That had the potential to be a difficult task, and it would be even more complicated if the Sunny crew were mixed in with their masters.

Frazzle had spoken to the station Sunnys at length. There was a large contingent of Pugs on the station, including the crews from the four FTL ships. They mainly stayed in their residence area, but the ships each held a skeleton crew capable of flying them in emergencies.

Apparently, the Sunnys' improvised planetary shield wasn't quite as effective as I'd initially believed it to be. There were so many rocks flying around randomly in the system that once in a while, one was on an unlucky trajectory that would somehow find its way through the semi-overlapping deflection fields. The station was a few minutes below the shields, which gave them a little warning if something was coming. They'd take that time to move their ships if it looked like the object was going to pose a danger to them.

As we approached, we could see that the disc was shielded on the side it presented to space. This made it look even more frisbee-like. The only exception to the frisbee look was the docking ports. They were arranged around the edge of the disc, with the four enemy ships occupying every other port. This left four additional ports. I instantly decided that some of my ships would dock at them. If we could physically link to the station and invade simultaneously through the transporter system, it would provide the maximum element of surprise.

We had approached to within a thousand miles. The Marines on each ship were ready to go, and it was just in time. I'd conferenced with Rudy, Holmes, and Joe, and they agreed with my initial plan to mix up our attack. Rudy and Joe would go in and dock immediately, separated by two Pug ships. Frazzle had arranged with the station for each of them to attach between two of the already docked ships.

Their Marines would exit and head directly for the Pugs' ships, dispersing in two assault groups, one for each of the two adjacent ports. We hoped that they'd be able to fight their way onto each of the four ships, preventing them from detaching and fleeing.

Holmes was to dispatch his strike force in a shuttle that would dock at one of the station's several shuttle ports. These were underneath the massive shield on the planet side of the structure. Their job was to take the shuttle-craft that were currently attached, preventing anyone from trying to escape.

My ship would hang back, providing cover for the docking ships, while my marine force went through the transporter system. They'd enter the station, arriving near the control room, which was their objective. They were to capture and secure it. There were likely to be Pug-bears in or near the control room, so Kasm's force would go through the transporter first. With any luck, they'd be able to deal with the Pug-bears, allowing the Marines the freedom to go after the Pugs without having to worry about the nasty aliens' mental control.

I thought the net effect would be so confusing that the Pugs, never quick thinkers, would not respond well. We'd shortly have control of the station and the four FTL ships if all went as planned.

We were almost ready to start our attack when Frazzle exclaimed from his seat at the control boards, "Dec! Come see dis!"

He pointed at the video monitor, and I quickly stepped over to his position. I was rewarded with a close-up view of the Pugs' ships. Two of them initially looked strange, and I glanced at Frazzle inquiringly. He pointed with one hand while he increased the magnification with the other.

The two ships were armed! Either the Pug-bears or the Pugs had realized that opposition in space required ship-mounted weapons. It was probably the Pugs' idea. The Pug-bears were only oriented towards individual physical fighting, but the Pugs were familiar with significant battles and could plan a little better than their masters.

Regardless of which species had come up with the idea, my ships were no longer the only armed ones in the fray. It was bad enough facing the small armed shuttle-craft that the Pugs had flown against me in my first space battle, now we had to face ship-mounted weapons that could undoubtedly draw on the massive power of the FTL's reactors.

My first thought was to have Rudy direct all of his Marines towards the armed ships, but after a moment, I compromised. His orders had been good, and changing them right before the attack would cause confusion. Instead, I moved over behind Liz, who was operating the weapons computer.

She looked up at me, her lower lip held between her teeth, a gesture she sometimes used when she was concentrating. I reached over her shoulder and pointed at the two armed ships.

"Liz, look at those. They're armed. Set the system to target those ships and lock it on them. If they start shooting or even move their guns, take them out," I ordered. I didn't want to risk having them shoot at us. The cannons they'd mounted were anti-matter projectors. A direct hit would be deadly, and we couldn't afford to lose any of our ships.

She gasped in dismay and quickly locked the targeting designators on the two ships.

Inspecting the enemy under high magnification revealed that they had mounted four cannons towards the front of their ships, near the rear edge of the bow shield. Not a bad arrangement, I reflected. They were able to fire straight forward with all four of the weapons simultaneously. My mounting system allowed for three forward blasts, the two waist guns, and the bow gun. In addition, their guns were gimbaled like ours, so they could swivel to cover a wide range.

This might not be as easy as I'd planned. I hoped the marine attack would be sufficiently disruptive. It would be far better if the enemy fell before getting their ships moving.

Rudy and Joe were approaching their docking stations, their ships gliding smoothly toward the grapples. As they hooked up with the station, first Rudy and then Joe clicked their radios three times. The Marines were on their way.

My strike force was waiting at the transporter. I turned to Frazzle and asked, "Is the transporter set for our Marines to board?"

He nodded affirmatively.

I mentally contacted Kasm, "The docking ships are attacking. You're clear to board."

His mental voice came back clearly, "On our way." I caught a passing thought that he hadn't intended to send, "This should be fun!"

Holmes' ship was just passing into the shadow of the station, moving out of sight below it, and I could see his shuttle detach as it headed for the shuttle port.

Our attack was moving, and our timing had been good so far. I drew a couple of calming breaths. The thought came to me that all plans are good until they encounter the enemy. What happens next is usually decided by the commander who thinks more quickly and can adapt to the unexpected circumstances that are sure to arise. It also helps to have a good communication system to coordinate your forces.

I extended my mental senses to try and encompass the entire attack. The strike forces that were to invade the four ships were just ready to pass through the locks into the ships. The shuttle assault force was spreading out over the shuttle-bay floor and had already captured several of the attached craft.

I checked on Kasm and found him in the full fury of battle. His Sim-tiger force was faced with a combined group of Pug-bears and Pugs. The Sim-tigers were hiding while the Pugs shot at them, practically raving in their desire to get at the Pug-bears. The Pug-bears were attacking mentally, trying to freeze his forces in place.

Their attack was affecting the Marines. Unshielded humans usually couldn't cope with their mental commands. I drew a deep breath and concentrated, trying to force my mental shielding out to cover all of my men. I could feel it starting to work, and then, suddenly, my effort was joined by Liz. She had sensed what I was trying to do and was adding her mental energy to the task.

Her reinforcement helped, and I could sense the Marines starting to shake free of the Pug-bears' thrall. They were mainly still outside the area where the Pugs were shooting, and a couple of them raced into position and started shooting back.

Their shots startled the Pug-bears, and they lost control of the rest of the men. My shielding effort became easier as more Marines reached cover and started shooting.

The Pugs had been standing in the hallway to the control room, completely in the open, and the Marines' return fire was devastating. The few survivors fell back quickly around a corner to regroup.

That was too much for the Pug-bears. Their natural fury took over, and they charged out of the control room directly down the hall towards my forces. They advanced quickly but then ran head-on into Kasm's group.

The mental images I was receiving became blurred with the intensity of the fight. I tried to keep up my shielding but realized that it was unnecessary. The Pug-bears were too furious and too hard-pressed to use their mental attack.

I gasped and popped back into my normal mental mode, realizing, as I did, that I wasn't hovering over the battle but was still standing on our bridge. I was sweating, and my hands were shaking. I glanced at Liz, and her face was pale with the strain she'd been under, helping me.

I grimaced at her, and in return, she lifted her lip in a grin that looked more like a snarl.

The communicator suddenly came to life as Rudy called, "Dec! We've got two of their ships, but there's hard fighting in the other two. We're pinned down and not making progress. We've got the outermost two under control. The two middle ones are full of Pugs, and they're causing a lot of trouble."

Just as his message finished, I saw a cloud of debris fly away from the docking grapples on one of the two ships. It had broken free of the station and headed out, its Em-drive on full, dangerously close to the station. It figured; it was one of the armed ones.

Chapter 31

The Pugs' ship passed over the station's top, heading away from the planet/moon. It was on a trajectory that meant it would move closer to the giant planet in its haste to escape.

"Frazzle, get us after that ship!" I yelled.

He did. We instantly accelerated at maximum and turned to a parallel course. We were about a hundred klicks out, and our turn placed us on a gradual intercept course. Our ship jumped ahead under full power, heading towards the gas giant's farther horizon in pursuit.

The dust and rocks formed a continuous flare as they bounced off our shield. So far, we had struck nothing that the shield couldn't handle, and I mentally prayed that condition would continue. As we moved inside the station's orbit, the dust thinned, although there were clots and streamers along with thicker patches.

The orbital shield system made a noticeable difference. The smaller objects were far less likely to bull their way through the overlapping shields. Those that got through were moving at a shallow angle towards the shields and filtered through the gaps between their overlapping configuration, usually ending up in orbit around the moon.

The Pugs were staying ahead of us. It looked like their ship was at least as fast as ours. If it were a newer generation, it might even be faster. I wondered if their transporter was active. Perhaps we could get on board that way.

"Frazzle, can we link to the ship's transporter?" I shouted.

He flinched. I realized I was practically yelling in his ear from excitement.

"I checked dere system. Not working. Maybe dey turned it off, but we can't use it," he answered.

That was out. We'd have to link up or, most likely, shoot at them.

Just as I thought about shooting, a heavier patch of dust in front of us developed a hole through its center. They were shooting at us!

I didn't know if they were nervous or their system wasn't as accurate as ours, and I didn't want to wait to find out.

"Shoot! Liz, shoot!" I shouted.

She triggered the weapons, and our fire-control computer released a triple burst from both waist guns and the bow gun simultaneously.

The enemy ship was moving behind a thicker patch of dust as we fired. The dust dissipated most of our anti-matter burst, and I thought that we'd missed them. Their ship rolled, veering as if it was changing course. As it continued its roll, I saw through the dust that we had hit one of its FTL vanes. The sudden mass shift caused by losing half the vane had caused the instability.

There was a sudden faint flash ahead of us as another hole burned through the dust. Frazzle gave a chirp of alarm, and our ship shuddered.

We'd taken a hit somewhere. I hoped our hull was intact and was somewhat gratified when Frazzle squeaked out, "De small shuttle gone!"

They'd burned off our shuttlecraft. As much as I hated to lose it, it was lucky for us it had taken the bulk of the charge.

Liz had been adjusting the weapons system, working on another firing solution. The guns fired again, burning a momentary hole through the now thickening dust cloud.

The dust masked the Pug ship for a moment. The cloud was thick, and we couldn't see them. I looked at the weapons control monitor and saw that it was tracking two objects.

"Liz, what happened? Did they launch a shuttle? What's that second thing?" I asked.

She hesitated, trying to get the system to focus through the interference, then answered, "I can't tell what's going on. We need to get closer."

That was something I was reluctant to do. They'd been a little too accurate for me to want to risk another hit. The edge of the dust cloud was approaching rapidly. It would be better to wait until they cleared the obstruction.

"Liz, aim at the edge of the cloud and wait for them to come out," I sent. I was going to give her the order out loud but then realized that I'd thought it before my mouth was ready to speak.

She nodded and made an adjustment.

There was a glint of reflected sunlight as the enemy ship passed through a thin part of the cloud, and then it sailed out into complete visibility. Liz tensed, ready to shoot.

"Stop!" I shouted.

The Pugs' ship was a wreck. The shot had cut it into two separate pieces, and these were what we'd detected. Both pieces were now spiraling around, headed for quick oblivion in the nearby atmosphere of the gas giant. As we watched, the pieces skipped off the upper reaches of the atmosphere and then plunged downwards, shedding red-hot metal and burning debris as they went. The pieces quickly disappeared into the thick cloud cover.

Frazzle turned our ship, and we headed back towards the station, grateful that our encounter had been no worse.

Damage control had sealed off the partially destroyed port, and our hull was secure. We were going to miss the small shuttle, but there were several on the underside of the station, and I hoped we could pick up one of these as a replacement. We stayed at battle stations. There was still fighting going on, and the second armed ship had not yet fallen under Rudy's control.

As we approached, I had a moment to think. If the Pugs were going to come after us with anti-matter armed ships, we'd need some kind of defense. The problem was that the stuff destroyed anything that it struck. Our bow deflection shield might shed part of the beam, but the anti-matter traveled at nearly light speed, and at least part of it would get through the shield and create damage.

We were getting closer to the station when Rudy called in again, "We've got control of all three ships. The Pugs are all dead, and the Sim-tigers and Marines have finished off all the Pug-bears. I'm trying to reach the shuttle bay assault team to check their status."

A little later, he called again with the news that the shuttle bay was under our control, but no functional shuttles were left. The fighting had damaged all of them.

As he finished, I suddenly formulated an idea. The dust had acted to attenuate the anti-matter charges. What if we could use our point-gravity control to hold a cloud of heavy dust or maybe metal filings out as a shield? Perhaps that would weaken an incoming anti-matter shot enough to minimize damage. The problem lay in getting it into place to intercept the beam. That might be a challenging task, but I thought the Sunnys could probably figure out a way to accomplish it. They were very creative with issues of personal safety.

Chapter 32

Rudy and Holmes had left to visit their two assigned planets, and my two remaining ships were now heading for the most distant Sunny world. It would take almost twenty days for us to arrive, and we were now on the nineteenth day. I expected our ship to drop out of FTL early in tomorrow's day shift.

We'd left the unarmed two of the three captured ships in the care of the Sunnys. In addition to one of our Sunny pilots, I had insisted on crewing the captured armed vessel with a small group of Marines along with a couple of Sim-tigers for back-up, and in case any Pug-bears happened along. We'd made sure the ship was supplied, and the crew had taken it out to the extreme edge of the system where it would discretely hang around on watch until we returned for the trip back to Earth. I'd initially planned to re-visit the first liberated (I hoped) planet to check on the yeast's progress rather than the second, but I reasoned the second would do just as well. We'd pick up the armed ship then.

The other two ships had been turned over to the Sunnys with a warning to keep them from being recaptured. Telling them to stay away from the Pug-bears was probably unnecessary, but I couldn't help myself. I wanted to make sure they were careful. It wouldn't do to allow those ships to fall back under enemy control.

There were only two other FTL ships in the Pug-bear fleet as I currently understood it. If they showed up, I was prepared to attempt their capture. If not, we'd eventually have to go hunting for them. Leaving the Pug-bears with the capability for space travel was a sure recipe for trouble. I'd spent a lot of effort to isolate the troublesome creatures, and I wanted them to remain isolated.

My only alternative to that strategy was to drop a planet-killing-sized rock on their heads. Due to a possibly misplaced sense of conscience, I didn't want to go that far. I didn't want to be known as the first human who had destroyed a planet and an entire alien species.

Liz and I were sitting in the cafeteria when Kasm sauntered in, followed closely by Jefferson. I felt a little pang at the sight. It wasn't actually like I'd lost my cat, even though he spent a lot of his time with Kasm. He still slept with us more often than not, but during his waking periods, he was most likely to be found hovering around the big, green-striped creature. I guess hanging with the Sim-tigers made him feel like he was part of an invincible pride.

Kasm trailed his manipulating hand over my back as he walked by. He seemed to be rather fascinated with our musculature and smooth skins. If he hadn't been an alien, I wouldn't have put up with being petted. As it was, he patted us about as much and in much the same way as we patted Jefferson. It might have been humiliating, except that I knew he really cared for us.

He got something from one of the food synthesizers that provided raw meat or a reasonable facsimile and returned to curl up on the floor near our feet. Only then did he begin to communicate.

"Dec, Liz, I've been thinking," his thoughts came through clearly. "We now have enough starships to control the Pug-bears and Pugs. I think that my planet needs at least one."

He hastened to add, "It's not that we're interested or maybe even able to fly the thing, but I think Tukoli needs its own fleet for defense. It would place us on a more nearly even footing with you humans and the Sunnys."

I replied out loud, "Yes. I can see that. I've been thinking something like that also. You see, I believe that our three species would benefit by cooperating. Your people and mine get along well, and together we can provide a measure of security for the pacifistic Sunnys. We may be able to establish some form of interplanetary trade. I don't know what the Sunnys or your people need or what your planet has to trade, but we can figure that out later. If we established regular traffic back and forth between our planets and maintained a joint force for defense, it might give us the security and means to build our civilizations into something more than they are now."

He mused for a bit and then sent, "I see what you mean. One thing from Earth that I know all of my people would like is venison. During my time on your planet, I've gotten kind of addicted to deer meat. It's a delicacy unlike anything on Tukoli."

He sighed, "I suppose that we'll need some arms also. We do like your swords. That's a given, and I think we could use some specialized anti-matter projectors if they were designed for our use. Dangerous beasts, like the Night Stalkers, can't always be avoided, and it would be nice to have a weapon that would stop them."

He was indirectly referring to the deaths of his mate and son, and I caught an overtone of sadness in his thought.

Liz spoke, "I'm sure that could be arranged. In addition, I expect that at least some humans would like the opportunity to visit Tukoli or perhaps even live there. Our species usually likes adventure, and some would surely enjoy the opportunity to explore your planet."

I said, "That's true. Don't forget the Sunny planets. If we can get rid of all of the Pug-bears and Pugs, they might become attractive places to visit also."

We all looked up as Frazzle walked in. He had a business-like air about him that led me to expect him to start in about our arrival tomorrow. Instead, he started on almost the same topic that Kasm had brought up.

"Dec, you give the two FTL ships to the Sunnys. I talked to dem, and we will be very careful with the ships. Pug-bears never going to get their control back," he started.

I responded, "That's good. I'd hate to have to do all of this again."

He looked at Kasm momentarily and then said, "Maybe we all works together. Maybe we make agreement to be big family with three different peoples. We Sunnys can make technologies that humans and Sim-tigers can't do yet. You learns, but maybe we can trade our machines for protection."

He paused again and then thought of something, "And, fish. Yes, definitely human-world fish." He licked his lips and added, "Dey good!"

Kasm looked at me, and I caught his thought, "Bargain hard, Dec. He has something else in mind also."

"Frazzle, that's just what we were discussing. I believe that our three species would do well to form an alliance. We could trade goods and services, including defense," I said.

Frazzle smiled with his tight grin. The Sunnys didn't show their teeth when they smiled. Possibly that was too aggressive to suit them.

He said, "We can always use some of the food from your planet. We likes de fish and maybe some of plants too. I think we can make alliance like you say. Sim-tigers maybe don't have as much on their planet for us, but they good fighters and can provide protection."

Despite my prior thinking about mutual defense, that statement seemed to imply that defense might be necessary.

I asked, "If we can isolate the Pug-bears and Pugs, is there anything else that we have to worry about?"

Frazzle made a churring noise in his throat, "Errrrrr, maybes. Dere some sign of other creatures far out past our boundaries. We never contacted. Then the Pug-bears took over, and we been slaves. I don't know if there be a potential problem or not, but better to be safe."

This was news! I had been primarily concerned about another Pug-bear break-out, with maybe the remote secondary possibility that the Pugs might one day develop into a threat on their own. However, if there were other aliens somewhere, we would eventually encounter them. There seemed to me to be a possibility that we'd have about an equal chance of cooperation or conflict, depending on what each species wanted. As Frazzle had said, "Better to be safe." Also, better to be prepared, I thought.

I concluded, "It seems like we have the beginning of what we could call the Inter-species Space Confederacy. The details will have to be worked out, but from our experience together, I know all three species can cooperate and work together for mutual benefit."

"I like that," Liz interjected. "The ISC. It seems promising. Let's make it happen!"

Frazzle nodded in solemn agreement while Kasm reached out and patted Liz on her thigh. It was enough to make me grin. Maybe it would work.

Chapter 33

We dropped out of FTL before I'd gotten through with breakfast, and I carried a kind of protein bar into the bridge, eating hastily. I was raising the bar for another bite when I saw the display monitor. It was amazing. I suddenly realized that my hand was halfway to my mouth, and my mouth was hanging open. I closed it with a snap.

It seemed like each solar system we visited was even more impressive than the last. This one was incredible. It was a binary system, and the two stars were close together. So close, in fact, that there was a colorful steam of gas flowing from the smaller member of the pair to the larger one. The result was spectacular. The larger star was emitting a constant barrage of flares and radiation. The smaller star showed large dark storms on the side away from the stream of its life's blood that was being slowly ripped away.

There was only a single planet left in the system. The closely orbiting stars had eaten all of their planets save the most distant. It had somehow managed to bump its orbit far enough out to be momentarily safe. It was so far away that it orbited both stars in a strange elliptic path. The seasons on the planet must be crazily variable. At times, it was far from both stars and then close to the smaller, yellow one, then far again, then close to the large, reddish one.

It was evident that this system couldn't be stable. It would inevitably reach a point where the cannibal member of the stellar pair had absorbed enough mass to go nova. The primary question was, how long would that take? The secondary question that popped into my mind involved the overall level of radiation here. Would we be safe if we moved into orbit around the Sunny planet?

I shot a glance at Frazzle and asked, "How can your people feel safe on that planet?"

His answer was interesting. "We's calculated dat the big sun won't get ready to 'splode for over a thousand years. We got time to live here and study the evolution of the system. The colony here was going to be just for science studies, but the Pug-bears came, and they don't cares about that. They probably won't even think about leaving until the star blows up. Many of us going to die if that happens."

"Well, how about the solar radiation level? Is it too high for us to approach?" I continued.

"We be safe if we come into de planet orbit, but not to go closer to the stars," he said, waving his hand at the screen in emphasis.

"It still looks to me like there might be a lot of radiation in this system," I said, unwilling to let the topic go. I didn't know if the Sunnys were as sensitive to radiation as humans. Maybe they could ignore levels that would cause us problems.

"Well, de radiation is high in space, but de planet got an iron core spinning, that gives a lot of magnet protection. But Dec, don't worry. The ship has heavy shielding. Our deflection shield won't let extra radiation through and –"

He stopped with a chirp in mid-explanation, then continued, "Oh! I never telled you this. The deflection shield is strongest at front of ship, but it goes over all of the skin of ship. Too weak to protect against Pug weapons, but it will protect against some radiation. Still can't get too close to the stars. The gas going from the little one is high in radiation, and when it hits the hot part of atmosphere of the big one, it makes lots of particles fly out. Very bad for life if too close or unshielded."

Liz had wandered in and overheard the tail end of our discussion. She knew a lot more about astronomy and physics than I did, and, as usual, she couldn't help displaying her knowledge.

"We call the outer part of the star's atmosphere the corona. It's a thin plasma that is much hotter than the inner layers," she said, unnecessarily in my opinion.

Frazzle blinked and added, "Yes, de inner layers of gas not so hot, but then go through a transition zone. Zone not very thick, but gas much hotter on outside than inside."

I shook my head, "Well, that clears that up, but I want to know, is the radiation around the planet much higher than around other Sunny planets or Earth?"

Frazzle waved his hand in dismissal of the notion, "Not much. Big star sucks up most of the stuff from small one. Planet get only little more than if it goes around one big star. We be carefuls not to fly through polar zones of big star, though. Radiation spikes dere."

We still had to finish our mission. I decided to take the radiation issue on faith and directed Frazzle to head for the station. While we'd talked, we'd traveled to within a few light minutes of the planet.

"Let's get on with the bombing mission, Frazzle," I said. "Are there any ships in this system now?"

He glanced at the monitor and answered, "No. Science shuttles only, but they not flying right now. I don't think the Pug-bears care about science much."

"How about the station, are there Pugs or Pug-bears on it?" Liz asked.

Frazzle hummed under his breath and then said, "I call. You wait a bit, and we find out."

He was as good as his word. He got on the comm and was shortly talking to a rather excited Sunny. They chattered and whistled for a few minutes, and then Frazzle's shoulders dropped in dismay. He turned to us and said, "De station full of Pugses, also some Pug-bears there. Only one Sunny there left alive. Pug-bears got mad, killed all 'cept him. He hide in science shuttle. Take it off the station and is now following station in orbit may be behind it a minute or two. Pug-bears don't find his mind yet, so he still free, but he's worried they might find him. There be Sunnys and some Pug-bears on planet surface, too."

"Let's see if we can pick him up. Can you locate the shuttle," I pointed at the screen.

He adjusted some of the sensor controls and then chirped in excitement, "Got him!"

I called Joe and asked him to hold his position in orbit around the planet. He responded that his shuttles were ready to start with the yeast dispersion program. I gave permission, and they launched, heading downwards.

Frazzle was working on centering the science shuttle on the screen. When he got it lined up, we accelerated in its direction.

"We be there in a few minutes. I get docking grapples ready to lock on," he said.

"Let him know we're picking him up," I ordered.

I picked up the intercom and alerted the Marines that we'd shortly have company. I wanted them to be there to meet him. I didn't think there was any chance of treachery, but it wasn't out of the realm of possibility for the Sunny to be under the control of a Pug-bear riding in the shuttle with him.

When I finished, Frazzle looked at me and said, "I never think of something like dat. You got devious mind, Dec. I call one of us to be there too. If that station Sunny come in and see only you humans, he might be too afraid. It best to have one of my peoples there too."

"I always try to think of the most unpleasant tricks the enemy can play, Frazzle. That way, I'm prepared if they happen. I'm also happy when they don't think of them," I said, grinning.

Liz snorted but didn't comment.

We approached the small shuttlecraft, and it passed over the bridge window, gliding along about a hundred feet off the surface of our ship. Directly there was a distant clang and thud as the grapples locked on. About a minute later, one of the Marines called in on the intercom, "We've got him. Heading for the bridge now."

They came through the transporter shortly after the call. The Sunny's eyes were wide, and his nostrils were distended, showing that he was frightened.

It looked like he was just on this side of panic. The reason became apparent. Kasm came out of the transporter right behind him.

The Sunny was smaller than average. I looked a second time and realized that he was very young. He'd been lucky to survive the Pug-bears' rage and even luckier that he knew how to fly the shuttle.

Frazzle stood up, and the small one dashed over to him. They embraced, and the little guy looked over Frazzle's shoulder at me, his eyes wide and dark.

Frazzle turned, letting go of him, and indicated Liz and me, chirping and whistling for all he was worth. The smaller Sunny visibly calmed down. They were easy to panic, but they shifted their emotions far more rapidly than humans.

He let go of Frazzle, walked over, and hugged my leg, chirping.

Frazzle said, "He thanking you for saving him."

I reached out mentally and very gently touched the little one's mind, "You're safe here. There is no one on this ship for you to fear."

He jumped, and then his eyes flashed over to Kasm. He pointed at our green-striped friend, and I received a weak query, "What about him?"

Kasm understood the problem and casually sauntered over to where we were. He patted the small Sunny on the head as he walked by, then patted Liz on the shoulder and lay down on the floor beside her.

That seemed to do it. The young Sunny relaxed. He knew he was safe.

The Sunny colony on the planet was not very large, but enough Pug-bears were running around on the surface to make it impossible to hunt them down individually. We'd have to use the yeast technique.

Shortly, our remaining shuttle was also on its way down into the atmosphere, bearing a load of fungi. We'd be here for several hours while it joined Joe's shuttles and disseminated its load across the surface.

That left me with another problem. What was I going to do with the orbital station full of Pugs and Pug-bears? I really couldn't see any reason to try and clear it manually. We'd probably lose men, and that was something I didn't want to do.

Neither did I want to shoot it out of existence. The planet-bound Sunnys would eventually need to evacuate the system. The stars might be stable for another thousand years or so, but there was no predicting exactly how accurate that number was.

To get off-planet, the Sunnys could transport up to an FTL, assuming that one with transporter capability arrived to pick

them up. If it were an older ship, they could transport to the station and then board the docked ship. That meant that it would be a good idea to leave the station intact, if possible.

We gradually overhauled the structure. We came up to it from behind, gradually approaching in a slightly lower orbit. As we got close, I could see that it was one of the starfish-shaped ones. The Pugs were all in their own wing, and the Pug-bears were in theirs. I checked mentally, and aside from a small group of Pugs operating the control bridge, the residents were isolated in their particular habitats.

I briefly wondered what future generations of Sunnys would say about me in their histories. Probably something along the line of 'bloodthirsty,' I assumed. Hattie was currently sitting at the weapons station. I thought about replacing her, wondering what effect shooting at essentially helpless sentient creatures would have on her psyche.

I started to ask her to move, but before I could, she asked, "Do you want me to shoot the station? If it's full of the enemy, we have got to take it out."

I belatedly remembered the cold way she'd shot the Motherland soldiers and realized that she wasn't someone who needed protecting.

"Yes, Hattie. Let me designate the arms we need to perforate. I don't want to destroy the entire station. We just need to shoot holes in, let me see..." I projected my mind outward to the station, locating the targets.

"Here and here," I said as I used the fire-control computer's laser to point at the two occupied habitat arms. "Try not to disintegrate too much of the mass. It will throw the stations' rotation off and maybe cause it to fall apart. I want to leave it so that the Sunnys can repair it if they need to."

She carefully set up the topside waist gun and then triggered two very brief bursts. They were deadly accurate. I looked closely and realized that the girl had out-thought me. I'd only considered shooting small holes in the arms. She'd shot a hole in the leading edge of one and the trailing edge of the other. The venting atmosphere from each hole imparted angular momentum to the station, but the two jets were in opposite directions and nicely canceled each other.

The station shuddered but didn't noticeably change orbit or rotation. I projected my mental sense in time to catch the final frenzied thoughts of the Pug-bears. Then there was nothing left alive in the structure.

We waited around for some hours until the shuttles had dumped their loads in the atmosphere. Frazzle transmitted trap-making instructions down to the surface Sunnys along with the message that they'd have to hold on until we could get some reinforcements here to help them.

They were overjoyed at the news that the Pug-bears would gradually lose their intelligence. They were more than ready for freedom.

Once the shuttles were picked up, we turned and accelerated out-system, heading towards our rendezvous with the other ships.

Chapter 33

Our two ships exited faster than light mode, shuddering a little as they returned to the different state of being that we thought of as reality. I'd thought about FTL travel a little and, although I didn't precisely understand what happened, I did know that the ship's matter somehow changed. I thought its energy wave traveled, re-materializing at the end of the voyage when the engine shut down in response to the computer's signal that we'd arrived near our destination.

As far as humans were concerned, traveling along with the ship in its energy state, reality hadn't changed. We still existed and interacted as usual. I wondered about the temporal distortion that I'd thought would be a part of FTL travel. Frazzle put that to rest for me.

"De pieces of light, when it seems to be particles –" he started.

"Photons, you mean?" I interjected.

"Yes, photons, you calls them. Dey have no time. From their perspective, time doesn't pass. Only from our side, we see they take time to go from place to place. The waves in the basement of space that the FTL engine puts our own wave pattern on top of, those waves travel much faster than light. Maybe a billion times faster or more. Our wave pattern is carried by those waves, and we go much faster than light, not a billion times 'cause they slippages, so we don't go so fast, but faster."

He looked to see if I was following him. I nodded as if I was, even though I was somewhat confused. It seemed like he was saying we were using the torsion waves in the quantum plenum in much the same way a surfer uses ocean waves. They served as carriers for our signal, but I didn't understand the 'slippage' idea.

He continued, "So, de photons don't think time passes. We have to think time passes, 'cause that's how we're made. We can't see no-time. For us, it is impossible to understand. So, when we go FTL, we see time passing, and from outside observer position, it does pass, but we go very quick, quick so that not much time passes. This means we get where we want quickly, and our time passed that we think passed mostly matches with the time passed for outside observer."

"You mean that if we think we're traveling for ten days, an outside observer would also see about ten days passing as we traveled?" I asked.

"Dats about right. Maybe some time don't match up exactly, but about the same."

That was the extent of what I thought I understood. He went on to talk a little about patterns in the universe's basement and how those patterns served as templates for what was now and what was in the future, as he put it, but I didn't get much of that.

What I did understand was that our voyage would seem to take about the same time for us as it did for those people we left behind. I hadn't worried about it previously until I'd traveled to Kasm's planet and back. Then, I was a little surprised to find that people hadn't aged. I mean that I hadn't even considered the twin-paradox at first, or I would have been in agony, worrying that Liz would grow old and die while I was gone. She hadn't, and I learned from experience that the time went at the same speed for both parties. So, I expected to get back to Earth and find things about the same as they were when we'd left, only maybe different by about two months.

I figured Jake would still be holding off the Motherland Army. I hoped that they hadn't decided to attack again. If they had, he had the armed FTL, which should make the difference. There was no way they could withstand the firepower it mounted.

We arrived back at the second Sunny planet. The initial inspection didn't show any changes in the system. There were no ships docked at the orbital station. With this assurance, we put out a call for the ship we'd left to guard the system. They didn't answer the radio call quickly enough to satisfy me, so we tried the Ansible. That got results. They were currently at the far side of the star, nearly a light-year away from where we'd dropped in. We both headed for the Sunnys' orbital station under Em-drive at maximum acceleration. Once we'd gotten up to a reasonable speed, one where we'd be in transit for about fifteen hours, we shut the engine off and coasted until it was time to decelerate.

When we arrived at the station, we settled into orbit nearby, and Frazzle, and I used the transporter system to the station. We came out of the portal to find we faced a large group of excited Sunnys. They were practically dancing in the hallway that led to the transporter, and the noise level was deafening.

Once we'd gotten them calmed enough to communicate effectively, Frazzle determined that the exuberant greeting was due to an event that had just happened on the planet's surface.

They told us that there had been no immediate result from our spraying yeast indiscriminately around the place and, although they were hopeful, the Sunnys continued life, as usual, working for the Pug-bears and putting up with their erratic and fierce behavior.

The Sunnys had managed to secretly start creating trap systems according to the instructions we'd left, but they had no hope of them working and were, in fact, fearful of deploying them. If an intelligent Pug-bear had found out about the traps, the Sunny population would pay a high price.

The thing that they were happy about was paradoxical. There had been a slaughter, and several Sunnys were killed. They were excited about this sad event because the deaths were due to a previously intelligent Pug-bear which suddenly and irrevocably reverted to animal behavior. The individual in question was the elder on the planet, and it had been in the process of giving them a series of orders regarding production quotas.

Suddenly, right in the middle of the group meeting, the creature had suffered a sort of fit, shaking and then falling to the ground. When it stood up again, it didn't communicate. Instead, it attacked the Sunny delegation and killed most of them. It was still lurking around the city and attacking randomly, showing no sense of purpose.

It sounded as if the yeast were having some effect. We advised them to begin setting the traps and avoid contacting the Pug-bears, if possible. If the yeast were taking hold, the rest of the creatures could be expected to suffer the loss of their symbionts and regress to simple feral behavior. It didn't lessen their dangerous nature, but the loss of their grafted-on intelligence would make them far easier to avoid and to trap.

During the next twenty-four hours, the Sunnys worked at setting traps, and by the time that I'd come back on day-shift, the Pug-bears were stumbling into the traps regularly. The Sunnys held such animosity towards their former masters that they overcame their antipathy towards violence enough to celebrate whenever they were able to pull a dead Pug-bear out of a trap and reset it.

When the reports from the surface came in, Frazzle hastily collated them, ran some calculations on the results, and then informed me that the Pug-bears would probably be about ninety percent gone within a week. The Sunny population was free and only had to worry about feral Pug-bears.

Without their symbionts, though they might kill an individual Sunny, the feral creatures were no longer a threat to Sunny civilization. They had been reduced to the status of wild animals. The yeast was a success.

The only drawback was that Ian wouldn't let us forget that it had all been his idea. Fortunately, he wanted to stay on the planet to study the local ecosystem, and the Sunnys encouraged that idea. I think they wanted to make sure that at least one of us stayed so that we'd have to come back again.

He went down to the surface on one of the planet's shuttles. I'd insisted on arming him heavily. The locals could manufacture power packs for the anti-matter weapons but currently didn't manufacture the weapons themselves. Those were all created on a different planet.

We'd been at the station for a week when Rudy and Holmes showed up. A single ship dropped out of FTL far out in the system and then called in using the Ansible system. It was Holmes.

He and Rudy had gone to their first assigned planet, and the yeast bombing had gone smoothly with no problems. They'd spread the stuff and cleared the local space station of Pugs at the same time. There were only a few shuttles there, and they'd been all at the station when the Marines had attacked. The shuttles were captured, isolating the Pugs and Pug-bears on the planet's surface.

Rudy and Holmes had then gone on to their second target. Here a serious problem had arisen. One of the two remaining Pug FTL ships was docked, and it had been armed.

It disengaged from the station before they could get close enough to capture it. Then it played cat and mouse with them around the numerous moons that orbited the planet. When they finally thought they were narrowing in on its location, it fired one telling shot that impacted Rudy's large ship's FTL vanes. Then it dove for the planet, skimmed the atmosphere, and entered light speed as soon as possible. Their escape seemed to have really angered Rudy.

Holmes was kept busy taking Rudy's crew off their ship. Without FTL ability, our spaceships were little better than shuttles. They were limited to in-system work only. Luckily, Holmes' ship had enough room for Rudy's entire crew.

There was no repair facility there, so Rudy's ship had to be left with the Sunnys. I reckoned that we'd try to pick it up as soon as we could find a way to ship a spare set of FTL vanes and an engine since there were no readily available replacement parts in that system. Meanwhile, Rudy's people boarded Holmes' ship and finished dumping yeast on the surface.

Their voyage back to rendezvous with us had been tense. Rudy didn't enjoy riding as a passenger with Holmes in command. He'd lost his ship and failed to damage the enemy, and his ego was suffering as a result.

Nor did

Holmes enjoy Rudy's constant complaining. He told me privately, "I've never seen someone so angry. I'm actually glad to get him off my ship. I thought a couple of times that he'd try to take over and go off after the enemy all on his own."

Rudy came storming through the transporter onto my ship when they were close enough. By the way he held his mouth in a tight line with the corners down-turned, I could tell that he was still furious at the loss of his vessel. He started in on me right away.

"Dec, I lost my ship! Those damned Pugs! They out-maneuvered me. There were a whole lot of small moons or rocks orbiting around that planet, and they ducked into them. I didn't want to follow. It looked like a meat-grinder in there, so I tried to circle the mess and pick a way to get inside, nearer the planet. I figured they'd come out on that side. They did, but not where I expected them. Our sensors couldn't track them through the mess, and they popped out and shot my tail off then ran."

"Calm down, Rudy. It could have happened to any –" I started to say, but he interrupted.

"Don't tell me that, Dec! I was stupid! I thought that my ship was more than a match for them. They only had a single anti-matter cannon. They shouldn't have gotten away from me. I want you to accept my resig –"

This time I interrupted, "No! I'm not going to let you resign, so you can get that out of your mind right now! You're going to take charge of the other ship we've got here. I don't have enough experienced people as it is. I can't afford to let you slink off in embarrassment."

He spluttered, "Embarrassment! That's what you think – No, I'm not embarrassed. I just lost – I mean I – Well, maybe you could do better. I don't know."

He was shaking his head in discouragement.

I said, "Look, Rudy, we're all improvising here. No human has ever engaged in combat in space. The rules are different. It's not like fighting on the ground or even exactly like airplane combat. The thing is, the anti-matter weapons are so destructive that even a partial charge will do a lot of damage. We need some kind of countermeasure, and I think I may have come up with a way to shield against anti-matter to a certain extent, but I need your help to work it out and also to work out a set of strategies for spaceship combat. We have to have some set way to operate in the future. We can't keep doing things by the seat of our pants."

Rudy just shook his head, negating my reasoning.

"Dec, I'm not a fighter pilot. I'm just an old insurgent fighter. Besides, if you can get the last Pug ships settled, there won't be anyone to fight in space," he said.

I grinned a tight grin and answered, "Well, maybe that isn't true. Frazzle indicated to me that there is another species out there. He doesn't know if they're hostile or not."

His eyes grew large as he answered, "Really? We're not done yet?"

"I don't know about that. We'll just have to wait and see. Besides, I'm going to need you. I strongly suspect that we haven't seen the last of the Motherland group, and there will probably be more like them in both Europe and Asia. We'll have our hands full getting Earth back into order."

He replied, "That's true, I guess. Look – I just made a mistake. I'm going to try and work out ways to keep from making another one."

I smiled, and we shook hands. Then he remembered something I'd said.

He asked, "What do you mean that you know how to shield against anti-matter?"

I replied, "I'm not sure it will work, but I've got an idea. Using our point gravity source to hold a bunch of dust as a physical shield should deplete the anti-matter burst. It might only work once unless we had access to more dust, but once should be enough if it allows us to shoot back."

He thought about it for a minute.

"That might work. Maybe we could rig some way to blow dust out of the hold in a cloud, then grab it with the point gravity. We could carry a bunch of dirt in one of the holds, possibly enough to shield us against repeated shots."

He was speculating, but it might work. We'd just have to test the idea.

We got underway the next day as Rudy took over our latest capture, and we headed to Earth. I wanted to regroup, check on Jake, then work out my confederation ideas. We desperately needed a new way of organizing ourselves.

Current human existence was tenuous, and we needed to rebuild. To do that, we needed a new structure. I didn't want to reinstate our old politics – there was too much wrong with them.

Chapter 35

I figured that what I'd been calling "Our Space," the rough area occupied by the Sunnys, the Sim-tigers, and humans, would require some governing force. That was the point of what Liz was now calling the ISC. I wasn't too concerned about the form of organization that either of the two other species chose. The Sunnys had a lot of experience organizing themselves over several planets, and there weren't that many Sim-tigers. They were widely dispersed on their planet, and Kasm had assured me that they no longer fought as they'd done in the past. Their groups always cooperated in the allocation of hunting territory. If they could just bring that attitude into space, we'd have no problem with them.

It was the human tendency towards in-fighting that had me worried. If space travel became widespread, we would have groups setting up their own empires, pirates, space Vikings, colonies of hippies, Amazons, militant feminists, and who knows what else. Total chaos wouldn't work into my plans smoothly.

Likewise, humans, now faced with aliens for the first time, needed to come together and act with a unified front. I suspected that our species is unfortunately too diverse to unify completely. One man's meat is another man's poison, so to speak. A political organization that works for some people won't work for all. It never has in recorded history. Trying to impose an organization on the discontented ones by force would lead to the same, sad set of errors we've always made. There would be wars, people would be killed, and humanity, as a whole, would be vulnerable.

During the voyage, I discussed the problem with Liz. We came to the not very astute conclusion that what worked in space should also work on the planet. In short, if we could form a confederation with the other species, we should be able to form one on Earth.

That way, the individual groups making up the confederation could have their own form of rule within their own territory. I didn't care about that, as long as they allowed people to emigrate if they didn't like the local rules. Eventually, the best set of rules should end up with the most citizens as long as people were free to choose.

While humans currently only held our home planet, I figured we'd extend our reach as quickly as the Sunnys could provide FTL ships to us.

I didn't like my name of "Our Space," so I sort of redefined the term 'Oikumene.'

The word is usually used in science fiction to refer to the human-inhabited worlds of the galaxy. As such, it seemed a little ostentatious to me. We only held one world, but if I included our allies – well, that was a different story. Together we held eight worlds if you didn't count those of the Pugs or Pug-bears, and I wasn't minded to count them. However, Oikumene seemed to be the way to describe our joint space, and I decided to use it.

If humans were going to expand into space, we'd need organization quickly, or we'd end up suffering the consequences in terms of interplanetary strife later. I couldn't see how that would benefit us.

Now, as to Earth, Jake's Eastern-slope group and our small community were loosely allied. If we could somehow either get rid of the Motherland group or make peace with them, that would bring over half of the old United States back together.

Several kingdoms and other groups were scattered off in the mountains to our north and west, and I thought they'd probably fall into line with the confederacy idea pretty quickly. I didn't know anything about Europe, Asia, or – well, I didn't know anything about the entire rest of the world. Still, I was prepared to use space power to enforce peaceful organization. The one thing I didn't want was a group like the Motherland Army terrorizing and stealing resources. If they were peaceful, that would be alright. If not, we'd see what it took to pacify them.

I looked in the mirror when I had this thought and wondered, "Am I going to turn into what I want to stop other people from being?" I didn't want to rule the world, though. I just wanted to give people the opportunity to live peacefully and prosperously. I hoped my organizational idea would lead to that.

Then another concept came to me. Our planetary system needed its own force. The ISC could serve for the three species, but we needed an Earth-space Protection Force to handle our own problems. I didn't want humans to feel antagonistic about the other species if the ISC had to intercede in human space affairs. Plus, we would shortly need someone to ensure that there was some standard of decent behavior in our own solar system. As I mentioned, I didn't want pirates or whatever.

That might work, though. Each species could have its own space force under the auspices of the ISC. That would keep the ISC small in size, and it could mainly serve as a coordinating organization, only pulling everyone together in the event of a significant emergency.

I told Liz about my ideas, and she commented, "So, now we've got two organizations in space. We need one on Earth. It could be a confederation like you say, and its role could be kind of like the ISC or maybe the old UN."

I was not too fond of the UN reference. That was a deeply flawed organization from its inception. The basic idea was well-intentioned, but it had quickly become corrupt. The general democratic structure ensured that. Democracies are always subject to distortion caused by self-interest.

No, we needed a robust coordinating organization on Earth, and it needed to be independent. How could I find a man who was saintly enough to run it and not be corrupted by power? Then it hit me, the Earth-space Protection Force – I'd taken to calling it the ESPF by now – would be responsible for planetary coordination of the various political entities. Maybe that would provide a little control for corruption.

After considerable thought, I got discouraged. I was pretty sure that whatever I could think up wouldn't be good enough to prevent ill-intentioned people from finding ways to screw it up. However, it didn't seem like I could do any better, so I decided that this would just have to work. If the ESPF started causing trouble on Earth, the ISC could step in and straighten things out. It wasn't perfect, but there were enough layers that I thought it could be self-correcting.

I hoped that the influence of the two alien species would also have the effect of overruling the human tendency towards self-interest. The Sunnys, especially, were altruistic in outlook and were likely to mediate disputes fairly. At least that was my hope.

Chapter 36

As soon as we arrived in Earth orbit, I placed a call to Jake's headquarters, hoping to speak to him. We'd left the smallest FTL spaceship in his care, and it appeared to be missing. Our sensors couldn't detect it anywhere in the system.

Of course, a solar system is a big place. The ship could be anywhere and be very hard to detect, especially if the engines were shut down. Even when running the Em-drive didn't give off much of a signal.

My major fear was that the Pugs had shown up again and recaptured the ship. I was worried about that, but then an alternative occurred to me. Perhaps he'd used it to strafe the Motherland group and flown too low. The ship wouldn't survive going deep into the atmosphere. As good as the deflector shield was, the friction of all of that air would most likely slow the vessel too much for it to regain orbital velocity. The Em-drive relied on a constant acceleration for its speed. It didn't have enough thrust to kick the mass of the ship out of a deep gravity well.

Our call to Denver was finally answered. I was a little surprised to hear Judith's voice. I replied, "Judith, is that you? Where is Jake? Oh, and where is his spaceship?"

Her voice came through with a little static, "Dec! I'm glad you're back. I don't know where the Warlord is. He was going out to get an asteroid. The Motherland gang has been moving our way in strength, and he decided to do what you told him. You know, drop rocks on them."

I grimaced. Of course, he'd do something unexpected like that. I should never have mentioned KEWs to him. I asked the next important question, "How long ago did he leave?"

I had kind of hoped that maybe he just took off to explore or something, but if he were looking for rocks, he'd probably have headed for the asteroid belt. There were closer objects, but most likely, he wouldn't know how to find them.

She answered, "It was four days ago. I thought that he'd be back by now. The enemy is practically knocking on our door. They're right back where they were before. Denver is surrounded on the east side."

The Motherland Army! Their self-styled President was rapidly becoming my primary irritant. He was going to have to be removed from control. It seemed like all he wanted to do was to expand his territory at the expense of those already living in the areas he wanted. That kind of behavior was exactly what I did not want in my planned confederation.

I took a deep breath, calmed myself, and asked, "Can you hold out for a couple of days, or do you need assistance immediately?"

"We're fine for now. They haven't gotten completely organized. My scouts have reported that the Motherland Army looks like it's waiting for some heavy artillery to arrive. It's still a couple of days away from their lines, so they probably won't do anything for at least that long," she said.

The radio clicked momentarily, and then a burst of static came through. It was pretty loud, and it continued.

Frazzle looked at me and made some adjustments, then said, "Somebody down dere is jamming. That's a primitive transmitter, a jump-gap sparker. It makes lots of noise and drowns out other signals. Not too hard to build, so I 'spect they could make it work if they have battery power."

"Can you get a signal down to Judith so we can finish planning?" I asked.

"Not unless she got another kind of radio. The one at the Warlord's place is not good for that. It's human-made and old. I don't think it can get through the noise."

I was disgusted, "Rats!"

Frazzle jumped in startlement, "What! Where be rats?" He looked wildly around.

I couldn't help myself. I snickered at him a little, "No! Not any rats here. It's just a saying. It means I'm frustrated."

He visibly relaxed. "Not good to joke about dem bad things. Long time ago, before Pug-bears, when Sunnys came to your planet, we got some of rats on our ship by accident. Very hard to get rid of. We have to put on suits and open ship to space to get them out. They eated lots of wires and caused big problems. Sunnys now got rules to keep from happening."

I grinned, "Well, you can count on my cooperation. I don't happen to like rats, and I definitely don't want any on our ships."

I changed the subject, "Let's move out to the asteroid belt and see if we can locate Jake's ship."

He turned back to the control panel, "'Okay. I do."

We proceeded under Em-drive thrust, outbound towards the region between Mars and Jupiter. There was no sense going at maximum acceleration since I didn't want to have to slow down radically when we got there, but we didn't waste any time. The trip would only take a few hours at the speed we were traveling.

I wanted to insert into the asteroid zone at a shallow angle and then gradually turn inward towards the arc of its orbit. I was determined to find Jake, even if I had to circumnavigate the Sun completely.

I figured that he would have headed straight away from the Sun towards the asteroid belt. That was most logical. The ship should be located in a relatively small portion of the zone if he'd done that. I couldn't imagine that he'd gone to the other side of the Sun to find a suitable rock to convert into KEWs.

We passed Mars' orbit uneventfully. The planet was currently far around the Sun from where we were, so there was nothing to see until we got closer to the myriad of small and large rocks between Jupiter and us. Even then, there was be little to see. Our asteroid belt has a lot of objects in it, but they are small, and space is vast. You'd have to be very unlucky to hit an asteroid, even if you took a random path through the zone.

A little after we passed Mars' orbit, the detector pinged. There was something out there. It was faint as if the ship's power was barely on. There was no engine signal and, when we tried, no response to the comm signal.

Frazzle approached the location cautiously. It was in a slightly denser area of the belt, and there were a couple of larger asteroids hanging around, spinning on their mindless path. The pings grew steadily stronger as we approached.

We moved past a large, wobbling rock, and there it was. Not something I'd hoped to see, though.

The view out of the bridge window was horrifying. Framed against the backdrop of Jupiter and its moons was Jake's ship – what was left of it. Pieces of it, small and large, were floating in a loose swarm. A little beyond the wreckage was another ship. It was drifting slowly towards the wreckage of Jake's. It was intact, save that a large portion of the hull had been dissolved, including the majority of the bridge.

Liz gasped at the sight and turned to me, her eyes wide and dark, "What happened? Is – is Jake gone?"

"Frazzle, is that one of the Pugs' ships?" I asked, pointing.

"Maybe. I don' know, but it must be," he concluded.

Jake must have been occupied trying to figure out how to capture a rock when the Pugs came along. There had been a battle, and both ships were destroyed. I wondered how he'd let the enemy get so close, but then I thought that the Pugs might have thought they were approaching one of their own FTLs. They would probably have tried to raise him on the comm, so... I really had no idea what happened. All we knew was that both ships were now total wrecks.

We poked around, investigating the wreckage. The weak signal was coming from the Pugs' ship. I checked mentally, and there was no sign of life in either of the two. Both had probably been opened to space before anyone could don a spacesuit. We did see some frozen Pug bodies, but there wasn't a sign of humans anywhere which was a bit of a mystery.

I was forced to conclude that the humans had all been caught in an anti-matter beam. The fact that Jake's ship was in fragments seemed to lend credence to that idea. It still bothered me, though. There should have been at least one human body remaining. I was left with a disturbing feeling that there was some kind of mystery there that I was not going to solve.

Nothing in the wreckage was worth salvaging, so we turned sadly back towards Earth, wondering how the Denver area would cope without Jake.

The only good thing about the situation was that Jake had somehow destroyed one of the last two Pug ships. Now there was only one to worry about.

Chapter 37

Judith didn't take the news very well. She was shocked at first and then angry that Jake had gone off and gotten killed, leaving her to face the rapidly gathering enemy. I don't remember her exact words when I contacted her on the comm, but they were something along the lines of: "That blasted fool! He was always too daring. He shouldn't have been up in that stupid ship anyway. Why did you have to give it to him? We need him here right now!" But with a lot more profanity.

The Motherland Army had finally brought up most of their big guns and were engaged in periodic shelling of the metro area with mixed effect. I estimated that at least half of their hits destroyed buildings that were overdue to be knocked down, so it could be argued that they were doing Denver a favor. Even so, Judith's nerves were shot. Even though no shells had landed near the stadium headquarters, she was a nervous wreck.

The sky over Denver was mostly overcast, so that we couldn't use the monitor's telescopic capability with any great degree of success. Even the infrared overlay didn't help much, although I could make out blurs that were either groups of men or animals.

The lousy weather was unusual for the area. The front range is ordinarily sunny and clear, but this was one of the few times it wasn't. As a result, I felt the need to get down there to see the strategic situation for myself.

I held a video conference with my captains and decided to fly down in the smaller shuttle. It was armed and able to do high-altitude surveillance, so it was the natural choice for a brief recon. Frazzle, and I headed down to the shuttle bay, leaving Liz in the command seat and Hattie sitting at weapons control.

Liz wasn't yet trained well enough to fly the ship in FTL mode (nor was I). She'd been working with Frazzle, learning how the thing worked. One of the problems she'd encountered was that many of the controls were Sunny specific and challenging for human fingers and reflexes. She could run the monitors and use the Em-drive, as long as the navigation problems weren't tricky. She'd probably have trouble flying it to another planet, but she could maneuver it around Earth-space. If she had difficulty, one of the more knowledgeable Sunnys would be able to provide some assistance.

Kasm was waiting when we reached the shuttle bay. I looked at him questioningly.

He spoke aloud in his low, growling tone, "I'm going to come with you. I'm bored and, besides, you might need some help."

I knew from prior experience how stubborn he could be. Once he made up his mind to do something, it was nearly impossible to convince him otherwise. I decided to make the best of things and waved him ahead of me as Frazzle opened the port and climbed into the pilot's seat.

The shuttle was small and not really suited for a Sim-tiger. The seats were set up for, I guessed, Pugs. I sat in the co-pilot's seat, and Kasm tried to get comfortable behind the two of us. There was a clash of metal as the grapples let go, and then we were drifting away from the body of our ship.

Frazzle whipped us upside down with respect to the ship's orientation and accelerated hard towards the rear. We lost orbital velocity quickly and began heading downwards into the atmosphere.

Despite how many times I'd reentered Earth's atmosphere, I still enjoyed watching the black emptiness of space begin to turn to the blue of home. We were halfway around the world and beginning to fly like an atmospheric craft. The descent into the Denver area was still to come. We passed over the western coast of California and the Sierra Nevada range. I could see the gorge of the Grand Canyon, and then we flew over the Rockies.

We'd thought to land and conference with Judith, but as we came over the Front Range, I got the idea to do a little reconnaissance.

I looked at him and suggested, "Frazzle, let's fly out over the plains and see if we can get an overview of the invaders' position."

He dutifully swung wide, passing over Colorado Springs and moving eastward in a gradual turn towards the north. As we flew, I could see groups and clots of men on the ground. They mainly were hanging around their camps in the bad weather. They'd been there long enough to set up tents and fires along with picket lines for their horses. It looked like they were well organized.

A little to the west of the camps, there were artillery batteries. A group of the guns fired as we passed overhead, and I could see the flash and smoke. One of the weapons blew a perfect smoke ring that lasted for a moment before it dispersed.

We'd flown up to a point about due east of Thornton when someone on the ground launched a rocket at us. Frazzle was better prepared than he had been the last time. He jinked the ship violently, and the missile went by on the right side. It started to arc around to re-target us, but he accelerated, and we shot ahead, our leading-edge turning bright red from the friction with the air. The shuttle was capable of outrunning the relatively slow rocket, and we did. I could see the thing nose down towards the ground far behind us as it ran out of fuel.

It sailed along an arc that terminated near one of the batteries of guns, exploding when it impacted the ground. I hoped it'd done some damage when it went off.

Shortly after that, Frazzle pointed out some dust off to the east. We circled and investigated, finding a convoy of steam tractors pulling baggage wagons loaded with supplies and ammunition. I could see pallets of artillery shells on some of the wagon beds.

This was too good an opportunity to waste. I activated the plasma cannon, and we flew back to make a strafing run. Fifteen minutes later, there was nothing left of the supply convoy. The plasma bolts had caused the steam boilers to explode with almost as much force as the artillery shells. The drivers mainly had run away when they saw us coming, but a few fool-hardy men had stayed to take shots at us with their rifles.

Some of the bullets had bounced off our shuttle, but it was hardened to withstand meteor strikes that carried far more kinetic energy than a rifle could muster. The ones who had hung around long enough to shoot at us perished in the explosions as our plasma bolts traversed down the long line of wagons.

We resumed our course and circled north, coming up to the mountains over what remained of Boulder. The barren strip we'd burned across the town was a convenient point to turn back south towards Denver.

We flew over the metro area and landed in the football stadium. I could see Judith, along with a group of men standing in the end zone waiting for us to climb out. Frazzle cut the engines and opened the hatch.

I started to move, but had to duck as Kasm, unable to contain himself any longer and desperate to stretch his legs, literally jumped over me, bounced off the flight surface, and leaped down to the ground. Frazzle, and I followed more sedately. Judith waved as we approached, as did the men standing beside her.

I wasted no time in amenities, "Hello, all of you. We've been out over the plains looking at the army investing the town. There are maybe forty or fifty thousand men, most of them mounted along with, I think, ten artillery batteries."

Frazzle interrupted, "No, deys twelve batteries. You missed two cause you looked out the wrong side. I counted twelve."

The others grinned at his statement, and I shrugged, "Well, I stand corrected. The Sunnys like to be as exact as possible, so it must be twelve batteries. We saw a convoy of supplies and took the time to wipe it out, so maybe they might run a little short of ammunition for their big guns."

That was an understatement. There had been at least twenty wagons of ammunition, much of which had exploded when struck by the plasma bolts and tractor debris. With any luck, the guns would run out of ammunition, and bombardment would cease until the Motherlanders could bring up more shells.

We went inside and arranged ourselves in a conference room to discuss matters. They had rigged a steam-powered generator, and actual electric lights illuminated the place. Jake had always found it necessary to meet in rooms with windows or use torches. The electric lighting was an unexpected luxury that I was pleased to see. Maybe our species wasn't going to just fade into obscurity and disappear after all.

Judith started the meeting by introducing her staff. I'm afraid that I didn't pay much attention. I was looking at a large map that was posted on the wall. It showed the Denver area, and someone had marked the locations of the enemy camps reasonably accurately.

"Dec, uh – Dec?" she said, trying to get my attention.

I jerked. I'd been thinking about how to wipe out the camps.

"Yes?" I answered.

She said, "We think they will attack in a few days. My scouts have informed me that at least another twenty thousand men are heading this way from the Goodland area. It'll take them a while to get here, and they'll need to rest for a day after they arrive, but then they're sure to attack in full force."

I thought about it for a moment, then asked, "Has the shelling been doing any damage?"

"Not much. They've knocked down a lot of houses, but you know that most of the outlying subdivisions are vacant anyway. Most of our people have moved closer to the mountains. The shells have started some fires, and we're just letting those burn out on their own. Otherwise, they haven't hit anything we can't do without," she answered, then continued, "Of course, we don't have very much by way of things we can't do without. Our men are mostly holed up in valleys or gullies, so the artillery hasn't bothered them."

Kasm had remained silent, but now he spoke, "What kind of force do you have?"

His deep, growling voice caused everyone to turn and stare. Judith stuttered a bit. I don't think she had realized that he could speak English.

She shook off her surprise and answered,

"We've only got about twenty thousand, total. There are still some fighters filtering over the mountains. We sent out riders to try and recruit help from the groups and towns to the west, and quite a few people have taken us up on our request."

Kasm said, "You don't have enough to stand and fight. We don't have enough people in our ships to make a difference, either. My people would make a good raiding party for night work, perhaps, but I don't want to have to make a stand in the daylight where you humans can shoot at us."

He looked at me, "Dec, we're going to have to use the spaceships. We must shoot at them with the anti-matter weapons."

I stood slowly; then, I pointed at the wall map.

"Maybe there's something else we can do that will discourage them even more. Remember, we burned them out with anti-matter the last time they attacked, and they've come right back."

Judith asked, "What do you have in mind?"

I smiled a tight smile and answered, "Maybe if we drop KEWs on each of their camps, they'll get the message. We can hit each camp accurately, and if we do it at night with a sizable mass, it might kill nearly all of them."

One of the staff members, an older man with a full beard, said, "Wait a minute, now wait just a minute. What's a KEW?"

I hadn't realized that they might not know.

"Kinetic Energy Weapon – basically, it can be anything we want to drop on them. A piece of rock, for example, falling out of orbit will be moving at thousands of miles per hour when it hits. If it is fairly large, the impact will be the equivalent of hundreds of tons of explosive."

He thought about it for a moment, then asked, "Where will you get rocks? Do we have to haul them for you? Will you need any particular kind?"

I grinned at his naivety.

"No, one thing our solar system has is plenty of rocks. They're floating around in space, mostly out past Mars. We'll go and pick up some asteroids, drag them to Earth and break off a few chunks. Those will do very well. The enemy somehow believes they can avoid an anti-matter strafing run. Their camps are situated well back from where we made our first pass. Maybe they don't know what hit them that time and think they're safe where they are. If so, vaporizing their camps might be more effective, although I hate to kill that many humans. There aren't enough of us as it is. It's stupid, but they aren't going to quit unless forced to. Anyway, the KEWs should cause a great amount of destruction, and those who aren't killed will be unsure of exactly what happened, except they'll know that their camps suddenly were vaporized. They're most likely going to think we hit them with atomic bombs. I think that will do it. It should be very demoralizing."

Judith shook her head, "I can't believe that we're sitting here talking about killing thousands of people. I was a defense lawyer before... before the EMP blast. I tried to help people. I don't like this very much."

The bearded guy responded, "You'll like it even less if those Motherland people defeat us."

She was quiet for a moment and then nodded, "Yes. I guess you're right. We need for them to leave us alone if they won't be peaceful."

I thought of their President and said, "I don't think they're going to be friendly, no matter what we do, Judith. They seem to be dead set on conquering and killing everyone who wants to live independently of them. We've got to hand them a huge defeat. One so intimidating that they'll forever leave us alone afterward. Wiping out their army is about the only way to do that."

Chapter 38

After the meeting, we returned to the ship and were now back out in the asteroid zone with the entire squadron of fours ships. Holmes and Joe were already towing small asteroids back towards Earth, perhaps a couple of hundred feet in diameter. Rudy and I were in the process of grabbing a couple more rocks. We locked onto them with our gravity point-source and began to move, catching up with Holmes and Joe.

We slowly came up to speed, pulling the extra mass. The rocks slowed down our acceleration, but the EM-drives gradually built up velocity, and we began the traverse back to Earth orbit. The plan was to insert the rocks into high orbit and then cut them into smaller pieces. I didn't want to leave their masses intact. That would be irresponsible. If one of the large rocks became unstable and its orbit decayed, it would do extensive damage when it impacted Earth's surface.

We'd re-counted and discovered sixteen major camps set up by the Motherland Army, along with several smaller ones, including artillery batteries. We intended to cut the rocks up into carefully calculated sizes, so we would have enough to hit all of the camps with enough mass to wipe them out.

I wanted to break the rocks up into smaller pieces that were the right size to keep the impact force under control. The gravity point-source projector conveniently had a sensor that indicated the mass of the item being towed, which allowed us to calculate the rock's average density. The only problem was the sensor used Sunny units, so we had to translate, but that was easy with a computer.

I needed to calculate the density of each asteroid and then use that single number for calculating mass by volume. This gave approximately the right size for cutting the pieces. The computer would calculate the velocity attained by the piece on its descent from orbit, and that, paired with the mass, would give us the impact force.

I wanted to keep the damage localized to the immediate camp area, so I decided to try and keep the yield of the KEW's impact equal to about a kiloton of TNT. I thought that should be adequate to vaporize even the largest camp.

We eventually eased back into high orbit. The rocks had made the necessary braking and maneuvering more difficult than usual, but we finally got in position and shut down the engines. The next step was to figure out how we would cut the things down to size.

Frazzle, when asked, was somewhat vague, "I never did anything like dis before, Dec. Maybe you send out Marines, and they use anti-matter rifles to cut the asteroids up withs. We don't haves any cutters that will cut that big in our shop."

I sighed. His suggestion was something I'd already thought about but hoped to avoid. The potential for accidents was significant. The anti-matter bursts would have to be aimed carefully. If someone missed, the destructive matter would continue until it struck enough ordinary atoms to dissipate. If some of those normal atoms happened to be currently holding the configuration of one of our other spaceships or another Marine, the result would be unpleasant, to put it mildly.

The other thing I worried about was whether there was any potential for the asteroids to shatter unpredictably. We'd carefully removed all angular velocity from each of them so they were sitting still in space and not rotating. That was about all we could do to minimize the possibility of flying fragments, but if one of the rocks had some kind of internal stress, it could conceivably break apart, throwing pieces around. That could be dangerous.

I finally decided to use a minimal crew of men with only one anti-matter weapon. They'd work on one asteroid at a time, cutting it carefully and removing one piece at a time. That was the best I could do, aside from moving all of our orbiting ships from the line of fire, something that we'd already done.

I was also going to be part of the crew myself, despite Liz's arguing against it.

She said, "You're our leader. Can't you delegate this kind of stuff? I'd think that you'd at least have the sense to let your men handle this. They aren't idiots, you know."

"This is dangerous, and I decided that I wasn't going to ask any of my men to do something I wouldn't. If we can cut one of the rocks with no problems, I'll leave them to do the rest. I want to be there at first to see how it goes," I replied, whispering so as not to disturb our children.

It was the early part of alt-shift, and we were resting in our cabin. The kids were asleep, having exhausted themselves earlier playing in zero-g in the hold. They were getting so proficient that I allowed them to go in when others were exercising there. Both children were more than capable of staying out of the way, although, if the truth be told, watching their antics did sometimes make me nervous.

All on their own, they were developing ways of moving that those of us who had been gravity-bound during our childhoods would never have created. I'd noticed some of the Marines watching Michael carefully and then trying out some of his moves. The kids were going to have a huge advantage over older people at zero-g maneuvers.

Liz seemed to forget about the KEWs and snuggled closer to me, sighing.

"It's been a long time since we could relax together," she said as she moved her head on my shoulder.

I felt the need to be defensive. It had been a long time, and I didn't want her to think it was because I didn't love her.

"Well, I've been busy and apprehensive about the entire situation. It's so complicated, and there are so many moving parts, what with the Pugs and Pug-bears, our relationships with the Sunnys and Sim-tigers, and then those blasted Motherland Army people. Their President gives me indigestion. He's a severe pain in the ass," I said, getting louder as I continued.

She put her finger over my lips just in the nick of time. Rowan was stirring around restlessly. I'd disturbed her.

"Listen, Dec, you don't have to be defensive around me. I know how much stress you've been under, and I understand. There are some times when I wish we were still in our little cabin, though," she whispered.

I moved my lips close to her ear and whispered back, "That reminds me. There's something we need to do, and now might be a good time."

My breath moved the tiny hairs on her neck, causing her to have goosebumps. She giggled a little and rolled over so we could kiss.

I forgot my worries during the next few minutes and had a wonderful night's rest as a result.

We were suited up and waiting for the loading bay port to open. I checked in with each of the four men using our spacesuit radios.

"Okay. Is everyone ready to go?" I asked.

They checked back with affirmatives, and I proceeded to review my instructions. "We're going to jump to the nearest asteroid. Frazzle has pulled it close, so it'll be no more than fifty meters. Go slow with your jump, just like in training. I don't want to have to chase anyone down just because you hit too hard and bounced off. Once we're on the asteroid, we'll use our adhesive packs to glue our tether lines to the stone," I said. They all nodded with the bobbing motion imposed by their spacesuits.

I continued, "We'll wait on the asteroid until the ship moves away. If we knock any fragments loose, I don't want to damage the ship accidentally. Once they're a few miles distant, you will stay behind me and watch as I use the anti-matter rifle to separate a piece of stone. I intend to keep it fairly small, so once it's cut loose, you can push it away from the asteroid. When you push it away, push it ahead in orbit and not towards the ship. We'll cut the pieces and push them out in a line where the ship's gravity point-source will be able to grab each piece easily."

The port was now open, and we jumped out, one at a time, floating slowly towards the large mass of rock that hovered in space nearby. It was interesting. The rock was larger than I'd thought it would be. It was ten meters from end to end and shaped like a spindle. The waist was about four meters across, giving it a spaceship-like look.

I led the way across, landing softly near the middle part of the rock. There was probably a tiny amount of gravity associated with it, but I couldn't tell. I carefully pulled myself hand-over-hand to the large end, and after some fiddling around with my utility belt, I managed to glue my tether to the rock.

The adhesive was supposed to set up instantly, so I braced my feet and tugged at the tether. It held. I was shortly joined by three of the men, but the fourth guy missed his jump. He didn't miss by much. He stretched out, reaching for the rock, and glided past about three inches too far away.

He was drifting slowly away, waving his hands in a vague swimming motion as if that would help. I checked my tether to make sure the other men were clear and then carefully jumped directly at him. You might think this would be easy, but I had to jump quickly enough to catch him before he got farther away than my twenty-meter tether line, but not too quickly. If I hit him too hard and missed my grab, the impact would push him away faster.

He continued drifting away but stopped waving his arms when he saw that I was coming after him. I kept checking his distance and the length of my remaining rope. I might just make it, but – no. I was going to be slightly too late. It looked like I would hit my tether's end about five feet short of his position.

So far, he hadn't said anything over the com save a quick gasp and a curse under his breath. Neither had I.

I realized that he was holding his tether in one hand, and I called him, "Carefully throw your rope to me. I'll pull you back with it."

He jerked when I spoke and then quickly shook out the rope and tossed the anchor end my way. It went past me and then recoiled. As the coils moved back towards him, one of them got close enough for me to grab. I did and held on as tightly as I could.

I reached the end of my line at that moment, and it jerked me to a halt. It had a slight stretch in it, but the jerk still hurt. The result was I started back towards the rock, dreading what was to come next. I grabbed hold of his tether with my other hand, now holding on with two.

He hit the end of his rope, and that painfully jerked me backward away from the rock. The impact had slowed but not stopped his drift, and we slowly moved away, taking up the slack in my line. Then it tightened up, pulling me back, and as it did, his mass came full on the line I was holding. There was a moment where I thought I might lose my grip. I tightened my hands and arms in anticipation, but we were both drifting slowly back towards the rock the next second.

One of the other men caught my tether and reeled us in like two stupid fish. We got back to the rock and finalized attaching everyone. Now we had another task, and it might be even more ticklish.

"You three stay on this end of the rock while I try to cut a piece off of the other end," I ordered.

I drifted away from them and ended up floating about two meters away from the rock near the far end. Our mishap had imparted a little angular velocity to the long stone through the jerking on my tether, and it was now slowly pivoting about its center of mass, moving away from me. I detached the anti-matter rifle from its clips, pulled it down and under my arm to my front. I adjusted the focus, narrowing the aperture so that the anti-matter wouldn't spread. Then I took a breath, hoping for the best, and fired a pulse, sweeping the weapon across the point I hoped to cut.

The anti-matter worked as usual. There was a sparkling effect as atoms annihilated each other, a few at a time, and then the point that I'd aimed to cut disappeared. The beam hadn't widened much, and the cut was clean. The loose end of the stone didn't move in relationship to the rest of the rock.

I called up two men and had them jointly shove the free piece away from the central mass. They pushed it in the direction we were moving so that it would float free but remain roughly in the same orbit, slowly moving ahead of us.

We repeated the operation, changing the pushing crew when the original two got tired. It took an hour or so, cutting carefully, but we ended with ten chunks of rock that were approximately the same size. They were strung out over a kilometer or so, gradually drifting apart. There hadn't been any sudden splintering or shattering due to a release of internal tension, and I was glad that possibility hadn't materialized.

Frazzle brought the ship close, and we unhooked the shackles from the tether adhesion points, leaving the flat pads and loops attached to the last piece of rock, then we jumped back through the open bay door. We slowly drifted down to the floor under the light gravity when we passed through the door.

The dismantling of the other asteroids went reasonably smoothly and proceeded in much the same fashion, although I didn't actively participate. The whole operation took two main shift periods. The only hitch was that one of the Marines got his hand smashed between two loose pieces. The injury broke some of his fingers but fortunately didn't break the seal of his spacesuit.

We had our ammunition, and now it was time to use it.

Chapter 39

I called a video conference early in the third shift. I needed to assign targets for each ship. Coordinating the attack was going to require some careful work. Each ship could handle only one KEW at a time using its gravity point source, so we weren't set up to simply vomit the things out like a machine gun.

Aiming was also going to be difficult and would require a delicate hand on the controls. The computers could calculate the trajectory, but the gravity point-source controls were strictly manual since the Sunnys had never thought of such use. They were designed to pick up objects close to the ship and only had some limiting automation that would prevent damage to the ship itself. Otherwise, you could do whatever you wanted with the object you held. That meant someone had to manipulate the rocks and actually throw them. To do this and hit a target, the timing had to be perfect. A miss that hit friendly lines would be a disaster.

I reflected on the desirability of being to aim our shots. If the old GPS satellites were still working, perhaps we could have used them. Maybe we could use the weapon-computer's laser to designate the target, but that would only work if we had some way to steer the rocks on their way down. That would mean that we'd have to engineer some kind of guidance system that could track the laser and adjust the trajectory of the rocks. After batting the idea around, I gave up. We didn't have the facilities or time to develop such a device. Perhaps we could eventually create aerodynamic KEWs with fins, but all we had right now were non-aerodynamic rocks. We just had to figure out how to throw them accurately.

We discussed the operation for a few minutes, not coming to any conclusions. Once again, Frazzle showed his grasp of technical matters, which solved the problem.

He waited until there was a break in the conversation and interjected, "We not use point-source to throw dem rocks."

"What do you mean?" Holmes asked, looking at him through the monitor.

"De point-source too hard to aim. You have to thro' lots of rocks for practice and still, maybe miss. We let the ship computer calculate trajectory for place on surface we want to hit and then move ship straight toward that point. Computer be accurate. Only thing you got to do is turn off point source at right time. Not so hard," he finished and drew a deep breath.

I could see that might allow for more accuracy than trying to keep the point source manually aimed correctly.

The whole concept was more difficult than I'd initially thought. Rifle fire is considered accurate if repeated bullets strike within one minute of angle at, say, five hundred yards. Here we were trying to hit a spot that would be over two hundred miles distant, and we needed to be very precise, within meters of the desired strike point. I hoped that we'd be up for the job. Frazzle's suggestion sounded like it would solve the problem. The ship's computer could calculate a trajectory that would point the ship directly towards a desired point on the surface, compensate for the Earth's rotation, and drop the rock precisely.

I assigned targets to each ship. There were sixteen major camps, and we'd go for those first. Each ship would drop their rock in sequence and then return to the higher orbit to pick up another rock. Then it would dive towards the next target and release. We'd move through four cycles of this to strike at the major camps. There were also over twenty small camps we intended to target. But I doubted they'd wait around. They would be moving out quickly once they figured that we were attacking and that they were next.

The fifteen Motherland artillery batteries were still pounding away at Denver, but they wouldn't be easy to break down and move. We'd leave them for last.

I called to let Judith know we were ready to attack. She was relieved. "Dec, I can't stress how important it is for you to stop them. The constant bombardment has caused a lot of problems. Many of my men have been killed, and we've lost some of our equipment, including a storage depot of TOWS. That hurt us badly. Plus, I've had men starting to desert. The waiting period has been too long, and they're getting nervous," she said over the radio.

"I'm sorry, but cutting the rocks into the right sizes was more difficult than I'd thought. They vary a lot in mass so that the strikes will have different yields. I couldn't figure out a way to get them cut precisely with the limited equipment we have on hand," I replied.

"I don't care if they are big or little. The bigger, the better," she replied, "My scouts think the enemy is showing signs of attacking, perhaps in the morning," her voice came back.

We were just about ready to go. I'd been planning on waiting until daylight down below, but we had about two hours before that would happen. It sounded like we'd better move now before our targets did.

"Let your people know we're starting our attack in thirty minutes," I told her.

Joe was first up on the KEW rotation. His ship was dragging a blackish chunk of stone that revolved slowly about a hundred meters off its port side. We watched as the ship initially braked and then accelerated downward on its computer-controlled trajectory. It dove down for seventy kilometers and then turned back up towards a higher orbit. We hadn't been able to actually see the KEW release.

Joe came on the com, "Weapon released. It shouldn't take long, now."

Holmes went next. He followed the same maneuver. Then it was Rudy's turn.

We could see streaks in the atmosphere as the two rocks began to super-heat. I wondered what the fall would look like from the ground but then realized that I hoped that I'd never get to see it from the target's perspective.

Rudy had to follow a slightly different path. Our orbit was taking us across the area the Motherland Army occupied. Joe and Holmes had dropped their KEWs as we approached, but now we were getting close to being overhead. The required trajectory had changed, and Rudy's ship computer took his ship in a different path. After dropping his rock, he climbed back to orbit and headed out to get another one.

It was our turn. Frazzle switched to computer control, and the ship made an abrupt shift in attitude. Then it accelerated quickly. It was good that we had our artificial gravity field's internal inertia damping effect. Otherwise, I don't think humans could have survived the sudden movements.

We watched from the bridge as our vessel headed Earthward in an odd path. It didn't seem like we were going in the right direction to strike our target, but it was hard for me to estimate the effect of our orbital velocity. As it was, it looked like we were going to throw the KEW backward, away from our target.

There was a sudden buzz and flash from the computer, and Hattie released the KEW at that signal. Her reaction time was swift, and our calculations had factored in the fragment of a second that it would take a human to turn off the point source. The big chunk of rock floated quickly away from us, looking as innocent as you please.

The computer turned our ship, and we moved back up. Frazzle took over and headed us out to pick up our next stone.

The largest monitor had been switched to track the target area on the surface. As we regained our orbital altitude, there was a bright flash from the ground, followed by three more as each of the four rocks struck.

I left the rock gathering for Frazzle and called Judith, "That's the first four. We're reloading and will be back for another pass in a few minutes."

She replied, "That was earth-shaking. My head is still throbbing from the noise. Are you sure you're not dropping A-bombs?"

"Just rocks," I reassured her, "I hope we're being accurate."

"It looks from here like they fell in about the right place, but I can't tell," she said.

I signed off, and we maneuvered back in a higher orbit, burning our Em-drive at full power to set up for our next pass. The subsequent three passes went smoothly, and we re-targeted the smaller camps.

Midway through the process, Judith called, asking if we could stop.

"The explosions have been murder down here. Are you sure you haven't been dropping nuclear weapons?" she asked.

I answered, "No atomics, just KEWs. We could drop smaller rocks, but we need to have enough yield to wipe them out."

Her reply was a little discouraging, "I don't think there's any doubt that you've wiped them out. Many of the downtown buildings have fallen from the shaking, and we just had an earthquake. It was pretty violent and knocked down a lot of other stuff. Now we're getting after-quakes. If you keep up, I'm afraid that you'll wipe out the entire town. Please stop."

I considered. We'd gotten the main camps and part of the smaller ones, but we needed to hit their artillery. Then a happy thought hit me. We could fly shuttle sorties to take out their guns.

I called a halt to the KEW bombardment with a sigh of relief. I hadn't realized it, but the strain of worrying whether we were going to drop a rock in the wrong place had worn on me to the point that I had a splitting headache.

I glanced at Liz, and she stood up and came over to me immediately, concern in her eyes. She sensed that I wasn't operating at full capacity but hadn't realized why until that moment.

She grabbed my arm and pulled me into a hug, saying, "Dec, you're a bundle of nerves. Relax. You've stopped the bombardment, so there's nothing to worry about at the moment. Just –"

Her next utterance was smothered as I turned my face down and kissed her gratefully.

Chapter 40

We sent all of our shuttles down to Denver and spread out from there, looking for any remaining artillery batteries. There were several, but the Motherland gunners had run away for the most part.

The KEWs had killed a lot of men simply with the concussion wave. The high-velocity impact was fierce. The camps had been mostly vaporized, and a lot of debris was left surrounding the impact craters.

We flew out to the east and observed some small groups of men fleeing but didn't bother them. I thought that their stories would probably be a great deterrent. Anyone hearing about the KEW bombardment would have to be a total fool to try another attack.

It seemed like the Motherland Army threat was gone. If they managed to pull another force together, well... rocks were cheap. I wouldn't wait until they were so close to Denver, though. We could hit them out on the high plains just as easily. There were fewer things to damage with a poorly aimed shot out there.

For her part, Judith sent out armed scouting parties and patrols to bring in the remaining guns and supplies. She wanted to add the cannon to the city's defenses. If that made her feel better, I didn't want to discourage her, but, as far as I was concerned, all of the cannon in the world were nothing compared to the destructive power of one of my spaceships.

Judith and I jointly made plans for additional patrols far out to the east. She'd sent out some scouts immediately after the Motherland's defeat. They tailed the survivors back to the old Kansas-Colorado border and then set up a watch for any repeat incursions. So far, there were none.

My contribution to the intelligence-gathering effort was to fly daily sorties with one of our shuttles. Our spaceships also provided coverage from orbit, although it was not continuous. Our orbits were such that we covered the high-plains region four to five times daily.

The orbital video was good enough to detect individual men, but it was easier to simply set the computer to alert us to larger groups heading west. Otherwise, we'd be constantly checking out individual travelers.

The area decimated by the Motherland Army's invasion wasn't heavily populated. The invaders had chased many of the residents away and killed many of the rest who were fool-hardy enough to try and stay. Even so, most of the refugees were now filtering back to their homes with the intent of rebuilding. This created a considerable amount of westward traffic that we needed to inspect to prevent any infiltration by the enemy.

We used the computer to create a target list for the daily shuttle flight to check on. The shuttle often found groups in distress, under attack by remaining invaders. The pilot usually made a couple of passes with the cannon when that happened. That customarily solved the problem. The Motherland survivors had apparently learned their lesson. They'd attack a group of farmers, but the sight of the shuttle sent them running for cover.

Rudy and I took one of the mid-sized shuttles back to the east coast to check on the Motherland response to their defeat. We'd waited for a couple of weeks to give them time to hear the news and to formulate a response.

What we saw didn't give me any great feeling of security. They were gathering more men. Extensive camps surrounded the Washington DC area, and there were long-supply trains of wagons bringing food to the gathered forces.

The Motherland President hadn't accepted defeat, and I expected him to send his army back towards the mountains. It would take them some weeks to arrive if he did since they were limited in speed. That should give us enough time to respond. This time, I planned on responding quickly. I wasn't going to allow them to get so close. If they showed signs of moving towards us, we would use KEWs to strike their camps at night.

Flying over the Washington area, we tried the radio and eventually got through to their President. He was no more conciliatory this time than the first time we'd rebuffed his invasion forces. The guy simply gave me a headache. I considered how best to get rid of him, but we had no idea where he was. Somewhere in Washington, of course, but most likely not in a location where we could reach him easily.

The entire conversation was one-sided. He spent the whole time making various threats about what was going to happen to us. When he paused for breath, I delivered an ultimatum, telling him that we'd wipe out his forces again if they persisted in invading.

The message had no effect. He just made more threats, so I turned off the radio. I could only take so much of the bombast anyway. It was starting to make me angry, and Rudy was looking at me out of the corner of his eye the way he did when he thought I was about to do something stupid that I would end up regretting. I figured it was time to head back.

We flew directly up to orbit and docked with my ship to let me out, then Rudy and Whistle continued around the globe to their ship. Liz was waiting for me when I got through the airlock.

"It's about time you made it back here," she said, "I'm getting tired of this. All we're doing is floating around and around, and it's boring."

I replied, "Look, Honey, the Motherland forces are rebuilding, and I feel like I've got to keep an eye on them. We don't want them taking Denver. Grand Lake will be next after that, and I don't want them messing with our cabin."

She said, "That's just the point. We now live in this spaceship, and, as nice as it is, I'm tired of it. We aren't making any progress towards rebuilding human civilization, and we aren't going to be able to simply retire to our cabin. What are you going to do?"

She was right. Thinking about it, I realized that I'd been marking time in a way. It was past time to start implementing my organizational plans. I figured I'd start the process with Judith. The next day, I flew down and met with her.

It was a cool, clear day, typical for Denver. Now that the automobile-caused smog had cleared, Denver was clear and pleasant most of the year. Judith and I sat in the upper seats of the old stadium and discussed my concept of a confederation.

She agreed with me that it might be a way to rebuild gradually. Neither of us thought that the surviving human settlements would willingly renounce their autonomy instantly. It had been over five years since the EMP event, and the survivors had lived through some difficult times. They had gradually formed groups, and each had its way of dealing with problems.

We decided to send out messengers to spread the word that Denver was open for trade. Anyone who wanted to join in the confederation could send representatives, and we'd form a deliberative body. There would also be a promise of mutual assistance for everyone involved.

I gave her my list of basic principles, expecting some argument, but she read through it and agreed without any quibbling. I hoped that other potential confederation members would feel the same.

Since Judith was a capable administrator, probably more so than Jake had been, I left it in her hands to get the ball rolling. It wasn't something that I wanted to do anyway. The last thing I could see myself doing was becoming some kind of governing authority and dealing with long lists of human problems. Besides, I had another couple of organizations to create. I was intent on my vision of the Inter-species Space Confederacy and the Earth Space Protection Force.

Chapter 41

The Earth Space Protection Force was relatively easy to organize. I cheated. I gave the problem over to Rudy and Holmes. It wasn't too long before they had come up with a provisional organization based on our current resources. We'd need more ships, but the Sunnys, now freed of the Pug-bears, for the most part, were starting up their long-neglected industry, and it would simply be a matter of time before they started cranking out FTL ships at a higher rate. We discussed things with them via Ansible, and they agreed that it was desirable to create more ships quickly.

We also had to find suitable things to trade for the different groups and a means of exchange. I didn't want to create yet another fiat currency. Those had never worked out for humans, and I didn't want to have the same problem again, only magnified by involving three species. However, that was something for the future.

The first thing I needed for the Earth Space Protection Force was a base. I didn't want it to be on Earth. That would create too many opportunities for politics. We discussed various moons in the system but finally settled on Ceres. It could be argued that it is a planet, although a tiny one at about six hundred miles in diameter. There was also some speculation that there might be a considerable amount of water frozen under its surface. If so, we'd have no problem generating enough breathable gasses for our base.

The thing that convinced me was its low gravity. It was low enough that our FTL ships could dock in cradles on the surface. They were unable to enter a large planet's gravity well, but Ceres had a, you might say, very shallow well. It would save a lot of transporting back and forth. That was convenient since we'd just about ceased using the Sunnys' transporters.

I had never felt comfortable with the things, and now that I knew more about them, I felt even less at ease with them. The idea that there was a certain amount of noise injected into the signal each time you went through one led me to conclude that I didn't want to subject anyone to possible long-term effects. Besides, Frazzle told me that the Sunnys usually didn't use them. They'd only made so many of the things because the Pug-bears demanded them for the convenience of their empire and the Pugs.

We now restricted ourselves mostly to shuttle transportation, although a transporter trip was not out of the question in an emergency.

That would be a huge advantage if the FTLs could dock on Ceres. We could set up repair facilities. To convince myself, I grabbed a calculator and applied the formula for the surface area of a sphere. The planet was large in terms of surface area, providing millions of square miles of usable surface. I figured that would be more than adequate for our purposes.

I got Frazzle to take us out to Ceres. It took a few hours of medium acceleration and then deceleration. When we arrived, it wasn't as impressive as I'd hoped. The asteroid or planetoid – whatever, looked small until we'd come up quite close. There were some bright spots on the surface that I first thought might be Pug-bear domes.

Frazzle assured me that the Pug-bears hadn't gone to Ceres. The spots must be something else. As we got closer, they turned into what looked like scattered areas of some kind of ice. I was curious and couldn't wait until we'd landed, so we fired a laser at one of the spots. The resultant vapor showed us that it was primarily water-ice with traces of methane and some other compounds. That would be good enough. We could use that. I hoped there was a lot more buried in the crust.

I asked Frazzle how the Pug-bears' domes were created, and, once again, he surprised me.

"Oh, dat. That's easy, Dec," he waved his free hand in a circular motion. His other hand was on the ship's control yoke. "We gots plenty of dome machines in the small hold."

"The small hold?" I asked, "Where's that, and why don't I know about it?"

It turned out that the small hold was minimal, and I'd walked past it numerous times, thinking it was some of the ship's machinery. It was a room-sized storage area adjacent to the cafeteria. The door was locked with a heavy-duty mechanism, and perhaps that's why I'd ignored it. It didn't look like something you wanted to open casually.

It turned out that it wasn't entirely safe in there. The so-called dome machines were a little dangerous. You set the thing where you wanted a dome and retreated a suitable distance before activating it remotely. You didn't want to be too close when it began working.

The machine created a spherical field that quickly broke down molecules in the surrounding rock and dragged them into a clear-lattice structure that eventually covered the entire sphere. The domes weren't actually domes at all. They were just the top halves of buried spheres. The molecular lattice was both transparent and incredibly strong. The machine layered lattice upon lattice until the dome structure was several centimeters thick. The thickness wasn't needed to contain the relatively small pressure of the internal atmosphere. It was intended to ward off any strikes by debris or rocks.

Frazzle proudly informed me that the domes would withstand most micro-meteorites and when combined with a variation of the ship's shield, they were nearly indestructible. We loaded up a bunch of them and hauled them over to the surface of the small planet.

The gravity was strong enough that you could walk – sort of. It would do until we could get an artificial gravity generator working. That would allow us to increase the gravity to nearly earth-normal. I belatedly realized that I'd never questioned the stronger gravity in any of the domes I'd been in before.

Titan was large, but it really wouldn't have earth-like gravity, yet that had been the case when I'd first been there before blowing the place up. I now understood that there had been a gravity generator in operation.

Domes placed close enough to each other would conjoin, leaving neat openings. Careful placement would create a usable habitat and, eventually, I hoped, an entire city. Distant domes could be joined by tunnels or possibly by transporters if you wanted to use the things.

We unloaded the machines, and Frazzle carefully supervised their placement. Then we climbed back into the shuttle and rose off the surface at his request.

"We be safer dis way," he said. "The machines' fields don't differentiate between atoms. If you too close, they will take your atoms as well as the rocks. That's why the small hold is always locked. Not good to accidentally set one of these things off in the ship."

I replied, "I can see why –"

I paused, awestruck, as the fields began working on the surface. The things created a veritable rainbow of colors as they manipulated and moved the atoms into the dome structure. It was a fantastic light show.

I reflected that while human technology was close to that of the Sunnys in some ways, in other ways, they were far beyond us. I glanced at Liz and Hattie to tell them how amazed I was, but it wasn't necessary. They were as astounded as I was. Hattie's mouth was open with a half-smile. It was apparent that she found the colors entrancing. They were probably the most beautiful thing she'd seen in her life.

Once the domes were set, we had to install an airlock. The lock was another piece of genius Sunny engineering. It came in a small package that unfolded into a door-sized structure. At Frazzle's direction, we carefully placed it against the dome, and it somehow adhered to the lattice structure. When he activated the electronics, it cut the lattice bonds, leaving a piece of the dome that could be adapted as an inner door.

We installed the lock, entered, and took a quick tour through the connected domes. There was probably enough space in the ten domes we'd set up to house over a thousand people. It looked like Ceres was going to be the new headquarters of the ESPF.

I wondered how hard it would be to figure out a work schedule oriented around its nine-hour and four-minute "day." Initially, it seemed like we might work every third such day with one day off and one for sleeping. I guessed that people would probably adjust their circadian periods to fit the rotation period.

Frazzle installed some additional equipment inside to generate an atmosphere. There was enough ice in the crust to use for that purpose, and the atmosphere machine immediately began emitting a metered mixture of gasses. The atmosphere generating equipment was a variation of the dome-making machines adapted to drag molecules out of the crust and release them. A certain amount of heat was released at the same time, so the temperature issue was partially solved in that way.

The atmosphere machine was something that Frazzle had to adjust. It pulled material from the crust a distance away from the domes and could be set for any mixture of gas desired. He set it for an atmosphere that was a sort of compromise that all three of our species could easily breathe. The temperature would eventually have to be regulated with an environmental control unit, but we could leave it for the time being. It would remain warm enough that the atmosphere wouldn't condense or freeze.

We returned to the ship to wait for the domes to fill with air. Meanwhile, I called Rudy and requested that he bring the rest of the squadron to Ceres. Frazzle was anxious to have more Sunny help than our small contingent provided. Between the four ships, there was a sizable amount of equipment that we'd need to make the domes habitable. This was all stored in various lockers and holds that we humans hadn't known about.

Frazzle sort of apologized about that, "Dec, de use you puts the ships to so far not been setting up colonies. Each ship Sunnys build have some colony equipment, and Sunnys never think to tell you about it. Now we need all equipment we can get. The other ships

have parts for fabricating a dock structure and houses inside domes. Also important is Rudy's ship has an environmental control unit. That will keep temperature set right."

I just shook my head in amazement. The Sunnys were certainly thorough in terms of preparation.

"Frazzle, did the Pug-bears know about this equipment on the ships?" I asked.

"No, dey just leave all work to us Sunnys. We had to make everything work right or be killed, so we were careful to include plenty of equipment," he replied matter-of-factly.

I was disgusted, "The Pug-bears are just stupid, despite their grafted on intelligence!"

He looked at me with a funny expression, and I revised my statement.

"Well, I mean, they may have a certain amount of intelligence, but they didn't care about Sunnys."

"Dat's right. They thought that they could always get more of us, and they could do until you freed us. We grateful for that," he nodded in understanding.

It was near the end of my day shift, so I met Liz and the kids in the cafeteria. We ate and then took the children to the main hold for some zero-gravity playtime. Halfway through, Hattie and Kasm showed up, coming through the hatch together. She had her hand resting casually on his back as they came through. It looked a little unusual to me, and I glanced at Liz. She gave me a cocked eyebrow that meant not to comment, so I didn't.

The two proceeded to join the zero-g fun, playing tag with Michael and Rowan. We let the game go on for thirty minutes before deciding it was time to make sure the kids got some sleep. Leaving Hattie and Kasm still flying around, we returned to our quarters.

Once there, we concentrated on getting the children to sleep, but after they'd nodded off, I asked Liz, "What was that all about, anyway?"

She knew what I meant.

"I don't know if you've noticed. You've been busy with the domes and stuff, but Hattie and Kasm have seemed to hit it off in some way."

I was puzzled, "What does that mean?"

Liz sighed, "Hattie has never been able to open up to me. I think that her horrible experiences have made her afraid to have a human relationship. Maybe she thinks that humans are too easy to kill. She's been gradually spending more and more time with Kasm. He seems to enjoy having her around, so I haven't said anything."

I considered, "Maybe I'll have a conversation with him. See what he thinks is going on. I'm sure he means well."

It was a little disconcerting. I didn't know how intense their relationship was or what direction it was taking. I knew from experience that Kasm was a good friend and one that was more mentally similar to humans than were the Sunnys. I just wanted to make sure that neither of them had unreasonable expectations of the other.

I was reminded again that socializing with other intelligent species was not what humans normally did. The whole alien relationship thing was something that I was still trying to figure out.

Chapter 42

The next day shift, I happened to find Kasm in the hall outside the cafeteria. This was probably as good a time as any to talk. I restricted myself to mental communication in case someone happened by.

I didn't waste any time on formalities, "I noticed that you and Hattie seem to be working on some kind of relationship."

He looked at me, communicating a feeling of mental satisfaction as he did, "Yes. She reminds me of those I've lost. You know she lost her family also. We have something in common."

I replied, "I can see that. What I'm curious about is how you see your relationship with her developing."

"Dec, you and I have a strong relationship. You know I'd do anything to protect you and your family," he sent. "I have killed to protect you, and I'd do it again." He paused, thinking, "I guess Hattie is like that with me. In some strange way, I think she's a lot like my dead mate."

He hastily added, "I mean mentally, of course."

I wasn't fast enough to edit my thoughts, and he got an image that I didn't intend to send.

He looked at my face in return and sent, "You know, don't you that she's been sleeping in my cabin?"

"No, I didn't," I replied, "Are you, uh, can –"

He interrupted, "No, I know what you're asking, and the answer is we both enjoy the other's presence, but we've made no effort to be physically intimate."

He paused, then continued, "I believe that we could be. I mean, I've seen you, and my physiology is not that different in that respect. But she's content just being near, and so am I in some strange way. She fills a void in my heart that I never thought would be filled."

I was first shocked, and then I thought it over, and maybe it wasn't so shocking after all. What was important here? They were both sentient, capable of deciding what they wanted and making emotional bonds. Maybe physical differences were the least important part of it. And, besides, maybe it wasn't any of my business as long as they were both happy about the situation.

"Look, Kasm, I don't want her to be hurt, that's all," I said.

He responded, "That's not my intention. It's the last thing I would do. I was a little hesitant about her moving in with me, but I decided that if she could put up with my alienness, I could put up with hers. It's not like you humans smell bad to me."

He grimaced at me with his lips pulled back, "At least most of the time. You could try to avoid passing gas when I'm around."

That wasn't fair, I'd only done it one time when I was feeling a little under the weather, but it hadn't made a favorable impression on him.

I answered, "I'll try to restrain myself. It doesn't smell good to me either."

"Then why do it?" he asked.

"It's not something that we mean to do. It's just how our intestinal system works," I tried to explain, wondering how we'd gotten so far off the track.

"Why don't you not worry about it, Dec? Let's just let us work out what we want on our own time. I promise you I only want the best for her, and I'll come to you if there's any problem," he sent.

I spoke to Liz about the conversation when I had a chance. She'd had a brief moment alone with Hattie and had engaged in a similar line of discussion. Liz and I thought so much alike, and I should have known that she'd satisfy her curiosity.

She said, "Hattie didn't have much to say about them. She told me she was staying in Kasm's cabin and that he made her feel more secure than she'd felt for a long time. I think he's such a capable fighter that she more or less automatically gravitated to him. You're already taken, you know, so she grabbed hold of the next candidate.

I grinned, "I see, but don't you think she should be more interested in another human, one of the Marines, for instance?"

She replied, "Maybe not. I think she's so fearful of losing another human that she won't emotionally bond with a man. She doesn't have the same fear about Kasm, so I sort of understand it in that manner."

I wasn't willing to let it go yet, "She's still a child. She's maybe only seventeen. Will she change her mind?"

"If she does, she does. That 'still a child' stuff doesn't cut it any longer, either, and you know that. Humans have been getting married or mating at much younger ages for our whole existence. We've only recently set some artificial limits on what society defines as appropriate ages for various activities. I think she's capable of finding her way."

I agreed, "That's sort of what Kasm told me. He said that they'd see how things went, and he'd come to me with any problems."

Liz paused and then said, "One thing that you might do..."

I waited, but she didn't finish. I finally prompted her, "Yes?"

"Well, I think it might be a good idea if you tried to transfer some psychic ability to her," she finished.

I considered. It would be possible. I'd opened Liz's mind to the latent human ability. She was pretty good at it. The other people I'd tried to train had various degrees of success. Some were fair, none were good, but over half had simply resisted, and I hadn't been able to help them make the breakthrough.

"I'll try," I said, "It would be the best thing I could do to help her interact with Kasm."

His native mode of communication was mental, although his telepathic voice wasn't powerful from my perspective. He could talk to me, and after much effort, he'd finally been able to send to Liz a little. The chances of him and Hattie communicating were slim, but if there was any chance at all, I now realized that I owed it to both of them to try.

"I'll do it as soon as I can arrange the time," I said.

We kissed, and she returned to check on the kids while I went on to the bridge.

The rest of the squadron had arrived, and the Sunnys were busy working on the habitat. They'd drafted all of the Marines and some of the Sim-tigers to help carry things inside the domes. The place was taking shape, starting to show signs of becoming the headquarters that I'd envisioned.

There was a group of Sunnys working outside the dome, creating some kind of structure that I presumed was destined to be a docking gantry. The Marines and Sim-tigers were all working inside in the pressurized part of the habitat.

When I arrived in the bridge, Frazzle was there.

"Hi, Frazzle," I sent, "What's happening?"

He was gradually becoming inured to human mannerisms and replied, "Not muchs happening, just building de system."

I nodded.

He continued, "We going to need more help. Can we get more humans from Earth to come and work? Dere not enough Sunnys and Marines to finish this place quickly."

"What kind of help do you need?" I asked aloud.

"We needs men dat can do building. Maybe some scientists or technical people who can be trained to operate the environment systems and engineers who can help build the docks for the FTL ships. We also need to work on hangers for shuttles and maybe farming in some of the domes for food and whole bunch of other stuffs, too," he said.

I realized then that putting together a settlement was not as simple as checking into a motel and then going down to the attached restaurant when hungry. There was a lot to the system.

This was precisely what I didn't enjoy doing. I'd always prided myself on my ability to take direct and immediate action to solve problems, but I'd never really liked setting up systems and administering them. I'd have to get someone appointed to run things pretty quickly. I didn't want to be that involved, as long as stuff worked and we could survive.

Besides, I still had to work on the overall structure of the Earth Space Protection Force with Rudy and Holmes, and then the Inter-species Space Confederacy posed an equally important problem. I was determined to get both organizations set up and functioning smoothly. The problem I had was finding suitable people to work in the organizations. I thought that maybe I could convince Judith to help out if she could be pried out of the Denver administration job. Still, it was a problem that I had to deal with personally, and the thing was, I didn't enjoy it at all. I had my doubts about exactly how effective I'd be as a result.

After some thought, I put my concerns aside in favor of another idea.

"Frazzle, can we scoop up some dust and store it in one of our holds? I want to experiment with using it as a defense against anti-matter shots," I said. I'd been thinking about my previous idea of using it and now seemed to be a reasonable time to try out the concept.

He answered, "I can do dat. The gravity point source can reach far enough to get some of the dusts off the surface. There is a place near the domes where there is lot of dusts in a depression. We fly by. I grab bunch of dusts and pull it into the small hold. It empty now, anyways. All the dome machines on the surface."

It took fifteen minutes of maneuvering to cruise by closely enough for the point-source to reach. It pulled back nearly a ton of mostly rock dust with some ice particles mixed in.

I didn't want to dilute our atmosphere if the ice melted and released any methane or some other noxious gas, but Frazzle assured me that he'd keep the small hold sealed and unheated so that the dust would remain in its frozen state. We discussed the operation and concluded that we could pressurize the hold and simply blow the dust back out in a cloud. Once outside the ship, it could be gathered up by the point source and moved into position as a shield. We'd try it out once we reached a suitable distance from Ceres.

At that point, Frazzle again brought up the need for more help, and we agreed to take our ship to Earth on a recruiting mission. We'd head for Denver and see how many people wanted a chance to work on Ceres or crew our ships. I had some doubts that we would get many volunteers, but Frazzle was right when he said we needed a lot of help.

Chapter 43

The Pug-controlled FTLs dropped out of faster-than-light speed near the Earth, well inside the Moon's orbit. No one had given the Pugs the message about the efficiency of KEWs. Instead, they had loaded their ships with extremely powerful nuclear bombs. The disruption of the Pug-bears' plans had angered the Pugs extremely. They had their own plans that included gradually taking over the Pug-bears' empire. Now that was not to be, and they were out for vengeance.

The Motherland President sat in the Oval Office in the old White House. It was a building that had been a palace in all but name, and now that he'd renamed it "The Palace of the World," even that distinction had vanished.

The old building was shabby and in disrepair, but the President didn't notice. His mind was not entirely connected with reality, and he often saw only what he wanted to see.

He turned to look out the window, gazing over the rows of gallows on the unkempt lawn and fondly looking at the hanging bodies. He had many enemies, and it was good to know that he had the power of life and death over them. Besides, the population would be less likely to revolt if they were constantly reminded of the fate of those who displeased him.

His mind wandered back to his main problem. Somehow the foolish people who lived in Denver had defeated his army...his mighty army. He'd hung most surviving generals as an object lesson to the rest. The men he'd promoted to fill their places would do better this time, he was sure.

He looked up toward the horizon, gazing past the distant oblisque of the old Washington monument at the clouds. Something had caught his attention. Something was falling from high above. He looked hard and then saw a brilliant burst of light inside one of the clouds a few miles away.

He started to say the phrase that many people had heard and subsequently rued, "Someone will die for this!" However, there was only time for "Someone will die –" before the first wave of the bomb's blast smashed through the building, carrying fragments of the monument with it. The intense light and heat instantly crisped him into ash that blew away as if he'd never existed.

The blast was huge, releasing over eight hundred kilotons of energy. Almost instantly after the detonation, the center of the explosion reached approximately five times the temperature at the center of the sun, approaching two hundred million degrees Fahrenheit.

The next thing to happen was a sphere of superheated air began expanding outward at over a million miles per hour, creating a vast compression wave that preceded the fireball.

In the next second, the initial fireball expanded to a mile in diameter and cooled to a temperature that was about four thousand degrees hotter than the surface of the sun. This incredible heat and light instantly ignited fires over a circle of about ten miles in diameter. This flaming wave of fire reached the "Palace of the World" shortly after that, shattering the windows and instantly evaporating all of the water contained in the Motherland President's body.

The Motherland President had been allowed only a split second to see the fireball blaze brighter than ten thousand suns before his eyes melted and his skin vaporized. Shortly after his body converted to ash and blew away, scattered by the blast, the fireball caused fires over an area of nearly one hundred square miles. Those fires forced huge masses of heated air high into the stratosphere, creating a vacuum effect and pulling all the air from surrounding areas into the center of the fire zone.

The fires ignited by the initial detonation began to merge, and within ten minutes after the initial blast, the entire center of Washington was aflame.

This giant fire dwarfed the energy output of the nuclear bomb many times over.

At this point, the firestorm was just getting started, creating rising winds of over three hundred miles per hour. The vacuum effect increased exponentially so that cooler air rushed inward towards the center of the blaze at more than hurricane velocities, uprooting trees and dragging people and entire buildings into the flame.

The city streets filled with horizontally driven fire moving at such a velocity that it broke through doors and windows, burning the contents of all buildings that had missed the initial destruction. The moving air had an average temperature of several hundred degrees, and its impact produced a lethal firestorm. Nothing remained standing, and no one survived within that area.

The structures directly below the initial blast were vaporized, and all buildings within a couple of miles of ground zero were crushed. High-rises were ripped open, and their flaming contents were dispersed widely, contributing to the flames.

The light from the fireball was so intense it melted the asphalt in the streets, and all metal surfaces within a mile of the blast began to run as the metal quickly liquefied.

The blast-induced winds spread out over the district, igniting fires and knocking down buildings, melting aluminum surfaces, and charcoaling the skin of all who were unlucky enough to be exposed to the direct light and wind.

Within fifteen seconds, the blast wave had traveled three miles, and the winds had died to a little over two hundred miles per hour. Fires raged everywhere over the area within ten miles of the blast epicenter.

Ten miles away, the flash was still powerful enough to cause third-degree burns for anyone exposed. No one who was within that incredible firestorm zone survived. Even those far underground died from fire-created gasses, while those who weren't deep enough simply baked alive.

Once the firestorm had died out, the area was too hot to allow anyone to pass through. The ground and roads maintained an oven-like temperature for days.

The next phase of the horror began as the dust and debris drawn upwards into the stratosphere began to fall back to Earth, tens and even hundreds of miles downwind. Everything that fell was radioactive, and that poison would linger in the Earth, killing and mutating every form of life for years.

The Motherland President didn't know it, but his death was one of millions. The Pugs had exacted maximum vengeance for Dec's actions. Washington DC, New York, LA, Singapore, and Tokyo all burned within thirty minutes of each other as the bombs fell from low orbit.

After suffering the terrible effects of the EMP attack years before, humankind had just been struck with what might prove to be a mortal blow.

Chapter 44

The ship was unloaded. There was no additional equipment left on board, and everyone had gone down to the surface of Ceres, including Liz and our children. The Sunnys had made quick progress, and there were now enough finished rooms to hold everyone.

The dome system had plenty of space for apartments far more luxurious than the ship's cabins. I could see that we'd have to engage in heavy recruiting if we were to begin to fill the domes. There would also be the need to continually find more Marines and spacemen, especially if the Sunnys could deliver more ships.

Frazzle and I were in the bridge, heading back to Earth. We'd already gotten up to speed and were rapidly leaving the vicinity of Ceres. There was no need for us to have help. I could do all of the talking, and we'd need as much space as possible to transport people, so just the two of us were aboard.

I was finishing up speaking to Liz on the radio when Frazzle made an exclamation, "Oh-Oh! Dec! Look at dis!"

I turned to the monitor to see that he had it focused on Earth. The distance was extreme, but it was evident that there had been an enormous explosion. We could see the flickering of the fading light emitted.

"Dat's fusion reaction!" he exclaimed. "Somebody just set off big bomb on surface."

There was a second pulse of light followed closely by a third.

"Two mores goes off! Very bad for peoples on surface. Would it be de Motherland peoples who shoots them off?" Frazzle was so upset, he was wringing his hands together.

"I don't know. They might have some bombs left over, but I don't know how they'd deliver them. I don't think they have any missiles or airplanes that could do it. Perhaps they were set off on the surface by a timer or suicide bomber –"

He interrupted my speculation. "No! Look dere," he pointed at the distant planet with one hand while increasing the magnification with another. "It's another FTL. Maybe de Pugs dropped bombs."

I momentarily wondered if we should get more help but then decided it would take too long. Frazzle could fly, and I could shoot. We needed to get there quickly and stop whatever was going on. Otherwise, it didn't look good for Earth.

As I thought that, another explosion went off on the surface. I turned to Frazzle to tell him to speed up, but he anticipated my order and had already set the ship to maximum acceleration. We'd be there as quickly as possible.

"Let's arrive with plenty of speed," I said. "I'd like to fly past them and shoot before they can get ready for us."

"Dey likely to know we coming before we get too close. De Em-drive not very detectable, but they see us if they're looking," he responded.

"You're right, but maybe they think we're out of the system, or maybe they're only concentrating on the surface. Let's hope we get lucky."

He muttered over his shoulder, distractedly, "Lucky, dat's what we need to be."

The trip seemed to take longer than ever. Once we began decelerating and our rate of approach slowed, I was practically shaking with anticipation. Belatedly, I realized that it might be a good idea to get into our vacuum suits. We donned them, leaving the helmets open. I seated myself at the weapons console, and Frazzle continued his piloting.

We approached the Moon's orbit, coming past it on the dark side. The enemy FTL was just coming around the Earth towards us in a low orbital pass. I thought they were preparing to drop more bombs and, in an attempt to forestall them, I fired a long burst of anti-matter.

They were on a bombing run and, although my shot missed their ship, it struck the bomb, destroying it. They immediately turned towards us and accelerated. Their ship was armed, evidenced by a sparkling blue ball of plasma that came flying towards us.

We could see it coming from almost the instant they shot. It approached rapidly, growing in size. At the last moment, Frazzle wrenched the ship into a sharp turn causing the internal momentum compensation to stutter slightly. I was jerked out of position and ended up sliding across the deck and fetching up against the stanchions of the seating in the back of the bridge.

Frazzle dove our ship down towards the atmosphere in an evasive maneuver as the plasma ball flew past. I scrambled across the floor on hands and knees until I could grab the framework of the weapons station, then I dragged myself up and into the seat. Once there, I got the targeting laser locked onto the enemy ship and triggered off another burst. This one came from one of the waist guns.

The enemy FTL managed to evade the shot somehow. The anti-matter burst wasn't as easy to detect as the plasma shots. It could only be seen when it reacted with ordinary matter, and I didn't know how they got out of the way.

Nor did I know if a Sunny or a Pug piloted the enemy ship, but whomever it was, was a master ship driver. Their ship spiraled around and followed us down into the upper reaches of the atmosphere, still firing, but to no effect.

I desperately tried to get the targeting system locked on again as Frazzle threw our ship back and forth, avoiding the plasma bursts. At one point, my display showed the surface right where one of the atomic bombs had exploded. It looked bad.

The bomb had gone off over mid-town Manhattan, and there was now a colossal firestorm burning out of control all the way out to Queens. I couldn't see any of the tall buildings on the island. I figured they'd all been flattened.

I knew the death toll would be tremendous, although not as large as it would have been a few years prior. Since the EMP burst, our society had been forced to spread out. Cities no longer could depend on regular, bulk food deliveries and the people who still survived had less of a tendency to congregate in large urban centers. Nevertheless, there were still plenty of city dwellers, and from what I could glimpse, most of them had just been wiped off the face of the globe.

We skipped out of the atmosphere over DC. It, too, was burning and must have been the target of one of the other two bombs. I guessed that would be the end of the Motherland president's attempt at empire-building. Without their central control, they'd fall apart.

We circled in a tight turn, coming out with a clear shot at the enemy's tail section. The targeting system flashed red as it locked on, and I triggered a long burst from our bow gun.

My shooting was more accurate this time, and a chunk of their tail section disappeared. Their Em-drive flashed and then blew apart as its containment vessel ruptured. This should have been the end of the battle, but they somehow continued to shoot as they coasted away from the Earth.

One of their plasma bolts finally struck us directly on the bow. The bow deflection shield largely dissipated the plasma ball, but enough leaked through to disable the bow cannon. It had been recharging, and the anti-matter containment chamber blew. The result was terrible. Anti-matter sprayed out in a jet directly towards the bow plate.

The cannon's base disappeared, and a large chunk of the bow plate vanished with it. The ship's emergency lights went on, and a siren started. The air pressure immediately started dropping. We'd been holed.

Frazzle and I sealed our helmets and turned on our internal air supplies. I briefly congratulated myself for my foresight in donning our spacesuits. The ship's warning lights continued to flash, but the siren gradually faded out as the atmospheric pressure in the bridge dropped towards zero.

I refocused on the battle and fired another shot from one of our waist guns. It struck their bridge area and opened the ship to space, blowing a lot of debris and some bodies out the opening. We were too far away to see if they were Pugs, but I assumed that was the case.

I was just beginning to congratulate myself again for winning the fight when Frazzle came on my suit's com system, "Dere's another one of dem! Watch out!"

The enemy had another ship! I'd thought that there was only one left in existence, but somehow there had been two. The enemy ship had appeared over the horizon on the far side of the ship I'd just destroyed.

The second ship was closing with frightening rapidity. To make matters worse, it was armed with anti-matter weapons rather than plasma cannons. I knew this because part of my initial target's wreckage suddenly disappeared with a burst of light as the new enemy's anti-matter burst struck it.

Frazzle was ahead of me and had blown the small hold's doors open. The next thing I knew, a mobile cloud of dust suddenly appeared between our ship and the approaching enemy. He'd activated the point source and dragged the dust in place as a shield.

The enemy shot again, and there was an enormous flare of light as the dust absorbed the anti-matter. It worked, but now there was a large hole through the center of the dust cloud. I fired back right through the hole.

As soon as my shot had gone through, Frazzle reconfigured the cloud, closing the hole. There wasn't another flare, so they hadn't fired a second shot.

By now, the enemy ship had moved past our location and was starting to recede. I took another shot at them with my tail gun as it came to bear.

Frazzle was starting to move the dust cloud around into position to protect our tail, but he was too late. They'd fired another shot as they went past, and it slipped in before the cloud shielded us. Our Em-drive vanished, as did all three of our FTL vanes and the tail gun.

We were now drifting in space in an airless ship. Thankfully, there was still power, and we could still fight with both of our waist guns. Frazzle had gotten the remains of the dust cloud into position between the enemy ship and us. It was a little late but still necessary since they'd fired a second shot as they started to decelerate.

The dust cloud flared and vanished. We now had no shielding, and their next shot would probably take out the rest of the ship.

I aimed both waist guns towards their position and fired a long burst. Somehow, I managed to miss their hull while disintegrating their anti-matter cannons. They had turned and were coming towards us but could no longer shoot.

I watched, belatedly realizing that my shot had taken off part of their FTL vanes and somehow damaged their attitude adjustment jets. Their ship was slowly rotating as it moved forward. They were unable to steer and didn't have Em-drive power either.

I knew that I shouldn't relax, but I had the brief thought that this would be easy. They couldn't shoot, and I could. Of course, things went wrong immediately. As I was locking the targeting computer onto them, our reactor blew out, taking most of the rest of our aft section with it. The guns both went down instantly. The only one that had battery back-up was the bow gun, and it was gone. I'd thought about installing batteries on the waist guns but had mistakenly felt that ship's power would be adequate.

The Pugs were headed directly at our position. They'd managed to accelerate before my shot had disabled them, and they were slowly approaching our position.

Frazzle turned to me in the dim, red, emergency illumination and said, "What's we do now, Dec? I can't fly. Maybe shuttle okay, but the computer is down, and I don't know."

I answered, "They are still coming, and there's a chance they'll figure out they can shoot at us with hand-held weapons. Let's go. You check on the shuttle and get it ready, and I'll try to get an anti-matter rifle to shoot at them before they think to shoot at us."

He was out of his seat like a little rocket, flying across the bridge in its now zero-gravity state. The pathway to the hold was longer without the in-ship transporter, but there was still a way to get there. I followed him quickly down the long hall.

We entered the main hold, and Frazzle shot over to the manual lock controls while I searched for weapons. The weapons locker was empty. Not an anti-matter gun to be found, neither pistol nor rifle. I suddenly remembered that the Marines had taken their weapons when they disembarked and transported down to the Ceres habitat.

I searched the locker again and finally found a practice sword left by one of the Sim-tigers. It was a Katana, but not a very sharp one. It had been used to strike targets, and the blade was in rough shape. There was still a bit of an edge, and the point was serviceable, but the thing wouldn't cut nearly as well as a sharp sword. It would have to do, though. There just wasn't anything else.

Chapter 45

I took the practice Katana and exited the hold through the now opened lock. Frazzle was headed across the surface of the ship towards the shuttle. The craft looked undamaged, but I couldn't see its far side.

I could, however, see the approaching hulk. It was coming directly towards us, spinning slowly. The surface of the ship looked funny. I stared for a moment and then realized it was covered with Pugs in spacesuits. There were maybe fifty of them.

I headed for the shuttle, but I could see that the ships were drifting together quickly. The Pugs were launching themselves towards our ship. I didn't know if they thought it was flyable or if they just wanted to continue the fight, but I did know that I was pretty angry and wanted a chance at them.

Fortunately, they weren't armed with anti-matter weapons. Some were unarmed, and some had splinter guns, but I wasn't too worried about those things. They weren't quite powerful enough to pierce a spacesuit unless they happened to strike precisely on a vulnerable joint. My chances were pretty good that they'd be unable to hurt me with the splinters.

The first Pug came gliding towards me, and I automatically oriented so that it seemed like he was flying upwards while I was looking downwards towards him. It was a simple matter to strike him with the Katana.

The sword might have been dull, but I swung hard, and a jet of atmosphere came out of his suit, spinning him around and away from me. I got my feet underneath me, using the built-in attachments of the suit's soles. The second Pug struck the ship nearby, bouncing off at an angle that placed him within my reach as he glided past.

I lunged with the sword, and the tip entered his throat. When I pulled it back, a gush of Pug blood followed, boiling as it exited the hole. That was two down.

Then there was furious action as the next eight or so of the creatures struck. They had timed their jumps better and didn't bounce off the surface.

I fought through them like swinging at a stream of fish approaching me. Each swing took the closest one, leaving me in position to strike the next as it approached. I was conscious of my hoarse breathing. The suit wasn't adjusted for my level of exertion, and it was shorting me on oxygen. It was getting progressively harder and harder to catch my breath. I'd have to slow down to breathe, and there were still maybe twenty more Pugs on their way.

I paused, trying to breathe. As I did, five more of the creatures landed on our ship and headed towards me. As the first approached, I saw that it was armed with a knife. A glance showed that the others were similarly armed. They wanted to kill me and had the means to accomplish that task. My mind suddenly flashed over to pure survival mode. I'd previously been fighting systematically, but now my instinct took over.

I took several slow steps off to the right. This reoriented their attack so that the first one was now between me and the others who were following. I stuck him in the chest, holing his suit. That gave him something more urgent than killing me to think about.

He thrashed about, getting tangled with the following two as they tried to bypass him. I slid forward, striking one with a forehand swing and then using the rebound to strike the second with a backhand.

The first one lost his hand to the blade, a wound that was a death sentence. The second suffered a shattered faceplate and lost all of his air at once.

This left about eighteen more for me. The ones already on my ship slowed their approach, waiting until the latecomers landed. As the others gained a foothold, they gradually spread out to surround me.

It looked bad. I had an advantage in reach, but there were way too many of them, and I still hadn't gotten my breath. My suit just wasn't delivering enough oxygen. I momentarily thought that if I lived through this, I'd have to get Frazzle to install some kind of emergency override to allow the suit to perform at a higher level.

Two of the creatures rushed me from opposite sides. That was a mistake. The first got the sword point through his brisket, and the second got a back side-kick that launched him off the ship, sending him spinning off into space with no way to return. That was just as good as an immediate kill as far as I was concerned.

The others paused momentarily, then came on. Glancing around, I realized that I might have a better chance if I retreated into the ship. The opened lock was immediately behind me. I'd inadvertently back-tracked as I'd fought, and it was now only a few yards away.

I continued stepping slowly backward. I couldn't hear the Pugs, their com systems were tuned to another channel, but they were obviously trying to coordinate their attack. Some of them split off to either side of me and started circling. I jumped forward and spitted the closest one, then turned and ran to the open lock. The ship's emergency lighting illuminated the inside of the hold with a dim, red witch-light. I remembered that the Pugs came from a dim, red star system. The lighting would favor them, but I still thought I'd have the advantage.

I jumped through the opening, just as two of the creatures also reached the lock. We flew into the hold in close proximity. My extensive practice with the Marines in zero-gravity came through. I shoved one of them with my foot, launching me towards the other in such a way that I could hit him with my sword. It cut through the leg of his suit, leaving me free to roll into position to bounce off the far side of the hold.

The one I'd kicked slammed his head against a girder, cracking his faceplate seal. Two down.

The rest were watching, clustered around the opened hatch. They slowly moved through, sliding around until they stood inside the hold. The suits' sole grippers worked on the inside of the hold just as well as on the outside of the ship, and the Pugs showed no inclination to launch themselves in my direction. They were unused to zero-gravity battle and were simply trying to keep themselves oriented as if they were fighting on the ground. That was a grave disadvantage for them. I had no such limitations.

Now that I was inside the ship's body, I felt more at ease. Outside, I was forced to keep my surface orientation. I couldn't jump off the ship without floating away, out of control. Now, inside, there was always another wall to bounce off. The only thing I had to make sure of was not to fly through the open hatch.

I picked the farthest, most isolated Pug and launched quickly in his direction. He looked up at me as I approached, snarling through his faceplate and lifting his knife. It was a useless gesture. I slammed him on the top of the helmet with the Katana, splitting it in half.

The rebound rotated me, and I extended my legs to bounce off the nearby wall, moving across the hold as if I were flying by the rest of their group, just above their reach. I slashed another helmet, causing me to rotate again while the Pug thrashed around, entangling two of his fellows.

I managed to straighten myself out in time to hit a second one on the shoulder. My strike caused a small leak in his suit, and he dropped his knife, grabbing at the leaking slice in an attempt to slow the pressure loss. I was now rotating horizontally in a flat spin that placed me in the position of approaching the next enemy with my feet first.

That wasn't optimal, but I just bent at the waist and pointed my sword downward between my feet. The point entered his throat and got caught, almost jerking the sword out of my hand as I glided on over his body. I managed to hang on, but his corpse came flying after me before the Katana slid out of the wound. The extra weight changed my center of balance, and I began to rotate rapidly, feet over head, turning backward cartwheels towards the nearby wall of the hold.

By drawing my legs up and then extending them, I first increased my rotation, then slowed it at the right time to get my feet between me and the wall. I hit with a slam that hurt my knees and threw me off balance towards the far corner of the space.

There were seven Pugs left now, and they weren't showing any signs of wanting to quit fighting. The blasted creatures were true warriors. I give them that. For the most part, they didn't know the meaning of surrender.

My current status wasn't optimal. There had been so many bounces and changes of direction that I was feeling disoriented; the room seemed to be spinning wildly. I was flying towards a corner, and I had no idea how I should try to land. As a result, I crashed into two walls in a way I hadn't done since I'd been a beginner at zero-gravity combat.

It stunned me, and I floated away slowly, trying to fight off a sudden urge to vomit. My vision had gone momentarily black when the back of my head hit the wall, and I was still seeing flashes of light in my left eye. That was bothersome, but what was worse, one of the Pugs had finally figured out that he could jump out into free-fall to try and catch me.

He sailed up as I rotated slowly across above him. I managed to thrash my legs in such a way that I met his jump with my sword point, impaling him from the shoulder through to his waist. The sword was locked into his body, and the leverage was more than I could hold this time.

He rotated away, ripping the Katana from my grasp. My vision flashed one last time and then cleared as I approached the far wall of the hold. I stuck out a foot and rebounded gracefully, heading back to the other side, near the ceiling.

There was a Pug there, and I guess that he thought he had me. I had no weapon, and I could see him show his teeth as he prepared to thrust his knife home.

It was time for some basic judo. I caught his wrist and levered my body around to place his arm in an armbar. My legs came down across his torso, and I pulled back with all of my strength. I could feel his other arm slam onto my left

leg, but it wasn't enough. His suit's shoulder joint released with a popping sound. The fabric ripped, and his arm broke as the air rushed out of his suit. I let go, grabbing the knife as it spun by my face.

The others were headed my way fast. They'd all jumped towards me as I grappled with their fellow. I threw the knife at the first one, striking him in the chest with the point. He glided up, and I bounced off his body in a way that sent me towards the recently skewered corpse to retrieve my sword. That left the other aliens flying towards a location where I was no longer waiting for them.

They were five in number, and as I pulled the sword out of the corpse's grip, it occurred to them that I was, somewhat incredibly, winning the fight. Two of them threw their knives at me. One missed by a long distance, but the other knife came flying right towards my chest. I swiped at it with the sword, contacting it blade to blade. The knife's spin slowed, and it bounced grip first off of my chest. Good enough, I thought.

The impact slowed me so that I drifted into the middle of the hold. This time, the three armed Pugs decided to jump me all at once. They carefully moved into position and then jumped, timing their launches to strike me all at the same time.

I whipped the sword through one's arm, setting his knife free along with his hand. The backslash took out the second Pug, leaving me moving along a path that was too far away for the third to be a problem. He looked over his shoulder at me, grimacing as he receded towards the far wall. Suddenly, his grimace turned to a nasty grin, and he pointed past me.

I turned and realized that I was drifting on a perfect course right for the middle of the open hatch. There was nothing I could do. I was too close. Even if I threw my sword to try and push me back towards the hatch, the reaction would be too little, too late.

I drifted through the hatch and away from the ship heading towards a slow death.

Chapter 46

I was dead. I knew it, but my heart refused to acknowledge the fact, even though it was just a matter of time before I was out of air. Out of the corner of my faceplate, I could see my crippled ship receding into the shadow of the Earth. It was losing altitude, and I thought it would enter the atmosphere within another orbit or so. The Pugs may have chased me out and left me floating in space with nowhere to go, but their prospects weren't any better. They'd become flaming bits of wreckage long before I was dead.

As I floated, I reached out with my mind and contacted – Frazzle! He was headed towards me in the shuttle. He'd managed to launch it in the fracas. He'd accelerated rapidly away to ensure that none of the debris from the Pugs' ship struck the lightly armored shuttle. The result was that he'd quickly left our vicinity and was now working his way back down towards my orbit from several thousand miles out.

There was something funny, though. I could sense some additional mental activity from off in the other direction. I turned my head but couldn't see anything for a moment. Then I made out a brief flash as some polished surface reflected moonlight for a moment. There was another ship headed my way.

I waited, trying to determine what ship it was and who was coming. I didn't think that any of our other ships were near. I tried to contact the faint mental activity. For a moment, I thought I was making progress. Then, shockingly and abruptly, I was thrown out. This was like no mental defense I'd ever encountered. It was as if I'd been physically thrown through a door, and a stone wall had then dropped down.

I tried again. Nothing.

The flash repeated a few minutes later, and I could suddenly see something moving closer to me. My eyes refocused, and then I could make out a little more. The object was not one of our ships! It was partly translucent, but most of it was jet black. The result was I couldn't figure out the shape, only getting an intimation of its strangeness. It continued to approach, moving slowly.

At this point, I didn't want to be picked up by that thing. I didn't know who or what was inside, and I didn't want to find out. Whatever it was, I couldn't touch it mentally and, if given my preference, I'd rather hang around waiting for Frazzle.

As if my thought had invoked him, my suit's comm system crackled, and his voice came through.

"I got you on de screen. Won't be too long before I get there, but Dec, something coming behind you. What is it?" His transmission came through clearly.

I replied, "I don't know, but I can't contact them mentally, so I'm not too anxious to find out. They must be some other kind of creatures. They're not Pugs or Pug-bears, or Sunnys either."

The strange ship seemed to have detected the oncoming shuttle. It flashed again as it turned, and then I could see the shape a little better. It was still difficult to make out, but it looked very long, and the angles were all wrong. The shapes were ones that neither Sunnys nor humans would use in design. This was definitely someone else.

Whoever it was didn't wait around for the shuttle to get close. The ship started to move outwards away from the Earth. It didn't fool around, either. One moment it was there, and the next, I was frantically trying to move my eyes fast enough to track the thing. It accelerated almost instantly, leaving behind a quickly fading phosphorescence, possibly dust particles super-heated by its rapid motion.

Frazzle called again, "I getting close. You get ready to catch hold. De other thing leaved fast. I tracked it past the moon, but it gone now."

"Do you have any idea what it was?" I asked.

He paused for a moment, then answered, "Not sure. Dere be some reports of other ships from way out. Far away. Sunnys not contact, so I don't know. Maybe this one of them."

I was getting my old tingling sensation down the back of my neck. My warning sense was going off, and I suddenly had an insight. The brain implants! They'd seemed to be much higher tech than anything the Motherland people should have been able to build, and they weren't Sunny-made. Maybe there was another player in our local drama.

My train of thought was interrupted by the frightening view of the shuttle careening towards me at a high rate of speed. It looked like the thing would run me down, and I drew up my legs instinctively.

It was all perspective, however. Frazzle had done a masterful job of intercepting my path. The shuttle rapidly slowed and came to a halt relative to me, but about ten meters away.

Frazzle radioed, "I got close. Wait a bit and I moves closer. Maybe you can get foots on hull where dey grip."

For once, I was ahead of him. I'd already launched my Katana downwards toward the Earth, and the opposite reaction was gradually moving me towards the hull. Since I out-massed the sword by a factor of at least twenty, my movement wasn't very swift, but I was moving in the right direction, nevertheless.

A couple of minutes later, I was able to stretch out my right leg and get the gripping part of my suit's boot onto the shuttle hull. From there, it was just a walk in the park. Well, maybe a little more complicated, but still, it only took another minute to access the hatch and get inside.

The cramped shuttle had never looked so good. Frazzle pressurized the compartment, and we removed our helmets.

"What was that ship, Frazzle?" I didn't want to let the topic go. It seemed even more critical than his rescuing me.

"I don't know if it was de ones I heard about from other Sunnys. If it was, they lives off far away, past the farthest Sunny planet. Maybe two, three hundred light-years. Nobody knows for sure. I heard that their ships goes faster than Sunny ships, and dat's all I know," he said.

"I think they've been spying on us and our problems with the Pug-bears. They may be the source of the brain implant devices the Motherland people have been using. I don't know where else they would have gotten hold of something so sophisticated," I said.

Another thought formed in the back of my mind. I vocalized it, "If the implants came from them, they must have been making a study of human brain structure. I don't see how an alien race could just whip out a device that was capable of controlling another species without a considerable amount of study, and ..." I trailed off, appalled. "They would have to study human anatomy, and that probably means they've been kidnapping people and dissecting them."

Frazzle just nodded solemnly, his eyes wide.

I shoved the thoughts back into my mind for later processing. There was nothing I could do about it at this moment.

"Let's get down to Denver and see what's left of the Earth. Those bombs may have done a lot of damage," I said.

Frazzle said, "I counted five 'splosions with de instruments before we leave the ship. They were big ones, and maybe lots of dirty particles fall out and spread all over. We have to check."

It occurred to me to ask, "Is there any way to calculate if the fall out will make the planet uninhabitable?"

He glanced at me, then turned back to the controls. "Maybe. We got instrument on shuttle that reads radiation. We fly round de Earth on way to Denver. Maybe gets enough data to figure out if there is a big problem."

I started to say something but then just shut my mouth in dismay.

He sensed my feelings and hastened to console me, "De bombs be dirty, but I don't think they enough to really uninhabit the Earth. Dec, don't worry. I sure your planet will still be good for human home."

Well, that was a little consolation. Frazzle was far more knowledgeable than I was on such topics. I resolved to accept his statement at face value, at least until contradicting data showed up.

We circled the globe gathering data and then landed at Denver before the shuttle computer had finished integrating the readings.

Chapter 47

The bombs killed almost everyone within twenty miles of the blast centers, and the fall-out accounted for hundreds of thousands more. People died from radiation sickness, cancers, and just plain starvation since no one could be found to transport supplies into the high radiation zones. It was a bad time for humanity. Compared to the enormous death toll brought on by the EMPs a few years prior, the current number of deaths didn't seem significant. It wasn't as large a number. You had to calculate the toll in terms of the population's percentage, which gave a different picture. It was horrifying.

The EMPs had killed somewhere on the order of half of the globe's population, although first world nations suffered the most, with nearly ninety percent of their population dying within a year. The fusion bombs the Pugs had dropped killed millions of people. The only blessing was that the destroyed cities were sparsely populated due to the EMPs. It could have been worse, but only a little bit.

The dust clouds spread the radiation over vast areas, sometimes polluting the soil for hundreds of miles downwind. That made it hard to raise crops and even harder to trust that the food on your table was wholesome and safe to eat. Most people were reduced to subsistence farming and, since they were forced to garden by hand, they didn't raise enough food to feed anyone outside their immediate family.

Denver had come off well, as had Grand Lake. I was happy about that since Liz and I had connections in both places. However, the cities struck by the bombs and the adjacent areas were decimated. The destruction of Washington DC totally disrupted the Motherland forces.

Their disintegration was greatly augmented by the sudden, surprise deaths of most of the commanding officers. The officers had been implanted with the brain-monitoring devices, providing the now-defunct president with direct control.

The system had been connected through some kind of radio linkage, and when the central processor in DC was destroyed, the implants all exploded simultaneously. This left the Motherland forces without any command structure, and their armies quickly dissolved into small bands of marauders who gradually migrated back to wherever it was that they'd originated.

The roving bands of disconnected soldiers caused many problems since they continued their pillaging ways. Only now, the residents of the lands they passed through stood up for themselves. The people hadn't dared fight back before when the army was intact. The repercussions had been too dire. Now the farmers and townspeople formed militias and successfully defended their territory.

Judith's people spread out from Denver and chased all the marauders out of their territory. Meanwhile, following my suggestion, Judith carried on a long series of negotiations and meetings, setting up a large web of confederated states and kingdoms. The western half of the continent was home to over two hundred different political entities ranging from democracies to kingdoms to various groups of loosely allied anarchists.

Each entity sent a representative or two to Denver for a conclave. Since they were, by and large, people with pioneering spirits, they adopted the old mountain-man name of "rendezvous" for the meeting. They used the time to hammer out policies and ways of working together covering trade, mutual defense, reconciling differences and disputes, and how to handle immigration and travel.

The lands that had been part of the Motherland empire began to select their own representatives and the second annual rendezvous promised to host people from all over the continent. The rules allowed anyone who represented a significant group of people to participate, so there were Canadians and Mexicans along with people who had been citizens of the old United States. It was even rumored that many of the island states in the Caribbean would send representatives.

We were kept busy providing support services around the world. Initially, our few shuttles had to do the job, but I put in a request for more shuttles with the Sunnys, and within a few months, Earth sported a fleet of Sunny-built shuttles that kept everyone connected.

Europe and Central Asia had followed the same pathway, although they'd had a rocky go of it due to ingrained, ancestral enmities. There were groups of people forced to live together in artificial nations who were now anxious to declare their independence. This led to some small wars and brush-fire conflicts. However, we suppressed these as soon as we found out about them.

It was usually easy to stop such conflicts. A KEW or two dropped for demonstration purposes was adequate to bring the combatants to the peace table. The result of all of this rearranging and political activity was that my idea of the Earth Space Protection Force was kind of shoved onto a back burner. There just wasn't much time for planning since we were kept busy for months simply acting as peacekeepers.

Eventually, the relations became stabilized. This was primarily due to Judith. She turned out to be good at negotiating and structuring the complex web of relationships between all of the various political entities. My only fear was that it might prove challenging to find a replacement for her when one was eventually needed.

The result of the first rendezvous was that Judith resigned from ruling the Front Range state and allowed herself to be elected as Chairperson for the Earth Confederacy.

I thought that using "Earth" in the name was a little ambitious since many areas had not joined, noticeably the majority of South America, India, Africa, and almost all of the Islamic states.

The Chinese were interested but had not committed themselves as yet. That was partly due to the Japanese, who had jumped at the chance to become part of the confederation. The old animosity between the two groups had raised its head, and there was still some work to be done there, although I thought that Judith was making progress.

Judith agreed to the chair position with the provision that she'd only serve for five years. After that, there would be another Chairperson who was to be appointed by the representative members. The thing I most liked was that any malfeasance was to be punished severely. The representatives agreed to hold themselves to the highest standards, so there would be none of the old order's foolishness of the representatives holding themselves above the law that applied to the common people.

Within the confederation, each political group was solely responsible for the laws within its borders and also for its own economic system. There would be no interstate or international or inter-group – whatever you chose to call it – financial aid. Responsibility for yourself was the rule.

By the time the second rendezvous rolled around, most of the remaining groups had joined, and now the name "Earth Confederacy" seemed to fit. I'd been a little overly pessimistic with my worries of warring states. The setbacks humanity suffered and the massive death toll had served to concentrate people's minds. It was rare to find a person now who didn't know what was going on politically. People didn't have the luxury to live unproductive lives, which led to a renewed sense of personal responsibility.

The other component was the knowledge that we were not alone. That was something that everyone now accepted. Humans had begun to understand that we could no longer afford to indulge in conflict among ourselves. There were other species in the Universe, and we'd seen that some of them did not mean us well. We now had a reason to stick together.

The Pug-bears were no longer a problem, and that was one blessing. They had been successfully isolated on their home planet, where the brewer's yeast had strangled their grafted-on intelligence. I didn't know if academics in the far distant future would praise me or damn me for my actions, but I was sure that I'd done the right thing. Those creatures were too vicious to be allowed to continue along their path towards inter-stellar dominance. The few that still survived on the Sunny planets had been confined to zoos by the Sunnys. They didn't want to forget how the creatures had made them suffer, and so, the zoos were set up to remind them that they'd escaped a horrible slavery.

The Pugs willingly settled down on their own planet, doing what they did. We sent in a group to treat with them, and they eagerly agreed to some small amount of trade. Their interests were a little too divergent from those of our three allied species to provide more than a minor basis for cooperation. They didn't live long, and, as a result, they were mainly preoccupied with status and breeding rights. They were primarily interested in metallurgy as it applied to hand weapons since they intended to continue their iron-age, battling ways.

We hoped that we'd eventually manage to build up a Pug merchant class whose status was based on economic rather than fighting ability. That would allow us to wean them away from their ongoing violence gradually. Unfortunately, it looked like it would be a long-term project.

By the time the second rendezvous had finished, we had managed to organize the Earth Space Protection Force into a more formal structure. We centered our operations at the Ceres base, and the place was constantly humming with arrivals and departures.

It not only served as a base for the shuttle fleet we used to maintain order on Earth, but it was also rapidly becoming the port-of-call for all Sunny vessels. Thus far, the Sim-tigers had been content with signing on as crew on human-operated ships. The Sunnys were just a little too timid to attract the cat-like people, although a few Sim-tigers worked for the Sunnys in security positions.

I'd been surprised at the number of people who volunteered to leave Earth. There had been a resurgence of the pioneer spirit. This was, I thought, due to the destruction of the civilization-imposed structures that suppressed that type of attitude. Apparently, a tendency towards pioneering is somehow built into the human genome. Some of us, at least, seem to be risk-takers and wanderers.

There was now a lot of interest in exploring our solar system. As we received shuttles from the Sunnys, various groups managed to work out terms and were granted ships capable of asteroid mining and exploring as far as the Oort cloud. This activity had yet to produce any significant economic results, but the scientific progress was creating waves in what remained of our academic circles.

Life had been found on some of Jupiter's moons and some of Saturn's. It was single-celled or whatever the analog would be, but still, it was exciting. As an aside, I was a little bemused by the fact that scientists could get fired up about a single-celled alien organism when we had fully functioning, intelligent aliens as partners.

I was a little more interested in the discovery that at least a few comets bore some form of life. Single-cell organisms had been discovered living a weird life on comets. They were similar enough to earthly life forms to lead scientists to speculate that we may have found our remote ancestors.

There had also been some mineral discoveries, but nothing too exciting until the first gold-bearing asteroid was found. That changed things. The asteroid didn't have much gold, but even a little was enough to create a modern-day gold rush. We were inundated with requests for shuttles by wanna-be prospectors. They were so anxious that some of them even took their chances in human-made spacecraft.

It wasn't challenging to create a ship that would travel in space, as long as you didn't have to enter a gravity well. The Sunnys provided gravity units and shielding, so neither null-g nor radiation was a problem. This allowed people to fan out across the system rapidly.

Some were good at their new occupation, and some were not so good. The number of Darwin Awards in Space rapidly increased until the communal body of knowledge reached a sort of tipping point. Then the deaths decreased. This was either due to better preparation and more knowledge or due (as I sometimes thought) to the fact that all of the really stupid people had already killed themselves. Despite the declining death rate, one of the ESPF's main tasks was to provide assistance and rescue for people who'd gotten in too deep (or out too far, if you prefer). We were kept remarkably busy rescuing miners from all sorts of crazy predicaments.

There had been no sightings of any other odd spacecraft since the one that Frazzle and I had seen. I'd only told a few people about that. It didn't seem to be something that should be spread around at the moment. If the owners of that ship had been responsible for the brain implants, their plans had been disrupted by the Pug attack on my ship. Until and unless they showed up again, we decided to keep their existence low-key.

Frazzle had reported them to the Sunny governments, and they filed the report with the other information, sparse though it was, about the potential problem from the distance species.

It was alter-day shift, my sleep period, and my family and I were in our quarters on Ceres. The kids had been asleep for an hour. Liz and I were lying in bed discussing the future, and Jefferson had curled up at the foot of the mattress in a tight ball.

It's funny how cats can arrange themselves into such a small package yet look so relaxed. I could hear him intermittently purring whenever we paused in our conversation.

Liz looked at me and commented, "As long as we're talking about the future, when are you going to realize that you're the de facto administrator of the ESPF? You can't keep making plans to jaunt off and rescue some itinerant miner every hour or so. You're needed here. The Sunny trade has picked up. They're bringing FTL ships in more and more often, and there's still a huge number of people who want to emigrate from Earth."

I sighed, "I know. I feel like I'm getting stale, sitting at a desk. That's not how I want to live, but you're right. There's so much going on. Maybe we need a competent administrator like Judith."

"Yeah, maybe, but you're the one whom people respect. Right now, the job is yours," she responded.

"You're right, you're right," I repeated, "The only thing is, I've got another problem on my hands, too. I'm worried about formalizing the relationship between our three species. We need some form of space navy to protect us, the Sunnys, and the Sim-tigers. For all of their ferocity and battle ability, the Sim-tigers are sitting ducks right now. If some aliens wanted to bombard their planet, there is little they could do about it."

She continued, "The same can be said about both humans and the Sunnys. The Sunnys need protection, and human tech isn't worth much."

"Yes, I know, but you're wrong about human tech, at least in the computer field. Frazzle says that our computer knowledge is easily as good as theirs. It's just that all of our systems were destroyed by the EMPs. Of course, now that we have the Sunnys' aid, maybe we can get going again," I reflected, then added, "We need to get the idea of the Inter-species Space Confederacy formalized, and we need it to have its own space navy. It need not be very large right now. I can't see the need for more than maybe sixteen FTL-capable ships. We should maybe have a couple stationed at each of our occupied planets. The Ansibles can provide instant communication in the event of an emergency. Still, it would be better to have a couple of armed ships handy near every planet. FTL travel just takes too long, especially when the distances are as great as they are from one end of our area of space to the other."

Liz cocked an eyebrow and asked, "Why so many ships, and what do you mean, 'emergency'? Do you think that we may have other aliens attack? Maybe the people who were flying the ship you saw?"

"Well, that and we might have some humans eventually get the idea that they could become pirates or space Vikings or some other kind of raiders. An armed ship could easily loot one of the Sunny planets. Maybe even loot Earth, providing that there was no defense," I said.

"What about Kasm's planet?" she asked.

"That too, but there's not much there to loot at the moment. Maybe if you wanted some weird beasts or thought you could kidnap some Sim-tigers and force them to fight for you, but..." I trailed off.

It wasn't likely that anyone would try to loot the Sim-tigers' planet, but they did need protection from potential aggression. They could be bombed into oblivion easily. Who might be disposed to commit such an act escaped me at the moment, but it was certainly possible.

Liz interrupted my thinking by leaning over and kissing me. I kind of resisted at first, still intent on the ISC, but she quickly prevailed, and my thoughts turned to more pleasureful activities.

Jefferson stopped purring and raised his head in mild reproach with a meow. When we didn't stop our movement, he jumped to the floor and curled up there. At least it wasn't shaking.

Chapter 48

This section of the Oort cloud was densely populated with pieces of ice and rocks of wildly varying sizes. The objects primarily traveled in non-conflicting paths, but occasionally, two would end up on intersecting paths, and the collision would result in fragments flying in all directions. Navigating through the area was a little dicey, and most miners tended to stay away, preferring to investigate less active parts of the cloud.

At the moment, a large rock was traversing the area. It had previously smacked into two ice balls, throwing ice and rocks in a spray ahead of it. The rock had built up a large amount of ice on its leading side from the collisions, enough so that when it eventually left the cloud and headed for the sun in a cometary path, it would undoubtedly display a spectacular tail as the ice began to vaporize. With its current path and speed, this event would occur some twenty thousand years in the future and the math calculated out to a nearly perfect chance that the thing would strike the Earth.

Based on the current state of affairs there, the future residents would be most likely to view the comet as an interesting astronomical phenomenon rather than the harbinger of doom that it would be to a primitive civilization. The Earth was now closely guarded by a series of powerful spaceships, and deflecting such a comet would not tax their capacity. It would be more on the order of something you do before lunch on an off day.

Still, the solar system is vast, and humans were busily engaged in exploring every part of it, even this dense and dangerous part of the cloud.

The spaceship came flying through the cluster of ice and rocks rapidly, avoiding the smaller objects in an almost casual manner that bespoke expert piloting. It slowed as it approached the large rock, maneuvered so that it was heading in the same direction, and gradually settled into a parallel path a few hundred yards away.

An ice ball was in the direct path of the rock, and rather than fool around with the spray of debris caused by the impending collision, the ship's anti-matter cannon vaporized the chunk of ice, clearing the path. Inside the cabin, Hattie leaned back in her chair and said, "That should give us enough time to look this thing over thoroughly.

Her partner, Kasm, turned his green-striped, furry face towards her and spoke in his rumbling voice, "Even so. But let's not waste too much time on this object. I detected some other interesting-looking rocks another million miles off in the spin-ward direction. We should check them also."

Hattie replied, "If we keep looking at these things, eventually we're bound to get one that has some valuable minerals. It'd be nice to go back to Ceres with a big enough find to buy our own ship."

Kasm grinned, a rather frightening grimace which showed his fangs, and mentally sent, "You just want to impress Michael and also show Dec and Liz that you're capable of doing more than flying FTLs to the Sunny planets."

She smiled back. Receiving his mental communication was second nature to her. They'd been together for the past ten years, bound in an emotional relationship that neither was precisely able to describe but which provided each with a degree of support and intimacy that they were unable to find in members of their own species. She wasn't able to send mentally. Dec's training had allowed her to "tune in" to Kasm, but she had never learned to use her mental voice.

"Well, maybe that's part of it, but I'd still like to own a ship out-right, rather than leasing one each time we come back from an interstellar voyage," she said.

"Leasing is a little advantageous, though, you must admit. We don't have to worry about storage while we're gone, and we can usually find the latest model to lease." He changed the topic, "It would be nice to spend one of our vacations on the surface with Dec and Liz in Grand Lake, rather than constantly exploring. I want the chance to get on the outside of some mule deer meat."

She snorted, "Just open the freezer. There's plenty in there, nice and rare, just the way you like it."

He curled his lip, "No, you know perfectly well that I'd like to go hunting and kill my own."

"I know, I know. Just... Well, I enjoy exploring. Somehow I've never really regained my attachment to Earth after my parents –" she faltered.

He reached out with his secondary manipulating arm and stroked along her neck and shoulder, easing the tension as he'd done many times in the past. She sighed and leaned into his hand.

"Don't worry about it. I enjoy exploring also," he paused, looking at the instruments. "Look at that! There's something on the backside of that rock. The rock is wobbling a bit, and it just came into view."

She leaned forward, searching the display, and then said, "There's part of a spaceship there. Looks like a mining or exploration vessel, but there's also something else. There's something weird about that rock."

Kasm attentively adjusted the instruments and, after a moment, he said, "It looks like the entire rock is hollowed out. The mass isn't nearly enough for the size. I'll use the deep scan, and we'll see."

He turned on another console and waited a moment for the reading to stabilize. "That's confirmed. The... it looks like the rock has been converted to some kind of habitat."

Hattie was already moving for her spacesuit. "We'd better go out and look this over. This could be our big score. Not minerals, but information. Who knows, maybe an alien artifact."

He cautioned her, "Yes, but we're not the first to discover it. That spaceship looks like it's an older Sunny model. There may be someone there already."

She shook her head negatively, "The ship is just a fragment. Look at the nose section. It's completely crushed. The ship could have hit some object a long way off and drifted onto this rock. There's no way someone would still be living in that wreck."

The two donned their suits, Kasm requiring some help from her as his suit was considerably more complex due to his six-limbed anatomy. Then they exited their ship and jetted across the intervening space, landing near the wrecked ship.

It was an older model, one much smaller than their leased vehicle. They carefully explored it and discovered that the ship was a total wreck. The nose section was crushed, and the back of the vessel was broken, showing that it had come in at some speed.

It had landed in a shallow crack in the rock, and the engine section had broken entirely off on impact. The only thing hopeful was that the passenger compartment seemed to be undamaged. It was buttoned up and looked airtight, although there was not a speck of power emanating from it.

Kasm's mental voice grabbed her attention. He communicated exclusively mentally when in a spacesuit. It was far more efficient for him.

She replied via her comm unit, "Yes, I see it. There's a track leading from the ship to that formation over there. There must have been a survivor or two, and they went back and forth several times. Probably carrying supplies."

His mental voice said, "That's what I make of it. Let's go see where they were going, but be careful."

She smiled. He was always warning her to be careful, but he'd take some of the most outrageous risks himself. She keyed her comm, "You be careful, too."

He snorted mentally.

The track led through the organic snow for several hundred yards, around a high promontory, and into a dark crack. They cautiously entered the shadow cast by the rocks and climbed over some rough stone to find themselves in a large, open depression.

Hattie observed, "This looks like it was manufactured. It's too regular to be the result of some chance collision."

Kasm responded by pointing at what was obviously an airlock. As they neared the entrance, it was apparent that it was not made for a humanoid. Even their old enemy, the Pug-bears, would not have used such an entrance.

It was narrow and quite tall. If the shape was representative of the creatures that had built the thing, they were maybe two times as tall as the tallest human but barely as wide as a man.

Kasm paused, "I don't think I'm going to fit into that opening, and I don't want you going in there by yourself. Too dangerous."

She was fumbling around with a control panel that was at the top of her reach. She finally jumped up against the weak gravity and caught hold of a loop-shaped handle attached to it so that she could inspect the panel more closely.

There was a knob there, and she turned it both ways with no result. Finally, she pulled on it, and the lock responded by opening suddenly. The narrow entrance snapped back into a wider configuration, opening to a room with a slot on the floor. The original users had apparently stepped into the room and then dropped down into the slot.

She cautiously advanced and looked down. About a foot down in the slot was a platform with gaps around it that betrayed a deep and dark opening. Further inspection revealed a mechanism that would lower it into the surrounding rock. The gravity wasn't much, and the mechanism wasn't very sturdy looking, a fact that did not increase Kasm's confidence.

She paused indecisively. "I think I should go down and see what's down there. Whoever it was that crashed here went down and came back for more loads several times, so I should be able to get out. Besides, If I get stuck, I've got my anti-matter pistol. That should be sufficient to shoot a hole in the rock that I can exit through."

She looked at him. His bulk was magnified by his spacesuit. It was doubtful that he'd fit through the entrance.

"You'd better wait with the ship. You can get me out with it if I can't get out on my own," she added.

Kasm sent a mental impression of resigned, extreme displeasure, "Okay. I can see that you're going to go in, regardless of what I think, so just be careful. I'll crack this rock like an egg to get you if you get stuck.

Be sure and keep your locator on, so I'll know exactly where you are."

He'd do exactly that, too. The spaceship's anti-matter cannon could easily shoot a hole entirely through the rock, intersecting the hollow interior. She felt reasonably safe as she stepped onto the platform and activated the mechanism with a turn of another knob.

The floor sank into the hole, and the tall opening snapped shut simultaneously. It was momentarily dark, and she felt a little panicky, but then the slot opened up, revealing a low illumination. The ambient light was almost ultra-violet, and it made it hard for her to see until she adjusted the filters on her suit.

The platform came to a halt as it reached the bottom. She paused and activated her comm, "Kasm, can you hear me?"

His mental voice came back quickly, "Your signal is a little weak. There must be some kind of shielding between us. Take it slow and check with me before you enter any rooms. I don't want to lose communication. It won't help if I can speak to you, but you can't speak to me."

His thought was tinged with worry, and Hattie smiled to herself. He'd been the perfect companion for her over the years. Caring, yet not too demanding. They had lived together on so many ships that they'd developed their own means of coping with each other's alienness.

Kasm was, for all intents and purposes, clothed by his stripy fur coat. She usually wore a standard jumpsuit, just for warmth, but had no qualms about sleeping nude in the same cabin with him. They often ended cuddled together in the same way that a human would cuddle with a cat or dog. Their relationship was far more than platonic. It was not physical in the sense of sex, but they were bound emotionally. She'd lost her parents, and he'd lost his mate and cub. In some way, she'd filled her emotional void with his presence, and he'd managed to do the same with her.

Michael often joked that the two of them should go ahead and get married. They were so close that some people cocked an eyebrow at their relationship, probably wondering about the propriety of it. It didn't matter to her what they thought. As far as she was concerned, Kasm just was there when she needed him.

She turned down a long hall, illuminated by the same lurid, purple light. As she reached the end, it turned a corner, and she jumped back. There was someone there!

CHAPTER 49

Hattie paused, leaning against the corner, and glanced around at the dimly lit upper reaches of the narrow hallway. The proportions of the hall were odd. Perhaps weird or alien would be a better description. The wavelength of the lighting was not optimal for the human visual system, either. She'd been almost sure that she'd seen someone at the other end of the hall when she looked a moment ago. Her heart was still pounding from the surprise.

She tried to send a message to Kasm, but her comm unit now showed no signal, making her wish again that Dec's mental training had worked to a higher degree for her. She felt terribly alone at the moment. If she could transmit her thoughts to Kasm, it would be a great comfort.

She pulled her anti-matter pistol and checked the charge. It was ready to go. She steeled herself and looked around the corner again.

There was a figure that had now approached about halfway to her location. She started to raise her weapon, but there was a sudden flash from the figure, and a wave of nausea struck her, then she momentarily saw the floor approaching her helmet. Her vision blacked out, and she distantly felt the impact as she bounced face-first in the low gravity. Her arms and legs didn't seem to want to cooperate, and she couldn't move.

Then someone grabbed her arm and rolled her over to her back. Although her vision still had black rings from the bright flash, she could see a little. The figure was wearing a standard space suit, a model favored by both miners and explorers.

Suddenly her comm crackled, and a man's voice came through.

"Well, well, well! Look who's come to rescue me. A cute, little lady. Don't try to move, Miss. You won't be able to, anyway. The stunner charge takes a few minutes to wear off. You're lucky I used the lowest setting. The higher ones can be fatal, so don't try anything," he said. He went on talking over the comm, although he was now addressing himself.

"I'll just drag her down to the hide-out, that's what. The lights are better in there, and I can see what I've got. It'll be better to get my helmet off. Don't have too much air in the suit anyway. Maybe she's got a ship. Maybe I can get it and get off this rock. Got to get somewhere so's I can cash in on ..." He trailed off.

Suddenly his faceplate came down so that it almost touched hers. Her vision had cleared a little, and she could see a heavily bearded, frowning face studying her. He didn't appear to be much older than her despite the beard.

"You just forget what I just said. You hear?"

Nothing of what he'd said seemed to make sense to her. The stunner had created a mental fog, and things just weren't making sense. She said so. "I – I d-don't – I mean, what are you talking about, and who are you?"

He grinned, making a rather unattractive leer that did more to unsettle her than it did to establish him as trustworthy.

"I'm not talking about nothing, so you just forget what I said, you hear?" he said, shaking his head.

She ignored the confusing double-negative, realizing that he was trying to cover up his revealing self-dialogue. She repeated, "Who are you? And, where did you come from?" Without giving him time to answer, she continued, "How long have you been here?"

He leered again, "Just you wait until I get you in the hide-out, then you'll get answers. Say, you got people waiting for you topside?" He'd just realized that she might not be alone.

"Yeah. I got people," she huffed, "You'd better treat me nice, or he won't be happy, and you don't want to see him mad."

"You ain't in a position to threaten me," he snarled. "You can't even move yet."

In that, he was wrong. She'd been gradually regaining her neural functioning and could now see perfectly. Her arms were tingling but seemed to be movable. She barely twitched them to test, and they responded without moving the surface of her suit. She could tell that she'd dropped her pistol, though. Still, there were things she could do. She lay still, waiting.

He paused, thinking, then continued, "You say 'him.' You got a boyfriend topside?"

She kept silent. Perhaps she should have implied that many people were waiting for her. Anyway, Kasm was probably the last thing this guy would expect to see. And, if he hurt her, Kasm was the last thing he would see, too.

He grabbed her left arm and unceremoniously dragged her down the narrow hall. Her view was of the distant ceiling, and she was able to see that the dim, violet light was varying in a rhythmic cycle from violet to purple and back. They reached another corner, and he dragged her up to an airlock door, then cycled them both through.

Inside, the light was more indigo than violet, a little closer to human-normal than before. He wrenched off his helmet and began to unlatch hers.

Panicked, she started to struggle, trying to keep her helmet on, unprepared to risk the atmosphere in the place.

He stood up and pulled a rod-shaped weapon from his belt, snarling, "Stop fighting 'less you want another charge!"

She instantly quit moving, lying back and watching him alertly.

He ordered, "Now you take that helmet off yourself since you recovered so quick. The air in here is fine. I used ship's stores to fill the place myself."

She looked at her instrument display. The air was high in carbon dioxide and low in oxygen, but the ambient pressure was about what she maintained inside her suit. She could breathe it for a while. She complied with his request and slowly removed her helmet.

His eyes widened as he saw her face, unobstructed, for the first time, "Say, you're more than just cute, Missy. You're the best-looking female I've seen in months." He leered at her, then continued, "In fact, you're the only female I've seen."

Hattie was unimpressed, "Look here, what do you mean by shooting me? I come in here, innocently investigating whether there were any survivors from the wreck out there, and you don't even give me a chance to say 'Hello' before you knock me out."

He grinned again, "That's cause I was expecting someone else. Someone not so cute as you are. I wasn't going to let them get the jump on me. I been here for nearly two hundred hours now, and I know the inside of this place pretty good. If they come, there's some stuff I can use to discourage them but good! Just you keep real quiet about what you've seen in here, alright?"

She reflected. It was evident that he wasn't quite right in the head. Maybe the stress of being stranded had affected his thought process. It would probably be best to humor him.

"Alright. I promise I won't say anything about this place. I haven't seen anything anyway. Just the hallway, this room, and whatever it was you shot me with," she said.

"That's a stunner. It's got different settings. The high one kills instantly. I got rid of –"

He stopped suddenly and bit his lip as if to silence himself. He glanced around the room and then returned his attention to her.

"You got a ship out there? Right?" he asked.

She nodded, not saying anything.

"I need it," he started but then changed his approach as he realized how that sounded. "I'd like to arrange for passage back to the asteroid belt. There's a mining base I need to get back to. Maybe I can trade you some things for a lift, huh?"

Her curiosity was piqued, "What things?"

He scrabbled in a dirty canvas pouch that was strapped to his suit and pulled out a small, silver-encased mechanism, extending it for her inspection.

"This here is a brain implant. All ready to go. It's self-installing, you just –" He stopped, wheels obviously turning behind his eyes.

"Maybe I ought to put it on your head. You don't feel anything. It deadens the nerves, and I'd be able to..." He trailed off again as he realized that her expression had become implacably hostile.

"Well, it was just an idea. No, that's not the thing to do right yet," he finished.

Hattie had been getting more alarmed as the mostly one-sided dialogue continued. The guy was crazy. He'd apparently killed at least one of his fellows, and he could just as easily kill her, or perhaps worse. She didn't want one of the implants in her head. She'd seen the nasty things explode and kill their bearers. She didn't know if this guy could control the implant, but it wasn't anything she wanted to find out about, either.

She desperately thought about her options. Her muscles were completely back under her control. She thought about overpowering him but decided it probably wouldn't work. He was a large man and looked powerful. She gave that thought up and smiled her most fetching smile instead.

"Did you find anything else in this base? I think it's interesting. Who do you think made it?" She continued smiling.

Her smile seemed to have more effect than what she'd planned. He looked stunned for a moment and then began to almost jabber in his eagerness to answer her questions.

"There's lots of stunners and some other things that may be some kind of weapons, but I don't know what they are. Lots of implants, too. This is some kind of storehouse for those things. They were going to use them on Earth before they got the wind up and left the system," he said.

"Yes, but who were they?" she quietly prompted, still smiling.

"Oh. That. They're the – the – Oh, I can't say their name! I'm not supposed to –" He stopped suddenly and clapped his hand to the side of his head in obvious pain, then added slowly and with effort, "They... uh, they lef'...left."

She looked at him with her best concerned look. He held his head and glanced wildly around the room again, then dropped his hand. As he did, she could see the tell-tale scar behind his ear. He was implanted! No wonder his behavior was erratic. She wondered how to proceed for a moment but then decided to continue trying to extract usable information.

"Never mind about who they were. It's not important. What's important now is that there are just the two of us here, and you need help," she said.

He refocused on her and tentatively smiled, "Yeah. You can help me alright, Missy. I need quite a lot of things. Maybe you'd like to take me out topside to your spaceship and introduce me to your man friend. I'd like to meet him," he said, unconsciously stroking the stunner rod at his hip.

Hattie paused. This guy was almost too obvious. Either he was plain crazy the way he appeared to be, or he was playing an even deeper game, using the presumed craziness as a shield.

They both started. The airlock activation light had just come on. It was flashing a bright yellow as the lock mechanism slowly opened. The man jerked the stunner free from his belt and fired it into the crack.

The lock opened fully, and the limp body of Kasm rolled out, his spacesuit clattering on the hard floor. The man jumped back in surprise, "What the Hell is that thing? I never seen – no, wait. It's one of them alien tiger things. Is it with you?" he asked.

He bent forward to look closely at Kasm and not pay attention to her. This was the chance for which she'd been waiting. She stood up quickly and swung her helmet with her right arm as hard as she could. The helmet massed about three kilos, and she swung it fast. It slammed into the back of the guy's head, and he went down as if someone had struck him with a bowling ball. He landed directly on top of Kasm's recumbent form.

The stunner apparently had not affected Kasm as much as it had her because the Sim-tiger rolled and grabbed the limp body with his manipulating arms. Kasm continued his roll, ending up on top of the guy and ripping the stunner free in the process. It rolled across the floor, and Hattie scrambled to retrieve it.

She looked at the object. Despite being alien in manufacture, the controls were obvious. There was a knurled ring, currently set to the first gradation, and a single button. She pointed the tip at the wall and pushed the button. There was a flash, and her arms tingled.

Kasm looked at her, and his mental voice came through, "Stop that right now. The impulse reflects from the wall. I felt it hit me when you shot it. Just point it at this man and shoot him if he starts fighting."

"I'm so glad to see you!" she gasped. "I didn't think I was going to get out of this situation. The guy's crazy. He's been here too long, and besides, he's got one of those brain implants in his head. He's not rational. He was probably going to kill you and me if he could. And, and how did you get in here?"

Kasm growled. The deep bass sound didn't transmit well through the suit speaker, coming out distorted and tinny. He sent, "He's not killing anyone now –" His words broke off as the man heaved and thrashed around. Suddenly the guy held a large knife that he'd pulled from his canvas pouch. He tried to stab Kasm, but the Sim-tiger grabbed his hand, and the two momentarily yanked the knife back and forth.

Hattie danced around, trying to get a clear shot with the stunner. Kasm's weight didn't count for much in the low gravity, and he was suddenly thrown off as the guy drew up his legs and kicked. The Sim-tiger lifted into the air and spun around, slamming down on his back, still holding the man's wrist. The impact jarred Kasm enough so that the man could wrench his knife hand free. He rolled into a kneeling position, lifting the knife over the recumbent alien.

He was just starting to come down with the knife when Hattie shot him with the stunner. She'd stepped forward and triggered it off as it contacted the scar behind his ear. The expected flash of the stunner was magnified by an instant explosion as the implant detonated. Blood flew out his ears, nose, and mouth and his eyes bulged out as he collapsed. The blood continued to flow over Kasm's spacesuit.

The Sim-tiger stood up quickly and stepped back, unperturbed. He sent, "Good. That's settled. Now let's take a look around here and see what this place is."

Hattie didn't say anything. She was too busy crying in relief.

CHAPTER 50

It seemed like I'd been sitting at my desk for hours. Actually, it was only about ten hundred in the day shift, so I'd been in my Ceres office for just a little over two hours. The problem was, I was bored. Acting as administrator for the ESPF and the ISC wasn't quite what I'd set out to do.

I was preparing to go for another cup of coffee when my assistant, Elliot, came bursting in.

"Dec, we've just received a communication from Hattie. She's coming in, and she's found something!" he said.

"Okay, El, calm down a bit and tell me what she found," I requested.

He was so excited that he was practically shaking. I guessed that he was nearly as bored as I was and something a little out of the ordinary was more than welcome. The constant stream of ships back and forth from the Sunny planets and Tukola took up most of our attention, but nothing was exciting about them.

Trade went on smoothly, and I was rarely called to intervene. The last bit of excitement was a reputed hijacking in the Kuiper zone. It amounted to a minor dispute between two competing mining groups when we investigated. One had decided it would be advantageous to accuse the other of piracy. There was nothing to the charge, and I ended up making the accusing party pay the investigation and travel charges.

Elliot took a deep breath, steadying himself, and then continued, "She wouldn't say much, but apparently, she's found some alien artifacts."

I straightened up. This might be an exciting day after all.

"When is she due?" I asked. Travel time using the Em-drive system was variable. If you went all-out, it would boost your velocity nearly to light-speed. That wasn't efficient for in-system travel because you ended up spending as much time braking as you did accelerating, and you posed a true hazard for other ship traffic. No one appreciated being in the path of a thousand-ton bullet traveling so fast that it could hit you before you could properly see it. My office tried to discourage that sort of thing, and we'd promulgated a sort of de facto speed limit for in-system travel.

Most of the ships maintained a steady speed of one-fifth light when the distance was greater than one AU. If you were traveling less than that distance, the limit was one-tenth light.

I knew that Kasm and Hattie were somewhere out in the Oort cloud, fooling around on vacation. They took it seriously and claimed that they were exploring, but as far as I was concerned, their exploring was just an excuse to get off Ceres and away from everyone else while they weren't working.

Truth to tell, Hattie wasn't very comfortable around other humans. She'd never been what you might call an easy person to know. Her relationship with Kasm had further changed her. Her mental processes were now divergent from those of mainstream humanity.

I had no problem with either of them or their relationship. They were always together, and I suspected they were each dependent upon the other in their own way. I never probed mentally. That wasn't something that I felt was ethical.

Elliot answered my last query, "If they keep their speed down, it will be several days before they get here. She wouldn't tell me what she found. All she said was that it was important. She gave me the impression of wanting to keep it quiet."

I responded, "Yeah, you know how the rumor mill works around here. If anyone thought somebody had discovered something valuable, there'd be another gold rush, and we don't need the hassle. Some of these newbies would take off without proper supplies, and we'd just end up rescuing them."

He nodded and left.

About an hour after lunch, there was a knock at my door, and Hattie and Kasm paraded in at my call.

I stood up in surprise, "What? How did you get here so fast? You didn't use FTL, did you? Did you wait until you were almost here to send your message?"

Kasm had a smile on his cat-like face. It looked like he'd just had something delicious to eat, a canary perhaps. His mental voice filtered into my mind.

"We found something good out there. An alien base belonging to the creatures that brought the brain implants. It's deserted, but they left some technology that is a long way ahead of where the Sunnys are. I think you'll be interested –"

Hattie interrupted excitedly, "We found a big base with lots of stuff stored there, but best of all, there was a ship!"

I drew a deep breath, held it an instant, and then carefully asked, "What kind of ship?"

"Oh, nothing special, just a little shuttlecraft. It's not very comfortable for humans, and it has no environmental system, no air, and no heat. We've been in our space-suits for a couple of hours, now –"

I interrupted her in turn, "A couple of hours! Where's your ship? How far did you come?"

She grinned and said, "Oh, our ship is still at the comet. The shuttle is amazing. It's got the ability to tunnel into FTL with no start-up velocity. It's simple to operate, too. You just pick your destination, trigger the tunneling apparatus and then drive through to your destination. Our trip here really only took about a minute. We were traveling in real space the rest of the time, trying to look like any other spaceship coming to Ceres. We didn't want anyone to look at us very carefully. The ship does look odd."

I suspected that I'd seen one of those ships before. It had approached me when I was floating in space after destroying the final Pug ship. I sighed and said, "All right. Let's go down to the dock and see this alien ship."

Hattie jumped up eagerly and led the way. Kasm following behind. After a bit, he turned aside, saying, "I'll be right there. I just need to check on something."

We arrived at the secondary dock. The alien ship had been moved inside a hangar and was lying there, brightly illuminated by banks of lights as a mixed group of human and Sunny scientists went over it. The Marines had set up checkpoints preventing unauthorized personnel from approaching too closely.

I turned to Hattie and asked, "Is this all your doing?"

She replied, "Yes. I figured that it needed to be kept under wraps as much as possible. I asked for the Marine guard, and Michael notified the research people as soon as I told him. They demanded immediate access to the ship, so he agreed. That's what you'd have done? Right?"

I had to admit that it was. They'd taken immediate steps to secure the prize and to start investigating its capabilities. I was starting to feel as if I wasn't necessary. It was kind of sad, but also kind of good. I realized that I trusted both Hattie's and Michael's judgment. They almost instinctively knew what to do in most situations.

We approached the ship and paused so that I could look it over. It was long with odd curves. It wasn't human or Sunny in origin.

A young man whom I recognized as being from the physics lab, although I couldn't recall his name, glanced up at us from a position near what looked like the ship's engine. He stepped towards us and said, "Hello, Administrator! This is the most remarkable thing I've ever had the opportunity to investigate. The technology is better than ours, but most of it is understandable or nearly so. Some of the components are cryptic, but we'll tease their function. As I understand it, this thing can jump immediately into FTL status without the need to accelerate first. It'll revolutionize our space travel."

He turned eagerly back to the prize as I snickered to myself. It had been only a few years since the Sunny technology had revolutionized human space travel, and now this youngster was telling me that a new revolution was at hand. Suddenly a familiar, furry face poked through the odd-shaped hatch at the front of the ship, and Frazzle appeared. He, too, was excited.

"Dec! Dec! Dis ship has some good advances over Sunny ships. It go faster and is easier to control. You set destination, and it jump there with no delay.

We can use this to speed up in-system travel. No more waiting for speeds-up and slows-down. No worries about traffic conflicts. It got a detector for proximities. You can't collide with something even if you tried. It like Sunnys went the wrong way on some parts of technology. These peoples went a little different way and got better result. But..." Frazzle paused to gasp for air. He'd spoken the entire time without a breath while waving his webbed fingers wildly in the air.

He continued, "But I's understand how this works. We can use it. Just need time to change our ships. Dec, dis changes everything!"

I smiled at him and thought to myself, "This changes everything."

I hadn't realized that Liz had tuned in to my mental stream from our apartment, but there she was, "Changes everything? What everything?"

I was about to answer, but I was interrupted by Kasm, who had walked up behind us as we looked at the ship. He patted me on my rear and thrust his large, toothy head between Hattie and me, wrapping his manipulating arms around both of our waists. Hattie sighed and leaned towards him, trailing her hand over his head in an intimate manner that I would not have used with him. He pushed his head into her hand.

I replied to Liz, "Things change. Years ago, I followed a drunk, and I found you and then all this," – I mentally visualized our confusing lives – "happened."

Her thoughts came back to me, tinged with love and a sensation that was like a mental snuggle, "I like that kind of change. It has given me everything." There was a heavy mental emphasis on "Everything."

I sent back, "Yeah. The only time a person doesn't have change is when they're dead, so I guess change is a good thing."

She left me with a sense of mental laughter and the thought, "Change happens."

My eye was drawn to a motion at the far side of the hanger. Our battle-scarred Tomcat was parading across towards us. There was gray fur on the sides of Jefferson's jaws, but he was still healthy and confident. He walked purposefully towards us, his head up, eyes bright, and tail erect with a little crook at the tip. He was followed closely by an escort of two half-grown males, both wearing his distinctive orange coat.

I thought to myself again, "Change happens."

They were followed at a distance by a bold kitten from Jefferson's latest conquest's litter. It walked slower, obviously slightly intimidated by the large, echoing space. About halfway across, it stopped and made a querulous, "Meowp!"

I laughed. He sounded exactly like his father.

Change happens.

The End

Dec's Notes on Principles for the Human Confederation

I've become convinced that humans desperately need a new way of living together. Not that we haven't already tried just about everything possible. The reality seems that every form of organization or government works for a while and in the circumstance in which it arose. Unfortunately, circumstances change, and sometimes they change radically.

When the circumstance under which a form of organization arose changes, the organization becomes dysfunctional to a greater or lesser degree. When that happens, people usually try to get along until the disconnect between what is and what is needed becomes too painful, then a paradigm shift happens. This can be moderate or extremely painful, laying waste to vast areas of the Earth and disrupting millions of mostly innocent lives. One needs only to look at history for examples.

On average, bad stuff happens to society every 80 years or so, and kingdoms or nations last around two hundred years, give or take some before they become too disconnected from the prevailing circumstances and fall into the dust bin of history.

At the current instant in time, western society seems to be heading into the Crisis period predicted by Strauss and Howe's 4th Turning theory. This means that we're due for a dust-up in terms of our society. It may be greater or smaller, but it looks like it's going to happen. (For those readers who encounter this book years after it was written, you can either congratulate me on my prescience or chuckle at my pessimism. In either event, I hope you enjoyed the story itself.)

It would be nice to come out of the other side of this period with a structure that more closely preserves the notions of individual freedom that the US Constitution was supposed to support. That is one of the major themes of the Gaia Ascendant trilogy.

Instead of having human society blow itself up (again), I provided the Pugs and Pug-bears as disruptive agents in book one (The Time of the Cat). I didn't initially have that in mind, but they proved to be intent on killing all humans, and their EMP attack and subsequent atomic attacks came close.

With that externally generated reset to our lives, I was then faced with an opportunity to rebuild. For a while, I thought that I'd allow the survivors the luxury of sliding into a post-apocalyptic life. Still, the Sunnys and their high technology showed up unexpectedly in the second book (Second Wave). They needed rescuing from the same villains (Pug-bears). Still, They were also able to boost our tech, allowing me to move the story forward into a universe where humans were free to travel in space and friendly alien races willing to interact with human society. The Sim-tigers had fought off the Pug-bears but were vulnerable to any attacking force that had the means to bombard their planet with KEWs (something the Pug-bears and Pugs apparently hadn't considered).

The entire second book avoids the organizational issue. It deals with the discovery of the additional alien species in an adventure format that turned out to be somewhat similar to Homer's Odyssey. The underlying social issue that manifests in this book, which becomes even more evident in the third book, is that "People are People" regardless of what form they take. Dealing with alien life-forms reduces the differences between humans to the point of absurdity. (And, I find it absurd that we hold differences in belief, opinion, culture, language, sexual orientation, gender, skin tone, etc., against each other.)

The presence of the Sim-tigers and the Sunnys meant that the surviving humans had to come up with some organization that allowed for the membership of three different species. The underlying theme hides below the adventure story in book three (Confederation).

I had initially had Dec write a long list of principles in one of the chapters in the middle of the book. When my wife found out about this, she informed me that most readers would quit reading right there. She was, I think, totally correct. It was very disruptive to the story flow. Even so, I thought that perhaps readers would want to delve into Dec's thoughts to a small extent.

That's the point of this appendix. Below, you will find the original ideas that occurred to Declan as he was pondering how best to set up and organize not only human life on Earth but also in space, including the more significant issue of dealing with three different species.

Here's his list of principles:

1. The libertarian non-aggression principle prohibits the initiation of force against others. Aggression is an attack on another person's life, liberty, or justly acquired property and is always illegitimate. Personal property rights are included since it seems to be a nearly universal fact that people sacrifice their time to acquire property. Since time is all an individual's life is, confiscating their property is tantamount to stealing part of their life.

2. The non-aggression principle is the only proper view regarding the Use of Force in society; this is based on an absolute commitment to the concept of private property as an extension of the individual's life force.

3. Fully free markets are essential for all transactions and relationships that do not conflict with the non-aggression principle.

4. For a society to thrive, some minimal form of governance (intrusive government doesn't meet the criteria of "minimal") is required.

5. Such governance is best provided first by family and kin, thereafter extended to larger groups based on locality groups. Central organizational principles fail because no one individual can know everything. It's best to allow small groups to adjust their governance to meet their local situation.

6. Voluntary governance may be further extended via contract. The right to contract on any matter must be absolute, as long as the object of the contract is not in violation of the non-aggression principle. If unilaterally subverted, such contracts must become void. That is to say-- a government may not redefine the rules in such a way that harms the governed.

7. Individuals are responsible for their own choices. To ensure that they have the right to choose, they need to be secure in life, liberty, and property. A wild animal will fight to preserve its life as part of the natural order, so it's only fair to allow humans that same right. Taking a life is a violation of their right to live. Since life is measured by time and effort, taking someone's liberty or property is, in essence, taking part of

their life. They have the right to preserve their liberty and property as a logical extension.

8. Thomas Paine once wrote, "There are two distinct classes of men in the nation, those who pay taxes, and those who receive and live upon the taxes." The idea of government-enforced taxes (along with their unfortunate tendency to become more onerous over time) amounts to a violation of the right to life. It essentially enslaves the population as they become tax-serfs and forces them to devote much of their irreplaceable, life's time working to pay off their government-imposed debt.

9. Government is not necessary for individuals to survive and flourish. In this, I agreed with Frederic Bastiat. In the final two years of his life, which ended in 1850, he wrote a slim book titled "The Law." Modern political "scientists" have largely argued against his simple principles, but one can easily use sophistry to disparage any point of view. He wrote: "Force has been given to us to defend our own individual rights. Who will dare to say that force has been given to us to destroy the equal rights of our brothers? Since no individual acting separately can lawfully use force to destroy the rights of others, does it not logically follow that the same principle also applies to the common force that is nothing more than the organized combination of the individual forces? If this is true, then nothing can be more evident than this: The law is the organization of the natural right of lawful defense. It is the substitution of a common force for individual forces. And this common force is to do only what the individual forces have a natural and lawful right to do: to protect persons, liberties, and properties; to maintain the right of each, and to cause justice to reign over us all."

10. Bastiat argued that the only proper role of government is to provide for the common defense. It most definitely should not try to organize other human endeavors, notably economics. It has historically proven to be unsuccessful at such tasks.

11. Society has a way of spontaneously arising. After the EMPs, Grand Lake developed its own organization. It had some continuity with the way things were before, but there were no laws for all intents and purposes. Much of the previous body of law had been dropped, and no one missed it.

12. One can argue that during human history, humans have opted for more and more freedom while simultaneously developing a more complex society. Things like language, trade, and money developed without central planning or direction. In fact, the efforts of various

nations to centrally plan economies have consistently failed. Unconstrained society does a better job. People know what they want and need on a daily basis and don't require some remote bureaucrat to tell them. Free markets and trade, along with no restriction on mediums of exchange, are necessary if the people are to avoid governmental control.

13. Libertarianism assumes a society of liberty under general laws. Individuals are free to pursue their own lives so long as they respect the equal rights of others. Individuals are subject to broad legal principles that develop spontaneously. They are not ruled by arbitrary commands issued from on-high. The few rules must protect the freedom of individuals to pursue happiness in their own ways and not aim at any particular result or outcome.

14. Equality of status is not assumed. Each individual must be responsible for his own decisions and actions and not rely on government to force parity of results. It's only when the government forces redistribution of earned wealth on the basis of political pressure that groups become embroiled in conflict with other groups as they contend for a piece of the political spoils.

15. History showed that unconstrained government obeyed only one rule – the rule of continual growth. That rule was paired with the gradual draining of power from individuals and accumulation by the government as the original contract was subverted. This is a hazardous slope to start down. The end result always led to tyranny, the death of much of the population, and the eventual destruction of the government itself.

16. Along the same line, war always brings death and destruction on a grand scale. It disrupts family and economic life and inevitably puts more power in the ruling class's hands. That explains the origins of most wars and why rulers don't share the popular sentiment for peace. While free people have to defend themselves against common threats, the role of government has generally been one of creating the problem in the first place. At the same time, resolution of the conflict often is due to the combatants exhausting both the resources and their will to continue fighting.

This is the extent of Dec's initial list. I hope it provided you, Dear Reader, with at least a few concepts to consider.

Author Notes

I'd been reading The Fourth Turning by Strauss & Howe before starting this first segment of the Gaea Ascendant series. The book was published in the '90s and contains a well-researched presentation of the authors' generational theory of history. It impressed me greatly since it offered explanations and predictions of our current political and social environment. The predictions seem almost like a script that today's politicians are following, and, unfortunately, it's not a very nice one.

I don't want to go into details of their work. I'm pretty sure that I wouldn't do it justice. Still, the parts that influenced me in writing the Gaea Ascendant series have to do with resolving our present phase of social and political development – that which will be known as our history in the future.

The authors argue for a four-phase, roughly eighty-year cycle. We're now in the fourth phase, and it has always resulted in a crisis in the past. They point out that there are several potential culminations to the current crisis. Only one of them offers some hope.

The outcome that will not happen is just a continuation of the status quo. This will involve the same or similar political and social leadership growing gradually more and more corrupt due to the intractable structure of politics, debt, money, and enrichment of the elite and their cronies. It's a safe bet that the system will break, and this result will not prevail.

Another outcome involves a war. The fourth turning has often ended with earth-shaking wars, not just regional conflicts, but wars that involve large portions of the globe. This has left the system cleansed and ready for a reset in the past, but now that we have weapons capable of exterminating all of humankind, it's not a result that one would voluntarily seek. However, if it happens and there are still people afterward, the existing social order could be replaced by a new order that may or may not be better than the current one.

The true threat is that this crisis could be the end of humanity. It could destroy everything leaving our civilization destroyed and inflicting a primitive life on the few survivors. This was the idea behind the ending I used in The Time of The Cat. Mankind was set back centuries due to the aliens' use of EMP devices. I refer to this in the first quote at the beginning of chapter one of Confederation. This outcome created a complete collapse of culture, politics, and society, leaving humans in most of the world living a seventeenth-century lifestyle.

Unfortunately, rather than alien attack, we are far more likely to be faced with social stupidity, human evil paired with malevolent ideology, and the lack of adequate foresight as we create such things as drones paired with artificial intelligence.

I guess whichever way it plays out, we'll have to do what humans have always done: survive by catch as catch can.

As Dec concludes in Confederation: "Change happens."

Namaste,

Eric Martell

About Author

Eric S. Martell set out to become a scientist when he was five. He has a PhD. in experimental psychology. When personal computers came along (way back in prehistory), he became adept with them and spent years in software design, working on projects that ranged from early childhood learning software to military training. He has been trained in various types of energy healing, is an expert in real estate investing and sales, and holds a black belt in Tae-Kwon-Do. He is also a pilot, scuba diver, guitar player, outdoorsman and is addicted to both science and science fiction.

Eric's science fiction books offer both believable science and compelling characters set against realistic action. They are carefully researched, and while his fictional science sometimes strains against the bounds of current knowledge, it is always plausible. His stories cover alien invasion in an apocalyptic setting, political structure, space travel, advanced weapons, quantum physics, hunting, war, romance, time travel, and alien worlds.

He's been published in a series of anthologies and has published many full-length science fiction novels. His writing goal is to provide his readers with stories they cannot put down, and he takes readers' suggestions seriously.

Notices about new books, free short stories, opinion posts, and preview pages for many of his books can be found on his author blog at **EricMartellAuthor.com**

<u>A request for you:</u>

I make every effort to ensure your reading experience is enjoyable. This involves multiple editing steps, interior book layout, design, and using a professional cover artist/designer. Even so, it is becoming more difficult to find readers. If you liked this book, please leave a review and tell your friends.

Reviews may be left on the platform of your choice or emailed directly to me through my blog.

Thank you,

Eric Martell

Venice, 2021

Also By Eric S. Martell

The Time Equation Series

Heart of Fire Time of Ice

Paradox: On the Sharp Edge of the Blade

All the Moments in Forever

Time Enough to Live

All Things in Time

The Belter Series

The Pirates of the Asteroids*

The Belter Revolution

Cyber-Magic Series

CyberWitch*

Nano-Magic

The Gaia Ascendant Trilogy

The Time of The Cat

Second Wave

Confederation

Other Books

Dustfall*

Asterats and Other Stories

*Florida Authors and Publishers President's Award Winner